M000308131

Take Me With You is those of us who call o. who we are and who we are supposed to be. Through characters that show us the fierce and expansive meaning of family, Vanessa Carlisle illuminates the myriad lives of interconnected people informed but never broken by the injustices of their race, gender, sexuality or class status. Kindred, the character who is the driving force in this immersive and provocative novel, is the daughter and sister of all the people who have raised her: her incarcerated father, lovers and friends in the sex work industry, and the social activists who empower and educate her. This is a book to read and share. Deft and powerful from beginning to end.

— DANA JOHNSON, AUTHOR OF *IN THE NOT QUITE DARK* AND *ELSEWHERE, CALIFORNIA*

TAKE ME WITH YOU

VANESSA CARLISLE

For the Hookers Army

ISBN (pbk) 978-1-947041-78-3
ISBN (ebook) 978-1-947041-80-6
Take Me With You text copyright © Vanessa Carlisle
Edited by Peter Wright

All rights reserved.
Published in North America and Europe by Running Wild Press. Visit Running
Wild Press at www.runningwildpress.com Educators, librarians, book clubs (as
well as the eternally curious), go to www.runningwildpress.com.

CONTENTS

PART I

1

WHAT ARE YOU?

What are you?

It is a wrong way to address a human being. It is a weapon.

I asked Carl, What are you?

It was the last time we talked before he went missing.

I remember gripping my phone and yelling into it. He had called from his favorite pay phone in downtown Los Angeles, near Pershing Square. He was broke and full of theories that scared me and he was sleeping outside again.

I was living in Brooklyn with my girlfriend Nautica. I was on my way to work, about to meet a new client at the apartment Nautica had converted to a rent-by-the-hour dungeon. I carried a bag of my BDSM gear over one shoulder. I was wearing heavy makeup for playing my Domme role, annoyed at running late.

Carl was trying to get me to send money to a nonprofit he was working with in Skid Row. For something I didn't understand and didn't trust. I was angry at him for pitching me instead of connecting with me, angry for so many other, older reasons, tired of hearing his ideas for revolutionary projects, tired of worrying about him. I remember the yelling, and the words.

"I'm not a bank," I said. "I'd help you out if it was for a doctor, or an apartment, or shoes, or whatever, but this? This is crazy! What *are* you?" I said.

"How about *you?*" he said back. "Didn't I teach you anything about the movement?"

I told him he'd taught me plenty, and hung up.

No one expects a loved one to disappear, especially not when you're pissed at them.

When I tell people what I do for money they often want to know how I got here. What happened to me that landed me in sex work. Why would I do it?

I tell them, a lot happened to me. Also, it doesn't work like that. You don't get recruited by the escort agencies from a secret roster of girls-who-got-hurt. Some kinky people were abused, sure. But most weren't, just like vanilla, normie, non-kinky people. Some strippers go to college, some don't. Some porn stars write books or raise kids or build incredible dioramas for model trains. People who do sex for a living are just as different from each other as people who don't.

Still, cause-and-effect logic is irresistible. We want to understand things, to make them like other things we understand. People assume there has to be a deep psychological reason someone would choose to go into the sex industries, because they themselves are afraid that the veil between normal life and life as an outsider is thin. And it is, of course, thinner than a sliver of a pill, thinner than a second.

Those people are endlessly dissatisfied with my answer about how I started doing sex work.

There was this time in my life when I really needed money and I don't care about being naked or people seeing me naked. Then, other opportunities came and I said yes to some and no to some. Then I met a girl I fell in love with who did a different, kinky thing with sex and money and I followed her lead. I don't think there's anything wrong with me, and I don't need a "reason" for what I do other than the fact that it seems to suit me better than other jobs I've hated. To search for a cause, an original trauma, a single reason I became who I am? It's insulting.

And yet. When Carl went missing, I started searching for the cause. I went back into my childhood and listened for clues. I combed my memories, recent and distant, and I tried to figure out how I had let it happen. How I might have even been the cause myself.

So of course, it starts with my mother.

Raw beef was my mother's answer to weakness of any kind. Caught a cold? Lost another job? Bright red, barely-seared steak would appear on the dinner table. It was a special meal, and it meant someone needed to get stronger.

"Get all the iron you can," she would say. "Drink that sauce."

But it wasn't sauce. Carl had sauce.

Mom had to let Carl cover his steak in A1, and she had to let him cook his as long as he wanted, because he was a grown man who she loved and who loved us both very much. He got to do some things for himself in his own way, she told me. I told my friends my mother taught me to drink blood.

We had been living with Carl since before I could remember. My friends knew him as my dad. But he wasn't married the normal way to my mom. Mom and Carl told me "common law marriage" was a real thing that happened to people who had lived together long enough in California. So they were married, but different.

And he was Black. He told me his black was capital-B Black, but not everyone wanted to call themselves capital-B Black even if they looked like him, so I should always remember to respect whatever people called themselves. My mom wasn't capital-B Black, she wasn't black, she wasn't brown, she was white. She never said the word capital-B Black, she only said "African American."

When I was eight-years-old, a fifth-grader told me Carl wasn't my real dad and it scared me. He seemed as real as me or my mom. I felt feisty at dinner.

"Carl doesn't drink his sauce," I said. Carl looked up from his plate at my mother, and they shared some meaning I didn't understand, but I knew I wasn't in real trouble. He straightened in his chair and patted the back of his hair. His hair was still dark and springy, then. He let it grow out sometimes, two inches or so, and twisted it and untwisted it in the back when he was thinking. He patted it when he thought something was funny. We had a round table, with mismatching chairs. It was a small circle just big enough for our plates, and underneath, all our feet met in the middle. My mother's feet were always in stockings or slippers because they were tired. She would rub them together and make a scratching sound I hated. My feet were tan on the top, lighter on the bottom. Carl's feet were brown on top, almost as light as mine on the bottom, and he had man-problems with his toenails that made them thick and yellow.

"You eat how your mother tells you to eat," Carl said, meeting my eyes. He winked. His eyes were a brighter brown than mine, with gold threading through them. His lashes were long, dark, curled. "I had a mother who did the same for me, and we're both lucky for that." I imagined his mother, a rounder version of him, in a flowery housedress with a giant bottle of A1 in both hands and a lot of gray hair in a bun.

"Is she my grandma?" I said.

Carl scratched his cheek. He shaved in the mornings, and by the evenings, his whiskers bothered him. "She would have loved to be your grandma, baby. She died when I was a young boy." I hadn't known that. It was hard for me to imagine Carl as a boy, because he'd always been a grown-up.

My name is Kindred. Sometimes Carl called me Kindee.

We were living in Studio City then, back when it was still a cluster of hedged-in sound stages and industrial stucco apartments, before Universal Studios landscaped the area into a theme park. Both Carl and Mom worked too hard or worried about having no job, alternatively, depending on various blame-worthy influences: the economy, racism, sexism, your drinking, no-your-attitude, depression, not trying hard enough, the unfairness of the world, the rich white men who made it so, each other, themselves, the bosses, but they never blamed me, although I often expected them to, as I stayed awake listening to their adult concerns issuing so quickly from their angry, exhausted adult mouths. Our apartment complex sat behind a Mission-style archway with reddish clay roof tiles. The exterior had been painted an absurd mint green, and it was part of a collection of six absurdly mint green units that faced inward to a thin strip of concrete and weeds. I loved that apartment. It had one bedroom, so I slept in a pile of blankets on the couch, every night except Sunday. Sunday I got to sleep in the bed with Mom.

"How'd she die?" I asked Carl.

"Honey, just drink your sauce," Mom said. She straightened up and rolled her shoulders. Her sandy blonde hair was parted unevenly in the middle and sat on her back, limp and thin. She wore blue eyeliner until after dinner. Her eyes were squinty all the time. She said someone in our family was a Cherokee princess, that was why. Carl said that was a bedtime story white people told to feel better about themselves.

"It's blood," I said. "It's gross."

"Stop it," Mom said. "It's good for you. It's called 'myoglobin,' the thing that makes it red. It's not blood."

I crossed my arms.

She sighed a little. "It's expensive, baby." She patted my knee under the table, gave an effort of a smile to Carl, and looked back at her own cut of meat.

I didn't move to drink the blood, which I remember because "it's expensive" usually worked on me.

My mother waved her papery hand, dismissing me.

"My mother died in a car accident," Carl said. "When I was eleven."

"Who took care of you?" I asked.

"My dad and my aunties did," Carl said. "I'll tell you more about them all sometime." Carl returned to his meal.

Mom tipped her plate and slurped in a way that seemed somehow both defiant and dainty. I thought I saw a greasy stink of blood rising from her wilted hair.

I didn't drink it, just because I wanted to.

These are the kind of stupid things I ache to take back now that Mom is dead and Carl is gone.

My memories are a little worn and tattered, and I don't always know what is true and what I made up. I know I wasn't always defiant. I started keeping a journal just after that dinner, and I never stopped. The journals tell a story of my growing up, but they don't tell the story of my mother, who started working at fourteen and didn't stop until she was too sick to move. They don't tell the story of her relationship with Carl, who fell in love with her when she was still young and vibrant, still staying up late to argue his ideas about politics and the movement, still singing "Singing in the Rain" in the shower. I can't tell all their stories now, but I can try to find that thread of sense that explains how I got here.

My mother told me money was like sugar: it seems like the best thing in the world until you have too much. Then you get sick. She told me to make sure I had enough to live on, and if I could do that, to share. But don't ever stockpile it, baby, she said. You can't take it with you. Carl loved it when she talked like that.

On Sundays, Carl would get the stereo going in the morning, and I would drag our cleaning bucket from under the sink. I divvied up some clean rags. The bucket was full of homemade concoctions: a vegetable oil and lemon juice mixture for dusting, vinegar-water for counters and glass, bleach-water for the toilet, shower, and sinks. Mom made the solutions in old hairspray bottles and mason jars and labeled them with permanent markers like they were potions for Alice to find in Wonderland. *Dust with Me! Clean Counters with Me!* She drew spirals and hearts and stars and smiley faces on them.

When the first trembling notes of the *Rondo Alla Turca* sparkled through the place, we would brandish our rags and dance. The game was the same every time. In time with the triumphant chords, I dusted everything from my height on down to the fraying carpet edges. I ran the rag over books and avoided piles of handwritten notes, mail, newspapers, and sketches from Carl's projects. He dusted above me, pushing his finger in between each book on his shelves and slowly circling the TV screen where I had usually left a streak of debris. Mom wiped down the kitchen table with vinegar water. We stopped cleaning when the music ended, even if we hadn't finished everything.

When it was time to stop, we played Miriam Makeba's song: "Pata Pata." Carl would sing and twist around the living room while I threw myself in half-spastic shapes onto the couch. Thump! Recover, reset. Thump! At some point right before the end of the song, Carl would scoop me up mid-leap, get into a horse stance, perch me on his side, and I stood on his thigh for a thorough flourish in our end pose. Ta-daaa!

My mother clapped, jingled the car keys, and all three of us would scavenge the couch and other piles of stuff for loose change. If we found a dollar or more, Mom rewarded us with a drive down to the In 'N Out burger in Hollywood. Sunday nights for a while I got to drink a milkshake and spend the night in the bed with Mom after the cleaning dance. For that one night a week, Carl slept in my spot on the couch, curled against its scratchy nap, under a quilt his dead mother had made.

It was in that apartment, sometime close to that steak dinner, when I told Mom and Carl that kids at school were teasing me, saying Carl wasn't my real dad. Instead of laughing it off, Mom and Carl sat me on the couch for a chat.

They nodded at each other, and held hands.

"It seems like you are starting to have some questions," Mom said. "About where you came from."

"I already know," I said. Because we'd already talked about sex.

"I don't think you do," Mom said. "Because we've never talked about this."

Carl said, "I hope you know I love you like my own flesh and blood."

Like.

"I had you by myself," Mom said. "I mean, I got pregnant by a man, but he wasn't ever going to be a dad." My mom didn't love my biological father, she said. She wanted to have a baby. "It was a wonderful affair," she said. "He was like a movie star. Gorgeous and romantic and left me alone when I told him to."

His name was Alex. She showed me a card he'd written her. He wrote that he was "honored" she chose him to help her make her own family. His handwriting was unfamiliar, difficult to read, black loops exuberantly covering the inside of a glossy card with a waterfall on the front.

Mom didn't invite him to my birth, didn't put his name on my birth certificate, never considered him a family member or even a father, but "more like a sperm donor." She fell in love with Carl when I was a baby, and he fell in love with both of us, and that's how we were a family.

It was unreal, insane, and obviously true.

"So my real dad didn't want me?" I said. I picked at the mustard yellow couch. It had turned beige in the middle from my sleeping on it.

"No, honey, that's not it. He didn't want a baby at all," Mom said. "He was happy to help me have you, because I wanted you so much!" She put the card on the floor. "Also, I don't think it's fair to call him your real dad. Carl is your real dad."

"No, he isn't." Was she stupid? And Carl had never wanted me, he'd accepted me because I came with Mom, I thought.

"You deserve to know as much as we know about where you come from," Carl said.

"You don't even have a picture of him?"

Mom shook her head. She seemed embarrassed. She'd been fine keeping pictures of him in her head all these years, never thinking I might want one.

I looked at the gold flecks in Carl's eyes, his strong shoulders. My mother was so pink and wispy.

My heavy brown hair didn't come from either of them. I felt

very stupid. A precise shade of betrayal descended, a saturated gray, which deadened the room. Mom opened her arms to me, her creamy skin looking stretched over thin blue veins from elbow to wrist, and all I had to do was lean slightly toward her, which I did, and she swept in to hold me and kiss the top of my head. But inside my ribs I felt hard and untouchable. I felt like I might pass out.

"Alex was a kind person and I'm so grateful you are mine," she said.

I hated her voice, and it scared me.

She kept talking. Alex had blended back into the world, without a fuss, about a month after she was pregnant. I asked where he was from, and she didn't know. He'd just been her lover, someone willing to get her pregnant and then, goodbye and good luck.

Mom spent the next eight months "getting ready to be a parent." Mom met Carl when I was six months old. He moved in after about a year. Carl is your father, she told me, even though he didn't make you with me the way some of your other friends were made by the men who lived with or visited them. She knew two of my friends didn't have fathers in their lives and she reminded me I was lucky to have Carl.

I finally had words. "You lied to me!" I wrestled out of her lap, stood, and faced them both.

"We never lied to you," she said, and I searched my memory for a time when Carl had said anything about not being my father. "We waited to talk to you about this because it is complicated, honey, and maybe we waited too long."

"You lied," I said. "You let me believe something that you knew was a lie."

Carl watched the ground. He knew I was right.

"Are you worried about who you'll look like?" Mom said. That hadn't crossed my mind until she said it. "Because you shouldn't be. You are a beautiful girl." She pinched my side and I swatted at her hand, as hard as I could.

"Kindred!" Her eyes were huge.

"Give her a break," Carl said to her. I couldn't look at him. "I love you," he said to me. "And I'm sorry. You're right. We should have talked about this all along."

Liars, I thought.

"So I'm sorry we waited," he said. "I bet you're angry with us both now, and want to know more than we can give you about the man who helped you get born."

Mom deflated. I flared. I yelled some things, like "I'll never trust you again," and ran into the bathroom.

My alienation reverberated from bones to skin, prickly, hot and cold. The dark hairs on my forearms, thin and straight and unlike the blonde fuzz that covered my mom's, were suddenly strange. I sniffed my arm. I smelled like myself, but I couldn't get used to it. I stared at my face. I was just another brown-haired kid, until that moment.

The kids in third grade asked each other a question that sounded wrong: "What are you?" I'd told them what my mom told me: I was "a human being." Or, "made with love, and perfect." When they demanded to know my race, I told them I was all kinds of things: a flying rainbow! A donkey dog! A Skittles tree! I'm a pink and purple zebra! I'm a bowl of pudding! Because Carl had told me race was an invention, like unicorns. It wasn't real. It was like Santa Claus, and people liked to believe it, but it didn't help anyone.

But the kids listened to how I talked, what shows I watched. They knew I couldn't understand Spanish. They decided if I was in or out. "What are you?" No one was ever surprised that I had a white mom. They were surprised I had a capital-B Black dad.

I couldn't go back to school. I said I needed new friends. I couldn't face the kids.

I will never know how much I influenced our next move, because we moved at least once or twice a year anyway. But this one meant a new school, and there, I told people Carl and my Mom both had adopted me.

A few weeks after they told me about Alex, Mom scolded me for avoiding talking to Carl.

"You are breaking his heart," she said. "The only thing he did to you was love you better than Alex ever could have."

I knew she was right about that, and I ached to explain myself. It had nothing to do with Carl, really.

On Carl's birthday that year, I wrote a long, impassioned letter declaring my familial loyalty to him and gesturing frantically at desires I couldn't name. He wrote me note and slipped it under my door.

dear Kindee-cool,

Thank you for your letter. I love you and I will never stop. Never. No matter how many changes we go through together. I promise.

one of your dads,
Carl

The news that I had a biological father out there in the world taught me something important: all lies are ongoing, causing continuous, compounding damage, unless they have been directly corrected by the liar. When you have a longstanding habit of honesty with someone, you can relax when you're with them, because you are not expending energy trying to tell them the "right" story, which is a fiction, which takes energy to produce. You can be yourself in real time with a person you are honest with.

My mother had good intentions. She thought she was telling me about Alex at a good time, perhaps a little late, but it had never occurred to her that I would be so hurt by what she felt was only a slight adjustment to the story of my life. She thought I would maybe feel some relief, because I didn't look like Carl and I was old enough to notice, and this explained why.

I did not feel relief.

I lost respect for her. I learned that keeping enormous, life-altering secrets for years was both possible and painful. I realized that for trust to exist among people, the clearing up of old lies must occur. It may hurt more to hurt less.

Later I was disappointed to discover that most people lie about how well they know their own history of lying, and then forget when they're lying about "small things," and then defend their integrity and honesty in the present, no matter what.

The most terrifying kind of lie is the one you forget you're telling. I am, right now, telling lies I have forgotten, and I now believe they are truths. I left them running like a white noise machine. Of course, I might get caught, someone could yank the machine out of the wall. The shock of silence, the sudden intimacy, a revealing of a truth, and therefore a revealing of the lie: this is the only real nakedness I have ever felt or feared to feel. To have a forgotten lie exposed.

Secrecy is power. Pulling the plug on someone else's lie is also power. My sadism emerges when I realize I have the opportunity to yank someone else's white noise machine out of their wall, to expose them, to show them their own state of denial or delusion.

My mother believed herself to be a good person. To protect that belief, she would perform incredible feats of irrationality, denial, and dishonesty. She never, ever apologized to me for lying about who my father was. I asked her for it, when she was dying, and she couldn't do it.

"I still don't think I did anything wrong," she said. "You were too young to understand."

2

THE RUNAROUND

I was nearly finished with my sophomore year of high school when Carl got arrested. It was a Tuesday afternoon. I got home from school and Mom was pacing with the phone pressed into her ear with both hands. It was not something I'd ever seen her do, and at first, I laughed. She shot me a look that disintegrated me. Her hair was pulled back into a long-day ponytail, tight at the base of her skull with thin blonde flyaways framing her face. She rubbed her cheeks and eyes and switched the phone to her other ear. I sat in the living room, watched her pace and make calls, and listened.

"Carl Baker," she said over and over, "B-A-K-E-R."

My name: Kindred Powell. Mother: Helen Powell. Father: "Alex," last name unknown. Acting Father: Carl Baker, who, from the sound of things, was currently being held in a jail or a hospital, or some other institution where people didn't like to help a common-law wife with a different last name. I felt a surge of fear and dread. Also, I was hungry. I thought: Carl would want me to eat.

Mom was on hold again. "What's going on?" I said.

"Give me a few minutes, baby," she said, "I'm about to find out."

She blew past me into her bedroom and shut the door.

I waited for five minutes, counted carefully on the green microwave clock.

I knocked on her door, asked if she wanted dinner. She told me to make whatever.

I poked around the kitchen and tried to make an adult decision with our options. I could definitely boil water. I made a box of Mac n' Cheese with all butter, no milk. It plopped into our bowls and shined yellow. I put the pot back on the stove and covered the last lumps. I wondered if Carl would be home in time to eat it before it went sour.

I yelled, "Come and get it or regret it!"

It worked.

"I can't believe this is happening," she said, emerging from the bedroom. She put the phone next to her place and lowered herself into the chair like her back hurt. Her eyebrows were locked into a very-upset shape.

"What." I sat across from her. She looked at her bowl.

"Carl's choices are catching up with him," she said. She shook her head. "It was just a matter of time."

"Tell me what happened," I said, as evenly as I could, "don't tell me what to think about it before I know what happened."

She crumpled a little and complied.

Carl had been delivering weed. He was driving my mom's 1979 Toyota. He was late. His contact had been paging every two minutes. He made an illegal U-Turn. When he got pulled over, the cops threatened a search. He didn't consent. The cop outside Carl's window put his hand on his gun, told Carl he smelled marijuana and that was probable cause for a search. Carl said he had a hand-rolled tobacco cigarette in a bag in his pocket, and they were welcome to pat it down to see. At that point, some bad things happened.

More facts: the cops made him get out of the car, patted him down, searched the car, and found the weed. They were talking shit to him. He talked back. They knocked him against the car hard enough to split his eye. They kicked him, to get him to the ground. They handcuffed him, booked him somewhere downtown. He called home and gave Mom some of that story outright and some in general terms, and then later, when she tried to get in touch with the jail about posting his bail, they said he had been moved, but when she called the other place, they said he had never been there, and he wasn't scheduled to come. I had arrived from school during the time when she couldn't locate him.

"So they finally stopped dicking me around and found him. He's at a jail in downtown LA now," she said. "And, he's going to have to sleep there tonight."

"He's not getting OR'ed?"

She seemed surprised I knew to ask that question.

I reminded her I was in high school now and I'd seen people get picked up for alcohol, drugs, racing, fighting...

"No, he's not," she said.

I asked why, and she said she didn't know, she was just following his instructions. He told her to bail him out in the morning.

"What? Why can't we go get him and bail him out tonight?"

"It doesn't work like the movies," she said. "For some reason they haven't set a bail amount for him yet, we don't know how much we'd have to give them, and so until that changes or he's seen a judge, we can't do anything."

I asked how long he'd been selling weed.

"He doesn't sell it," she said, as if "selling it" were a less respectable job than the one he had.

"How long has he been driving weed around, so someone else can sell it, then?"

"Years," she said. "On and off. When one of us is in between jobs." She got up from the table and took her half-full bowl to the sink. "I'll clean up later," she said. She walked to the bedroom with the phone, but left her door open.

I guessed I had sort of known this, without ever being told. Carl had people. He met them sometimes after work. He didn't smoke weed in the house, but he smelled like it, and I knew, finally, what it smelled like because I'd smoked at school with my friend Angie and it had reminded me of Carl. My mom really thought I was an idiot, I thought. I wondered if she'd made Carl promise not to tell me.

She made a few more calls. I took out a notebook and started drawing a vampire-sex scene for a comic I was working on.

"Kindee," she called from her room, "we need to cut school tomorrow morning and go to the jail, ok?" As if she would miss a little school, too. I didn't want to go to school, but I also didn't want my mom to need me so badly.

Within a few months, I found out that she seemed weak that night because she had started to feel sick. She was tired all the time, didn't want to eat, and it was getting harder to do her day-and-night job work schedule. She didn't know cancer was growing in her stomach. She just knew she felt bad.

Like at most of our places, I slept on the couch at that apartment. It was a futon that I rarely unfolded, so I could burrow in and feel held on one side. Later that night, when we'd finished our private bathroom-time shifts and she'd broken a bowl and cursed and cried and cleaned it up and told me to wear nice clothes tomorrow, I heard her sobbing in the bedroom. I wound

my quilt tight around my head. Angry with Carl, and afraid for
him too. Angry with Mom. Angry at the rotting smell that
wafted into that apartment on trash night, angry with the world
for giving me such a shitty array of options.

In the morning, Mom told me our plan was to bail Carl out and
then wait for him to be released. She was wearing work clothes.
Her stretchy black pants were slightly lighter than her stretchy
black button-up. Her lipstick was already creeping into the tiny
wrinkles around her mouth. She had washed her thin hair and
she smelled like Suave. I wore a clean black dress that came
down to my ankles and heavy black eyeliner.

"We look like the Addams Family," she said.

"I'm not changing," I said.

She shook her head and packed her purse.

I offered to drive and she agreed, another abnormality. I
only had a permit then.

Luis BailBonds' storefront was across the street from the
jail. We parked and fed a meter. "Let's get this over with," she
sighed, and took my arm.

Through the hand-painted glass front door, we entered a
large open room. Inside smelled like coffee, microwave
popcorn, and Styrofoam take-out boxes. The office had gray
carpet and white paint, some exposed pipes, and a few 1980s
movie posters on the walls. There were five large banker-desks
arranged in a horseshoe around the entrance, with folding
chairs facing each one, for the people like us. There were
workers at the desks, on the phone, shuffling files. They all
wore T-shirts and jeans, except for one older guy in a white
button down sitting at the desk at the back of the room. He was
the least busy, so I figured he must be the boss.

I walked Mom directly to his desk and said good morning.

It took him many sentences to say good morning back, while he fetched us a second "client" chair. He was Luis, and this was his place. He said things like "We represent the interests of families in need," and somehow, I knew he knew it wasn't true, but it wasn't strictly a lie, either. He looked like he was in his fifties. He wore a hammered gold wedding ring, and his hands were warm and dry when he shook mine. His black hair, graying at the temples, was combed into a stiff, flattering wave in the front, and he was clean-shaven, although I could tell he'd have a serious shadow by two PM. He was slightly thick in the middle, the kind of man who maybe once had a killer body but gave up working on it once he got a steady job, and his shirt had decorative stitching along the button holes. His English was accented and he spoke slowly and carefully to us, but then he excused himself to answer his desk phone during his own intro, and suddenly he spoke a fast-flowing Spanish without many consonants. His desk was piled with forms, carbon copies of forms, manila folders full of forms. Forms printed from something that left tiny holes along the sides.

"My apologies," he said, hanging up. "How can I help you two lovely ladies today?"

I pulled out a sheet of folded legal paper. Mom had taken notes when Carl finally got through on the phone, and we had his booking number, a few lawyers we'd called without getting through, and the name "Luis BailBonds."

"I don't know how he knows about you," Mom said to Luis, then seemed distracted by the framed poster for *Beverly Hills Cop*, signed by Eddie Murphy, on the wall behind him. "But if you can get Carl out," she trailed off.

"Break this down for us," I said to Luis. "What's the first thing we need to do to get a person out of jail?"

"Yes, we really don't have any experience," Mom said, wavering.

I made eyes at the guy and shrugged just slightly. She's upset, who knows what she'll do? He saw it, pressed his lips, took a long inhale, and leaned forward in his chair.

"Ma'am," he addressed my mom, "we are going to get your husband out of there as fast as we can."

She sighed and seemed comforted. I wasn't, so I stared at him.

He asked where Mr. Baker was, currently.

"The county jail at 450 Bauchet Street," she answered.

"Twin Towers?" he said.

"I don't know--"

"That facility is called Twin Towers, ma'am, is all," he said. He was already typing. The computer screen faced him only, and I realized that the room was set up so that clients could never see any of the computer screens unless they walked behind a desk. Luis made two phone calls and used Carl's name.

"Here he is," Luis said to himself, checked our scribbled notes, and then frowned. He clicked a few more things.

I asked what was wrong.

Nothing was wrong, just something about the arrest record, not how they usually, oh, actually it didn't matter. He got someone else on the phone. "Three thousand dollars," he said, and crossed his hands in front of the keyboard. "Felony resist."

"WHAT?" my mother's voice was too loud, too high. Luis's eyes fluttered briefly at the sound. Then he snapped into action. He pulled out his clipboards, he started talking it through. Three thousand was the bail amount. The full amount had to be paid for Carl to be released, and the full amount would be returned to the person who posted the bail when Carl showed up for his arraignment. If we didn't have three thousand dollars on hand to spare, he said, as if we might, because some people do, but no judgement if we personally didn't, we could pay Luis BailBonds a fraction of that amount and they would post the full bail. The bond to get Carl released, payable here and now, was ten percent of the bail, plus fees. "You will definitely see him today when you pay the three hundred-fifty right now," Luis said. My mom kept shaking her head in denial, so I nodded at Luis when he paused. Go on, she's just taking it in, I'm listening, go on.

A felony was a more serious charge than a misdemeanor, and so it came with higher bail. If we bailed him out before his arraignment, Carl would have to go to an arraignment at a later date, where his actual charges, which may be different from what he got arrested for, would be given to him. At that arraignment, our contract with Luis BailBonds would end, as the full bail would be remitted to them. Luis started talking just to Mom. "We hold your information here and you become liable for the full amount of the bail if Mr. Baker fails to appear at his arraignment."

"He will be wherever he is supposed to be," she said.

We needed three hundred-fifty dollars. No matter what, we wouldn't get that back. After a few more versions of the same explanation, Mom said she understood, and wrote a check. She looked at me with ashamed eyes.

"Well, there goes Christmas," she said to Luis. Then to me, "Because there goes half the fucking rent."

Luis told us to go home and wait for a call, but neither of us wanted to. Mom wouldn't go inside the jail, and she wouldn't let me go alone. So we amassed our change, fed the meter, pulled the crackly sunshade from the trunk, opened the windows, and camped out in the car. Luis assured us he would let us know as soon as Carl was released, and that it would likely happen before he closed his office for the day.

"It's nicer in here," Mom said, and put her seat back. I considered going into Twin Towers by myself anyway. It scared me. I wasn't eighteen. I could get Mom in trouble. I could get Carl in more trouble. I could get arrested. For what? It didn't matter, it wasn't worth it.

I kept thinking: Any minute now. I kept reading a hand-painted sign on the corner: Oil change, $12.99. The car got hot.

Mom said, "Every day we do things we can't take back."

I imagined scanning for Carl inside the jail, my legs sticking to a vinyl chair in an ugly waiting room where everyone else was also scared and stressed out, or a cop. I waited for Luis to appear at my window, watched every person who crossed that street, experimented with ways to stretch out in my slightly gritty passenger seat.

Luis let me use his office bathroom. I drew a tiny carica-ture of him on a paper towel with the Sharpie I always carried and left it in the cupboard under the sink for someone to find. I drew him with a big grin and stacks of money in his hands. I put a speech bubble above his head, "I help families in need."

One of the Luis BailBond assistants brought us two cans of Diet Coke and two granola bars. He didn't bend down far enough for me to make eye contact, but offered the treats through the window. He had hairless, brown forearms and visible veins puffing a bit over strong muscles. We took the gifts. I watched him walk inside. He seemed very relaxed.

Maybe an hour later, which I'd spent sorting car trash from important paperwork and scraping old candy out of the glove compartment with a broken hair comb, the same guy came outside for a smoke break. I got out of the car without waking Mom, and dared myself to bum a cigarette from him. If she saw me smoking, she would freak out, but it seemed very low stakes, considering the kind of shit Carl was in.

The guy nodded once and said "Hey," at me, like I was another guy. He said, "'sup." His name was Anton. He leaned against the wall of Luis BailBonds. I had my back to Mom and the car, which seemed reckless.

"Hey," I said, suddenly wanting, horribly, to be someone important to him, "My name is Kindred."

"Kindred?"

"Yeah."

He smiled, just slightly. "Never heard that name before. Kindred. Like family."

He loosened a cigarette and held out the pack for me to take one. I did. It was not my first smoke, but I was conscious of my fingers, which seemed enormous and out of control, and he had to ask me to hold still to get the thing lit. I took a deep drag and coughed as I thanked him.

He gave me a larger smile. His front two teeth were both pointing slightly askew, the right one partially covering the left. I wanted to make out with him and feel those teeth press into my top lip. "You don't smoke," he said. "Don't start."

"I smoke sometimes," I said.

"That's what I'm saying," he said. "Don't."

"I know, I know," I said. I took another, slower, drag. "Thanks for helping me out."

"Rough day," he said, nodding toward Mom asleep in the car.

"Sure," I said. I tried not to think about the gray, boxy specter of the Twin Towers, or Carl in there. "Can't wait for it to be over."

Anton nodded. "Fuckin' bullshit," he said. He held his cigarette like a joint, inhaled, flicked his ashes on the ground, and looked me in the eye for the longest moment so far. His irises and pupils were nearly the same color. He squinted a little in the sun. "What would you be doing today if you weren't here?" he said. "School? Work?"

"School."

"College?"

"Yeah," I lied. It was too easy. I was sure I saw him relax a little. That's good, my body said.

He scratched his neck and smoke uncurled from behind his head. He's so hot he's on fire, I thought, and suppressed a crazy person's giggle. I smoked. I looked at his shoes. Timberlands. Untied and clean. His jeans were dark.

"You like this job?" I asked. His T-shirt had shapes and symbols on it I didn't recognize.

He shrugged. "Naw," he said. "Would you?"

"No," I said, glad to be in agreement with him. "Especially not if people like my mom came in all the time."

"She's ok," he said, "she's waking up." I turned back and saw Mom getting out of the car. I waved at her with my free hand, dropped my half-smoked Newport between my feet, stepped on it as I turned to Anton.

"Guess I'll go," I said.

He gestured with his own, not-quite-finished smoke. It meant, go ahead, I'm going to finish this.

"Bye," I said, and waved ridiculously at him as I aimed myself for the car.

"Don't start smoking!" he called after me.

Mom pretended to have seen and heard nothing. She asked if Luis had given me any news.

"No news," I said. "I'm going to take a nap, too, ok?" I curled up in the backseat, tried to feel the meager cross breeze, and fantasized about going on a road trip with Anton somewhere wooded and lush, pulling into an abandoned rest stop, and fucking him in the driver's seat, in the grass, in the bathroom, and when I got tired of that, we went to the beach, and fucked on a blanket, watched the sunset together while he fucked me from behind, far away from other people but not so far away that they couldn't see us, and when I got tired of that, I imagined standing in some undefined sensual swirl of softness, filling my mouth with his neck, biting down, and not letting go, no matter how he squirmed and screamed, and that was the best one, and I thought I must be really fucked up, to like that so much, but it was just in my head, so.

I woke up disoriented and nauseated by hunger. The light was lower. Luis and Mom stood outside the car. He handed her a card and told her good luck, call him anytime. I opened my door.

"Let's go," she said, in a near-normal voice. "He's getting released right now!"

We walked toward the door Luis had marked on the tiny map printed on the back of his business card. We rounded the corner and Carl was already outside, scanning the street.

He had two strips of stained medical tape holding his right eyebrow together. The gash was probably an inch long, directly horizontal, and swollen heavy. I was scared by how bad he looked. Mom started crying immediately. Therefore, I did not. Three large patches of blood had dried on his shirt. We got out and ran to him. He smelled like pee. He hugged us to him, all stinking and bristly, and we rushed him to the car, and I drove home, and Mom sat in the backseat and fired questions about jail, while Carl let his hand drift through the air out the window and kept his eyes on the sky. He answered with descriptions of unconscionable things that had been done to him by the arresting officers and then the jailers and then the property officer. He had either forgotten or no longer cared to lie to me about the weed.

He was angry. She was angry. I was angry, but also feeling

something new, something more sludgy, a slow and ugly style of fear, an intense pressure inside my chest, wrapping around my shoulders and creeping up my neck.

Mom asked him if he'd resisted arrest.

"No." He said. He went colder. "I was physically compliant the whole time."

"Then how do you have felony resisting?" she asked. "What's that for?"

"Goddamnit," he said, exhausted, "you tell me, huh? Who does the paperwork?"

"Cops," I said. "They get to keep the money they find, too."

"Don't be simple," Mom said, catching my eyes in the rearview mirror. "They can't do that."

"They do it," I said. I didn't tell her it had happened to a guy I knew from the parties I was going to.

"Thank you Kindee," Carl said. To my mom, "She's right, they take the money and don't look back. They hit me, baby, they knew they were going to and they went right ahead and there was nothing I could have done to stop them that wouldn't have gotten me killed."

"You don't know that," she said. "Don't say things like that."

"I do know it," he said, quietly, out the window.

"They don't just kill people," she said.

"They don't just kill white people," he said.

They stopped talking about it in front of me for the night. We got home, Carl took a shower, Mom opened three beers, handed me one with a hug, it was the first time she'd let me drink with them, and we got in their bed, because the TV was in their room, and watched some show about monkeys living in a city in Asia, with Carl in the middle and me and Mom cuddled up to his sides.

Carl pet my head a little. He was the only person I still allowed to touch my hair. "Sorry you had to go through all that today," he said into my head, and kissed my crown. "You smell like cigarettes."

"Kindee was my guardian angel," Mom said, eyes still on the TV.

"Weird, but, thanks," I said. "Sorry *you* had to go through all that," I said to Carl. There was so much wrong. I asked him how bad his eye hurt.

He made a growling sound in his throat. "It's talking to me," he said, "but not screaming."

When I left them to burrow into my pile of blankets on the couch, I heard Mom let out her panic. That apartment had carpet and thick walls and usually I could only hear raised voices or sex noises. This was different. Mom said, "I can't take it anymore" and "sick with worry" and "Kindred's future," and yelled "No!" a few times clear and loud, despite Carl's muffled responses. I lay awake straining to hear them until the sun came up and they went quiet. I wondered if they'd made a decision about something. And if they had, what it would mean.

The three of us went to Disneyland before Carl's trial. I didn't know where they got the money, and I didn't care. It felt like we were just a few steps ahead of all the bad stuff, that day. We laughed so much. Mom had her energy that day, her eyes were lit up and she and Carl were kind to each other. He brought us churros while we waited in the line for the Matterhorn.

"You seriously don't want to go on this ride?" I asked him.

He looked up. "Nope," he said.

"He's scared," Mom said. "He thinks the tracks aren't safe."

"Then why are we going on it?" I said.

"Because I think he's wrong," Mom said.

Carl smiled. "You risk your own lives," he said to me. "I'm going to sit on that bench and watch the people."

When we came off the ride, he was chatting with a woman, who looked like she was also waiting. She was pushing a sleeping toddler in a stroller, back and forth, back and forth.

"There they are," he said, arms out. "You made it!"

The woman nodded and moved off.

"You flirting?" Mom said.

"Of course not," he said. They kissed. I made sounds of disgust. They squeezed me.

I ate an orange creamsicle on Main Street and let Carl tell me how wrong it was that there was still a "cigar store Indian" outside the shops.

"Was Walt Disney a racist?" I asked.

"Come on," Mom said, "please can we just enjoy our day? Please?"

Carl shot me a look. It confirmed that Walt Disney was a racist, and also, that we'd talk about it later.

"Fine," I said.

And it was, for the three of us, that day, for a few hours, sort of fine. Mom needed to rest, to sit, to go to the bathroom more than normal. She didn't want to talk about it. She didn't want to talk about anything uncomfortable. I couldn't decide whether we were pretending Carl wasn't going to trial, or enjoying ourselves in the face of the fact that he was.

3

A BRIEF SUMMARY OF THE WORST
YEAR OF MY LIFE

After months of appearances and two public defenders hoping he would change his mind and take a plea deal, Carl finally got his trial. It was a four-day farce in which two cops lied on the stand and claimed he'd hit one of them and tried to grab his gun while resisting arrest. I watched Carl's neck muscles tense and twitch from my seat in the courtroom. I'd never seen him stay quiet when something was so wrong. I took notes. I got thrown out one day for chewing gum, paced the hall, and snuck back in when the jury shuffled through the door after their lunch break. I couldn't look away.

He was found guilty on all charges. The first charge was a misdemeanor possession of marijuana, which could and should have brought a fine with time served, since he'd spent the night in jail already. But they'd smacked him with felony resisting and assault on an officer, for which he'd end up serving thirty of thirty-four months first in Lancaster, later at Corcoran. The judge had perfectly thick white hair, which stayed tight in a hairspray helmet while he talked, and he looked only at his documents or the lawyers, never directly at Carl. He told Carl he'd been "lucky" not to have a record until now.

I had not understood that you didn't get to say goodbye. They just shoved him out a side door and we had to wait two days to visit him because of "processing."

During the first few months of Carl's sentence, my mom and I visited him every weekend. She was scared every time, obsessively checking her pockets for contraband cash or forgotten nail clippers, and shakily re-applying thick cocoa butter lip balm in the rear-view mirror while I watched the guard towers and picked at my cuticles. I had torn-up hands until years later, when a friend I worked with at the strip club told me having ugly nails affected my income.

After signing faded copies of visiting registries and getting patted down, metal detected, and questioned about our visit, Mom and I would sit in the noisy visiting room, at a plastic table, and Carl and I would talk about the book we were reading together. Mom would tap her fingers on the bench by her thighs and interject news from the outside.

Did he get to watch the news yesterday?

Yes.

So he knew about the tsunami in Japan.

He did. What was the update on getting her car fixed?

She'd asked his friend to come over last week but he never did.

Call again, baby, just call again.

He would turn to me. Kindee, how far did you get in that Angela Davis book? Did you read up to chapter three like we said?

I only got to chapter one. School's been hard.

The truly bizarre part about the whole thing was that none of us ever just started screaming.

. . .

"She's caught the darkness" was a way for Mom and Carl to describe a person who was depressed, bleak, hopeless. It was not the same as someone angry. For that they used "gone wild." You could go wild *on* someone, or on your own. While some people seemed to be going wild a lot, and that was considered a problem, for the most part people went wild for a brief time and then tried to resolve things. If you'd caught the darkness though, you had to actively begin to heal yourself or you were at risk. Darkness had to be actively encouraged to pass, or it might not.

Before the Worst Year of My Life, Mom and Carl had methods for handling it when someone caught the darkness. I don't know what all the things were that they did for each other but if it was one of them who caught it, the other paid more attention to me and made sure I was ok. If it was someone outside our house, they made calls, brought food, checked on people at their homes.

After Carl went to prison, Mom caught the darkness and I didn't know how to take care of her by myself. She sat at the table, staring at her hands, at the tabletop, at something just beyond the present moment, from the minute she got home from work until I went to sleep. I got tired of making macaroni and cheese, so I started putting salad dressing on the noodles, or peanut butter. She ate a few bites of things and thanked me but didn't move. She made it to work in the morning, so she must have slept sometimes.

Eventually, I confronted her.

"Mom, you need to snap out of it. Go grocery shopping. Do some laundry. This is nuts."

She seemed confused and hurt. "What?" She also looked skinnier. And the lines around her mouth were getting deeper.

"You're like a zombie and it freaks me out."

"That's hurtful," she said. She arched her back, stretched, and deflated again. "I'm thinking about Carl a lot."

"Yeah, well, we're not in prison!" I said, and leaned against the fridge. She was craning her neck to see me there. If she looked away, I'd consider the whole horrible thing done and go put my headphones on.

Instead she got up from her chair and came for me. "I'm so sorry, honey," she said, and brought my stiff self into a hug. She started crying. It scared me, and I disrespected her for it.

"Ok, ok," I said, and hugged her briefly back. Then I pushed her off. "Can you be normal now?"

"Sure," she said. She wiped her eyes.

"We're going to visit him in two days," I said. "He's gonna call you in an hour."

"Yeah."

"I'm hungry," I said. And I was sick of noodles. "Can we get pizza?"

"That sounds good," she said. She wanted to touch my face, my hair, I could feel it. She cracked four knuckles on one hand, then the other, and then went for her purse on the counter. "We can spend $12," she said. "Let's go to Little Caesars?"

"Yes!" I pumped my fist excitedly and got a smile out of her.

I turned on KROQ in the car so she could have something else to complain about besides Carl.

"This isn't music," she said.

"Welcome to the future," I said.

The smell of pizza inside a Little Caesars was a personal world of bliss.

"What can I getcha?" asked the guy at the register, with the silly hat on.

"A pepperoni personal pizza for me, please," I said.

"And for your sister here?" he said to my mom.

"Honey you just made my day," she said, genuinely, which I hated somehow. "I'll have a pepperoni one, too."

"You betcha," he said.

I went to a table while she paid. There were only two, and the other one was shared by a group of five people who looked a few years older than me. Three boys, two girls. Both of the girls were sitting on boys' laps. I wondered about that other boy, standing there with them. I imagined him turning to me and saying I was right on time and then running out of there with him and getting in a car with those people and driving away.

I sat across from them and looked at their feet. Vans. All of them. How did they afford them? I wondered.

I inadvertently made eye contact with the standing boy. He stared. I looked down.

He walked three steps and was at our table. "Mija," he said to me, "You want to come with me?" He was probably twenty. His brown eyes were dark, like mine, with heavy dark lashes that made him look sweet. His hair was black and combed back with so much gel I wanted to feel it crunch. His skin had been tanned darker on his forearms, maybe from skating, I thought. He wore long black shorts and a white T-shirt with a white tank underneath.

"No, she doesn't," my Mom said, approaching the table, glancing back at the register, like the goofball in the hat could help.

"This white lady belong to you?" the black-haired boy said to me. No one had ever asked me that.

"What the hell did you just say?" Mom said. He ignored her. He was still looking at me, waiting for an answer. His friends were watching. "I'm talking to you," Mom said to him.

"Yeah, she's my mom," I said.

"Oh my bad, mija," he said, and put a hand over his heart. "I thought she was like your caseworker or something. You have a nice evening with your moms." He nodded to Mom and bowed slightly as he moved away.

His friends all got up and they left. I watched them. The girls were wearing cut off shorts that showed the bottom half inch of their asses. I stared at those asses and wanted to touch them so bad.

Mom opened and turned our boxes the same way so their tops rested off the edge of the table.

I started eating.

"What was his problem?" Mom said.

I shrugged. "Maybe he thought I was into him," I said.

"Why would he think that? What did you do?"

"Nothing," I took a huge bite but then got afraid that somehow he'd read my mind.

Mom pulled a napkin from under her box and handed it to me. I used it. I swallowed. "I just looked at him," I said. I glanced outside. It was dark. There were cars in every spot in the tiny strip mall. The concrete was cracking out front of Little Caesar's.

"Ok, whatever," she said. "Let's eat."

Later that night she got sick. I knocked on the bathroom door while she was throwing up. She told me it was food poisoning but we'd eaten the same food and I was fine. She sounded horrible, in pain. She went to the doctor after two days of not being able to keep food in her. We missed our visit with Carl that week. Her friend Lynn from work came to drive her to the ER. She wouldn't let me come. So I sat at home until Lynn called and said she was coming to pick me up. That Mom needed to talk to me.

She had stomach cancer. It was in a late stage. This was not food poisoning or the flu. She was dying. There were other details. I don't remember them.

. . .

Lynn drove me to see Carl the following week with my papers that Mom had signed. She drove me many times after that too, sat just a foot or two away in the visiting room, read her book, and pretended not to listen.

Carl looked so sad. We sat in silence for a few seconds before he suggested we talk about Mom's diagnosis when we felt we were ready, but not force ourselves.

Ok, I said. But other than her diagnosis, which was death very soon, I didn't have much else to think about.

"What did you get up to last weekend?" he asked.

I told him I had grabbed a plastic Halloween costume feather headdress from some blonde chick's bobbing head at a concert and yelled drunkenly at her about sacredness and disrespect and eagles and chickens until her boyfriend beefed up next to her, at which point I threw the headdress at her and ran. Carl told me I'd done a good thing.

"No one learned anything," I said. "That girl looked at me like I was a monster, her boyfriend wanted to punch me, and when I left, they called me a crazy bitch."

"It doesn't matter," Carl said. "You're not trying to convert her to being a better person, you're trying to stop her from disrespecting Native American cultures by wearing a headdress she has no right to wear. And you did that. So, I call it a win."

"Probably her mom told her she had a Cherokee princess in her family tree," Carl said with a wink.

Another lie. Another translation. Another crack in my education.

Carl asked me to check out a book on the history of minstrelsy. He told me dressing up like an Indian was the same. "In my generation," he said, "everyone played this game called 'cowboys and Indians,' and the point was to kill each other."

"That's stupid," I said.

Carl suggested I read *Pedagogy for the Oppressed*. I read the beginning but it was too hard for me. I had caught the darkness. Loneliness. Back of the room. At school, I was a stranger. This doesn't apply to me. This won't help me. This isn't for me. This wasn't written to encourage me. The only exception was the biology textbook I read in Mr. East's class. I looked at diagrams of cells and imagined Mom's cancer, growing monstrous and brownish red in her stomach.

Read Freire, Carl said. Write to your principal and demand better education.

Carl told me that I could probably trust my instinct when I wanted to listen to someone. That my instinct not to listen was usually the one that went wrong. Not just me. Anyone. Listening is a sacred act, he said.

Listening is like letting someone touch you. The ears are open to anything that comes to them. You can't turn them off, he said.

It was confusing. Who to listen to? Who to trust? Who is teaching me, who is controlling me, who is helping me, who is exploiting me? I would sit in the back of my classes and try to figure it out. Listen to your heart of hearts, Mom said. Maybe I should study biology, I thought. Go into medicine. Heal people. Listen to yourself, Carl said.

But my self was often so disappointing. So cowardly. So broken. I couldn't listen to her very well. Anyway, in my head, she mostly screamed.

Read Angela Davis, Carl said. Read bell hooks. If you don't want to read what they assign you in school, don't. But read something.

I read and I didn't read. I got A's and then C's and then when mom got really sick, F's. I colored in pie charts, did math problems, and then didn't. I drew people wearing combat clothing. I drew people wearing wings and furry boots. I drew people having sex in hammocks. I read a few pages of the *Art of War*. I read a few pages of *Rules for Radicals*. I read Carl's letters. Sometimes, I wrote back.

Carl went to prison nine months before my mother died, and he didn't get out until after I'd moved to New York. He used to say any black man could go to jail just for living, but getting a prison sentence meant you'd pissed off someone in particular. After they sent him to Corcoran, he changed. He never blamed someone for "getting themselves locked up" again. When people at school or at the parties I went to or at mom's hospital asked me why he was locked up, I gave one of two answers. If I was mad at him, I said he got arrested for drugs that should have been legal but got locked up because he couldn't shut his mouth. If I was missing him or feeling mad at the system or the cops who had fucked with him, I said, "He was born Black in America and doesn't take shit."

Carl would call every morning, and I'd hear the robotic female voice of the collect-calling system announce that I was receiving his attempt, his reaching out, and most of the time I would answer and tell him that she was getting worse, but the morphine was at least making her comfortable. Sometimes we laughed over the things she said from her haze. Sometimes he talked about how the morphine probably felt to her, and I'd hear his longing, for something like relief. I didn't tell him I was taking a steady number of Vicodin I got from a kid at school, and that I knew the thick softness he was missing.

Occasionally I hung up on the California Department of Corrections, which had yet to add "And Rehabilitation" to its name, even though I knew it was Carl waiting on the line for me to accept the charges, that he would hear the click of me hanging up, and I usually lay still in bed for about an hour afterward, flattened by dread and shame and panic, until it was time to check on Mom.

At Corcoran, the gladiator games were just starting to make headlines. Carl had written me a parable about a cockfight in a letter, and I hadn't understood. He drew pictures in the margins of enormous men with cigars and roosters in cages. He wrote:

When the Big Man gets bored, he looks for blood. He finds his rooster, and he puts him in a cage. He takes his rooster down the road a ways, until he sees another rooster, owned by the next Big Man. He goes in to see the next Big Man and shows him the cage. The Big Men shake hands and light up their cigars. They put their roosters in a pit and let them go. The roosters don't know, because they have never known, that the Big Men are not their family. They are confused. They think the other rooster is their enemy. They try to kill him. One of them succeeds in breaking the leg, or gouging out the eye, of the other. Maybe one of them is killed. The Big Men laugh. They may even shoot a rooster who looks hurt. They hand each other money. When they get home, and someone wants to know what happened to the rooster? Where is our rooster? They shrug. Don't know, they say. Roosters like to fight, they say. Stupid bird must have gotten out. See, we need to cage him, they say. Otherwise he's a danger. Big Man counts his money. Maybe I'll do that again, he says to himself. That was a good time.

Carl stayed mostly safe, somehow, by making friends, casting himself as an educator, teaching other guys to read and analyze what they saw around them. In the main visiting room, I heard guys calling him "Pops" and he'd give a tough grin and say

"Boy, I'll pop you one!" and then change his face as soon as he was looking at me again.

My mom was dissolving into a hospital bed, choking, getting poked with thick IV needles, her face and arms full of tubes, and looking at me with eyes that begged for it all to stop. She must have done all the depressing paperwork while I was at school, at the beginning of the last hospital stay, or maybe she gave her power of attorney to her coworker. I was underage, and knew it was a stupid difference, between myself now and myself in two months, but the state said it mattered, so it did.

I was contorting with grief, furious with Carl for not being there with me, and discovering an impassable distance between myself and other people my age who didn't think about death or prison every day.

She called me a cunt, one night when I showed up late to visit her at the hospital, and she was yelling about my selfishness, and I laughed, out of the shock of it, the word "cunt" just hanging in the air between me and the woman whose cunt I'd emerged from, and I said something like "takes one to know one," and she said "fuck you," and I laughed again, because she was so frail and so angry it was absurd, and then she broke out and laughed too, and it made her throw up. I was drunk, and now I see the scene through the scrim of time and poetic irony: my mother there doing the vomiting while I did the drinking, both of us angry, both of us cunts.

For a while I went straight from school to the hospital on a bus, stared at my homework while I curled uncomfortably in a pink vinyl chair, and when a nurse asked who they could call to come pick me up, I would slip out, get another bus to our apartment, pass out, miss my first class, rush to the school, and do it again. I didn't talk to anyone about it but my friend Angie, the nurses, and Carl. I successfully became invisible in a sea of more loudly problematic or outstanding students. I migrated to the quiet wall at the back of the campus where the smokers didn't bother each other.

I considered busting the night nurses' cabinet door lock and getting Mom enough morphine to kill herself, because she'd asked me to more than once. I dreaded the moments when the nurses were away from the station, because I hoped I would do it and I knew I wouldn't and then I had to live with myself.

I never told her I wished she would die faster, but I thought it a few times, and I hated myself, then hated what my life demanded of me, then hated her for making that life for us, for me.

Mom told me she wanted me to be happy, find a man, get a job. She told me I was going to be fine, if I wanted it.

"Don't sell yourself short," she said. "Get your education. There's a lot of financial aid out there." She said these things on good days. On bad days she told me she regretted so much of her life. The last thing she said to me, before she entered her coma, was that she loved me, and that she had arranged for me to stay with Lynn until I was eighteen, and "be good." I told her loved her too. I promised her I'd be good. I held her hand, I lay in her bed with her, I cried against her papery skin and ate vending machine food for three days. The overnight nurses let me sleep there. I told her I loved her and stroked her hair and wondered what would happen to me and got scared, so scared of life without her. I knew I was definitely not going to stay with Lynn.

I wasn't there when she died. I was out getting drunk and walking in a mall with Angie, who had insisted I take a break and go into the world. She was thin and beautiful, a redhead who cut off all her hair, when that was still a big deal. She read philosophy books, and had what seemed like a lot of money. She had big perfect lips I wanted to bite.

I remember Angie that day, in a fluorescent mall-store filled with body products. She looked at the ingredients list on a small tub of natural shampoo. "Bananas," she said, "avocado, shea butter, some stuff I can't pronounce."

"If you can't pronounce it, is it really 'natural?'" I asked.

"Natural just means it has a less floral perfume in it," she said. "The natural bath products are for baby dykes like me."

I'd never heard her use that word and it sounded hard.

"If you were really trying to be natural you could just use olive oil for everything," I said.

"But that would be gross!" Angie said. She put the shampoo back in its rightful place on an artfully designed shelf made of distressed wood. She hesitated as she removed her hand, as if she'd considered, just for a split-second, toppling the whole pyramid of 4 oz tubs with a quick wave. "Let's go," she said. "I just hit my limit."

"I saw it," I said.

"Yeah," she said. "It happened very quickly."

We left. She dropped me at the hospital and I was told that Mom had passed quietly and without pain. The staff had moved my mom's body out already. But I didn't feel like I hadn't said goodbye. Not on that day, anyway. I felt guilty that she'd died alone and then certain that she'd waited until I left so I didn't have to see her dead.

They tried to get me to stay around because someone from Child Services needed to talk to me. I resolved to never be caught by them. I only had six more weeks until I was eighteen. I snuck out of the hospital and never went back. I craved the smell of that banana shampoo inexplicably and I gave in. I returned to the mall by myself, found the body product store, opened a tub, and inhaled hard. Sweet soft bananas held steady by the buttery avocado. A quiet cinnamon. It was a perfect smell. I wanted to smell it every day. But there was simply no way I could spend thirty-eight dollars on such an offensively tiny amount of that pleasure. A week later, Lynn picked up Mom's ashes and brought them to me at Angie's. She and Angie's mom spoke quietly. They both sat with me when Lynn gave me a small heavy box with my mom in it. There may be small bits of solid matter in there, Lynn said. Bone fragments. Part of a tooth.

"How much would you have paid for that shampoo in good conscience?" Angie asked me later that night.

"I could have happily paid four dollars," I said. I knew it right away.

"What if it wasn't your money?"

"Like, if I had a non-transferrable $50 gift card to the shop?"

"Okay, yeah," she said.

"I'd buy the tub of shampoo and a travel size with the difference."

"You make no sense at all."

"The shampoo actually smelled worse after I looked at the price."

"Of course it did," she said.

"No," I struggled, "*That's* the part that doesn't make sense at all!"

She sighed. "Nah, the price is the part that reminds you of the real bullshit. That shampoo's probably made of edible, food-grade bananas. Do you know how that company treats their factory or shipping or office workers? If the lowest employee in the company can't eat good fruits and vegetables on the wage they earn boxing up your favorite smell, then the price is fucking offensive no matter what it is."

"I doubt my sense of smell is that smart," I said.

"It would be so wonderful if all our senses were linked up with our sense of right and wrong," she said.

"I want to be like that," I said. "I probably could do it with a lot of practice. I think Carl might be like that."

"I think it takes a lifetime devotion to a serious meditative state," she said, "but that doesn't mean we bastard children of the end times shouldn't try."

I knew what she meant, but I couldn't help thinking: Shut up, Angie.

"I'm sorry," she said, as if reading my mind. "This is so shitty, Kindred. You got such a fucked-up deal in life right now. I hope you know I'm here for you, girl. I really am."

"Thanks," I said. She took me to see *Pulp Fiction* at a cushy theater, and bought us KitKats and Reese's and popcorn, and let me stare out the window silently the whole way home, and let me sleep in her bed with her. She stroked my hair and let me cry without telling me it was all going to be okay.

After Lynn dropped the ashes off they sat in a box on the kitchen table until Angie said, Kindred, honey, we got to do something about your Mom there. It's not right.

So we bought a can of Yuban. She threw the coffee away. I wouldn't have done that. But I wasn't thinking about wasting food right then.

Carl was still locked up when she died. He was being punished for something that happened on the Yard, and had been rolled up to a solitary unit during the last week of her life. When I went to visit him with her ashes in the coffee can, they wouldn't let me bring them in. So Mom waited in the car, and because I had nowhere else, I kept her in there for a long time.

I was used to sitting at a table with Carl, being able to hug him at the beginning and end of our hours-long conversations, but this time, I sat down for the visit in an unfamiliar gritty green cube behind thick glass and realized that they were punishing me, too. We put our hands on the glass like we were in a movie.

He looked bloated and gray. His eyes seemed heavy. He was sniffling and coughing.

We cried together, trapped in the glass, and he tried to get me to participate in a call-and-response poem he'd been practicing with me since I was tiny.

"We never hide to cry, you remember why?"

I shook my head and played my part at first. "Tell me why we don't hide to cry," I said.

"We never hide, even to cry, because we need our head up to lead or to fight."

I was supposed to say, "If we must cry, we cry with pride."

Carl had written the poem on an index card for me in elementary school. It was a totem against the bullies.

But I couldn't say it. It sounded insane. My mother was dead. Carl was as good as dead, stuck in that tomb. Lead who? Fight what? I had no sense of the pride he was asking me to feel.

There was a sharp moment of silence when I refused to answer his call, didn't give the response as it had been written for me. Instead I wrapped my arms around my head, leaned heavily down against the table, curled up to feel grief in spasms, out of his view, until I could breathe a little normally and raise my gaze to him. He held it.

Instead of concerned, or contorted with his own suffering, he seemed softly proud. He didn't console me. He didn't ask me any questions. He told me he loved me. He told he me would call at the normal time tomorrow, and I left.

The next day, at the apartment where Mom had lived with me, I sorted through my own things before I could touch hers. I left piles of clothes, papers, trash. I put other stuff in plastic bags and boxes. Angie and a few guys from school who did what she said came to help me move some of our stuff into a storage space. Mom had given me her debit card and the PIN and I got cash out to pay for it.

Angie quietly packed things she thought I would need, while I robotically touched and moved and maybe dropped things I couldn't make decisions about. I smelled Mom's clothes when Angie wasn't looking. I kept a sweater. I kept some of her cheap nickel-plated jewelry and a throw pillow that had always been on her bed.

After Mom died, I used Angie's as a home base, I often slept in my car, and I drank disgusting things, Southern Comfort and Coke, syrupy fruit liquors, wine coolers, whatever I could get someone to buy me cheap. I got my mail at Angie's. Her parents made a little pile for me on the table in the breakfast nook. I had sex with a few people who would let me spend the night and eat out of their refrigerators. I don't remember much of those days or weeks or months now, and I'm grateful.

Carl wrote me a letter every Monday and Wednesday. The Wednesday letters were "for shared study;" they were handwritten transcriptions of essays he admired, pages of his own ideas about politics and race and class war, book reviews, musings on television and films he had seen, and his hand-drawn art. Just before I quit school, I sent him the colored diagram I had to make of photosynthesis, instead of turning it in to Mr. East's biology class. He loved that one, and hung it in his cell next to a picture of us, the three of us.

Carl and I both had a version of that picture, Polaroids taken one right after another by another prisoner in the main visiting room. We bought the Polaroids for $2.00. Mom, Carl, and I posed in front of a hand-painted cartoon forest backdrop. Mom's hips faced forward, her torso twisted in, her arms clung to Carl's waist, and her neck craned toward the camera. Her eyes were on something else just before it. Carl's right arm held steady around her, from shoulder to lower back. Carl's left arm was tight around my shoulders, and my arms were pressed flat to my sides. Despite all the awkwardness, Carl and I wore identical, deeply mischievous facial expressions: our eyes settled directly in the camera, our mouths curved up to the left in a shared half-smile. He liked the picture. I liked it. Mom had thought it was a bad sign for my future.

On Mondays Carl would reflect on our conversations, write stories from his life, tell me things about my mom I didn't know and sometimes didn't believe, and occasionally, he'd let me in on how terrible things were for him inside. He complained about the slow, understaffed medical ward. He told me they had stopped giving him his blood pressure medication, and he needed me to write to the warden, which it took me two months to do. He got his medication reissued after that, and he was so grateful, and I just felt guilty.

Sometimes Carl's letters would arrive missing pages, or stuffed with a notice from the prison mail room: the "contraband" had been removed from the envelope. I complained to Carl, because it seemed ill-advised or stupid to complain to a corrections officer.

"Please stop sending me letters on *Revolutionary Suicide*," I said, on one of those collect calls. "They always take out the most important parts and now I don't know what happened to Pony."

He chuckled. "Did you get the theory though?"

"Not really," I said. "I can't tell if he wants me to kill myself for the people or not."

He laughed and said he'd try a different way.

His next letter was written entirely in the spaces between the lines of an academic text from 1958 called *The Dynamics of Planned Change: A Comparative Study of Principles and*

Techniques, authored by three presumably white male professors of social sciences at large Midwestern Universities.

Kindee,

Greetings my loved one. I hope you are breathing clean air, drinking clean water, and sleeping well at night. It was so wonderful to see you last week! I forgot to tell you how much I liked your new hair color. Very bold. Joe says he didn't recognize you, that's why he didn't wave like usual. (I say he never wears his glasses!) Well, on to our next topic.

This week we are going to talk about our feelings. I know I usually write about personal issues on Monday, but I think you'll understand why feelings are an appropriate topic for a shared study letter.

There are standards for acceptable feelings to have and for acceptable expressions of feelings you are having. The standards are enforceable through threat of punishment, expulsion from a group, or other forms of shame. We live in a world with many unspoken answers to who should feel what feeling, and when, and where, and why, and for how long, and what should be done about it, in order for group functioning to proceed smoothly. Some people live all their lives under one set of rules. Others must navigate the demands of multiple sets of standards.

Sometimes the rules are laid bare by a disturbance. Imagine: a loud public argument between two well-dressed, thin, beautiful white women at a shopping mall, a violent tantrum from an old person in a grocery store, a crying male politician leading a big meeting. These events are memorable because they show us what isn't "supposed" to happen under our current rules.

Rules about feelings are also expressed in idioms, advertising copy, religious clichés and the like: they are smuggled into our beliefs as a set of repeated instructions that scaffold our everyday language and pose as common sense.

When people are gathering around a shared goal of making a change to their current circumstances, particularly when they must challenge, confront, or provoke a power structure (like the government, a school board, or a greedy boss), they may choose to openly discuss their designs for an alternative, internal standard for handling feelings.

This brings us back to the beginning: functional groups must have agreement within them about how people are going to behave when they feel strong feelings.

If the agreement doesn't exist, or if it is broken, or if it is unfair and privileges the experience of one party over another, resentment happens. For instance, under the current dominant set of laws and rules about expressing strong feelings, no one is allowed to scream at each other without fearing arrest. But men get arrested for screaming at women much more than women get arrested for screaming at men. However, women get told they are crazy when they scream, which does them enormous harm in the long run, I think. Men are told that they are just letting off steam. So you aren't supposed to scream, no one is, but the social and political consequences for doing it are different, depending on your gender, in this case.

Here's a real-world example to think about:

The Black Panthers required members to memorize and behave according to the following "8 Points of Attention":

Speak politely.

Pay fairly for what you buy.

Return everything you borrow.

Pay for anything you damage.

Do not hit or swear at people.

Do not damage property or crops of the poor, oppressed masses.

Do not take liberties with women.

If we ever have to take captives do not ill-treat them.

In other words, Party members were *ordered* to keep their emotions under control, for the proper functioning of the Party, and, by joining the Party, members agreed to abide by a particularly restrictive set of rules for how they would express feelings. This made some members less vulnerable to provocation, as their self-discipline developed. It made others, however, more vulnerable to the poisonous tentacles of agent provocateurs, factionalism, and COINTELPRO (Did you read that article I sent you about all those covert, illegal operations of the FBI?), as they struggled to participate in serious Party activity while repressing big emotions like love, fear, jealousy, loneliness, rage. Repression is not the same as self-discipline, no matter how similar their immediate effects on behavior may be. People working to make real change have to be honest with themselves to feel real feelings, and take care of each other when strong or big feelings come.

That's why I don't tell you not to cry, Kindee. Just cry with your head up, and know what you got to cry about, and what you don't.

Next time, I'll write about the myth that oppression makes a people less fit to govern themselves.

. . .

I'll leave you with this idea from a social scientist in 1946:

"Intergroup relations in this country will be formed to a large degree by the events on the international scene and particularly by the fate of colonial peoples...Jim Crowism on the international scene will hamper tremendously progress of intergroup relations within the United States and is likely to endanger every aspect of democracy." --Kurt Lewin

Love,

Carl

Now that Carl is missing, I search for clues. For the first time, I read the printed lines he'd written his letter on, the words from *The Dynamics of Planned Change*:

Interdependence among the parts of a system is often associated with a fear that the improvement of one part can be gained only at the expense of another, and there is thus a tendency to feel threatened by any proposal for change except, perhaps, one's own.

Resistance based on threat is particularly a problem because of the psychological concomitants of a state of threat. These include constricted field of attention and a need to find some way of controlling whatever it is that threatens. The former makes it difficult for the threatened subsystem to envisage or believe in new and improved ways of operation. The need for control makes it imperative that existing sanctions be applied to punish the deviant or recalcitrant part and restore familiar patterns of control. Change, therefore, is the very thing which is most intolerable to a system or subsystem experiencing a high degree of threat.

On the other hand, it must be remembered that it is not pleasant to feel threatened and that pain can become a force toward change. The system experiencing threat will try first and most urgently to return to old and secure patterns of behavior. If this course of action is blocked off, however, it may be willing to try something new. In a state of crisis any change may be viewed as an improvement.

When I was seventeen, I needed food. I found my listening ear, I found my drugs, and there was always free alcohol. What was hardest to get was food, because the only way to get it was money, and that was the one thing I couldn't produce. I could talk about my problems with my friends, but none of them were hungry, or even knew what I meant when I said it. They thought I was referring to the situation in which you have a slight twinge of desire for something to eat. I couldn't get them to understand. I was woozy and confused and irascible and tasting metal. Groups of people would all split a check and I'd have to chip in my last cash even though I conspicuously drank lemon water and ordered no food, and so I would let go the small wad of precious dollars, because I couldn't bear the misperception that would happen if I refused to pay "my share" of the group bill. I did not want people to think I was rude, and I did not want to talk to them about being poor. I stayed the most at Angie's. I never said no to drinks, pills, bumps, weed, whatever. My joints ached in the morning's sharp edges. Sometimes I sat out on the street in front of my high school late at night, drinking, and left my stolen nips in neat empty rows on the steps.

As disgusting as it could be, my car felt like the safest, freest place I could be besides Angie's. I drained the bank account, utterly paralyzed by all the decisions I had to make and how terrible it was to make them. I had to keep looking at her name. I couldn't take her name off the account, because I was a minor. I occasionally called Lynn when I knew she wouldn't be able to pick up and left messages saying I was great, staying with a good friend, no worries, handling it.

When I told Angie about things like this, she would sink into herself and her face would tense. Sometimes she tried to help me solve problems. "Let's look at the classifieds for a job that accepts high school kids," she'd say. Or, "Maybe you should go to a free support group for people like you?"

Inwardly, I thought: People like me. Didn't she understand? I was bitterly alone, there were no people like me.

I said, "Ok, I'll look into that," and then didn't. Because I couldn't.

I would often find myself staring into space, hunched over and straining my neck, and not remember what I had been thinking about, but aware that my body was far too heavy and painful to move from where I'd settled. And that sensation of heaviness would ease when I was high on almost anything, especially alcohol, and I could at least try to think about feeding myself when the pain was a little less pressing. I ate plates full of chips at every party.

Even Angie, who saw so much, never saw me at the worst moments. Those all happened alone.

On my eighteenth birthday, I woke up in too much sun. I was sleeping in my backseat and wasn't sure where I'd parked. I tried to sit up and was immediately ready to puke. The painful throbbing in my head, the light stabbing through my eyes. I felt around for sunglasses, for water. I pulled myself up and breathed through a few more waves.

I felt the crying push up from behind my shoulder blades and sting my nose. Useless. Alcoholic.

Your real dad didn't love you and never tried. Piece of Shit. Your mom had a short stupid life, and so will you.

And so on. I cried so deep and so long, and with no calming rest at the end. The end was exhaustion, a delusional quivering hope that I might truly be dying *right now*, and then the realization that I wasn't, and so I'd have to get up and move, before a cop found me. That tiny shot of adrenaline my body could make was enough. I got in the driver's seat. The crying started again, this time faster. It scared me.

This is not my life, I thought. This is not a life. This can't be life.

I turned the car on and started driving, seeing a lopsided and loopy world through tears, half-hoping that the car would crash and I wouldn't have to be in charge of myself, wouldn't have to do adulthood at all.

I went to Angie's, told her I was hungover, let her judge, and then fell asleep in her cool, sweet-smelling sheets after she left.

Angie's house was a luxurious playground full of things I needed and things I'd forgotten how to want. The endless cold and hot water. The beds. The books. More than one kind of cracker to snack on. TV. I couldn't believe how much the TV was a part of her family's constant environment in the house.

Angie's parents moved through rooms and hallways without eye contact or touching each other. They would acknowledge me with nods, sometimes a "Hi Kindred," but we didn't have conversations, and that was exactly how I needed it to be.

They had a housekeeper named Flora who talked to her sister on the phone while she did the laundry once a week. She scrubbed and dusted and vacuumed with music on, swingy songs that sometimes inspired me to dance out to where she was at and help her. Flora and I occasionally took a shot of tequila together from the pantry, especially after cleaning the bathrooms. She threw Spanish words to me here and there, and criticized me outright for not learning them, and praised me with applause and loud sound effects when I got them right.

But I didn't always see her, because she could come over and do her entire routine without me waking up. She did the ninja thing that day, while I slept off the poison, but I knew she'd been there because she had washed the small pile of clothes I'd left on the floor.

When I woke up in the afternoon, I called Angie on her new mobile phone.

"Happy birthday," she said, a little too solemn.

"When are you coming back?"

"I'm hanging with some people at Danny's tonight," she said. "I'll be home late." My heart hurt. I was not invited, even though I knew all the people she was going to be with.

"Let's do something tomorrow," she said. "If you're not hungover."

We hung up, I got back in bed, and I watched *Home Improvement* until I fell back asleep.

At 4:30 AM, I woke up again. It was a good time to leave if I was going to visit Carl. Angie was curled against the wall, breathing sweetly through her mouth. I looked at her for long enough to realize that if she woke up and caught me I'd be embarrassed, then slid out of the bed, picked up my clothes (Oh, thank you, Flora!), and went into the bathroom. My hair was in a lopsided knot. My eyes looked hollow, rimmed with red. Like Mom's had. I showered and rubbed some of Angie's fancy products on my face.

I poked around Angie's parents' stash of special wines, left them alone, stole a half-empty bottle of Southern Comfort from the pantry, since I didn't mind it and no one would miss it, and pocketed the loose change on the counter.

I was eighteen. Carl didn't know I was not graduating, because I was the only one he'd hear that from now. It didn't matter, I told myself. People are all stupid and the only good ideas come from crazy people and addicts.

It took me nearly three hours to drive to the prison from Los Angeles. I bought a breakfast burrito and a coffee at a Jack in the Box, and stared into the wide orange morning in Santa Clarita while talk radio made the sounds of education and outrage.

It was after 9:30AM when I turned the car off in the visitor parking lot at Corcoran that Sunday, and realized in an uncomfortable crush that I had only ten dollar bills to bring in, instead of my normal twenty, because I'd finally tapped Mom's one account. Carl was going to ask me about that Angela Davis book again during this visit and I hadn't read any of it.

I wished I'd stayed drunk from the night before, the kind of drunk that doesn't fade quickly, the kind of drunk that you know people can smell on you but you don't care. You know you're stable enough on your feet they probably won't say anything, and when you start sobering up, the justification for staying drunk is physically self-evident. I swigged the SoCo.

Sunglasses were not allowed on grounds at the prison, and the light shot into my head as I took mine off. Carl was lucky I was coming to see him, I told myself. Fuck the book we were going to discuss. What could we have to say to each other about *Women, Race and Class*? Carl was now calling himself a Black Revolutionist. My mother was white. Midwestern, blonde, mayonnaise-loving white. They were a couple for sixteen years. How had that happened? My biological father was a one-night stand named Alex, origin unknown. I looked like my mother with darker hair and skin that tanned. She had always burned in the sun. I didn't care. Of course, I cared. I didn't care. I knew I should probably think about something or someone other than myself.

I swigged the SoCo hunched under my hair in the car, in full view of the guard tower. Maybe I'd hang out at a 7-11 or Burger King off the freeway and sleep somewhere new tonight.

My hair was getting long. I pulled a strand from the back and measured. It definitely covered my nipples. I had more split ends than not. At least I smelled like nice bath products, in addition to alcohol.

I kept my head down and watched the asphalt on my way to the line of visitors outside the first cage, where they'd check my ID and decide if I was dressed right. After the first visits with Mom I had realized that it was young women, my age to maybe early forties, who were routinely sent away to make themselves less beautiful or sexy. Women who came to visit in soft yoga pants were always sent away to change, even if the pants covered them all the way to their shoes.

When I'd been turned away the first time for wearing blue jeans, I'd discovered the women at Friends Outside, a little room set up at the edge of the parking lot with instant coffee and visiting-warden-friendly clothes to borrow. They had me throw on a pair of sweats over whatever I was wearing so my own clothes couldn't get lost.

"Too much shape on that one," a regular Sunday-church visitor had murmured conspiratorially to me once. She nodded at another female visitor, whose large cleavage and ass curves defied even the Friends Outside's largest women's sweatsuits.

"I ain't going back there to put on no men's shit," the woman had said. "Y'all can't do that to me. That's just wrong." Her body, which could not be hidden, was allowed in to visit after everyone else in the line went through. Just that time, they said.

Because I kept all my clothes in the car, I was in a much better situation going in.

As I made it across the parking lot, I checked the guard's cage and saw a broad-chested white guy, exactly the kind who made us all change. I wasn't wearing the wrong colors, but my tight black pants were ripped at the knees and thighs and my sweatshirt wasn't covering the shape of my eighteen-year-old ass. If he didn't feel lenient, he'd refuse to let me in to visit. I glanced at the people who had already made it through to the waiting room, and at the few who were in line in front of me. I recognized a few usuals. It looked like Diana had brought some new pictures of the girls with her, but not the girls themselves this time. Diana wore her beige suit. She always had shining ringlets, which she shook and patted until she saw her son. If I went to change clothes before getting in line, it might be another hour before I got processed, as Sunday morning visit slots always filled up. But if I made it up to the first cage and then got sent back to change, I'd end up even farther down the food chain. I decided to risk it.

A guard I didn't recognize told me to look up at him when he checked my ID. He seemed ready to question me, looked at my date of birth twice, checked the roster to make sure of something, maybe that my ID hadn't already been used that day? I couldn't imagine what else for, since I was such a regular customer. Framed by a thin, graying comb-over, his face was rugged, pockmarked and older than I'd imagined from farther away. There was no way he was going to let me in. Guys like him wanted prisoners to see women in Victorian hoopskirts and cardboard collars, or burlap sacks, if they got the chance to see women at all. His nametag caught my eye: *Seabury*.

I knew there were guards there making a gambling sport of torturing people out on the Yard. That the gladiator games were only ended temporarily, and had resurfaced in a new form. Carl had never given me any direct facts or instructions, but I knew I hated that olive-green shirt and the smell of Seabury's coffee-cigarette breath, and that I wished I knew how to make him feel it without getting myself in trouble. I was suddenly sure he was one of the dirty COs taking bets on the fights he set up.

"Who you here for?" he asked, still holding my ID.

I told him Carl's prisoner number. Then his name.

"You can't wear those pants inside the visiting room," Seabury said. "And, unfortunately, Friends Outside isn't open today. You'll have to change at home and come back before 1PM to get back in line." He tossed my ID in the space below his plastic protective window. I had to get on my toes to fish it out. Seabury was the one who would decide if Carl and I were going to see each other on that day, and so I was not going to run my mouth. Not yet.

Especially on weekends, guards *knew* how far the regular visitors traveled. Many of us couldn't go home and come back on the same day.

I took my ID, ambled to the car, hit the SoCo, changed into some of Mom's dingy old pink velour track pants behind my half-open door, and got back in line.

This time I was behind a man maybe in his forties. He was short, clean-shaven, with dark hair that went salt-and-pepper along his ears. He was wearing a collared purple shirt and flapping his hands just slightly in his pants pockets. It sounded like he was muttering prayers in Spanish.

I went through the process again. Seabury told me to turn around in front of him for a "visual inspection," then he buzzed me through the first set of doors, and watched my covered ass walk through them.

I handed over my ID to new officers, showed them my little plastic bag with dollar bills and pictures in it, went through the metal detector, got patted down, waited in a plastic chair, stared at the beige linoleum. Other visitors' feet shuffled and tapped around me. Dirty sneakers, sensible pumps, pantyhose encasing swollen ankles. The two kids there, girls in matching flouncy white Sunday dresses and saddle shoes, played a game of running between their chairs and the guard's desk until Purple Shirt asked them to stop and their responsible adult held them close to her and shushed them.

Aside from the little kids, I was often the youngest. This time a girl around my age with bleached blonde hair in a big ponytail argued with the guard about changing out of her off-shoulder sweater, tank top, and hoop earrings. She'd gotten past the first check. She told the guard behind the desk that his homeboy had let her through and she wasn't trying to get back in that line for some bullshit.

"I'm sorry ma'am," the young guard said, clearly unsure if "Miss" might have been a better move. "We have rules here that need to be followed."

"Then you better tell your boy out there," she pointed at Seabury, "that he don't know his own *dick* when it's right there in his *hand*."

I simultaneously admired her and feared she'd get arrested. The young guard responded to everything she said by repeating himself. She had to give up eventually. She stalked to Friends Outside, I presumed, wishing I'd caught her eye so I could warn her it was closed, but then, a half hour later, while I was pacing the side of the waiting room I hadn't been sitting in, she reentered, seething, silent, sans earrings, wearing sweatpants and a hoodie sweatshirt, in full make up, with her rhinestone sneakers, and she sat with her arms crossed and her eyes at the floor. Seabury had lied to me? Or did she have a suitcase in her car too?

I got called into the visiting room.

Carl looked straight at me when the door opened and smiled so excitedly, like a kid getting a present. His right cheek was puffed up and dark purplish black. He hugged me gingerly at first, then held me tight for a second once my face was on his chest. He smelled familiar, but with a whiff of something sourly antiseptic. He was wearing a white A-frame undershirt with his clean, pressed prison blues and his shoes were gleaming white.

"Glad you could make it," he said, pulling away and turning to find his chair. "Happy birthday!"

"What happened?" I asked, gesturing toward him.

"To my face?"

"Yeah, to your face."

"Well," he said, and glanced around the room, "I can't talk about it here. Understand?"

I didn't, since "here" was all around us, and the only place he and I could ever talk was "here," but it didn't matter enough to me to try and understand. He looked like he'd been working outside; the skin on his face and forearms seemed darker. His hands were cracked and dry, his elbows were ashy, and his hair was frizzing out of the rows someone had braided for him. His grays were visible.

"If you got in a fight, shouldn't you be rolled up right now?" I said.

He nodded slowly, then said, "That would be true if I'd fought on my own time."

"What's that mean?" I said. I was sick of code. "Just tell me what's happening."

We were in the large visiting room for people who got contact visits. We were allowed ten seconds to hug at the beginning and end. We sat across a low table on metal and plastic chairs that belonged in an elementary school. The walls were blue-gray, with wan sunlight coming in one side of the room through clouded windows. Later we'd take a little walk to the vending machines along the back wall, and I'd use up my ten single dollar bills buying Carl a burrito and candy and chips and soda.

"You don't look great," he said.

I thanked him, sarcastic and thick.

He didn't speak for an eternity, while I breathed through some nausea and shifted in my chair. He was watching me.

"What do you want to talk about?" I said.

"It's okay to just sit here," he said. "I could look at your ears for two hours straight."

"Shit, are you high?" I said. I heard my mother's voice come from my mouth. He must have too.

He kept focus on my eyes. "I haven't gotten high on any real shit since I got here," he said, "although I don't blame you for thinking it."

All this time, I'd never asked him if he was using anything in prison. It hadn't occurred to me that he could be, until that moment. The shift mattered--the fact of him living there, all the time, where someone hit his face and he couldn't tell me why, and there was an economy in which he could buy and sell drugs, suddenly felt newly real.

"What would you want if you could have any drug here?" I said.

"I can have any drug here," he said, glancing around again. "I guess that letter I sent with the discussion of the prison's black market wasn't that exciting for you, huh?"

"Not much."

"But if I had to stay inside the tomb to do this fantasy drug," he gazed somewhere up into his memories and desires, "I'd still do mushrooms before anything else."

I laughed, for real. "You're absurd," I said.

"You should try them," he said. "They can change your life."

"I have tried them," I said. "I was at Venice Beach. Not impressed."

"Who'd you trip with?"

"A friend from school."

"Angie?"

"Nah, some kid I never see anymore."

"You need to be with people you love and admire, who can encourage you to go new places in your head," he said. "It's good to have a sober person around to hold the reality, too."

"I don't have any of those people," I said.

"Cryin' shame," he said. Then he was infuriatingly quiet again.

I knew he knew I wasn't sober. I knew it hurt him. I knew he wouldn't say anything about it to me, wouldn't embarrass or expose me, wouldn't put me at any risk I wasn't putting myself at already. I hated him for his transparent sense of duty and loyalty.

I hated Mom, and then she died, but I loved her. Carl had too. It was a large thing to have in common. We both knew what her skin smelled like in the morning, and we knew how much she hated work shoes, and we knew how sad she got around bedtime, and we had pictures, of us three together, in which my mother beamed at one or both of us, her reckless blonde hair constantly blowing into someone's eyes, and her snaggle-tooth sticking out in most of them, and I figured if I was going to love anyone else living, and since I already knew I could love someone I hated and someone dead, I should go ahead and try to keep loving Carl, so I loved him guiltily, loved him angrily.

Something in my heart cracked open and spilled out my eyes.

"So good to see you," he said. Then he said it again, and it meant even more. "So, so good to see you, honey."

"I'm sorry it's been so long," I said to the floor.

He asked how I was holding up.

I said not too good.

Two hours later, I realized we hadn't done the vending machines and we'd talked only about me and my problems.

He'd been helpful, he'd been a good dad, he'd listened to me, but of course I hadn't told him everything. That I was not really in school anymore, that I was rarely sober, those were things I did not say.

"I know times are hard," he said, "But they are always hard for people like us, who are fighting the system that governs most aspects of our daily lives."

"I'm not even fighting the system!" I said. "I'm just trying to survive."

"But that is *your* fight, baby," he said, and patted my hand. "It's the most important fight you can be in, to survive, until you are ready to take up something else."

"You always act like I'm some kind of big protestor, an activist, like you," I said. "But I'm not. I don't care about waving signs or staying up late talking politics at the coffee house."

He smiled. "You know there's more to it than that."

"Sure," I said. "But I'm not doing any of it."

"No one is asking you to do anything you don't want to do," he said. But he was. I never wanted to go to Corcoran, it was so hard to get there, and so hard to get in, and so hard to deal with all the bullshit. But I did it anyway. He just didn't make sense, talking like that from inside that place. Or maybe he did, because he could imagine that everyone on the outside was making free-will decisions all the time when he couldn't.

"How's your political education classes going?" I asked.

"Slowly but surely," he said, and smiled. "Did you read my last letter about it?"

"No," I said. It seemed useless to lie about that.

He nodded. "I love talking about politics with the guys in here," he said. "No one knows what's wrong with their own country as well as a convict."

"I'm going to the vending machines," I said. "The usual?"

"Let's go look and see what they've got today," he said. "I'm not in the mood for beans."

He came with me to the machines, picked a sandwich instead of his normal burrito, then went back to our table, because he wasn't allowed to touch the money. After vending, I walked over to the microwave. Another visitor was using it, trying to press the greasy buttons with her long nails rather than touch them with the pads of her fingers. It wasn't working at first. She figured it out. When her food was done and she turned around, we acknowledged each other.

"Kitchen's all yours," she said. "You go ahead and feed your man, now."

"Right," I said. "Thanks."

I sat with Carl again.

"I want you to know I'm really proud of you," he said.

I had no idea what he was talking about.

"I know you don't believe you're doing anything important," he said. "But you are. You come out here and you nourish me for my own struggle. Every day you make it through the pain of losing Mom, you are doing something important. You just got to keep putting one foot in front of the other, ok? Stay committed to yourself."

I looked at the grime around the legs of his chair.

He hugged me again when I left, and I missed him, and I wanted to get away from that place, and I kept hearing his words in a loop on the way home.

Stay committed to yourself.

I smoked Angie's weed all day the next day while she was gone and resolved, again, to make some decisions. I had to get something together.

I had to at least try being eighteen before I gave up, I decided. Some part of me, still inspired by and admiring Carl, wanted to see if things would change, and that was enough.

4

SELF-RELIANCE

Just after I turned eighteen, I ran out of money for rent on the storage space. But when I went to turn in my key and say goodbye to the few small boxes of stuff and the yellow couch I thought I was losing, the night manager handed me a receipt and said my rent had been paid through another six months. I recognized my old biology teacher's signature on the receipt. Jonathan East.

Mr. East was a slightly shorter than average. He had light brown hair that stayed a little feathered on his head because it was so fine. He was fast and precise when he moved. He wore thin wire frames and button up shirts. Some days he wore khakis, the heavy kind that absorb things. Some days he wore jeans. He always wore the same pair of buttery brown loafers.

On the first day of class he stood in front of his desk with his arms loosely crossed. I looked at his fly and wondered about his penis. That day he was wearing dark khakis and a blue and purple plaid shirt, light cotton, short sleeve, with the top button undone. I guessed he was thirty.

"Some teachers think they should be the absolute authority

in the classroom," he said. "They think they rule a small kingdom. But I don't like envisioning you all as subjects, and I think historically kings get power by intimidating people." We shuffled around, not sure where this was going. "I'm not in charge of whether you go pee, or come to class, or do your homework, and it's your choice to pass or fail this class. So let's just say I know more about biology than you, and I'm going to try to give you some biology-related information for a few months, and you're going to try and remember the stuff we do together. Ok?"

Most people nodded and said "Ok" reflexively. I stared at him without moving, and so he noticed me. He asked my name.

"Kindred," I said.

"What do you want out of this class, Kindred?" he asked me.

I had no idea. "Um," I said, "I guess an 'A?'"

"How do you plan to get that 'A?'"

"I don't know," I said, annoyed now, "I guess I'll study."

"Perfect," he said. "That works for me."

He asked two other students the same question, and got the same answers. Point made. He turned around and started writing on the board. I looked at his butt. He did something to stay in shape. He was really looking good. His butt was round and firm but not all clenched up.

He turned around. We met eyes, his skipped away quickly. "These are the pages you are responsible for studying this week. There are ten pages per day of class. The classes will be relevant to each set of ten pages, in successive order. I suggest you keep up with the reading, because you will get a lot more out of the class that way. If you like to read ahead, you are equipped with the information you need. Any questions?"

We were all stunned at this. I remember it like it was a smell, or a loud startling sound. We didn't get talked to like adult human beings capable of making our own choices that often.

"Well, if you feel confused about anything, please speak up," he said. "For today, we are going to do a short and sweet experiment together to get you used to the procedure of the lab. When you come in to work on a lab project..."

I tuned him out and watched him move. I wondered if he was gay. Or a dancer. He was just so graceful.

"Kindred," he said. I'd missed the important part before my name. He was waiting for an answer to something.

"Sorry, I was spaced out," I said. "What are you asking me?"

He smiled. "I just told you two rules of thumb for working in the lab. Did you hear those?"

"Nope," I said. Someone stifled laughter. I looked down at my hands. I didn't want all this attention.

"Did anyone hear them?" he asked the class. Of course Vanessa had, and her hand was up and stretched irritatingly high, with just the hint of a wave in her fingers.

"Yes, what's your name?" Mr. East asked her.

"Vanessa," she said, a tiny bit cloying. "And the two rules of thumb are: 'your hands are dirtier than you think' and 'put the cap back on as soon as you can.'" She waited.

"Nice," Mr. East said. "Thanks for paying attention." ˌ

I went in and out of hearing the rest. I started looking through my book. I turned to the first of the pages we'd been assigned. My mind exploded. I was learning about plant cells for the first time. The illustrations were beautiful, vivid, strange, and I loved them.

Mr. East left me alone for the rest of the class. Later he told me it was because he saw me fall in love with biology on my own, and it was such a rare and beautiful thing he didn't want to disturb me.

And it was a rare and beautiful thing, for me to feel surprised like that. Interested, curious. Without fear. With no traumatic association with the thing I was looking at, because it was completely new to me, and seemingly, made just for me by people who knew what I liked. The drawings were all cartoonish, freehand, with crosshatching and squiggly shapes. The colors were a little faded because the book had been in use since its publication in 1976. Later of course, the cell drawings all looked like cancer to me.

I swear he winked at me that day, though. And he always maintained that he couldn't have. Wouldn't have.

How did I get here? How did I become who I am?

He had paid for my storage space.

I went to his classroom on a Friday, guessing that he wouldn't have plans after school. I wore a black mini dress, sneakers, and a black hoodie. I'd done my liquid eyeliner thick and heavy.

"Mr. East?" I leaned in the doorway.

"Kindred!" Wow, he was nervous. My body electrified. He was a pretty guy. There were still a few kids in the hallways.

"I just wanted to come say thank you in person," I said.

"Do you have some time to talk?" he said. "Can I get caught up on your situation?"

I was supposed to be at Angie's already. I told him I couldn't stay just then but maybe another time. He said okay, let me take you to dinner, and then wrote his phone number down and handed it to me.

"You can call me," he said. "I know you're really going through it. I'm so sorry to hear about your mom. Please call if you need anything at all."

Something in my heart twisted around at his kindness. I

believed him. And also, I knew, I just knew somehow, that he wanted something from me, too. I had no idea how he'd heard about my mom, or my storage space. Maybe he just wanted me to come back to school and graduate. Maybe he wanted to fuck. I called from Angie's bedroom later that day, and we made a date for the upcoming Sunday night.

The first time I went out to dinner with Mr. East was the first time I ate sushi. He smiled over and over again, without making me feel stupid. He taught me to use chopsticks. He ordered things that wouldn't scare me too much: salmon, tuna, avocado roll. He ordered a large Sapporo and let me sip on it.

We talked about movies. I loved the flavor of sushi rice. I thought things were going well, although I didn't really know what things I was dealing with.

Mr. East had waited until I was eighteen to ask me to dinner. I respected him for that. He paid for my storage rental, before he ever got to touch me. He was practical and kind and genuinely interested in my well-being. I thought he was ridiculous for caring about me, but he was helpful, and inoffensive, and nice looking. There was just something about him that was weird.

It was the penumbra of repressed shame he had for being a foot fetishist, the poor thing.

I took the attention, and the dinner, and the fleeting, friendly touch, and the thrill, and the confusion. I took it and it gave me reason to move forward with being alive. Mr. East gave me something strange, but it wasn't anything I didn't want.

As we left dinner he told me he'd like to ask me about something personal. He said if it made me uncomfortable at any time I could say so and the conversation would be over. He said I didn't owe him anything. I believed him.

"I would really like to worship your feet," he said.

"Worship?"

"I'd like to sit on the floor below you and touch and kiss your perfect feet, if you'd let me, for about ten minutes."

I laughed. I said sure.

He took me to his Ikea model apartment. He set me up like a princess on his couch, leaning on a pile of pillows. He put on some twenty-year old action movie.

"Are you comfortable? Do you want some water?"

I said I was fine, go ahead.

He untied and pulled my boots off slowly. He sniffed and stroked my feet gently first with socks on, then peeled my socks off and stroked and sniffed again. The first time, I was so fascinated by how unfamiliar it was, to see a grown man ecstatically sniffing my dirty socks, I didn't notice how much I liked it. It tickled a little. He sucked on my toes.

He missed a week after we'd seen each other for three consecutive Sunday evenings. I felt let down and angry. It wasn't just that I wouldn't get a good dinner. I wanted his mouth on my toes.

I called him and told him so.

"Really?" he said.

"Yeah, don't make me say it again," I said.

I did not know this was a fetish. I did not know it was a very common one. We never kissed. I never took any clothes off, and he only ever touched my feet and calves. I knew it had to stay a secret, and that it was fine by me. I was happy to let him put my feet in his mouth and on his face. It cheered him up so much.

Years later, my girlfriend Nautica hypothesized that he chose me because he knew I could keep something important hidden and "didn't have any personal boundaries." She had a difficult time believing my side of the story and wanted to call Mr. East a perpetrator, a predator, and dismiss the whole experience as one of sexual exploitation. But I wouldn't back down from saying he never exploited me.

It was difficult for her, to let me be a horny eighteen-year-old freely choosing to spend time with a recent teacher who really only wanted to kiss and touch my feet, and who paid for things. I knew what I'd wanted, and what I'd done, and how miserable and scared I'd been outside of those moments with Mr. East. I told her he helped me live during the Worst Year of My Life, and the only person who really knows what that could mean, was me.

Nautica had started working as a dominatrix directly through an apprenticeship with a friend of hers. She had no experience in any other sex trades. On the one hand, this made her an exquisitely powerful dominant: she never second-guessed herself or identified too much with her submissive. But she was also sometimes quick to dismiss the complexity of choices that people in precarious positions have to face. She just avoided precarity altogether, if she could. She knew I'd had sex for a place to sleep during that time and she told me I was a victim of every person who had ever "used" me that way. But it wasn't how I'd experienced those people, or that sex.

I never stopped thinking that Mr. East was really a dear man.

I tried to tell my story in group therapy, tell it to Nautica, tell it on a mountain somewhere in a letter I buried while hiking. I tried to speak my truth. But memories live in parts of me that don't speak. Layers of stories stack up under my skin. They communicate, emanate, in gesture, reflex, smell, secretions, heat. And no matter how hard I try to speak it, I cannot crush my body, that explosively colored, exquisitely textured orchestral circus, into only language.

When a lover I really want touches the inside of my thigh, thoughts and memories gush: this is sexiness, this is promise, this is interest, this is my body, this is your body, this is what it means to receive, this is the time to respond positively or negatively, this is the turning point, there is nothing else, there is no going back, this is a mistake, this is the best life has to offer, this could be rape, unless this is love, this is your weakness, you slut, this seems safe enough, this can't stop or I'll die.

Anyone who touched me after the Worst Year of My Life touched a place that was part garden and part ruins. The rubble is still there. If you touch my skin slowly enough, you can feel it.

Dear Kindee,

I admit that I am extremely angry today at this whole insane institution. The CO's here have no respect. I received the news that we were on lockdown just an hour before you were due for our visit, with no way to contact you. I knew it would be a horrible experience for you. I also don't know yet what the lockdown is for. This shit is arbitrary and malicious. Cages are torture enough.

I'm sorry you had to go through that experience of being turned away by the Sgt. I know you were able to stay calm and exit the situation without any more trouble than he'd already caused you.

They are pitting people against each other in here. You would not believe your eyes. The CO's do anything they can to cause friction among the population. Nothing has changed since the gladiator days. When someone snaps after all the abuse, they lock us all down and choose new people to systematically destroy.

Next time I see you, let's talk about the ocean for a while.

I'll tell you about the time I drove all the way out to Dockweiler Beach with one of your mom's house dresses wrapped round the front axle!

Please keep your head up for me and don't let the games they play here bring you down too much. I will do my best to stay positive.

All my love,
Carl

I got a job at a call center. I listened to people talk confusedly about their problems with their purchases from SEARS and I directed them to appropriate departments. I slept with most of the people in my office, and especially enjoyed Daisy, the first girl I had more than one hookup with. I still drank, but only on the weekends. I got skilled at alphabetizing, I went to visit Carl, I had dinners and foot worship evenings with Mr. East, I finally let go of the storage space and all that was in it, I studied a bit for my GED, so I could at least have a high school diploma, for my pride, for work, for something to feel not guilty about.

Angie got into Pratt, an art school in Brooklyn, and was planning to go. One night, late in the summer of 1998, we were smoking weed in her backyard, and after a silence, she changed my life.

"Come to New York with me," she said.

I had been preparing myself to say goodbye to her. I had been shoring up potential housing opportunities and telling people at the call center office that I would happily be someone's live-in nanny. I was about to get my GED.

"And do what?" I said.

"Does it matter?" she said.

"Ouch," I said. She held the joint to her lips, sipped the air around it, and passed it to me. She shrugged. She blew a cloud over her shoulder. More smoke than it seemed like she could have inhaled. "I mean, what are you doing here that you can't do there?" she asked. "Be depressed? Be a telemarketer? Get people to buy you drinks on the weekend?"

"I can't leave Carl," I said. "And I'm not a telemarketer. I work in a call center."

She was quiet. It had been a clear day, and it was just a little chilly, for a summer night. I wondered how long we were going to stay outside.

"You need a change," she said. She was confident. It sounded true. "You can stay in my dorm room until you get a job and a place. It'll be fun!" She nudged my knee with hers. We both wore shorts. I felt her skin like a lightning bolt, a terrifying surge of electricity that ran directly to my clit. I recognized the feeling, but it had never felt this strong with Angie.

"I do need a change," I said. I looked at her face. She was smiling in the dark.

"Pass it back," she said.

I hit the joint, exhaled, and leaned toward her. "What if I can't make it work?" I said.

"Make what work?" Her fingers grazed mine. Another electric shot.

"Like what if I can't get a job? Isn't it expensive to live there? I don't know," I could hear my mother's voice in my head. It was unbearable. My mother definitely thought I was crazy to have this conversation in the first place. Crazy to want to stay with Angie, whatever that meant.

Angie stretched her arms over her head and rolled her neck. "You'll figure something out, babe. You always do. You can do phone sex or something."

I laughed.

But she was serious. She brought the joint back down, tapped the end, and sipped. "You're a mess," she said. "I love you, but you're a mess. I think you could be happier, you know? I really think you could."

My body said: of course I could. (Kiss her!)

My body said: no, you can't.

Angie's face was backlit, haloed by the light inside, and she suddenly looked like a witch to me. And I wanted to be a part of her magic. Stupid, I thought. You're high.

"Just think about it?" she said quietly. Then, "Want any more of this?" she held the joint out.

"Okay, yes, I'll think about it," I said. I was already too high, but I took the joint from her anyway, to feel the tiny touch of her fingers. I took a last, silly drag off the dead pinch of ash and then stepped on it.

Angie put her hand out and beckoned, just slightly, for me to come closer. I scooted my chair as close as I could and we sat with our forearms touching, our knees touching, side by side. Inside, I was shaking. She turned her face to me, reached up to hold my chin, and gave me three slow, deliberate, soft kisses on my cheek. If I had moved my face even two inches, I may have shown her what she needed to see, the invitation, to kiss my mouth. But I couldn't. I was frozen, overwhelmed. I wanted it so badly and I couldn't move. So the moment passed. We waited in the dark there together for what felt like a very long time.

Angie moved to New York in August. I stayed here and there with other friends in Los Angeles through the fall. I worked six or seven days a week and sometimes studied for the GED. Every time we talked, Angie told me I should come out. And when I mentioned it to Carl, he said I should make my life count, and do what I felt was right for me.

"I'll miss you like hell," he said at a visit one Sunday, "no doubt. But if you're feeling like growing, and you want a new place for it, I understand that. You need to go ahead and grow."

So I took and passed the GED exam. I turned nineteen. I put everything I still owned into a duffel bag, I used my last two paychecks from the call center to buy a one-way plane ticket, I accepted $250 gift money from Mr. East for "expenses," and I moved to New York.

Carl and I worked out a regular communication schedule until he paroled. Then it got harder to get in touch with him. When he got out, he stayed with a friend and got a job on a painting crew and met with his parole officer and then when the apartment building had to be tented for bedbugs and the friend left town, Carl stayed with someone else. His PO didn't like the new situation because the new guy with the lease was also an ex-con. Carl couch surfed for a while. He eventually went to a shelter. That was when we worked out our phone call system: if I didn't pick up on the first call, he'd leave a message telling me when he was going to call back in the next few days so I could plan for it. If I didn't pick up on the second call he'd wait a week and try again. It worked for us.

I lived out of my duffel bag in Angie's dorm room for her last month of her freshman year of college. I found odd jobs in the back of the weekly papers or on craigslist, and ate meals she smuggled back from the cafeteria. I walked in Brooklyn, walked and walked. I tried to imagine people living in those strong stone buildings in 1895, 1915, 1945. I went to the park. I bought drugs sometimes from the same guys and sometimes we laughed together. I didn't touch Angie, but I wanted to. She had a guy she slept with, and when I was alone in her room, I masturbated with her vibrator. When the semester ended, we got a tiny apartment near campus. Finally, for the first time, I had my own room, and I could close the door.

. . .

Dearest Kindee,

I'm thinking of you in that big city, getting on subway trains and beating the heat. I hope you are happy and healthy. I'm at the nicer shelter tonight. I'm proud of you and Angie for getting a more permanent place!

I've been thinking about how we define "social problems" in this day and age. I'm in a minority here when I say that I think the existence of drugs is not a social problem. The existence of prostitution is not a social problem. The existence of socio-economic class, and the forms of violence that issue from the belief that there isn't enough in the world to go around, is The Social Problem.

I imagine the social scientists of the 1950s and 1960s, exuberant in their progressive ideas, believing that inclusion, representation, and a diversifying of the identities claimed by members of the power structure is/was/will be the arrival of lasting social change, and even peace. Peace through integration! If we can just get enough darker faces in the room, we can tell ourselves we've made it, finally, to equality. And I think a lot of Black people believed it, too. Inclusion was the goal of so much of the Civil Rights struggles. I imagine these scientists, who were 90% white men fifty years ago, telling their wives about their ideas. I wonder if any of their wives were feminists, Native American women, Black, closeted lesbians, or otherwise disposed to feel disqualified from the great white We, the "brotherhood of man," and his assumed inherent characteristics. His logic. His rationality. His connection with God the Father. His explicable psychology, as mapped by Dr. Freud. Everybody on board for white supremacist education!

Be suspicious any time someone tells you their theory about "humanity," my baby. There is truly no such thing except that we all need to get energy in (food), put energy out (shit, moving around, orgasm, sneezing), some of us make more people while we're alive, some don't, and ultimately, we'll all transform (die). All the rest is stuff we make up, and it may be truly wonderful or stupid stuff, depending on your point of view.

The thing about democracy is that in order to produce rational dissent, one must be considered a rational being. In other words, today all you have to do to silence the voice of a people is: make their problems individual, part of their own psychological difficulty, instead of seeing dissent or resistance as a natural response to oppressive structure. I am guilty of this myself. I told you and your mother more than once that you were too emotional. I apologize for this. I see it now as a sexist response to the way you were trying to communicate your resistance to what was happening to you.

I called your Mom irrational when she was crying about something I thought was small. I forgot all the time how much pressure she was under to work as much as she did, how hard she fought to make the life we had. I thought I knew what she could do better, and that if she just listened to me, it would work out. It's not a good way to relate to someone. It's patriarchy.

Watching the men in here deal with their emotions is sometimes demoralizing. The way they express themselves furtively, in secret, breaks my heart. They give each other shoulder and neck rubs sometimes, like in prison. Everyone living needs human touch. I know you understand this.

How can people say they care about "rational choice" in our explosive advertising culture? Can you make a rational choice toward disposability, disinfectant, deception, institutional inclusion, easy answers, maximum credit, weight loss, leaving big problems to those above you in a hierarchy that does not require your consent, denial of *both* the genocide perpetrated against Native Americans *and* their continued survival and struggle, addiction to distractions, violent war video games that emulate real covert war operations, the legacy of slavery and Jim Crow? These are things Americans find rational. Prison, Kindred. Prison is supposedly a rational response to the problems of "crime." I can tell you decisively that putting human beings in cages is not a rational response to any of our society's current ills. Shelters are cages too, in case you need a reminder.

And I know that most activists think that the goals of all rational actors will be, overall, humanitarian. So all we have to do is educate people about what's "wrong" with the system and they'll step up to fix it. But it's not true. Many people know about what goes on in prisons. They do not step up to fix it. Or, they try, but the people who want the prisons and shelters and mental hospitals to function but don't want to know what happens there, are the ones with the resources to decide whether I ate a peanut butter sandwich or hot lasagna on any given Saturday.

Let's say one definition of rationality is: making decisions toward your own survival. Revolutionary social change agents must assume that the goals of rational actors from oppressed classes will not overlap, overall, with the goals of rational actors from ruling/employer classes. Our interests are simply not the same. This is why Marx predicted, and still people speak of, a class war. People rise up when they are threatened enough and have enough solidarity, or when they are suicidally finished playing along with totalitarian regimes, or when they believe that the struggle might be temporary. It does not feel rational to people who have any preservable privilege to risk their station for the well-being of all. But it is a rational choice, if you believe that your own survival depends on the survival of your larger human community, or even the survival of species diversity on the earth. Point of view, see?

Huey P. Newton wrote that revolution is not an action, it is a process. It takes time. It takes many people, many decisions, many mistakes.

I wonder how much you identify with what I'm saying. You have lived in contact with real oppression, and also, with the owner class. I think you have seen many things I have not seen. I would love to read your thoughts. I hope I have made sense here.

We've had a relatively quiet few days here, which is why I can get these thoughts down.

Have you heard of Kurt Lewin? Did I tell you about his work? Another time maybe. You should look him up, he's a real thinker. I'm enjoying reading his old books again.

Whatever you do, please keep learning and growing.

If all goes well, I'll have a new job soon. I'm still grateful every day that I'm not locked down. I still get a little dizzy with excitement when I think about walking barefoot on grass, or driving on the highway with the windows open.

Please write back when you can. I can pick up mail here even if I check out and go somewhere else. Thinking of getting a tent. A friend has one and he's doing fine, and no one breathes down his neck all day and night like they do here. Then again, he's out in the madness all the time. The other night things got rowdy and Lionel tried to arrest a park bench. Somewhere on Skid Row, someone is screaming, always. That part doesn't get easier.

I miss you.
　　All my love,
　　Carl

5

FALLING AND RISING

Angie introduced me to KC, a friend of hers at Pratt who stripped a few nights a week at a club in Manhattan, and she convinced me to audition. It wasn't that difficult of a conversation. Angie told me I was a pretty enough girl and for sure I'd get hired if I could move sexy, KC told me how much she made on average per shift, and I considered the inconvenience of shaving most of my body hair off.

All three of us went down to the Kitty Stop, KC's strip club, for my audition. Walking up to the door I wished Angie wouldn't come in. I must have given her a tiny signal because she patted me on the lower back and told me she'd wait at a bar down the street.

"You're hot as fuck," she said, very seriously. It turned me on. I felt a little bad about it. "You will get hired." She pointed at an awning about a block away. "That's where I'll be. Come get me."

I thanked her.

KC was smiling very sweetly and gesturing for me to follow her up to the bouncer.

He was large and round, and he looked me up and down. I'd just gotten a haircut, so I had some funky layers around my face and length in the back. I'd straightened it, and put a little pomade on the ends. I was wearing mascara and black eyeliner, the same eye I did any time I was dressing up because it was the only one I knew for sure I liked. I had clear lip gloss, a French manicure, and was wearing jeans, boots, and a tight black T shirt without a bra. I felt good. I thought I looked like Joan Jett with a tan and an ass. The bouncer asked for my ID.

"Auditioning?" he said.

"Yep," I said.

"Good luck," he said. "You'll get it, don't worry. Have fun."

"Thanks Bear!" KC said to him. "See?" she said to me. "Easy peasy!"

I wore a black thong bikini I'd borrowed from KC with a stretchy cocktail dress over top. Easy peasy, I told myself. Remember KC's advice. Go really slow, breathe a lot, touch yourself.

The bar was smaller than I'd imagined. The stage was eight by ten feet with a pole on one half. One little flight of stairs connected the underground dressing room with the stage. The chairs were all black metal and vinyl, some of them fraying or even ripped, with lines of white stuffing pushing out of their cracks. The neon beer signs were hung at regular intervals, along with large posters for out of date Budweiser and Heineken specials. The walls were sided in dark wood, and the bar was made of the same. The varnish seemed thick and slightly gummy. The carpet was a dark maroon. There was one blacklight that ran along the floor of the stage, underneath the tipping bar. I felt very comfortable in there.

I was terrified entering the stage, but then the music started and the terror was replaced with something unfamiliar and much more pleasant. I reached for the steadying pole, found it, walked around it, leaned out at arm's length, and felt very quiet inside. I took everything off but the thong, and kept waiting for a moment of feeling naked that never came. I stayed on the stage for "Head Like A Hole" and "House of the Rising Sun" while the manager sat at the bar, tapped his clipboard, and occasionally wrote things on a form. It was nice to get some air on my breasts for a change.

And Angie was right, I did get the job. I also made eighteen dollars in tips during my audition, which seemed pretty good to me.

After I got dressed, I sat down with Mark the manager and half-listened to his speech about things I was allowed and disallowed to do in the club. I watched his wispy brown hair. I wondered if he'd fucked any dancers. He wasn't terrible looking. But he wasn't sexy. I realized he was expecting me to say something.

I asked him to repeat his question.

"What's your stage name?"

"Easy Peasy," I said.

"C'mon," he said, smiling. I smiled back. "Ok," he said. "Easy Peasy. You can always change it."

Mark put Easy Peasy on the schedule for three shifts the following week at the Kitty Stop and I took a slip of paper with the dates and times on it and shook his hand and thanked him.

I said goodbye to KC in the dressing room. She seemed genuinely happy for me to have gotten the job. She asked to see my schedule. "Try to get in on Thursday nights," she said. "We'll work together! It's a good night."

I thanked her and told her I'd wash her bikini.

I walked out of the club feeling light and strong. I found the awning Angie had pointed out. I found her inside. She was sitting with her back to the bar, swiveling just an inch back and forth on her stool, while she read a newspaper. I didn't feel the horrible need to repress sexual desire. I just felt love for her. She looked up and saw me. Her face beamed back. She shook and folded the paper. She was the only customer in the bar.

"I'm a stripper!" I said, and waved my hands in the air.

"You win!" she said. She applauded, and the bartender turned from his task at the register and clapped, too. He brought us a round of tequila shots on the house after waving past our fake IDs. They both laughed at my name. I still liked it.

Angie dropped into seriousness again. "I'm proud of you." She leaned in and kissed me on the cheek. "I can't believe you actually did it! You showed your tits and everything?"

"And everything," I said.

I liked the smell of the dressing room at the Kitty Stop. It smelled like girl sweat, cheap sweet fragrance sprays, vinyl, feet, and champagne. The fluorescent lights showed every red bump, every thigh dimple, every bruise. The bruises were my special menace. I tried oil-based face foundation make up to cover my bruises. I tried powder. I tried frozen spoons, massage with arnica gel, vodka poultice, and ignoring them. I took iron pills. I slept with a pillow between my legs. But I always had a bruise, somewhere. Luckily, there were always customers for whom the dirty girl was the fantasy.

KC and I should have been in direct competition because we were overall the same type—tanned white girls with longish straight brown hair, brown eyes--but our differences were complimentary in the strip club. She had enormous breast implants and I had small natural breasts. She had a tiny flat ass and I had a large apple bottom. Instead of competing, we usually worked together, snagging a pair of friends or golf buddies together and letting them fantasize about how we could be sisters.

But KC hated stripping. She drank a lot. She felt ashamed of it, talked to customers about how she was putting herself through art school and couldn't wait to quit. She was cynical and funny, utterly honest about how she felt about everything. She was also brilliantly angry about every piece of unwanted sexual contact she ever had in the club. During the first shift we worked together, she asked me fearful questions about what I would do if my family "found out" I was a stripper.

"My mother is dead," I said. "And my dad knows."

"Oh my God I could never tell my parents!" KC said.

"Yeah, well," I said.

"Your mom's dead?"

"She died when I was seventeen."

KC lit a joint in the corner of the dressing room, sucked a little too hard on it, and had to flick it out with her long pink nails. She blew her smoke into a toilet paper roll covered with a dryer sheet. "Wow, shit," she said, "I'm sorry."

"Thanks," I said, knowing I was now going to have to change the subject to save the conversation, "What's that for?" I asked, gesturing at the dryer sheet thing.

"It hides the smell," she said. I decided not to argue even though a skunk was now definitely in the room.

"How long have you had your implants?" I said.

"A little over a year," she said. "I don't know what I did without them. I know it's weird, but I wanted them from when I was like sixteen. I got them even before I started dancing."

Before I could say anything, Claudia entered. She was wearing the tiniest red bikini, a bespoke piece of magic. It was like four triangular pasties on strings, one on each nipple, a miniature merkin, and a triangle acting like a crown on her buttcrack. Her breasts were enormous. Her legs were so long.

Her dark brown hair was tinged with a reddish henna. Her irises were so dark her eyes seemed fully black. She had dark red lipstick on. Claudia was selective about who she talked to in the dressing room, and so I knew something important had happened when she turned her attention to me.

"Babygirl," she called to me, "please let me be the first to take care of your eyebrows. You'd be upping all us bitches a notch if you'd just tame those motherfuckers."

"Really?" I'd never thought about my eyebrows before.

"You surprised? C'mon girl, it is *time*." So I let her pluck my eyebrows for me.

Shhhhh, she kept saying, don't be such a pussy, it gets easier as you do it more, it won't ever be this bad again, I promise. I couldn't help jumping or tearing up. I bit my lip to stop the whimper sounds. But I also loved the attention, the way she stared intently at my face without looking in my eyes, her voice, our knees touching. That cluster of feelings, a little pain and an avalanche of unfamiliar pleasures, was so much better than the way I'd been feeling before. I made a choice to be always on Claudia's side.

"You look better," she said, and told me to look in the mirror.

"Wow, I can see my eyes," I said.

Her phone rang. "Hey bitch," she said. "I'm at work, honey! I just took my break with this new fish who needed some help with her look." Pause. "That's right, mama, I'm like the Mother Theresa of paint up here."

No one had ever called me "fish" before.

After I let Claudia pull out half my eyebrows, she taught me how to make a perfect smokey eye, how to test lipstick colors against my skin, and how to do contour makeup on my face that helped my features stand out in the dark club.

Claudia wore seven-inch lucite heels when the rest of us

were still wearing fives or sixes. She was the only dancer at the Kitty Stop who was allowed to police her own body without repercussion from management. The rest of us had to ask a bouncer for help if something went wrong. Management was supposed to take our side, but they usually took the customers'. Claudia had her own thing going on there.

When I first told Carl I was stripping, he asked if it was going okay.

Yep, I said.

He told me to pay close attention and take care of myself.

I asked him if that was it.

"What else did you expect me to say?"

I didn't know. Something more paternal, maybe. More worried.

"Let me tell you a story," he said. He told me he was twelve when he had sex for the first time.

"I don't think I want to hear this story," I said.

"Oh shush," he said. The girl was older. She thought he was more experienced. They were at a friend's house, in the bedroom. It was the afternoon, not yet party time.

"Come on," she said to him. They were naked together. He didn't know what she wanted him to do. "Stick it in," she said.

"I thought I already had," he said to me. "I just felt warmth and sliding around down there, I didn't know. I didn't know."

"This is grossing me out, but now I want to know what happened."

"I was making her kind of angry," he said. "She grabbed me and pushed me in her. I kind of froze. Then, immediately," I could hear the smile in his voice, "it was over, and I told her that was my first time, and she slapped me."

Why?

Because he had been rude. "You'll remember this for the rest of your life," she had said, "but I won't. You just lost your virginity by your damn self."

"Wow," I said, "that's brutal, and doesn't have anything to do with me working in a strip club."

Then came the end of the story. Carl did not have sex again until he was eighteen. He went to a strip club that was also a brothel, with a friend. He had sex with a prostitute who was very kind and informative, gave him confidence, taught him how to use a condom.

"Oh my God," I laughed. "That's not real!"

"It is," he said. "It's as real as my life."

I told him he was a crazy person but I loved him, and got off the phone. I was glad he didn't tell me he was disappointed in me or that he'd hoped I'd do better for myself. I realized I'd been avoiding telling him because I was ashamed that I wasn't headed back to school, in a job that had a future, or something. But Carl didn't mind. I used to write Carl snippets of conversation that I thought might entertain him, as if they were scenes from a play. Sometimes I would draw pictures of us, too.

(Inside Dressing Room. Claudia and Easy Peasy sit in chairs facing the long make-up mirror. KC stands a few feet from them, in the dancers' lockers.)

Claudia: Damn, I need to get myself a new fuck buddy.

(KC lights a joint, blowing the smoke through a dryer sheet into her locker.)

Easy: What about that Vegas guy?

Claudia: He's an asshole.

Easy: So?

KC: (coughing) Sometimes the assholes are the best for that.

Claudia: You're right. He's not an asshole. He can't take direction.

Easy: Oh no, he's bad in bed?

Claudia: You tell me. What's so difficult about: If I'm getting fucked hard, call me a dirty name. If we're making love and all the candles are lit... call me a dirty name.

Easy: There's nothing difficult about that. At all.

Claudia: That's what I'm saying, girl. I need a new fuck buddy.

I'd been dancing four and five nights a week for over a year when there was some kind of coup in management at the Kitty Stop. Most of the staff were just gone one day, replaced with new faces, and the only "old" people left were all the ones I didn't like. One night I was drugged. At the time, I felt like the manager was being extremely vigilant and taking care of me every time I came to. Later, I realized that he probably should have gotten me to the hospital, but chose instead to monitor me himself, because he didn't want consequences. A dancer got kicked off the schedule, presumably in retaliation for asking to see her contract, the one she'd signed when she'd been hired.

There was a big renovation that gave us a second stage, a second bar, and a second dressing room. The management arbitrarily decided which girls went into the old dressing room, and who went into the nicer, newer dressing room. Suddenly, we had an invisible class structure out on the floor with customers. The club got gnarled in ambient resentments, arbitrariness and anxiety about a conflict that seemed constantly just under the surface. KC got moved to the nicer dressing room but Claudia didn't. Management had informed me I was to move, too, but I ignored the instructions and stayed in the old dressing room until Claudia hadn't shown up to work for a month and I was invited into a champagne room with a girl who used the nicer dressing room and she decided we should work together a few nights this week while these guys were in town for this thing. I took the opportunity, started using the nicer room, and we made good money together. Claudia didn't respond to my messages. We didn't have any mutual friends. I asked other people at the club about her and got silence and shrugs.

For my twenty-first birthday, Carl sent me a necklace made of paper beads. It arrived the day before I was going to go out for my first legal drinking. Each bead was individually rolled into a tight coil, wrapped around itself, and glued. They were surprisingly solid-feeling and made a great sound when they hit a table, almost like rubber. The note read:

Dear Kindee,

These beads are made using an old guerrilla technique--I learned how to spin paper into these tiny rolls to get messages in and out of prison. A friend of mine started making these with scraps that blow around in the morning line at the free laundry. I designed the clasp. I hope you are celebrating your freedom today and everyday! My friend just lost his bed at the shelter because we tried to come back fifteen minutes after they closed the doors for the night. They make it hard to live here. So now we are going to go for a stroll and see what we can find. Missing seeing your face.

Love, Carl

There was no return address. The necklace clasp was a roughly sanded and twisted hook made from aluminum can tabs. I wore the necklace out on my birthday night. It got commented on, I'm sure of that. I was drunk before we hit the bars. Angie told me the following day that I'd said "depressing" things about my dad living on the street in Los Angeles to anyone who noticed the necklace. I kept it in a box in the bathroom after that.

I left the Kitty Stop for a nicer club near Wall Street, a few months after 9/11. I'd been told I would make twice what I made at the Kitty Stop by a stripper I met at some party and because I'd heard it was easy to get a sugar daddy there. I wore the same outfit I'd worn at the Kitty Stop: black patent leather six-inch heel boots, black thong, black bra, long black silk robe. Sometimes I added thigh-highs, a garter belt, or a cocktail dress.

I'd heard so many stories from girls who saw their customers outside the club. I'd gone to parties, I'd gotten paid to strip for groups of bachelors, but I'd never taken the offers for more money if I'd fuck. Finally I realized I didn't have a good reason for it, and I got curious. And I was tired of dancing. Dating for pay seemed obvious. I just had to find the right guy.

There was no fanfare after I found him. It was Angie who pointed it out: does this mean you're a bona fide hooker now?

I guess so, I said. I hadn't thought of it that way.

As long as you're happy, she said.

I wasn't sure I'd ever been happy for more than a few moments at a time, but that was so clearly not my customers' fault. Most of them, anyway. And I was sure I enjoyed the guy I'd chosen to pop my pro cherry with.

I didn't know how to explain it to anyone. It didn't insult me to get money for being someone's favorite person to relax with. I liked being good at sex. Brennan treated me like a person who was on her way to something else. He was in finance, a Wall Street guy, and I never understood his work but he had to be on his laptop by 7AM every day. He told me he had followed a path that was given to him by his family. He recognized that I had not. He told me I was surprising and interesting and powerful. When he touched my legs in our first champagne room, his hands were strong, warm, and sure. I liked it. Within weeks, we were going for drinks before my shifts. He would leave me for an hour while I primped in the dressing room, then meet me in a champagne room.

One night, I broke the rules, kissed him spontaneously.

"What did you make here on an average night before me?" he asked later, while he was settling his bill.

"It doesn't work that way," I said.

"What?" He furrowed slightly. He scribbled a tight spiral on his receipt and handed it back to the cashier. He thanked her politely and she said it was always her pleasure.

"Every night is different and sometimes you can't explain why you make money or not," I tried to organize a more respectable explanation, "so, I average my income by the month."

"Ok then, riddle me this: how much do you have to earn, on a night when the signs are pointing to your doing very well, for you to feel really good about working?" He reached out to his right and alighted on his champagne glass. He drew it into our eyesight, and sipped it without breaking from my gaze. I felt it in my clit like he'd touched me. We strolled away from the cashier and toward the door. The house lights were coming on.

"A grand," I said, which was a total lie.

"Done," he said.

"What does that mean?" I asked, suddenly aware of where his hands were, the heaviness of his belt, anything that might hurt me.

"It means I will buy you out of your next shift, and we will see how we feel about it, yes?"

I said yes.

He made love like a husband, holding my neck, gently propped on his pillows, pushing at a ninety-degree angle to my hips, not quite slow enough to tantalize, not quite fast enough to satisfy. I resolved to help him realize his potential. I resolved to live a life where at least I was having some fun.

Fun matters. It motivates people. It relaxes people. It helps people treat each other well. It distracts them from pain. Sometimes, it provides openings for new solutions when a problem seems insurmountable. When I focused on the fact of Mom dying, I couldn't have any fun. Even though she would tell me to leave the hospital and go enjoy myself, I couldn't. Carl would tell me to leave the prison visit and enjoy myself, but I couldn't. I didn't understand how they could ask me to do anything enjoyable in the midst of their and my suffering.

Eventually I came to understand that they wanted me to grow stronger. That they wanted me to take care of myself. That they hoped I'd make a life for myself that included happiness. Those trips to In N Out Burger on cleaning days when I was a kid? Those were an enactment of something Carl called Fun on Principle.

Yes, you need to get serious and put in your work, Carl said. But that comes easily to you, baby. What you need to grow on is how to enjoy yourself. You won't last a minute in the struggle if you don't know how to make yourself feel better when the hurt comes from the outside. Find things you like to do and do them. If someone hurts you, get an apology and a new plan of action, or leave. Keep yourself strong and healthy.

You have to make time for your kind of fun, your real fun, not someone else's fun. And you have to make time for it especially when things are looking real bad for you.

6

TRAMP STAMP

I made the decision to let Angie know I was attracted to her because the desire to kiss and touch and get in bed with her had become a daily problem, finally. I thought she might stop coming into my room without a shirt on, casually spooning yogurt into her pretty mouth while she talked about class. I thought she might have some compassion for my struggle to contain and manage myself.

Instead, she felt betrayed. Like I had been getting some lascivious pleasure from proximity with her that I'd been secretly hoarding. No, I told her, I've mostly just been suffering. She didn't understand. She called me dishonest. She wondered what my agenda was. We were in our tiny apartment. She sat curled into herself on her bed, hugging her knees. I sat on an egg crate she used as a stool.

I didn't know what to do. I had no agenda, I told her.

She accused me of trying to manipulate her into "playing wife" and "playing house" and fulfilling my fucked-up childhood trauma sufferer's need for family. Which may have not been totally untrue, but it was shocking to hear from her. Her face was harder than I'd ever seen it. She told me it was scary, that I could keep that information from her for so long. She acted like she hadn't known. Hadn't played up, or flirted, or enjoyed my attention at all for all those years. Hadn't used my affirmation to feel good about herself. Since high school. Hadn't she wanted me first? I thought she'd been sort of waiting for me to come around that night on the patio.

"I think you're overreacting," I said. "I'm not lying to you, and I never did. You were the first girl I ever felt this way about! I didn't even know I liked girls until I wanted to kiss you when we were fourteen."

"Well, I didn't think I was one of the girls you liked. You hid yourself from me," she said, her eyes meeting mine. I couldn't hold her gaze. "You hid and you lied and you did it so you could stay close to me, and that's the meanest thing. You didn't just give me the truth and let me choose what I wanted to do. I've been open with you about myself, and you haven't."

I said I thought that was what I was doing now.

"God DAMN it," she said, pressing her knuckles to her eyes. She took a breath. She was quiet. I looked at my feet. I had my toenails painted a dayglo pink that really popped under the blacklight at the club.

She asked me to look at her. "I don't think you should live here anymore," she said, and uncoiled herself. She went into the bathroom before I knew what to say. I waited for a few minutes and then realized she might be hiding in there until I left her bedroom.

So I left. I wasn't sure how I got so stupid. I started packing. I made an inventory of people I might be able to stay with. I tried to understand what was happening. Was Angie going to stop being my friend? Would I ever see her again? The panic rose. My eyes and nose burned. Idiot. You never should have told her, one voice said.

You never should have NOT told her, another voice said. She's right, you lied. You started lying in LA, back when she asked you to come with her to New York.

I was not ready to accept the wisdom of the second voice. I packed up angrily, hurt by Angie's response, terrified of not having her to come home to at the end of a double shift. I wanted the late-night ice cream, I wanted to be in the room with her while she made art. Another person taking themselves away from me at the moment I'd tried to get closer.

I'd gotten so used to it, the sense that I was attracted to her and she wasn't attracted to me, that it didn't even seem like a problem. If anything, it was just my cross to bear. I told her about it because it had become overwhelming lately. I thought about her all the time, and even when I was dating or messing around with other girls, I was thinking things like "I wish Angie wanted this with me," over and over. Maybe internally I'd just hit a wall. Wanted to grow, was the way Carl would have put it.

The morning after I told her I was in love with her, Angie left me a note in the kitchen telling me to move out within two weeks, take care of myself, she'd call me when she was ready to be friends again.

I packed up what little stuff I had in that one day, called one of the bouncers from the club who had a truck, and we got everything into a storage space ten minutes away, before six PM. I didn't yet know where I'd sleep that night. My plan was to take a subway into this gentrifying neighborhood in Bush-wick, get a really good tattoo from a place a dancer friend had recommended, eat some fancy food, and then never go back there, or back to the apartment I shared with Angie, again. I packed my sketchbook, a black sweater, and three hundred dollars in twenties into my bag. I drank an inch of whiskey from Angie's bottle of Jim Beam, before I went, for the pain. I figured that eventually I'd drop in to work and see if anyone invited me over after closing.

I exited the subway at Morgan Street and followed the directions KC had written for me when I asked about tattoos. I spotted a magical-looking storefront. A winding vine was painted all around the floor-to-ceiling glass. In graceful script, the sign read: Drink Me! A Juice House. Like Mom's home-made cleaning solutions.

Inside, I found large terra-cotta tile flooring and a purple couch. The barista greeted me enthusiastically and encouraged me to take my time reading the menu. He wore a black apron like they did at fine dining restaurants. It had straws sticking out of a pocket.

I ordered a shot of some special juice tonic with cayenne pepper in it that promised to invigorate and replenish me. It made my eyes water before it was in my mouth. It cost seven dollars and tasted like dirt on fire.

"Jesus!" I said, and slammed the paper cup down. "You didn't tell me!"

"Yeah!" said the barista, smiling under his bushy beard. "Wakes you up, right?"

I was still catching my breath. I thought I might throw up. "Water," I whispered.

He got me some. I drank it. Things moved around inside me.

"You got so much good stuff in there," barista boy said. "Ginger, lemon, cayenne, that's the part you're freaking out about right now, turmeric, royal jelly, omegas, amino acids..."

I realized he probably didn't know what he was talking about. Fancy juice was just another way for rich people to get high and feel righteous. I suddenly, intensely wished they'd just admit it. Maybe with some honesty in advertising I could enjoy the feeling of having just pounded enough capsaicin to shrivel a housecat.

"Can I get another glass of water, with some ice and straw and a lid?"

"Sure," he said, slightly deflated. He gave it to me.

I left and went two doors down to a bar that had no windows. I ordered a beer, pulled out my sketchbook and started doodling for my tattoo.

I wanted some eyelets and lacing on the small of my back, not too low down, so that the ends of the ties wouldn't be below my crack. I wanted it to look like vintage corsetry.

When I had a design that looked close to what I wanted, I walked into the shop and asked if anyone was free. The person running the shop that day was named Nicky, had thick plugs in their ears, a short military buzz cut, Dickies held low on their hips by a thick leather belt, and art on their neck that was so detailed I couldn't tell what it was at first. Eventually I stared hard enough to see it was a mass of seahorses. Nicky was surprised I had no other tattoos. She was a little worried I didn't understand the "implications" of my choice of placement.

"People have stereotypes," she said carefully, "about lower-back tattoos. I just want to make sure you understand what kind of ideas they might have. I mean, people have stereotypes about butches, too, and I flag the shit out of it anyway, because, you know, that's me. But I'm just checking."

"I'm already a tramp," I said. "I want to flag it."

She had no idea what to say to me, but obviously she was not going to turn me away since I had the dollars in my hand

and was old enough. So, Nicky locked the front door, set up the table for me, and started to work on a drawing, with my sketchbook next to her.

I sat on a slightly sticky vinyl couch and let my mind reach to Carl, and the drawings he used to send me from Corcoran. Maybe I should get one of his pictures tattooed on me, I thought. He'd made some gorgeous and heartbreaking still life drawings of his cell when he was in solitary. I could get one on my calf. I wondered if he was ok today. I realized I should tell him I was no longer living with Angie. I pulled out my phone, dialed the last number I'd had for him, and left a voice mail after the standard female instructional voice told me to. I told him I had to move out of Angie's, that I was still looking for a place, and that I wanted to check in and see how he was doing. I told him to call me. I had his favorite Skid Row payphone's number saved too, but that was for when he called me, not the other way around. He may never get my message.

"What do you think of this?" Nicky said, holding up a drawing. It was perfect, and I told her so. The lacing looked alive, like it had real weight, and I wanted it on me.

I lay on my belly on the table.

"I'm scared now," I said.

"That's ok," she said.

Then came the part where the buzzing needle entered, and the pain, the oddest and most delightful pain. Like someone massaging deep into my muscle, and cutting me too. Nicky kept asking me if I was doing okay. It struck me as unutterably sweet.

"I'm great," I said, in awe. I couldn't remember feeling that good for a long time.

It took about an hour. By the end of it, I had decided it was all for the best, me and Angie taking a break from seeing each other for a while. And I had decided to seduce Nicky.

So I kept my eyes on hers during the conversation about aftercare. I invited her to get a celebratory drink with me. She looked at the clock. The shop was supposed to stay open for another hour, but she didn't have any appointments, so she closed up. We went back to the bar I'd been in earlier. We drank. We talked about tattoos, mostly she talked and I listened and stroked her knee. She was so kind, and so excited about what she did. I learned about white ink, and debates among artists about the origins of traditional designs. I asked her if she was seeing anyone, and she said no, not right now, with that strain in her voice that people get when they are recently broken up.

"Take me home with you?" I said.

She looked a little shocked. "Really?"

"Yeah, really." I figured we both could use some sex and some companionship, and I needed a place to sleep. I did not share the last part.

I was right about us both needing the sex. Nicky was such a nice person, and I could tell by the way she fucked that she had been in a relationship for a long time with a person she'd really loved. She had a vocabulary of affection in her hands. She even cradled my neck as I came, so I could shudder as hard as I wanted to without bashing our chins together. She fucked me without hurting my tattoo. In the morning, she cleaned and inspected it. I stood naked in her shower, and she sat on the toilet so my ass was right in her face.

"Looks beautiful," she said, with a smile in her voice.

I shook it a little.

"God you're sexy," she said. And rubbed up the sides of my thighs. She asked if she could taste me. I bent over and opened up, held on to the tub, and enjoyed her.

• • •

Carl and I talked on the phone that night.

"Angie kicked me out," I said. I was drinking in a bar a few blocks from work. Sitting by the window with a beer.

"What happened?"

"I told her I was in love with her and she got mad," I said.

"That sounds like a Neil Diamond song," he said.

"Fuck you!" I said.

"I'm sorry honey, you're hurting, I can hear it. How long have you been in love with her? Long time?"

"Yeah, I guess so."

"You two are deep friends," he said. "I know it hurts now, but I believe you'll come around to some kind of relationship that suits you both."

"I don't know," I said. "She thinks I lied to her."

"Did you?"

I told him I hadn't thought about it that way. I thought I was just keeping my feelings to myself because she didn't want to deal with them. "I guess that counts as lying," I said. "I gotta go," I said.

"Ok, I'll call you next week," he said. "Hang in there sweet one. Maybe this is a good time to come visit me?"

I could afford it right now. And he'd been staying at an apartment, housesitting.

"You're still at that place in South Central?" I asked.

"I've got it for another two months," he said. "It's got a backyard, a lemon tree, and a dog. It's so nice here. Come spend some time with your old man."

I told him I'd think about it. And I did, for about another two hours, before I bought a ticket.

I called Angie and she didn't pick up. I sent her a text apologizing for being dishonest with her and letting her know that I understood why she felt that way. Told her I was going to go visit Carl for a while.

I knew I'd come back to New York. I liked it there. I didn't feel "done" with it. I was making money at the club, and seeing my Wall Street guy and a few other people on the side. I could find a place to stay. I always had.

Angie wrote back: Thanks for the apology. Say hi to Carl for me. Let me know when you're back.

I stayed with Carl in his little one-bedroom for four days. I took meticulous care of my tramp stamp while it was healing, and felt sure that having that tattoo saved me from something dark and nihilistic that had been threatening to suck me under. I loved Nicky's art, and craned my neck to look at it in the mirror every day before I got dressed.

Carl and I talked. He was working at a non-profit downtown, on Skid Row. It was a housing advocacy group, and he was happy running legal clinics and attending protests and teaching political development classes where people read Angela Davis with him. We drank together, smoked blunts, went for walks with the dog. He looked good. His hair was graying and his hands were more wrinkled than I remembered from the last time I'd seen him, but he seemed happy, in a quieter way. He didn't have a plan for where he was going to live once that apartment-sitting gig was up. I didn't worry about that. I told him about my feelings for Angie and he was kind. He asked me if I was ever attracted to men and I said yes, and then added, "But I really prefer women, I think."

"Do you think of yourself as gay?" Carl asked.

I told him I'd never been gay enough to call myself gay.

"But you're not straight," he said.

No.

"So, bisexual?"

"I guess so," I said. "Sure."

. . .

I got myself a couple back-to-back shifts for when I was home and made some plans to spend a weekend with Brennan, while sitting on Carl's temporary back porch. I told Brennan I needed a hotel room for a week because my housing situation was up in the air. He got me a room at some old executive's hotel a short train ride from the club. I thanked him a lot for that.

I told Carl about the gift.

"Thank the Lord for the sex industry," he said.

We high-fived.

"Your mom would hate me for saying that," he said.

"Good thing she can't care," I said.

He gave me a look, but he didn't say anything.

"I like what I do," I said. "Most of the time. And that's pretty good, for a job."

"I know Kindee. It's just the kind of job you can't do forever."

"No one does their job forever."

"Ain't that the truth."

On my last night in town, Carl asked me if I ever thought about going back to school. We drank Coronas on the porch as the LA sunset slid from orange to blue.

"Sometimes," I said, "but not often."

"I think about going back," he said. "But no one wants a violent felon in their program."

"You don't think you could make a good case for yourself being rehabilitated?" I said.

He shook his head. "I got real strikes, my girl. People don't forgive assault against an officer, no matter how far in your past."

Of course, that was probably true.

"I think I'd probably want to do biology if I went back," I said. "Or art. Like painting and drawing."

"Why not take a class or two at a community college while you're working?" he said.

"That's a leading question, 'why not,'" I said. "There are lots of reasons why not."

He smiled at me. "Maybe you'd like law school," he said.

"Maybe *you'd* like law school," I said. "I don't like school, period."

"I know you say that," he said. "But you're diligent with things that interest you. I don't think you ever had teachers who really encouraged you."

"Besides you, you mean," I said.

"Besides me."

I'd never told him about my foot fetish affair with Mr. East. "I had a good bio teacher in high school," I said. "It's why I still think about biology sometimes."

"New York State has a solid community college system, is all I'm saying. An education is something no one can ever take from you."

He'd been saying that since I could remember.

He drove me to the airport in the homeowners' Honda. I tried to remember the last time I'd seen him drive a car.

"Good to see you," I told him.

"You're my heart," he said.

When I got back to New York, I saw Nicky a few more times before she started dating someone who wanted to be serious and monogamous. That meant she had to lose my number. I was, per usual, happy for her and annoyed that I didn't get to date the new person, too. Why not all three of us? Why not?

No one ever had a satisfying answer. It just wasn't what people did. But it could be, I said.

"Well, if she ever wants a threesome," I said.

"I think I'd probably let her pick the girl," she said.

"Yeah, okay," I said. "If she wants a threesome with a guy, probably you should let her pick the guy, too."

"That's never happening," she said. "Take care of yourself," she said. "Hope I see you again sometime."

"Sure," I said. "You too."

Angie and I didn't see each other for two months. I'd been couch surfing, looking for a stable situation, working, and trying to handle my pain. She called me late one night when I wasn't working, told me she missed me and wanted to hang out. We were both awkward. We drank. We drank more.

I woke up in her bed with her, still dressed, but with a sinking sadness. I had no idea if we'd kissed or touched each other in any new way. All those fantasies, and I wasn't even there.

"Fuuuuuuck," Angie said, and put her hands up to her face in the morning. "Fuck, fuck, fuuuuuuuuuck."

"Yeah," I said. I couldn't ask her what had happened between us. I bet she didn't remember either. And I felt so tired.

She fumbled around a little and checked her phone.

"Goddamnit!" she said and lurched up and over to her bathroom. She started the shower. "I have to be in class in 20 minutes!"

My head hurt. I wanted to watch her shower, but we should probably talk about last night. I couldn't decide what to do.

Angie breezed past me, ruffled the back of my hair, and the air was sweeter where she'd been.

"I think I'm going to go to an AA meeting today," I said, and

I met her eyes. She was surprised. "I'm sick and tired enough, I think." There were always fliers for AA in the dressing room at the club. It had been in the back of my mind for years.

She put a neutral face on. "I think you'll probably hate the God stuff, but you should try whatever you want."

I didn't know what to say to her. What did she know about it? Did she think I shouldn't go? It was confusing. I crawled back under the covers and shut my eyes. After a few more minutes of dashing around the bedroom, she left.

By the time I got to the basement of the Methodist church just two stops away from my favorite pedicure place, my resolve had faltered. My self-loathing had arrived. I was one of the quiet people who held tightly to myself in the back row. I was prickly and scared and burning my own guts out with shame. My feet were exposed because I'd gotten a pedicure that afternoon, but it was obviously too cold for sandals. I felt somehow that I was just like Carl. I felt crazily young and stupid and sad and alone. And, I thought, my mom died almost six years ago. I should be better by now.

I drank bitter burnt coffee and chewed on the edges of the cup, then did it again. I tried to look at everyone without making eye contact, so I could figure out who to sit next to and who not to. Then I saw there were twice as many chairs as people, and I relaxed just a tiny bit. There was something about that, like when a super sexy stripper's eyeliner is just a bit off, and you feel like, oh, that's right, this is just a person. This was just a room full of people, I told myself. People who have some things in common.

I didn't take a chip. I didn't tell anyone it was my first meeting. I stayed wrapped in on myself in a corner chair. Two people tried to start conversations with me and then gently moved on after they let me know I was welcome. The only requirement was a desire to stop drinking, they said.

I had a lot of desires. I supposed that was among them. The desire to be drinking *right now* was also there.

Just hearing all the words and sounds people were making was almost too much. The volumes of grief and loss, the museums of fear. One of the meeting leaders casually mentioned that his brother and father died in a car crash when he was a teenager, on the way to his story about how the program saved his life.

There was a visiting speaker. That person looked like he could be teaching high school biology, like Mr. East. He said we all show up here dragging a closet. In it are shelves full of lies. Recovery requires a process of dusting all those lies off, looking at them, reckoning with them, to try and throw them out for good.

And then he said something about God that I had to tune out. He crossed his arms over his small potbelly and sat back.

The person sitting next to me started talking and I watched her perfect hot pink acrylic nails scratch at her black leggings absently while she spoke. Her parents had just come to visit. It was a terrible time at work. Her father looked old and it made her feel bad. "I'm really struggling," she said.

I sneaked a look at her face. She looked rich. Of course you want to get drunk, I thought. Your life is parasitic.

It works if you work it, they said. I heard Claudia in my head: "Yes, work it girl, work it!"

I sent Angie a message: I'm sorry for stuff. Let's get coffee soon?

She didn't write back.

I wanted to be finished with the part of my life where I struggled all the time. But didn't know what I needed to do to get the change I wanted. So I took risks. I tried things, let people convince me or pay for me or take me along. I had so few feelings besides a bleak despair or a quiet horror I started to develop tastes based on things that brought me relief. When something brought me real pleasure, not just relief from suffering, I was astonished and disoriented. I got taken by it. I tried to figure out how to have it more often. Later, Nautica would call this period of my life the Hall of Mirrors.

You saw yourself, but you saw yourself all misshapen, she said.

7

LOVE IS SELF DEFENSE

I got a room in an apartment shared by other dancers at the Top Hat. We drank wine together and cooked spaghetti and talked shit. A guy got his finger into my asshole one night during a lap dance, and although I got away from him, I decided I should get more proactive about my safety since the management and bouncers at the club never had my back.

I didn't understand, prior to arrival, that the weekend self-defense class I'd signed up for was going to be taught by a cop. After years of visiting Carl, seeing how cops treated girls at the clubs, and getting more afraid of them the more clients I saw on the side, trying to learn from one seemed like a bad move. But, the hundred and twenty dollars wasn't refundable, and, the most beautiful woman I'd ever seen was rummaging in her bag when I walked in the door, so, I decided to stay.

The class was held in a high school gym and had ten students. Seven of them looked young. A few of the students seemed to know each other, and spoke together quietly. Another young woman was alone, dressed all in black with shit-kicking boots on, and her face was serious. Then there was me, one older woman with salt and pepper braids tied into a big knot on the top of her head, and the most beautiful woman I'd ever seen, who introduced herself to the circle as "Nautica." She had bright almond color eyes, like Carl's, and little white freckles on her nose and cheeks, and she sat next to the older woman, on the other side of me. Nautica's natural, dark brown hair was pulled back into a pouf at her crown.

She had bright expressions and strong arms. She walked her high, round ass through the room with a swish that people had to try not to look at. I was distracted. I had to keep telling myself I was in the class for a very, very serious reason.

The teacher, Karen, looked like a ranch hand who chose her style in 1980. She had a wedding ring and talked about her "old man," so then I imagined she never got out of being married because she had kids--she had kept her sandy brown bowl cut, she had a huge face and thick hands. She wore a maroon collared shirt and told us that she was always angry that more women didn't know how to take care of themselves when the "bad guys got them."

The first exercise was about using our diaphragm to project our voice. We put our hands up in unison and yelled "NO!" at the front of the room. She kept telling one of the students, who was wearing a panda on her shirt, to "dig deeper" for her voice.

"You got to let 'em know!" Karen bellowed. "We don't scream here, we YELL."

"No!" tried Panda shirt. "No, no no!" She still sounded like a child. I cringed a bit for her and for Karen.

Nautica tapped me on the shoulder when it was time to partner up to practice escaping a choke hold.

"You wanna work together?" she said.

Did I ever. "Sure," I said. Trying to be cool. We introduced ourselves. I wanted to say something smart about her name but nothing came.

"Kindred's a unique name," she said to me. "Where's it from?"

"My mom just thought of it, I guess," I said. I wanted to tell her everything. Until then, I was picking up on the moves pretty quickly. Suddenly, I felt blank and clumsy.

"Begin!" yelled Karen. She started wandering around, checking on the pairs.

Nautica said "May I?" and when I nodded, she put her hands around my neck.

"Go ahead," she said.

"Oh right," I said, and did a sloppy version of the escape technique.

She smiled. "Try again?"

"Yeah, ok," I said. I did it right the second time.

"You do me now," she said. My insides jumped. Yes, please.

I put my hands around her neck. She was warm. I feared my hands were sweating, clammy. She shouted "NO!" and broke my hold.

Karen looked over at us, "Nice voice!" she said to Nautica, like a coach.

We practiced a few more times. Then Karen told us all to sit in a circle.

Nautica sat next to me.

"Let's talk about why women get attacked," said Karen, and she slapped her thighs. "Anyone want to guess?"

I raised my hand. She pointed at me.

"One reason is because we live in a culture that supports rapists and blames victims," I said. "And another is that rape is a tactic of war."

Nautica gave me a surprised, approving look.

"I don't know about all that," said Karen. "Women get raped because they aren't prepared to fight back."

Nautica raised her hand. "That sounds like victim-blaming to me," she said. "Like Kindred said," she added.

"Look," said Karen. "You came to this class to learn how to repel an attack, am I right?"

We all nodded and muttered some form of assent.

"Then trust me," Karen said. "I've been a cop for twenty-five years. You would not believe the shit I've seen, ok? I'm telling you that women don't fight back when they should, and it's a problem."

Ok, I thought. I can agree that's a problem.

"So you don't just come in here and yell 'no!' and punch one of my guys in his pads a couple of times over the weekend and then go back into your life acting exactly the same, ok?" Karen said. "You all need to practice what you learn here. This is about changing the way you carry yourselves. You need to know that you'll defend yourself out there, not just in here. You're learning street effective techniques, ladies. Use them carefully, but *use* them. Make a friend in the class and get together to practice."

After the class, I looked at myself in the mirror in the bathroom and pep talked myself into asking Nautica if she wanted to grab some food. She looked at her watch and then said yes! We went to a taco place near the gym. Over carne asada and Diet Coke, we studied for our certification quiz and got to know each other. We asked each other about strike points and defensive maneuvers. We drew circles on copies of body outlines: weak places, bony places. We drew tattoos and penises and breasts and eventually, the papers looked like fifteen-year-old boys had emptied libidinal buckets on them.

She asked, "What do you do for money?" and I told her I was a stripper.

"I knew I liked you," she said. "I'm a dominatrix. And the headmistress at my dungeon."

"I want to learn how to do that," I said, before I'd thought about it. "I'm also, uh, a regular hooker," I said. "Like, I see guys outside the club?"

"Girl you're brave," she said. "And in my dungeon we say what you do is full-service sex work, vanilla work, because some of the girls don't like words like 'prostitute' or 'hooker' used about them. You're like a sugar baby, or girlfriend experience, or whatever."

"What is that?"

She smiled. "You go on dates where you have to laugh at the jokes and wear nice clothes?"

"Totally. I get my guys through the club usually. See them on the side until it ends."

She whistled through her teeth. "I'm serious, I think that's brave. It's more emotional mess than I'm willing to handle."

"Thanks," I said. No one had ever said anything like that to me.

"I'll teach you to Domme if you want," she said. She pulled a card from her bag and gave it to me. A photo of a modern, low-light interior, paddles and floggers hanging from the wall. On the back, it said *La Jouissance: New York*, and there was an email address.

She said she liked what I said in class, about why women get raped. She asked me if I'd ever been raped.

"Not really," I said.

She laughed. "What the hell does that mean?" She didn't apologize for laughing.

"I've had a lot of sex I didn't want to have, but nothing seriously violent," I said. "I've had a lot of other bullshit, like guys touching, fingers in my bikini at work, um, waking up next to someone after blacking out and stuff like that." I paused. "But I've never called any of it 'rape' in my head."

"I think any sex you don't want to have is rape," she said,

"even if you're not willing to call it rape, I would be. And dudes sticking fingers in your body at work is straight up assault, if not also rape."

There was something both comforting and scary in hearing her say that. We both took sips of soda. A jukebox turned on, played a loud polka, and we had to raise our voices over it.

"I can't even use half of the stuff we're doing in this class at the club," I said. "I'd get fired and I can't afford to get fired. I don't know what I was thinking. No one teaches you how to get some dude's fingers out of your asshole quietly, discreet-like, and still keep a lap dance going, which is what I've tried to do. Anyway. What about you? You got raped?" I said.

She sighed. "I was raped, yeah," she said. "In college. And I don't believe in 'nonviolent' rape," she said. "My attacker was a person I knew who didn't beat me up before or after. He just snuck into the bedroom where I was sleeping, and I woke up to him getting my pants down, trying to push his dick in me. I was so out of it he was having sex with me before I really woke up and pushed him off. No one wanted to call it rape. But I became the Take Back the Night girl on campus after that."

"Right," I said. "What an asshole," I said. That had happened to me too, at more than one of those parties during the Worst Year of My Life. I hadn't called it "rape" or even "attempted rape" or even "attack" in my head before. It had seemed pretty normal, at the time.

"I don't like Karen," I said.

Nautica laughed again. "Me neither! What's your reason?"

"She's a cop," I said.

"You don't like that she's a cop?"

I shrugged. "My dad went to prison when I was in high school," I said. I did not say, he is homeless now. I did not say, he is an activist.

"Aha. Well, I don't love them either," she said. "But my

problem is I think Karen's a repressed lesbian and that shit just makes my skin crawl. Just relax and come out and get it done, you know? This is the twenty-first century. But I appreciate you. I don't meet a lot of white girls who hate cops."

I looked my plate and started sawing a corner of meat. "Not sure how to respond to that," I said.

"Why, because you're a repressed lesbian too?" she slapped me lightly on the arm. "No worries. I've got a cure for repression. I call it sex."

"I'm not repressed," I said.

"Perfect," she said. "Neither am I. Should we consider this our first date?" she winked.

"Yes," I said. And my heart actually fluttered. "Yes, we should."

She had to leave, but we kissed outside the subway for a brief and amber-scented second. I blushed about it all the way home. My roommates saw it on me the instant I opened the door.

"Aw shit," one of them said. "This one is gonna be bad for business!"

The next day Nautica and I struggled to break free of the grip of enormous men wearing full body padding. We yelled and punched and stomped and elbowed and went out for drinks afterward and burned our Rape Defense Class Completion Certificates into an ashtray in the back patio of the bar and had sex at Nautica's place. Her apartment was draped with luscious fabric and stacked with soft pillows and perfect candle-lighting. We'd made out on her couch for a while when she pulled back and said, "I want to fuck you."

"Yes me too, please and thank you," I said.

She twirled a piece of my hair and stroked my neck. "You've got this face," she said. "You're beautiful."

I thanked her.

"You also look like you've been through a lot," she said.

I asked how she could tell.

"I notice people for a living," she said.

I wanted her, and I didn't want to tell her about my life yet, but I wanted her to know me, and it was strange. I wanted to know all about her, too.

We had hot, slow, eye-gazing sex.

Oh shit, I kept thinking, I like her so much. I like her so much. I want this woman SO BAD. It felt like every heartbeat ached, every muscle fiber I had was stretching toward her. I was so painfully alive I thought maybe I was dying. She felt so good, it was terrifying. Luckily for me, she fell for me too.

After we had been dating for a few months, Nautica invited me to come sit in on an incall session at the dungeon she managed before I started taking my own, to see if Domme work appealed to me in practice as much as it appealed to me in theory. She told me she never did outcalls, where you meet the client at their hotel or home. "They come to me," she said. "It's part of the power dynamic." Watching her work was like getting hypnotized.

"Wear something tight but not slutty," she said. I wore a black cocktail dress and pumps.

She instructed me to arrive fifteen minutes before the session started, so she could walk me through her set up and her plan, and then she put me in the dressing room for the first twenty minutes so that she could "get him ready" for me to come in and watch the next half hour. Five minutes at the beginning for him to undress, five minutes at the end for him to get dressed again. A one-hour session is a snack, she told me, it's not a meal. It can be great, but mostly, it's forgettable. You need a longer session to get someone to "go deep."

I had a chair to sit in, a perfect view, and no job other than to witness, which was a gift she was giving both me and the client. They all liked to say they were healthy and fit, but he really was. It was something Nautica liked about him, because it meant he could take longer periods in more elaborate bondage. She had him in leather wrist and ankle cuffs, perched on a spanking bench with his belly on the bench and his knees on either side. Some shiny nylon rope crisscrossed over his midsection and his cuffs were attached to metal eyes on the bench with small padlocks. He was gagged, but she'd removed his blindfold so he could see me there. I liked the look of him immediately, so peaceful, so vulnerable.

"Hi honey," I said to him, and petted the back of his head. "What a sweet little guy."

"Isn't he?" Nautica said. She spanked him lightly. "He's a peach." Then she gestured that I should have a seat.

Her movements were sure and strong. She opened drawers, pulled implements out, inspected them, decided for or against, and built herself a small arsenal next to her submissive, where he could see. She talked to him in a soft, sweet, baby voice, one I'd never heard her use before, and petted and cooed at him. "I've already warmed him up a little bit," she said to me, "but I'm going to shine his ass now." He whimpered and wiggled a little.

She had chosen a piece of gear that looked like a monstrous ping pong paddle, leather on one side with metal studs showing and fur on the other. She started slow, tapping the bottoms of his feet lightly, tapping up his calf on one side, then the other, then up his thighs, then back and forth on his inner thighs. "That's what I'm talking about," she said quietly, as he strained against his bonds to open up more for her.

He likes it, he wants it, I kept saying to myself. He *paid* for it. It was a revelation to witness. I shifted in the chair and neither of them looked at me.

She tapped his entire body with the paddle before focusing a few hits on his butt. One. Two, a little harder. Three! The hardest yet, and then she rubbed him with the fur side.

I had expected more brutality from her, somehow. I had wanted to see her whale on someone and not give a shit if they were crying. I hadn't yet learned that masochistic submissives who like truly intense and hard corporal punishment from their Mistress were a specific style of client. This guy wanted some pain, and he could take some pain, but Nautica was a controlled, attentive, deep listener, and she never gave him more than he could take.

She was more conservative because he was paying her, she told me later. "You know better than anyone that I'm happy to make reckless mistakes with lovers," she said. "Because we learn things, we bond, we fix it, maybe we even find a new edge to flirt with, whatever. With a client I have to stay totally on top of what's happening the whole time. And so should you," she added, "especially you."

I watched her work the client up to a pretty serious spanking, and his butt turned bright red all over, with some purplish bursts in the center of each of his cheeks. "These are such beautiful roses," she cooed, rubbing him. She squeezed his flesh in handfuls, then let him go and patted him. He seemed to relax another inch or two into his bonds.

Behind him, out of view, she put together her work dick, an easy-to-clean patent leather strap-on harness with a long, thin, light brown dildo. She put a condom on. I loved that little pelvic tilt she got into, so familiar from men I'd fucked, rolling it on, checking, ready. She stepped in front of his face and slapped him very lightly with the dick, never letting him get it in his mouth, tap, tap tapping his face and telling him she was going to fill up his slutty little holes. He whimpered desperately.

She shot me a quick look that indicated I need to watch carefully. She'd arranged the bench so that the client could see her behind him in the big wall mirror if he held his neck up against the bonds. So he had the option of seeing her fuck him, but it was tiring for him to hold the position in which he could see. A little predicament.

She put on a black nitrile glove and massaged his asshole with three pumps of thick lube. She used the gloved hand to get her dildo positioned just right, then pushed in just a tiny bit, and let him wriggle to get closer. He'd opened up very fast. I imagined he had enormous dildos he stuck in his own butt at home. She pushed in slowly, until her cock was about a third of the way in him. She started moving in and out, pumped more lube on him, pulled her glove off, put another one on without missing a beat, and told him how good he was doing.

"Such a nice baby," she said to him, and spanked him. "What do you need? Tell Mistress what you need."

"Fuck me, please, please, Mistress, thank you, fuck me," he whispered.

She did. And because of the size of her dildo, and her own perfect choreographing of herself, she got none of his fluids on her body, only made physical contact with him using her hands and her thighs, and never touched any of the soiled stuff-- condom, any of it, with her bare hands. I was impressed and intimidated and grateful to see it. She trained me for a few months while I kept money coming in from the strip club and my vanilla clients, and then I got some pictures taken in one of her old corsets, posted an ad, and started taking my own submissive clients at La Jouissance.

I remember a letter Carl sent me sometime in those months.

Dear Kindee,

Science says it's good for us to laugh. Chemicals, brains, muscles, something. I believe, through my own experience, that people require pleasure to thrive. They don't need it to live. Survival does not require it. But to relax into joy, to sense something exquisite, to be rendered utterly tender, pleasure must be free to enter. Fun on Principle.

Self-created, self-sustaining pleasure is simultaneously privately experienced and politically relevant. Pleasures shared in a group are the organizing principle behind everything from religious observance to orgies.

I don't believe that everything happens for the best. I do believe that you can make the best of whatever happens. So why wouldn't you?

Back at Corcoran, one time we were on lockdown for four days. There was nothing enjoyable at all on the surface. The lights are painful bright and they keep them on all night. I woke up every two hours to the rapping on the doors, and I had to stand up and come to the window for count. We ate bologna with white bread and fruit cups. Sometimes peanut butter. I couldn't get comfortable in the heat during the day, and the cold during the night.

That institution was built to cripple a man.

It is so clear that when we react, they grow more powerful. Every time a prisoner finally breaks, fights back when he's being beaten, or speaks up at his parole hearing, etc., they retaliate immediately and viciously. I've seen a man be beat nearly to death by two CO's after he spit at them. Why'd he do that, you might ask. I ask you, does it matter? Even if he'd spit at them in utter hatred, does beating him nearly to death when he was unarmed and in handcuffs make any sense? That isn't self-defense, Kindred. (He spit because they called him a faggot. Now what do you think?)

I'm thinking about food, and not just because they gave us shit there. One way power is expressed in America: buying stuff. Thus, you feel powerful when you can feed yourself through buying individual portions of food. In America, an abundance of money does not ethically require that you then turn to feed others. This contributes to a culture of waste and unfair distribution of basic resources. Hollywood is getting gentrified, there's a new shopping center with a nightclub. On a normal day there, I am surrounded by very young white people who feel comfortable spending amounts of money daily on food that I experience as disgustingly large. It's wasteful. I keep thinking of Fela Kuti and wish I could listen to "Expensive Shit" today. Do it for me? I wonder what the next neighborhood target for "business improvement" will be.

I read about agribusiness and I'm shocked, Kindee. There are enough resources on this planet, still, for food and water to be freely available to everyone.

Therefore, food and water should be free.

When do you think you'll be able to come back out to California? I hope you are enjoying your life in NY. Send me some more pictures please. You can use the office address at the Downtown Action Center I gave you last time. Give my best regards to Nautica. I hope you two are taking good care of each other.

Love,
Carl

PART II
NINE YEARS LATER, 2011

8

WORKING

There was a slideshow playing on a large LED screen embedded in the back of the seat in front of me in First Class. Hawai'i pictures and facts.

I already had the money, so now I did the gig. My main concern was for it to go well enough for Jason to want to do it again, continue the Dominant/submissive relationship we'd cultivated, keep a good thing going. Getting a client was not the same as keeping a client. Nautica was excellent at the long-haul pro-D/s relationship. She had regulars in four major cities. I tended to attract curious one-offs or short-term flows of money from men in states of mania. I really wanted some more stability in my game.

I'd been seeing Jason for a few months, which was already an accomplishment, at least for me. He was recently divorced, seeing his kids every few weeks or so, living in a spare Manhattan apartment, working like a workaholic finance guy works. And exploring his submissive side. He'd come to me through my website. He told me he googled "experienced petite brunette Domme high end incall New York" and my ad caught his eye.

I got to do the first leg of the travel alone, First Class from New York to Honolulu. Then I'd meet up with Jason at the Hawaiian Airlines First Class Lounge and we'd get to Kauai together.

The seat smelled cleaner than coach. The informative slideshow was too pleasant, too welcoming. I overdubbed it in my mind. How precious is this natural resource! Let us rush to save it from the encroaching decimation of modernity's excess and return it to its historical, "true" state! But let us not remind mainland Americans that Hawai'i was colonized and annexed, made a territory and then a state, through theft and deception and violence.

A flight attendant approached. His teal shirt was perfectly pressed. He offered me guava juice or sparkling wine and handed me a complimentary in-flight entertainment device. My dude, that's just an iPad.

"How can you look so sour when you're on your way to Hawai'i?" asked the flight attendant. He was smiling, waiting for me to relax.

"Hawai'i scares me," I said.

He laughed. "Flying there, you mean?"

"No, not really," I started.

"I'm Stephen, and I'll take care of you, don't worry," he said, and he patted my headrest and moved on.

On my complimentary First Class iPad, I read about the Mala Wharf. I looked at pictures of the 1922 structure, a stretch of concrete.

It was to be a company asset for the Baldwin Packers, an export outfit owned by one of the Big Five families who controlled Hawaii's territorial economy. They wanted to ship more canned pineapple out on bigger boats.

But only three steamships were ever able to dock there. It was built against the advice of Native Hawaiians who were specific in their predictions: the waves would be too high and the currents too strong for ships to safely dock at the wharf. And they were right.

In my electronic tourist magazine, the Mala Wharf was then pictured today, a series of perilous angles made by shoddy concrete now underwater, reclaimed by coral and brightly colored fish. It had finally collapsed in 1992 during Hurricane Iniki.

The article exuberantly proclaimed the sunken bridge a "perfect host" to a "dazzling array" of sea creatures, and a favorite spot for families on boats and beginning scuba divers. And so an invasive corporate interest's dangerously bad piece of hubris was deftly recast as a site for environmental education and pleasant recreation. It felt insane. I made a mental note to tell the story to Carl when I was home. He'd love and hate it in that way that gave him life.

The person in the seat next to me was coughing. A wet cough. I didn't like it. It felt like an affront to First Class. I stole a look at him. Not as old as I'd thought. Wearing nice pants and flip flops plus a clean haircut. He would make a great client. I wondered who he already belonged to.

I swiped to the "Easy Listening" playlist. I recognized all the songs. I listened to "Lola" by the Kinks, able to hear all the lyrics clearly for the first time in my fanciful headphones, and felt nostalgic for any time or place that was more queer than the one I was in.

I looked good. I had the big dark glasses on, I'd smoothed all my hair down into a chignon bun on my neck, and my lamb leather travel jacket was just light and soft enough that I wouldn't look silly in a tropical climate. I didn't have any acne. My vagina was healthy and I wasn't menstruating. I had just shaved and shea-buttered myself into a slick silky-smooth version of my skin.

When I arrived in the airport lounge for elite travelers, I saw that Jason had put some effort in too, which was a good start. He was wearing his clean vacation traveling clothes, not a suit from the office, which meant he'd taken time to go home before he left. If he was in a good mood, the whole trip would be easier.

I resolved to stay on a path to actual relaxation, as much as possible, for the next three days. I knew for sure that I found it impossible to relax fully around a client. People took energy, period. I was the most myself around Nautica, and we had some friends I could be real with. But I had come to accept that I still found it impossible to relax fully unless I was alone.

Alone, I approached my own psychological labyrinth with deep, sincere, sustained effort. I'd tried biofeedback, yoga, meditation, journaling, reading, therapy, three different recovery groups. I felt like I'd come a long way from the traumatized child I was when I moved to New York. I knew desperation and depression. They were not my daily habit anymore. Nautica and I had good friends and a healthy bond. I was making steady money and when people asked me how I was doing, I said I'm really good! and I meant it.

Jason sat across from me in the airport lounge, flipping through magazines about things I didn't think he cared about, like cars, and I felt a little wave of affection for him, looking at the tiny curly hairs that poked out of the bottom of his shorts at his knee.

"I'm going to take you to a show on Friday night," he said, withholding eye contact until after he'd finished his sentence.

"What kind of show?" I smiled, no resistance here.

"A dance show, a real traditional luau!" he said, looking very pleased with himself.

He started miming something, like he was brushing ants off a counter, and then I realized it was supposed to be hula dancing, and I could have smacked him, but instead I said, "Don't." And he went back to his magazine, a little smug, a little chastened.

I should have seen that one coming. I prepared myself for the inward horror of him going up on stage and pretending to hula. He would be that guy.

Shake, shake, shake, the magazine got my attention. "Where'd you go?" he said.

"Nowhere," I smiled again. "I'm right here."

"I can't wait to stretch out on one of those hotel beds," he said, and stretched both his arms up and his legs out, taking up as much space as he possibly could. "Gaaaaaaahhhhhh." He sighed.

I would have loved to stretch and growl like that, right then. I uncrossed and recrossed my legs, drank a sip of water, and clenched my jaw instead. Because femininity mattered.

I gave up trying so hard and fell asleep on the second plane. I got a red nap-spot on my cheek, which Jason talked about three times during the trip. He also talked about how much he loved his childhood dog, who died around the first time he ever came to Hawai'i, such an important time in his development. When I woke up we drank a chardonnay and he whispered, "I promise this is the last shitty alcohol for three days!" and I whispered "Thank you," and nibbled his ear for a full second. Because I knew it was true and I felt sincerely grateful for that.

On the drive to the hotel he chatted up the driver and I enjoyed twenty minutes of not having to talk, the luxury of idle gazing out the window, tracking signs and place names, letting myself be amazed by how *green* and *how* green and how lush and gorgeous it was, it really was, after all this island had been though.

They gave me an orchid lei at the hotel and so I smelled like cum before we'd even entered the room. Jason was already in ecstasy, talking about how nice everyone was here. I did not remind him that racist cultural appropriation and the exploitative service industry was designed to make him feel good, to offer him ways to spend his money on feeling good, at great cost to others. I could feel him trying to signal sex before dinner, and I had to decide quick. I interrupted his unpacking routine with a hug and I touched his cock and balls lightly.

"I want to give you some really quality attention tonight," I said, looking in his eyes. He liked it. "So let's change, get some drinks in me, eat some lovely food, and get back here early tonight. Good plan?"

"Good plan," he said. I patted him and put my head on his shoulder.

"You take such good care of me," I said.

"You deserve it," he said.

There was something wrong in our power balance, and I needed to fix it. As I got ready for dinner, I reminded myself that I was a Domme. A grown woman with power. I was here to do a job, a fun job, not to feel harassed by everything. I took deep breaths and hugged myself. It helped a little.

We had a good dinner. He was obedient and predictable during sex. We had a hot tub on our floor. It made a difference that I was in shape and felt good in a bathing suit. It made a difference that he'd booked a massage for me for the following afternoon already.

Still, by the time the massage came, I was exhausted from giving him my full attention and biting my tongue.

I called Nautica from the locker room in the hotel spa.

"How's the hottest babe in occupied paradise?" she said when she picked up.

"I'm so happy to hear your voice!" I said, and suddenly felt like crying. "I'm tired," I said, my voice wobbling.

"It's ok baby, cry away," she said, a little softer. "It's tough to travel with people. Especially to tourist places with a violent colonial history. Which is like anywhere a client wants to go. When's your time off?"

"I don't really have it, except right now," I said, "I'm getting a massage."

"That's good," she said. "Make sure you get two hours alone tomorrow too. Feels like something I should have reminded you about. I know your dynamic is a little weird but you can exert your power to stay healthy. You can take some time alone and stay strong."

"Right."

"Take care of my Kindykins," she said. "Take Jason's money, get home safe, and learn what you can about how the rich people are doing their ugly things there."

"I will," I said. "Thank you."

"Anytime and forever," she said. We hung up. I texted her some hearts.

On the second night, we went to the show. I got lightly drunk beforehand, half aware that it was a way to cope with what I expected to be a well-produced display of sanitized "legends" made for white tourists, performed by young people from the area.

I was not surprised that the dancers were impressively skilled. Or that the costumes were fantastic. What surprised me was how much the music moved me, and how much history of pre-contact Hawai'i made it into the program. I clapped with everyone else and touched Jason's inner thigh when they were choosing "contestants" for the crowd-pleaser at the end. He stayed in his seat. I made it. I felt silly and confused, but I'd made it.

We went for a walk after the show, out on the beach next to the theater. We were aimless, holding hands, laughing, pointing at beautiful things for each other, "Look at that! (Gasp) Look at THAT!" A banana leaf taller than Jason. A big beautiful shell.

He lingered on my eyes longer than normal. Penetrating. A question behind his gaze.

"What." I said.

He shrugged. I wasn't going to get the whole story. That was okay. "I don't know anyone else like you," he said.

"Thank you," I said. And that was all I said.

We walked quietly for a few very long, very intense minutes. Then he pulled me gently toward him and pivoted so I was facing him and the water. He slid his forearms around my waist and folded his hands onto my mid- and lower back, suggestive but not aggressive. It was a nice feeling, and I went toward him, and we kissed passionately, the ignition lit. This was an important romantic moment of the trip and I'd nailed it. And it felt good, and we enjoyed each other.

On the last night of the trip we decided to stay in and take it easy. Which meant he wanted an extended BDSM scene. I had started to feel a cold coming on. I sent him to a beach bar for happy hour before our "night in."

Obelisks on fire. Thick deep music. The air was soft, moving, fresh, and warm. I knew that drinking and staying up late would tip me over into getting a full-blown cold, but this was the night, there wasn't another chance to perform as hard as tonight, right now. We sat in a large clamshell, upholstered in white suede and faux fur. Twinkle lights made perfect scallop shapes in the ceiling.

I leaned in and whispered in his ear, "This place is incredible. I've never seen anything like it." And it felt so good to say, because it was true.

I ached with an encroaching fever and my throat was sore. I drank whiskey in coffee. I tried to stay apace of our conversation. I wondered if he could tell I was sick.

While he was up paying the check, I gave myself another internal pep talk about being a good Domme.

In our room, I lit a few candles I'd ordered from the front desk on the sly and put on my Massive Attack Pandora radio station. I did some beautiful work on his back with his own belt. He liked a little cock-and-ball torture so I was kicking him with my going-out heels when a cough came on, and I had to go into the bathroom to stifle it. He wanted to switch after that, although neither of us mentioned me seeming sick. We had some basic, functional, hot-enough doggie style sex. We did not have a mad crazy BDSM evening, but, I felt that his orgasm, which was longer and more powerful than usual, was my accomplishment.

I blew my nose quietly in the bathroom and worried about how bad I felt, and then worried about breathing through my mouth or snoring. I rummaged in my toiletries for an antihistamine. A pink one! Sweet salvation in a plastic bubble, let me peel back your sacred foil.

I took the Benadryl with a swig of tap water, fixed my hair a little, brushed my teeth, checked my vagina, blew my nose again. I was prepared to sleep pretty.

In the morning, he asked if I was feeling alright. I sniffled and coughed. "I think I must be allergic to leaving Hawai'i," I said lightly. He recoiled just slightly. I was right to hide it then, I thought. And so I hid it as best I could, although I slept through both flights instead of making nostalgic romantic conversation about the amazing time we'd just had.

Once I was home from Hawai'i, I was sick, the sickest I could ever remember being. My throat was so inflamed swallowing made me cry. My muscles were run through with acid, burning, scorching, poisoned. My lungs were full of something dark and alien, which I could only cough up after long, violent spasms. I was scared of cancer, because I was scared of cancer every time I got sick.

Nautica turned our bedroom into a healing center within fifteen minutes. She was lighting candles and diffusing essential oils near the bed. She brought out lotions and pots of thick salve. She concentrated, reading labels, sorting, making choices. Occasionally she would ask me a question.

"How long have you had the fever?"

"This is the third day."

"You know how high it was?"

"No."

"Can you estimate for me based on how you felt?"

"102."

"Are you exaggerating?"

"Yes, probably, but I really feel the worst, ever."

"I know. I also know you are lucid."

I would do what she said. It was what I wanted anyway, to have her attention, to be the subject of her perfect problem-solving mind. Because if I was her problem, she wouldn't let me go until she'd solved me, and solved me creatively, and solved me well.

She told me to take my shirt off, lay on my stomach, and give her room to work. So I did.

She poured a tablespoon of minty oil into the small of my back and spread it evenly up my back, down the other side, up and down in reverse. It hurt me, in a way that seemed like a fever delusion, like she'd just scraped off a layer of skin. I sucked in some air.

"Ok," she said, and suddenly the feeling was gone.

"What are you doing?" I said. I half expected the answer to be "Magic."

"Trying stuff," she said. Which wasn't much different.

She added a little more oil. It smelled like lavender this time. She kneaded my aching muscles from my feet to my head and did some sort of lymph-draining stroking thing on my neck.

She worked slowly, methodically, adagio, a walk, a blues. She occasionally shook something, a muscle, a joint, as if it had stopped listening to her, and then returned to massaging it. She held pressure points in my hand and shoulders that sent sparking electricity down my arm and into my fingers, then she rubbed the spots with the back of her hand, in circles. She massaged my ass with her elbow, and I whined. It was so good. I had points of relief to focus on, places where the pain was subsiding, for the first time in days. She told me to flip over, leaned over my vagina, kissed my mound, and said something so softly I couldn't hear her.

She put some heavy herbal-scented medicinal salve on the bottoms of my feet and slid socks on me. It gave me hope.

"When you go to see a doctor, do you tell them you're a ho?" she asked.

"I thought I was supposed to say 'sex worker,'" I said.

She snorted a little. "You know what I'm asking."

"I'll tell a doctor I've had more than ten partners," I said. "If I'm there for a Pap smear or an STD test."

"I just wonder about whether they could help us more," she said. She moved to sitting next to me, pulled her nail kit from the side table, and started taking the polish off her toes. She scrubbed in short, vigorous circles with pure acetone.

"That can't be good for me," I said, about the stink of acetone.

"The last time I got a Pap smear the doctor asked me what kind of exercise I did," she said, ignoring my complaint. "He said my pelvic floor was 'very developed.' And he wanted to know if I did yoga."

"Did you tell him you do yoga?" I rolled to the window and opened it, breathed what seemed like sweet, sweet air. My senses were all messed up. "Can you put the fan on when you do the acetone thing?"

"Sure, sorry," she said. "I'll do it next time, almost done here."

"I think it's been five years since I had a Pap smear."

"The yoga doc was okay, you should go to him if you're due. I said he was right, I do yoga. I just wonder if he would have been looking for different things if he knew what else I do."

"Like what, though?" I asked. Outside of pegging her clients, Nautica had penetrative sex exclusively with women. She didn't let her clients near her orifices, except to kiss the outside of her panties. She was meticulous with her sterility practices in the dungeon, and as far as she'd ever told me, she'd never used a needle to shoot up.

"I don't know," she said. "That's kind of my point."

"I'm much dirtier than you," I said. "In terms of pathogens. What do you think I should do besides get STD checks and PAP smears? Tell them to look for signs of premature aging in my vagina?"

She made an amused sound and started putting her nail polish remover and cotton away. "You have to stop with that 'clean' and 'dirty' stuff," she said. "It's really bad for sexual self-esteem."

"Not mine," I said. "I'm a dirty girl."

"Maybe when you were nineteen."

"Definitely when I was nineteen."

"Ok, ok," she gave in. "I just wondered if you'd had more constructive interactions with doctors than me. Sounds like not.

So, you ready for what I think you should do next for this sickness you're in?"

I was ready for a nap. But I listened to her instructions.

Right around the time my cold resolved, Jason sent me a box full of cheap souvenirs from the Kauai hotel. There was something very sweet and a little bit insulting about it at the same time.

9

ENTER COMPLEXITY

I met Griffin at a bar in Bushwick. Nautica had canceled our date by text while I was on the train on my way to meet her. You can't check your phone outside in New York during the winter, and Nautica knew it. She also knew I'd end up at home eventually, whether she showed up to meet me or not.

I'd worked the front desk that day, which I hated doing. I did an intake interview with a new client, gave him an OK on his file, and then he'd immediately gotten an appointment with another Domme, didn't tip me, and I was trying not to feel insecure. It happened often enough that the new client doesn't choose the first Domme he sees, even if he likes her best. Many people have to try a lot of different Dommes to know what they really like, because of how intense the sensations are. Once you know the form, you can appreciate more subtle differences in practitioner. Also, some people are just sluts.

The problem with this guy was that he booked with Queen Gina, tried to get her to do a full toilet scene when they hadn't negotiated for it, and then came out of the session saying he didn't want to pay. Nautica usually managed beefs like that, and they were not something that happened that often. But she was off, so it was my problem. I stuck with our policy against refunds and the client called me a cunt and slammed both his hands on my desk.

"Sir, it's time for you to leave," I said.

"Who the fuck do you think you are?" he said.

"You need to go right now," I said. I walked around the desk so that I was effectively stepping up to him.

"I'll fucking leave whenever I want," he said. Which was stupid, because he was trying to get out of paying at the same time that he was refusing to leave.

I reached to his outside shoulder.

He was so angry that I put my hand on him to escort him out of the front door he flailed as if to hit me. I caught his hand and twisted it in toward his chest. He turned and dipped a bit, and I was able to move him.

"Fuck!" he yelled.

"Don't struggle," I said, and we took the four steps to the front door. I let go of him. He opened the door and went out, shaking and rubbing his hand pitifully. As I closed the door behind him, I heard him yelling.

"Fucking cunt bitch goddamn it I'm calling the fucking cops you'll be hearing from the fucking DA motherfucking violent piece of shit..." Finally, he stormed off.

And then Nautica flaked at the last minute.

So I planned to get a drink or maybe too many at a noisy, social place around people who would ignore me that night. It was one of the few things that sounded better than going directly to bed.

Walking from the train, I got to read the walls. The graffiti was sprawling and looping, curls brushing through circles and overlapping. Sometimes an image or a phrase would repeat and I'd imagine the street team, armed with stencils and spray paint and cameras and halogen lights, gleefully marking these blocks with their perfect Millennium Falcon or their nearly-unrecognizable Che Guevara sporting a Dali mustache. Then there were huge shapes, bright blue and pink, candy colors, and screeching yellow pillows, making messages you could only read from a block away. On an impossibly high outside wall near the bar, the word READ commanded everyone. The artist would never have been able to take a step back while painting it. The piece leaned very sharply to the right.

The bar Nautica and I were going to meet at played too much rock. It was also cheap and close to our apartment. The brick outside was painted dark green and then covered with intricate monochromatic renditions of fantasy animals' skeletons. A sphinx, a centaur, a flying skeleton of a dragon, a two-headed dog. I took a picture of myself leaning on the wall, next to the life-size unicorn bones painted there. I even pulled my warm hat back on my forehead so she could see my eyes. Then I went in. I sent the picture to Nautica's phone, asking if she wanted to change her mind. I had to blink a lot once I was inside because they also allowed cigarettes. The Myth House. It was just a little bit too hard to say. Because that was hip, somehow.

The beer list was extensive, written in chalk high up on a large blackboard bolted to the wall. The beer taps stood at attention in a long row of bright colors and symbols and logos, behind a thick wooden bar decoupaged with hundreds of old concert tickets. Low-watt, coiled lightbulbs hanging from the ceiling washed people in pallid tones. I looked at my forearm. Wan. The floor was concrete painted dark brown, and scattered sawdust added some kind of decorative flair. Brooklyn was so tricky that way, mixed-up: an asymmetrical number of mismatching glasses at an old dive versus a perfectly shelved array of three types of glasses at a hipster joint. Unintended consequence at the one, stylistic choice at the other. I tried to talk to employees and meet owners when I was confused about whether I was dealing with a stage set or a real gem. Where I was, the wood paneling wouldn't announce itself either as cynically self-aware 1970s-style procured from the "artisanal" decorator in town, or, as the original 1970s wood paneling that had been replaced piecemeal for the last thirty-odd years by the same family-owned lumber distributor. I had to let it go. Either way, the wood was nice.

I saw Griffin at the bar when I scanned the room. He was made mostly of bones and he moved lightly. I logged him and two other people as "cute," and moved in to place an order.

He tripped me, I fell on him, and it felt like he took something from my bag as I got up. He was deft. I blocked him with a right elbow and poked him a bit in the chest while he said a little chorus of sorry-sorry-sorry-I'm-so-clumsy.

"Hand it over," I said, recovering, and opened my palm.

"Hand what over?" he said.

"Whatever you just stole out of my bag," I faked a jab to his solar plexus. He didn't flinch. Strange.

"Jesus," he said. "Why so violent?"

"Give me my shit," I said.

He tossed a book at me. My journal. He was thin and jaunty, like an adolescent somehow. Sweet in his defiance.

He tried to get up. I clamped his bicep and pulled him down on his stool. He didn't resist. I let him go. I asked his name.

"Griffin."

"Is that a joke?" I said. He looked confused. No, it was not a joke. "You didn't just come up with that because of the painting outside?" I said.

Ah, recognition. "Other way around," he said. "They've got

everything but a griffin out there. Thought I'd help them out." He tried to smile but he looked too scared.

"What do you want with my journal?" Since he was so clearly full of bullshit, might as well see how he handled that question.

He stared into my left eye. His eyelashes were clumped, like he'd cried recently, and his nostrils were flickering. "I want to jerk off to it," he said.

My face must have registered genuine surprise. Griffin adjusted his posture, sat straight. I asked him what he was drinking, and then told him to order us two margaritas when he said beer. I wanted to do something to him, but I couldn't tell yet what it was. He seemed like he needed some punishment, to get back in balance.

After he got us the drinks and sat, we clinked glasses. "Okay," I said. "Now explain yourself." He was visibly uncomfortable. I liked it. He had straight dark hair cropped to keep a kind of mussed spikey shape on top. He touched his hair, patting and twisting, then he took a drink and wiped his mouth with the inside of his white T-shirt collar. He wore a gray hoodie over it, zipped mostly up.

"I'm trying to make a searching and fearless moral inventory of myself," he said. He looked like he'd just shaved.

I couldn't tell if he was kidding. It was probably a nice bar to be an alcoholic in. Lots of smiling. Lots of women. "Did I just push you off the wagon with this margarita?"

"No," he said. "I'm not an alcoholic."

"Well hi, Griffin, anyway," I said.

He seemed very serious. "But I am in recovery. I steal journals from women and use them for sexual gratification." He deflated just slightly. "It's kind of a new thing. I used to just be a regular klepto."

I didn't say anything.

He glanced at my face, then back down to his drink. "So," he cleared his throat, squirming. "I'm sorry for taking your journal. I shouldn't have done that. I go to SA meetings, and I'm really not looking forward to sharing about this."

"Well," I said, too amused to punish him just yet, "at least you know yourself. What's 'SA?'"

"Shoplifters Anonymous," he said. He tried to finish his drink too fast.

"Hold on," I said. He hesitated. I checked my phone. He looked away, as if to take stock of the bar in my absence. Nautica hadn't changed her mind, and wanted me not to wake her up if I got home late. So I was free to chat up this boy. "Don't run away in shame just 'cause you're a pervert and a thief," I said.

"I'm not a pervert," he said.

"Yeah, you are," I said. "According to everyone. Lucky for you, though, so am I." He gave me the first of many gratifying dimples.

"Why would you say that?" he asked, all tingly.

I told him he didn't deserve to know my kinks yet, but if he wanted to buy us another round and move us to a table I'd think about telling him a story. He bought us tequila shots and Tecate. He had a surprising wad of cash in his beat-up brown leather wallet. He moved our empty glasses over to the server's station, placing them on the rubber where someone could whisk them into the sanitizer. Then he put the new drinks on our tiny woodblock table and raised his shot, brandishing his lime wedge in his left hand.

"Are you a stripper?" I asked him.

"No," he said.

"Then what's the story with the cash and the good bar etiquette?"

"I manage a floor of an apartment building. One of the

dudes pays me his rent in cash. And I don't know, I come here a lot. I watch people. I try to be helpful."

We drank.

"Cash is so convenient," I said.

Griffin rubbed his nose with the edge of his sweatshirt sleeve. "Don't get used to it," he said. "No one's going to accept cash in ten years."

"Well, I love cash," I said.

"I met Dave at a party and he told me he was going to set himself on fire. Not my best choice for a roommate. But the cash is great."

I prodded. Griffin said Dave was determined to incite his friends to action against capitalism. He thought dying would make them all militant revolutionaries. This was before Occupy Wall Street, Griffin explained. "I argued with him for a few minutes before I realized that trying to talk him down from suicide was not going to work. He asked me to help him bring up some important items from the basement and buy him some beer and some gasoline." Griffin took a slurp from his Tecate.

"And you did it?"

Shrug. Sure. Apparently, Dave wanted his magazine collection to burn with him. A few hours later, Dave decided to live while on the phone with his long-distance lover.

"So you thought, 'perfect roommate?'" I said.

"Well, no," Griffin said. "I mean I knew he was a gamble, or something." A few months after he moved in, Dave set a fire in his room when no one was home.

I asked the obligatory question about whether he had hurt himself.

"Nah," Griffin said. "He didn't even really hurt the building that much. And he always pays on time. That's a big fucking deal for me. The place I manage is a shithole. Most of the people who live there are lice-ridden anarchists who think rent is evil, so they don't pay. I mean, I'm not stereotyping anarchists. Some of them are really clean and smart and stuff."

Then he asked for my name, so I told him. "Kindred."

"Awesome!" he said. "Do most people make a joke right away about being kindred spirits with you?"

"Definitely, white women do that," I said.

He nodded, "Yeah, that makes sense. I kinda heard it in my mom's voice when I thought it."

Somebody tumbled into us. Griffin's knees knocked into mine. That quick touch gave me a shot of adrenaline so strong I was surprised. The unsteady girl apologized, giggling and not sorry at all, and moved on.

Griffin excused himself to pee. I checked for my journal in my bag when his back was turned. It was still there.

The bar was filling with more people and noise. I texted Nautica that I'd met a cute boy and was going to stay for another drink. She didn't respond. She was probably asleep already. She had an early morning client tomorrow. She was the only one at the dungeon who took appointments before 9:00AM. When I showed up for my afternoon sessions, she would have already made her money.

I finished my Tecate. I'd planned on two drinks, and already had three. Might as well keep going, now that I'd done it.

Griffin appeared through a small crowd. He held two more shots of tequila.

"I see how it is," I said, as he handed me one.

"How is it?" he said, as he produced new wedges of lime from a napkin.

"I see you have been trying to read my mind," I gestured with the tequila.

"You had the body language of a person who intends to

keep drinking," he said, clinking glasses with me. He put the shot back and swallowed.

I told him he was good. He dipped his head to smile, and I reached over and scratched him behind the ear, like a puppy. He took it. He made eye contact. His eyes had a perfect searching look, a Please Take Me, the silent plea of the sexual submissive. I wanted to get my hands on him and make him squeal.

The precise moment at which I was too drunk to make good decisions passed without my noting it, of course. I let Griffin read a few pages of my journal, while I held it in front of him, without my knowing what he was seeing. Then I shut it and kept it in my bag between my knees. If he wanted to look at it, he would have to lower his eyes and look at my body.

He asked me to tell him about my parents.

"I already gave you a peek under my armor," I said, tapping my bag.

"I didn't ask you to tell me all your childhood trauma," Griffin said. "I was just curious about the people that made you."

"That *made* me?" I said, somehow offended. "I made me."

"Sorry," he said, putting his hands up.

I took a breath. He probably just came from old money or an intact family.

I told him a brief and clinical version of my Origin Story. He nodded and blinked and asked questions that didn't offend me. My hunch was right on--he had an intact set of rich, white birth parents. He wondered why I called Carl by his first name, if I also considered him to be my "real dad." He wanted to know if I'd tried to find my biological father. No, I told him, He didn't want me. What a waste of my fucking time for a conversation neither of us wants to have.

"Right on," Griffin said. "Seems like most people would

feel, something? Like, compelled? To search for an absent father," he said.

"I guess I'm not most people," I said.

"So Carl's in LA now," he said. "And where's your mom?"

"She died when I was seventeen," I said. "Cancer."

"Oh fuck," he said. "That must have been hell."

We talked about death. I told him it changed me, her death, but I'd stopped believing it was the only thing that defined my life. It was like LSD, I said. It made the world appear totally off-kilter and full of absurdity, and I started hating people who wasted time or lied about important stuff. Especially people with authority, like doctors.

He asked me what I did for money.

If I was unsure and wanted to stay closeted, I told people I was a make-up artist: it explained the odd hours, the suitcases, the cash. This time, I didn't choose a cover story. I wanted him to know. I wanted to see if he liked imagining me in charge of my clients. I wanted to see if he would treat me like a zoo animal. I wanted to watch him get turned on and then tell him no. It had been a few years since I'd gotten excited by a person with a penis who wasn't paying me. He was wearing the kind of denim that shapes itself in thick bunches when you sit down. And I resented that if he was getting hard, I wouldn't be able to decipher it.

When I said the words "sex worker" and "pro Domme," his eyes lit up.

"That's exciting," he said.

"Yes, it is," I said.

I told him about the relationship I was in with Nautica. I started off right, blunt and clear. Letting him know my situation in a way that would allow him some time and space to decide whether he wanted to pursue me. I was making sure he knew that I was in an open partnership with a woman who would always take priority over him. I told him we were in a commitment that allowed for us both to have lovers, even fall in love. We had worked through some shit over the years. "I'm telling you this because I want to see if we have some sexual compatibility sometime," I said. "And maybe even go on a date, but I'm not available the way single straight women are, and I don't lie to Nautica, so you have to consent to all that unless your instinct so far is that we're on our way to a one-night stand."

"And if it seems like a one-night stand?"

"Then what do you care about my relationship status?"

He laughed. "Wow." He put his elbow on the table and his face in his hand, poised to keep listening. "You've got this all planned out."

I swatted at his arm, like a teenager. "Don't make fun of my 'It's Complicated.'"

"Tell me about Nautica," he said, and swigged.

Somehow, as I was talking about Nautica, he asked me if she was a Domme too, and I just plowed on ahead. Hell yeah she is, I told him. She taught me everything I know. I gave away stories about the dungeon that could have gotten me and her arrested. Plus I told him the name of the place *and* the neighborhood, which was not something we did without a vetting process, and the only way I could explain it to myself, when the realization came crushing in on me as I peed unsteadily in the tiny women's bathroom, was that there was some good reason to trust him I'd be able to figure out later, when I wasn't drunk. But there was no way around it: all the Dommes at the dungeon signed an agreement so that Nautica could remind them of it, and we never outed each other or gave away each other's information like I just had.

Maybe, I thought wildly, I can introduce Nautica and Griffin before too much time passes and she'll feel inspired to trust him too and we can get excited about him together and get him to work there with us as a pro sub! That would be perfect!

I pulled myself together. I jostled my way through the people and got back to the table. The bar seemed utterly chaotic now, so loud no one could hear but somehow everyone was still yelling.

"I gotta go," I said.

"I'll walk you out," he said.

Just at the door to the bar, we both got out our phones. "You text me first," I said, and gave him my number.

He wrote, "This is Griffin. We met at Myth House. I didn't steal your journal." He seemed almost too delicate to touch. I had a quick flash of getting him on a spanking bench, tying him down, and Nautica fucking his mouth with a huge black dildo while I pegged him with my strap-on. In the vision, it was my personal strap-on, not the dungeon one I used on clients. Which meant something.

I hugged him. I felt it. I didn't want to let him go and I wanted to kiss him, too.

"Thanks for hanging out," he said, as we moved back into our personal space. He opened the door. Then he turned back, pulled my hand up and kissed it. It was silly. And it turned me on.

"Don't do that again," I said.

"Okay," he said, and seemed very happy. Then we were outside in the cold again.

"Get in touch with me," I said.

"I will," he said. "If it's okay with you."

I rolled my eyes and scoffed a little, but his deference was right on time. I started walking. We hollered goodbye. The wind pierced my ears. I burrowed my face into my scarf and shuffled through the cold to the building where Nautica and I lived. It was an old remodeled hotel, with thin wood floors and narrow stairways.

I puffed up three flights and stumbled outside the door trying to pull off my boots. I scuttled through the apartment, bumped into a box of my own stuff in the hallway, stripped in the dark in the bathroom, and flopped into bed with Nautica, my stomach churning around the tequila, the adrenaline, and the burning ball of guilt. I watched a grid of mortar lines spin on the brick side of the room. Nautica sighed in her sleep and scooted her butt up against my belly and I knew I'd suffer if I didn't make myself throw up. I went in the bathroom, knelt, prodded the back of my throat, and after a few retches, I had enough relief to spit, flush, rinse, floss, brush, swish, drink some water, dry off. Nautica liked the smell of blue Listerine because it meant someone was trying to be considerate of her. Recently it seemed we used it as a code that meant I wanted sex but didn't want to stress her out about it if it didn't sound good to her. If she could smell it on me, she knew where I was at.

I turned off the space heater on my way back to bed, with a flutter of annoyance at how she'd left it going full blast on a cheap acrylic rug, probably for many flammable hours. When I eased into Nautica's warmth under the layers of down, she made a sweet noise from within her dream, and reached back to pull me against her ass. I put my arm around her. She nuzzled, adjusted, and settled. I felt trapped against her soft solid body, terrified of waking her up and also, wanted to fuck her so badly I considered sleeping on the couch. It might be the only way I would sleep at all. But moving myself from that embrace onto the couch was too hard. Impossible. I willed every muscle to sink into the bed, and fell asleep with Nautica's right shoulder pressed to my mouth, her breath heating and cooling my arm.

In the morning, when I poured out my story, which was a mix of confessions and apologies and pieces of wonderment at how odd and beautiful this boy had been, Nautica's response was to cross her arms, fold her eyebrows down, concentrate on my every word, and stay nearly silent until I ran out of steam. Her hair was combed back into two buns and tiny frizzing dark brown curls fringed her forehead and temples. What she called her "winter skin" was still a few shades darker than her bright brown eyes. The tiny light spots around her eyes appeared like astrological patterns. She was wearing an orange silk robe, nearly lighter than the air, with a delicate pastel floral pattern around the sleeves and at the hem.

We stood in the kitchen, where we did most of our talking. It was small and rectangular and one side opened toward the hallway. If we leaned on opposite counters, we could get just enough physical space to argue. My headache was brutal.

"Well," she sighed, "Sounds like you fucked up and acted stupid." She turned to the coffeemaker and refilled her cup. I watched her familiar swoop to the fridge for the half-n-half. In one looping arc her forearm and wrist maneuvered the pour, the return, the fridge door sealing closed.

I apologized again.

"You wanna explain what all this guilt's about?" she said, turning toward me with the cup poised at her mouth. Blow, sip. "Is there more to it you aren't telling me? Because I'm pissed about you breaking confidentiality. You have never respected how hard I work to keep my identity safe. I'm also pissed at you getting drunk for no reason, but I'm thinking this is exactly your style of fuckup. So. I'm angry. But, I'm not shocked. What I don't want is to find out later that there was more to it and you were too scared to tell me."

I assured her I'd told her all the dirt. Then I said I wanted her to meet Griffin.

Suddenly, she was even more angry. "You want what now?"

"I want you to meet him," I said. "I really liked him."

"I don't have to meet all your people," she said. "He already irritates me."

"Don't blame him for what I did," I said. I realized then I'd left out the part about him being a compulsive thief. It didn't seem relevant.

She shook her head. She told me to leave her alone for a while to get ready. "You're stressing me," she said, "and I've got three sessions today. Two of them are back-to-back."

"You don't want any eggs?" I sounded like a child. The eggs, pan, and butter were out. She didn't answer, so I only scrambled two.

I lay on the couch, spooned a few bites in, and hated myself. I turned on the TV, and hated that more, which felt a little better.

Nautica emerged from the bedroom in her winter boots and black sweater-dress. Stiletto heels poking out from her black leather day-bag. Her short wig on, with the bangs combed perfectly straight across her eyebrows. It was 8:00AM and she was sharp.

"You look miserable," she said. She went into the kitchen, pulled the crackers and dried fruit from her cupboard, put them in her bag.

I leaned in the doorway between her and the front door. "I feel miserable," I said.

"Self-pity isn't sexy, honey," she said.

"I wish you didn't get introduced to Griffin through all this drama," I said.

"You sold me out last night," she said, pointing at my face. "And instead of being grateful that I didn't throw a fit, you want me to fucking squirt myself about some boy."

I tried to interrupt but she was already saying, "No, no, fuck you!"

Calm down, I said. I'd told Griffin all about her in a good way, too. She flinched and flared at every word. I couldn't make her understand.

"I didn't even do anything with him," I said.

"How'd it feel when he touched you?" she said.

I froze.

She saw. "See? You can't just talk to me about it," she said. "You're a coward and I'm through with this conversation."

The ball of guilt swelled. I was poisoned with it. I was a coward, that felt true. I told her I loved her again.

"You want me to feel loved?" she said, voice rising, "then clean up your own damn messes!" She reached into the sink, pulled out a plate, broke it in one slam to the edge of the counter, and tossed a half toward me, not to hit, but to startle. Then she stomped to the door and yanked it closed behind her. I stood frozen in the doorway, run through with adrenaline.

We hadn't had a fight like that for years. Our early relationship had required a lot of emotions and conflict and even a queer-friendly therapist who had helped us learn better communication, especially around jealousy and other lovers. We had been together almost ten years, and we'd been treating each other really well for most of it. I was in shock, shaking, terrified of what might come next. I searched desperately for a method, a tool, a totem of our love and health to bring her back to me. I could think of nothing useful. I cried. I got ready for work clumsily.

That night, she sat at the little wood table at the edge of the kitchen and held her bag on her lap. I'd had a text conversation with Griffin from the granite bathroom at the dungeon. I'd told him we may not be able to see each other right way because Nautica was having some trouble adjusting to the idea.

Our relationship had been non-monogamous from the beginning. When we started dating, she was seeing two other people. One of them was a longtime lover and friend who was still in our lives, who I had my own friendship with now too. One of them wanted to get more serious than Nautica did. Nautica and I matched up so well that neither of us remembered ever talking about "getting serious" --we just did. I had dated a few other people, mostly queer women. A few I'd really loved. We both had play partners, with whom we shared bonds of power exchange and BDSM interests, but no romance. Our friend circle was resilient, and when people broke up, they tended to figure out how to stay in touch and stick around. I had now introduced a reason for some old-fashioned jealousy into our lives.

Nautica saw the messages I'd written to Griffin without looking for them, when she was hooking my phone up to the speakers to play music. I'd meant to talk to her about it, it seemed like it shouldn't be such a big deal to respond to him back and forth a bit.

"What's this bullshit?" she had said, phone in hand.

"You're so suspicious," I said.

She pointed at the messages where Griffin called me "sexy" and "forceful."

"What's wrong with that?" I said.

She looked at me with an unfamiliar hurt in her eyes. "You're the cold one here," she said. "You really don't get that?"

I really didn't.

She slumped a little in her seat. She still hadn't put any music on and the silence seemed dramatic. "Then you should date him until you get it," she said. "But don't expect me to mingle. And don't ever double-book us. And if I get sick of it, I reserve the right to make you choose."

"Choose between you?" It sounded absurd. She was my home.

"I really hate talking with you about relationship stuff

sometimes," she said. She put her head on her arm on the table. It was a posture of defeat. She turned her head to the side, away from me, and said to the wall, "If I get sick of him, and you want to hang on, I'm not going to sacrifice myself and go through hell tolerating him to keep you happy. I will make you choose. I'm warning you now. I would not do this about a lesbian or a queer lover of yours. It is because he is just so much a boy. Clear?"

"I can't believe you're even thinking like this," I said. "This could be nothing. This could be a stupid drunk hookup that never even happens! And so what that he's a boy?"

She stared at me.

"Okay," I said. I wanted the argument over.

"You have to really agree to this," she said. "This is a boundary."

I said I'd agree to it, but it didn't sound right to me, given what we'd always said about our commitment to supporting each other being sexually free and independent.

"Sexually free in a queer world," she said. "Not free to bring heterosexuality into my homelife. Even if he's kinky."

"You're making that clear," I said.

She went into the bedroom.

Later, she came into the living room, where I had returned to the couch and television. She was naked, her hair tied up in a scarf, water beading on her chest. She must have already dropped her wet towel on the floor somewhere.

"I'm sorry for saying some shit I didn't mean," she sighed. "I shouldn't have said that I hate talking to you about anything. Especially relationship stuff. You're still my favorite person to talk to. And it was mean to call you names. I'm sorry about that too. You're not a coward. You're one of the bravest, most resilient people I know."

I thanked her. I could tell she wasn't quite done though.

"You know it hurt me that you broke our trust so easily, right? For a boy. It scares me."

"Yeah, I get that," I said. "I'm really sorry." I meant it more deeply somehow, and it got in.

"I always forget that people do mad stupid stuff when they get crushes," she said. "Especially you. Remember that baby girl you got all fucked up over?"

I didn't risk a response. That "baby girl" was a cynical twenty-one-year-old Smith college girl I'd had a major love affair with. Nautica had supported it until I started forgetting to do things I said I would do at home, coming home later than I said. I'd felt drugged with love for that girl, similarly to the way I sometimes felt for Nautica. But my love with Nautica was like a river. Constantly moving, and still always there. The "baby girl" had been like a firehose on Monday and a drought on Tuesday.

Nautica walked to me and reached for my face. Her fingers were wrinkled from the shower. She traced a heart on my cheek. "You haven't had one like this for a long time, have you?" she said. I shook my head. No, and we both knew that the last time I'd had a big crush on someone it wasn't that twenty-one-year-old. I'd fallen for a friend of ours, and she'd stayed close with us even when our romance cooled. Our community wasn't comprised of serial monogamists. It was a web of people who loved each other and let romance ebb and flow. There were a few couples and one trio who lived together and provided a certain kind of grounding for the other relationships. Nautica and I were one of those couples. I definitely was messing with the system by bringing Griffin into the mix.

"Let's fuck before you forget how much you like it," Nautica said. She smiled, a little sadly. She wanted the fight over too.

I followed her to the bedroom.

"I never forget," I said. I asked if she had something in mind. She told me to get my dick, and while I threw a few things around on the floor looking for my harness, she pushed the comforters aside and perched on the edge of the bed. "Get the new one," she said, which meant I was not going to be fucking her hard. The new one was black silicone, and bigger than my last, and I wasn't graceful with it yet. I found my stuff, ran into the bathroom, warmed my cock in the sink, fitted it into my harness, covered it in lube, and found her standing on the bed when I reentered the bedroom. She ordered me to lay on my back on the floor. I did. She looked at me from her height for a long moment. Then she stepped down from the bed, knelt over me, lowered herself onto the dick, and rode me until she came. Every time I moved to touch her she slapped my hands away, but when she got close to her orgasm, she leaned down to my face and kissed me for real, which normally pushed me over the edge right away, but this time, I wrapped my arms around her and wanted to cry. She came so hard I worried about slipping out and hurting her. But she held on, and I held on, and we rocked together until she was quiet. We held still there on the floor until it hurt my back, and then we crawled into bed, and I wriggled out of the harness and let it thunk to the floor, and asked her to go to the Brooklyn Museum with me soon.

"Sure," she said. "That would be fun."

Just as I was falling asleep, she asked me what time I was going in to the dungeon tomorrow, and I remembered that I was seeing a new guy. "Need to get out of here by 2PM," I told her.

"I'm out before then," she said. "Guess I won't see you until I get back." I'd forgotten she was going to Philly for a weekend rope suspension training. "If Griffin calls you up and wants to see you this weekend," she said, "go for it. Have fun. Stay conscious. We'll talk when I'm home. I trust you."

She kissed my head, turned over, and was asleep in six breaths. I lay awake for at least an hour, bouncing between pained gratitude for Nautica's grace and ferocious sex, and imagining some ways I might make Griffin beg me to keep going, please, please just don't stop. Nautica knew I was in something and she was going to love me through it, just like she had for the past nine years. And Griffin? He was like a puppy wearing a sign that said *Take Me*.

GRIFFIN'S APARTMENT

There was a crusted bottle of Soft Scrub and a fetid sponge, but no towel, in Griffin's bathroom. The floor tiles were loose, and I moved one back and forth a half inch with my foot while I peed.

He lived with so many people. There were piles of confusing shapes in the hallway. Vacuum hoses? Old plastic tubes for tennis balls? Brown packing tape peeling off big boxes that could hold the belongings of someone who has been gone for years. Matted cakes of cat hair collecting inches from the base of the wall. The remnants of a taxidermy kit Griffin said he usually tried to forget.

I asked about the taxidermy box. There was a crate full of cotton, spools of light brown thread, and coils of wire in various thicknesses piled chaotically on top of it.

Griffin avoided it and kept talking about the apartment. The old manager was responsible for most of what was wrong with the space, Griffin said. He put up plywood "walls" and rented half-rooms to people who couldn't and never did pay rent. He removed the water shutoff valve from one of the toilets, so it wouldn't flush. That meant there was one working toilet for all eight people who lived there.

"It made some sense at the time," Griffin said, "in my defense. Our water bill was too high and no one was home much. Most of us made a real effort to shit elsewhere."

"Why do you have a taxidermy kit."

He sighed. "I thought we were wasting a great opportunity by poisoning the rats."

"Opportunity for what?"

"Re-use. Profit. I ordered a beginner's taxidermy kit, like for squirrels or something. I watched tons of YouTube videos."

"Did you ever do it?" I touched the box. It was thick with dust.

Griffin smiled and pointed at a series of finger-smudges on the wall just to my right. I added my smudge to the collection.

"I wanted to make a series of dioramas with the rats dressed up in doll clothes and sell them to the hipster bars on the other side of Bushwick. I really thought I'd make money. And be repurposing the rats. I got the idea from an old taxidermy manual I got at the thrift store around the corner." Griffin pulled some masking tape from a corner of the box and peered inside. He saw what he wanted.

"And?" I asked. The story reminded me, somehow, of Nautica. Maybe because she had a collection of teeth.

"I sold three dioramas before they went out of style," Griffin said as he opened the box, just enough to wedge his hand in and retrieve a worn maroon book with faded gold leaf lettering. "You have to read this," he said. He backed down the hallway, dragging his hands on the sides of the wall, clicking and rustling his fingers on the thick paint. Rat sounds.

"What were the dioramas?"

One was a scene in which a mouse in a dress was laying on a divan with a tiny martini. That one was called Daisy.

I entered his room. The dust bunnies were gritty there too.

The second scene involved three rats, dressed up like the Three Stooges. The last one was the best, Griffin said. It was Jesus the Rat on the cross, next to the Rat Buddha, and a dancing Rat Krishna. "I made Krishna's extra arms out of a few different types of clay before I found one that looked right."

Griffin led me to his bed and pointed at the place where I was supposed to begin reading in the book.

PREFACE
The object of this book is to enable the reader
to gain complete mastery of the art of taxidermy.
We do not believe in the wanton destruction of
birds for ornamental purposes, nor do the laws in
most states, if properly enforced, allow of such
practices. We do believe, however, that at least
one person in every community should possess the
knowledge to enable him to correctly mount specimens.

Millions of birds are killed yearly in the United
States by accidents, such as flying against light-
houses, telegraph wires, or buildings, etc. Practi-
cally none of these are saved because there is no
one at hand who has the requisite knowledge.

If only a fraction of one per cent, of all the birds
killed accidentally, and those shot by sportsmen
and thrown away, could be saved and correctly
prepared,
it would be unnecessary to shoot thousands
that are now killed every year simply for museum
purposes.

We trust that this book may be the means of creating a taxidermist or an enthusiast in every section of the country, and that each one of them will
endeavor to persuade sportsmen to save most of
the game they kill. You will find that there is pleasure
in doing the work for yourself and profit
in doing that for others.

In the following pages we give you the results
of our thirty-five years' experience in all branches
of taxidermy. No trade secrets are held back;
everything is laid bare. We have endeavored to
omit nothing that would be a help to the student
and to avoid the introduction of any hindrances.

We have illustrated every point as fully as possible, and are sure that any faithful reader and
worker can in a short time do work equal to that of
the best. The text, every drawing and every pho-
tograph used in this book is new and made express-
ly for this work. We wish to give credit to our
chief taxidermist, Mr. N. F. Stone, who mounted
a large number of the specimens that are pictured;
while a young man, he is one of the best that this
country has yet produced, a natural-born taxidermist.

We shall be more than pleased if, by our work,
others can be produced.

Chas. K. & C. A. Reed.
Worcester, Massachusetts.
May, 1908.

We pored over phrases that tickled. We mused about how one comes to discover that they are a "natural born taxidermist." And how the environmentalists of today seemed to be missing something about the joys and pleasures of doing the work of preservation.

"But," Griffin said, closing the book, "There comes a point where you cannot hide the rotten core of a building with white paint anymore."

"What is that supposed to mean?"

"I was so horrified by the number of rats I was catching I had to stop doing it. I couldn't stuff them fast enough, and I had already started storing them in a separate freezer."

"Why not just stop catching them?" I said.

It had something to do with exposing oneself to the innards of urban spaces. Griffin couldn't un-see what he had seen. Rats were the living infrastructure of the city.

Griffin pushed a few buttons on his computer keyboard, pulled up his music, and clicked through a few ideas. I heard the first lonely strums of Bob Dylan's *Time Out of Mind*. Griffin skipped ahead to "Standing in the Doorway."

"I'm obsessed with this song," he said.

He sang along with Dylan, dancing slowly toward me, and traced small circles around the base of my neck, then kissed me lightly there, in between the words.

I felt hypnotized, seduced. I needed to get a handle on the situation.

"What is the defining feeling you have about your child-hood?" I asked him.

"Generally negative," he said. He nudged me toward the bed. I went, and pulled him with me.

"Get more specific," I said.

"It was apocalyptic at all times, because Jesus was COMING BACK."

"Oh no."

"My dad had a midlife crisis when I was in high school and wanted to improve on our already monstrous house. Frustration at the unattainable," Griffin's curved fingers brushed through his hair and landed lightly on my arm. He stroked where he'd landed and gave me goosebumps. He met my eyes.

"The unattainable Jesus?" I said.

"Sure, but even more so the American Dream," he said.

"Were they connected for him?"

He nodded. "Perfectly connected. When I was asking about how he'd made his money, all he'd say was 'God takes care of his children.'"

"Sounds frustrating, but kind of harmless."

"This is the same guy who went to build himself a new driveway on his unaffordable new house, and got halfway through before he realized he'd calculated his projected amount of concrete using the formula for area only, and his money was gone."

"I don't understand."

"He'd calculated incorrectly, and spent all his budget on not enough concrete."

It clicked.

"Because he lacked depth?"

"Because he lacked depth."

"So God didn't take care of him."

"Jesus, no." He smiled. He liked being clever. It was annoying and cute.

I told Griffin about my client Jason. How Jason liked to tell me "Some people work for money. Other people have money that works for them." He wasn't trying to point out that I was the former, and he was the latter, although it was true. He was one of those rich people who had worked his way out of poverty, made some truly brilliant and many lucky moves, and ended up a boss. He believed in the American Dream, because he felt he'd lived it. He couldn't understand how it might be unattainable to someone else, as long as they were "smart" enough. He prided himself on those things; he was smart, he was a good boss.

"A good boss is still a boss," Griffin said.

"What we want is not dominance but for the yoke to be released," I said. "Do you know who said that?"

He shook his head no.

"Huey P. Newton," I said.

"Lady, you're full of surprises," he said.

"You don't even know," I said. "You don't even *know*." I thought about Carl, and what he'd think of this place, these people. What he'd say to Griffin about anarchism, his choice to live like he didn't have the money he had, or repurposing city rats.

Griffin picked up my hand and intertwined our fingers. "Nice manicure," he said.

I kept my nails short and dark, easier to glove up and penetrate with.

He nodded thoughtfully, didn't ask for clarification.

I hadn't had vanilla sex with a man without being paid for it in years. It clearly made Griffin very, very happy. I wondered what Nautica would think. It was enjoyable, but it also felt strange, like a shoe with a tiny rock in it.

There were three quiet sleeping bodies in the living room in the morning as I left, two boys on two couches, and one black cat.

Carl called as I was shutting the door. I was headed to work.

It was our last phone conversation.

He asked me how I was doing. I told him I was fine. I didn't talk about Griffin, or being in some conflict with Nautica. I didn't want to discuss my love life with him that day. I felt vulnerable, on edge.

He sounded excited. "We're really getting somewhere with this project," he said.

We? I couldn't remember who he was working with. "Which project?" I felt like he always had three or ten he was working on.

"The stadium," he said. "We got some traction in our fight against the stadium here."

"Cool," I said. I had no idea what he meant but I didn't have the energy to pay attention so I let it slide.

Then he asked for money. I didn't want to send him any.

He tried to convince me, and reminded me that the money was for the project, not for him.

The conversation devolved. I told him I was tired of being his bank and I didn't want him to ask anymore.

He told me I was ignoring what he was saying and that he was trying to get some real work done down here goddamnit.

"Real work?" I said. "Real work? What do you think I'm trying to do? What kind of underhanded shit is that? You think you're some bigshot revolutionary and the rest of us are just idiots who should pay for you?"

"Kindee, I don't think that—"

"Oh yeah? I think you do."

"I'm not here for this."

"Then what are you here for? Huh? What are you?"

"What are *you*? Didn't I teach you anything about the movement?"

"You taught me plenty."

I hung up and fumed. Feeling guilty, angry, and hating it.

· · ·

Carl taught me there was nothing inherently wrong with being "taken in" by an experience. It can feel wonderful, to be surprised by something pleasurable, to be cast into an unknown place where the music is more poignant, the tastes unimaginably delicious, the affection deeply sincere, the ideas profound, the orgasm metaphysical. Carl told me to trust the feeling. I should feel grateful when I got taken by something or someone. When deep, unexpected pleasure comes and takes you, you are being most yourself: for an instant, unconflicted. Filled with only Yes.

But I must not chase it, or I would become addicted, a slave.

Nautica and I tended to enjoy and welcome new lovers because we wanted a large, loving, strong queer family. Our bond was unassailable and our friends supported our intimacy, even when they were dating one of us. We had always agreed that a gift of our open relationship was that we also got to enjoy it when our partner got taken by feelings for a new queer. Griffin was not in our script. Yet, I was getting taken in. I wondered how we'd stay in sync. It was the first time in nine years I'd worried that we may not be able to. Even if I walked away from Griffin that day and never saw him again, something had already changed.

Later, I told Nautica Carl had wanted money and pissed me off. It had happened before. I expected us to work it out. I expected us to talk again. He was supposed to call me back within a week or so and we would both apologize, he'd explain the project he was working on, I'd get inspired to support it, I'd send him some money, and the cycle would begin again. That was what life was supposed to be.

11

RESCUE

Two weeks after my fight on the phone with Carl, I woke up to a phone call from Griffin who had fallen off his bike. He sounded disoriented and sad and scared and so I went to pick him up in a Zipcar, wearing sneakers and sweats. We got him and his slightly busted bike back to his apartment. I advised him on proper wound care.

He had no idea that soap and water was the first line of defense against infection. He wanted to spray vinegar on his arm before even washing it. No one advises that, I told him. Where'd you learn that? He couldn't remember. He had a gash just below his elbow and another one on his pubic bone, where he'd gone over his handlebars. I told him he was lucky.

"It's not luck," he said. "I know how to fall."

"But you don't know how not to crash," I said.

Then I saw two clients, one of them new. The new guy was not new at all to BDSM, and wanted to tell me all about the other Dommes he'd seen and how wonderful they were.

"I've been at this a long time," he said. "I've had so many experienced, talented Dommes do sessions with me," he said. "I'm kind of addicted or something," he said.

"Have you ever been collared?" I asked.

"What?"

"Have you ever made yourself the sole property of one mistress?"

"No, never."

"So you reserve your right to be a slut."

He smiled. "Yes, I'm a slut."

He was utterly annoying, gave me no feedback, and I grew to hate him a little during the session, which was too bad because I needed one or two more regulars. He hadn't shaved around his anus. He said he was paranoid about marks. I said he shouldn't have any from what I did. It was difficult to care.

My regular guy was slightly withdrawn, not his normal effusive self. I sensed he was worried about something and I couldn't tell if it had anything to do with me. At the end of the session, I instructed him to sit on the ground and I let him rub my feet.

"You're so cute when you do that," I said.

"Thank you, Mistress," he said.

"Do you have something on your mind?" I said. "You weren't your usual self today."

"No," he said. "Nothing important."

"Then I'm disappointed in you," I said. "I was ready to forgive you for being boring if you had something serious going on."

He stopped rubbing, looked at me, and seemed horrified. Maybe I'd gone too far with the reprimand. Usually he liked getting a little slap on the wrist like that.

"I'm sorry," he said, tightly. Straining against his protocol.

He was angry with me! I took my feet away. Something bad must have happened to him.

"Go get dressed," I said.

So, maybe, that regular was done with me, too.

When I got home, Nautica was having an angry call with Kaiser Permanente. It sounded like they'd lost something important. An appointment? A lab test? I couldn't tell. She made eye contact with me, frenetic, loving, stressed, and then went back to the call. I went into the bedroom and flopped onto the bed. Annoyed. Resentful. Bored.

Take a shower, my brain said.

Fuck it, another part of my brain said.

You have body fluids on you, my brain said.

Not much, and so what, the other part of my brain said.

Nautica has made it clear she prefers if you shower after work, my brain said.

So I decided to do it. But I hadn't moved yet when the phone rang. Griffin again. It was after nine PM, and we didn't have plans to see each other again that day.

I answered. He sounded very upset.

"I'm sorry," he said. "I'm lost and I need someone with the internet to help me."

Hang up, a part of my brain said.

"What do you mean?" I said. "Where are you?"

"I got on an express train by mistake," he started.

"Don't tell me a story," I said. "Give me an address where you are."

He was in Queens. He'd never been to Queens. He sounded disoriented again.

"Did you get a concussion? Are you on something?" I said.

"No, I'm just stupid!" he said. "I'm in shock from the crash, I'm foggy, I don't know."

"That doesn't sound good," I said.

"Please just tell me what to do next?" he said.

"Ok, ok," I said. Then, I gave him directions to the train.

He called back in twenty minutes and told me that the station I'd directed him to was closed. The next station was going to be closed by the time he got there on foot. He didn't have any money on him for a cab. He never had had credit cards so he couldn't use any app-based car services. He was starting to panic now. Nautica was still on the phone when I left to pick up the same Zipcar, and rescue Griffin, again.

He was giving me reasons and explanations for the entire drive.

"It's not important," I said once. "It's ok," I said once. "Happens to the best of us," I said once.

He resolved to pay me back three times what I'd had to put into renting the car. While we were stopped at the gas station, he made me a small bouquet of hard green leaves from a hedge and some gum wrappers twisted into curly shapes.

"For my knight in shining armor," he said.

I took him home, again. I told him to stay there for a few hours so I could sleep.

"I'm sorry I called on you so much today," he said. "I wish I knew why everything is going wrong with my life."

You're spoiled and have no respect for how difficult it actually is to support the basic functioning of your own life because you've always had people doing your dirty work for you, I thought.

"I wish you knew what was going wrong, too," I said.

"Want to come inside and tie me up for a while?" he said.

"No," I said. "I want to go home and take a shower."

"Ok, I'll miss you," he said.

I gave him some kind of half-smile. I hadn't even put the car in park. "Goodnight," I said.

"Goodnight," he said, and I could feel him wanting some other comfort from me.

"Talk tomorrow," I said, and nodded toward his door. He got out. He shut his door. I lifted my foot from the brake before he'd really gotten out of the way. Although all the running around was annoying, ultimately it was a win for me. Griffin got what he needed, and now he owed me one. That was the power script we both liked best.

When I got home, Nautica was in bed. I took a shower. I slid in next to her.

"You ok?" she said in her sleepy voice.

"I picked such a baby to fuck with," I said.

"Yeah," she said, and sighed a little. "He's so in love with you now, though. That part has to feel nice."

"He's dependent."

"He's a young, unconscious submissive and a masochist," she said, as if that explained the whole day.

"You ok?" I said. "Your phone call with bureaucracy seemed heavy earlier."

"I was trying to get some records for my mom," she said. "It was really annoying."

"I'm sorry," I said. Most people I knew still had moms.

"Don't be," she said. "Not your fault." My eyes were getting used to the dark. I searched hers. She looked so sweet, and so tired.

"Let's sleep," I said.

She jutted her chin out a little and puckered. I kissed her. "I love you," she said, with a seriousness that surprised me.

"I love you too," I said back. "So. Fucking. Much."

We snuggled in and slept.

. . .

The following afternoon, I was headed to Griffin's to check on him. The sky was crooning orange. Some number from LA had called me seventeen times since six AM. The one voicemail from that number was garbled. The voice was masculine, but I didn't recognize it as Carl's.

I called back during the eight-minute walk from the train station to Griffin's building.

"Hello, is this Kindred?" he had a voice like a radio host, an intonation like Mumia Abu Jamal's.

I confirmed.

"Sorry to bother you," he started, and I braced for a piece of horrible news from a forgotten collections agency, "but I'm a friend of your father's. Carl Baker is your father, is that right?"

"Yes, Carl is my dad," I said, "what's going on? I haven't heard from him in weeks." This guy just said he was a friend, but cops lie.

"I'm Rodney," he said. "Carl's been tripping on the skirts," which meant nothing to me but sounded like romantic drama, "and Riley said she needs to stay out of it so she gave me your number to call if he got picked up."

"Is he in jail?" I asked. I put a finger over my other ear and stopped walking. I leaned against a heavily painted brick wall, wedged in between fruit displays and the door at a corner store. I tried to concentrate.

"No ma'am, I don't think so," he said. No one called me ma'am outside the dungeon. "I checked the sheriff's and he ain't in county. He's just gone, honey, like poof!"

"Where'd he go? Who are the skirts?"

"They're the fake-cops that patrol downtown Skid Row, they wear these colored shirts, we called them the 'shirts,' and then that sort of turned into 'skirts,' you know, no disrespect, it's just what we call them."

Right. Call them something feminine to insult them, no disrespect. "But he's not locked up?"

"No ma'am," he said. "He's just M.I.A."

"I don't understand. What happened to him?" Blocking my ear wasn't helping.

"I don't know," Rodney said. "One day he was here. Next day we all wake up before the skirts come roust us all and he's gone, which don't bother us, but then he didn't come back that night, or the next one. That ain't like him."

"So how long ago was that?"

"This'll be the third night he's gone," he said.

"Fuck!"

"He never said a word to me, but all his shit's still here and we're going to get moved off the block this weekend and I can't watch his set-up. They'll throw out all his albums and his books and everything, they don't give a fuck," he said. "I wouldn't worry about a grown man off on his own for a few days, but his phone is dead, too. And Riley said she don't know what he's doing, and she said she can't help, so I'm sorry I got to call you."

"He has a phone? Like a cell phone?"

"Yes, uh, yes?" Rodney seemed as confused as I was.

"Who's Riley? Who is looking for him?"

"I mean, I've gone to some of his spots, if that's what you're asking. No one's seen him for days." He cleared his throat. I wondered what he expected me to say. "Riley. Your sister? You haven't heard from her, I guess."

"I don't have a sister," I said.

Silence. "Shit. Ma'am, I don't know what to say. Carl told me she's his kid, she calls him Pop, I assumed you...I'm sorry," he said. "You must not have grown up together."

"You're sure you have the right person?" I said, but of course he did. Carl had given the man my phone number and told him I was family, that made sense. Who. The fuck. Was

Riley. "So you're asking me what to do about his camp," I said. "I don't know."

"You have my number, right? Do you want to just think about it for a little while and then call me back and tell me what you want to do with his stuff? I don't want it to get thrown away or for the rest of the guys to split it all up for themselves. Carl's my best homie down here."

"Yeah let me think a minute and call you back," I said. Rodney. Carl's best homie. Riley. Who called him Pop.

I thanked Rodney. We hung up.

Carl and I had a system. We'd been using the same system for years, since he was at Corcoran, when I'd been nearly impossible to get in touch with. Now, I usually answered on the first or second try. He knew my general schedule. We spoke about twice a month. I hadn't heard from him in two weeks. During that last conversation, we'd yelled at each other. We'd fought about something stupid. We'd said terrible things. I'd put it all out of my mind because we always figured it out eventually when we fought. My guts hurt.

I walked another block. The neighborhood was industrial, less people milling than in mine. Piles of plywood and weeds behind chainlink fences, un-sponsored street art. The best was an astronaut with a sandwich. His face was covered by the helmet so you couldn't tell if he'd realized it yet, that to eat the sandwich he'd have to stop breathing. Ground control, something's wrong.

I left a message for Nautica. "I think I have to go to LA this week," I said. "Something's up with Carl. I want you to come with me. I don't think you really can, though. Let's talk about it tonight."

She was teaching an intensive workshop at the dungeon for curious people who wanted ropes and sensation play added to their mostly straight, mostly vanilla sex lives. It was bringing in a big chunk of money. It was impossible for her to miss this event and then for us to still make our bills.

When I got to Griffin's, there were two sweetly greasy people in the front room who opened the door with their arms around each other, giggling. They said yeah, Griffin was home, and stumbled inside. Their T-shirts were ripped in strategic places and their denim shorts frayed unevenly on their thighs.

That ridiculous apartment, built of plywood and a hundred years of paint, had a floor that buckled under my boots and a ceiling that flaked red dust when people walked on the floor above. Two bare light bulbs in the hallway made me squint.

I opened Griffin's door, climbed the short ladder to his bed, and perched at the top. I breathed in the smell of him, like fresh bread, with a tiny sour edge. He was sprawled naked in bed with my journal next to him, dead asleep. I got the book and spanked his thigh with it. He buckled awake, gasping. He reached for the sheet but let go, on second thought.

"You have a problem," I said. Waving my journal.

"I know," he said.

"Well?"

"I'm sorry?"

"Want to make me a promise about how you're going to change your behavior?"

"I promise never to do it again, to anyone," he said. He looked terrified. We both knew he was going to break this promise, and that he would be punished, and that it would probably be our favorite fuck of the year.

He may have sincerely been trying to stop stealing. He'd been earnestly doing a moral inventory, and coming up with nothing, he said. His Shoplifter's Anonymous sponsor kept telling him to dig deeper. He was either a moral genius or a diabolical self-deluding arrogant dangerous boy-monster. The latter seemed so much more likely.

"You know what," I said, "I gotta go."

"Oh no! Please don't," he said. "I'll get up, I'm sorry I fell asleep!"

"No, really," I said. "It's not just that you're a thief who lives in a shithole, I have some other stuff going on I need to think about."

I left. I started home.

I couldn't understand. Carl was missing? He was beefing with the cops? Who. The fuck. Was Riley. I texted Nautica some kind of update.

I'm coming home now, I said. Carl's missing. I don't know what's going on.

12

DECISIONS AND CONSEQUENCES

Nautica was in the kitchen when I got home, doing dishes in her underwear. I came in and she toweled her hands in preparation to hug me. She turned her topless beautiful body my way and opened her arms and said, Come here, baby.

She held me, and we breathed together. We let go.

"Let's talk about what you wanna do?" she said. She threw on a sweatshirt and some slippers. I changed from my outside clothes into my sweatpants and T shirt. Pulled my hair up and took off some eye makeup from who knew how many days ago.

I sat in the living room. She brought us two mugs of tea.

We settled in on our sides of the couch, facing each other. I sat cross-legged, she had her knees bent up. She held her mug in both hands, blew on the tea, and sipped. She made eye contact.

She loved me. It was really unreasonable of her. I felt a shot of gratitude.

"Thank you for talking this out with me," I said.

"You're stupid," she said, with affection. "What happens to you affects me too," she said. "So what is it, exactly."

"I don't know," I said. "Honestly. I got a call from a guy named Rodney who said Carl gave him my number? He said he's missing. He also said he had another daughter named Riley, who doesn't want to be involved. I'm fucking confused."

"Holy shit."

She waited for me to go on.

"I don't know what to do," I said. "I feel like I should already be there."

"Sure," she said. "But what could you do if you were there?"

"Look for him? Maybe I can meet this guy Rodney and see if there's any information in his stuff? I guess his property is about to get stolen or seized or something."

"You'd look for Carl? Look for him how?"

"I don't know!" I said.

She took a slow breath and let it out.

"I'm scared," I said.

"I know," she said quietly. "I want to help you make a good decision and suffer this a little less, if I can."

"Do you have an instinct about what I should do?"

"One strong one," she said.

"What is it."

"That you should call the police in LA and report him missing before you do anything else. I think they might be required by law to check hospitals and jails."

"I can't do that. He would hate it if I did that. I would literally be setting the dogs on him. The people who have hurt him the most, looking for him."

"What if he's in a hospital? What if he's in a coma? What if you could know tomorrow exactly what happened and be able to start dealing with it?"

"I mean," I didn't know how to respond to that. "Okay, but..."

"But nothing. Carl taught you to hate the police, I get it." She saw me rising to defend myself and put a hand up and went on, "You've got your own reasons to hate the police, fine. But this is actually one of the few things that they *should* be doing with their time."

I looked at my hands. Dry skin in the fold between my thumb and index finger. Dry knuckles. I needed to moisturize before the skin got hard. Then I found the reason.

"If he's about to catch a case and took off somewhere to stay safe," I said, "and he gets caught up because I gave the cops a reason to put manpower into finding him? I won't be able to live with that," I said.

"Okay," she said. Sipped her tea again. "Are you saying you are completely and totally against the idea of reporting him missing at all?"

I sipped mine. Licorice.

"No," I said.

"But if you think you might file a report sometime, then you really should do it now. He's already been gone over twenty-four hours."

Of course she had a point. She always did.

"I just can't do it," I said. "I can't let being scared turn me into someone who relies on the enemy like that. I've got to find another way. That's why I feel like I should go out there."

She was shaking her head, just slightly. She gave me a sad little smile.

"He really convinced you," she said.

"You always say shit like that," I said, getting angry. I pulled my legs up into myself and held myself together. "Walking into a police station feels like asking to be traumatized," I said. "And, it's not just *his* theory. It's revolutionary theory. It's real history. It's his experience. It's my experience. The fucking cops are there to serve—"

"The interests of the owner classes," she interrupted.

"Yeah."

"I get it," she said. "I do. I think you're rigid and ridiculous but I also love you for this thing you do."

"What thing."

"You will go ahead and make shit harder for yourself if you believe it's the right thing to do."

"Going to the cops doesn't make shit easier on me," I said. "And it definitely won't make anything easier on Carl."

"It might," she said. "You don't know that for sure. But regardless, it sounds like you are ready to get a flight out there," she said.

I agreed that it did.

"In your vision of yourself going off to LA," she said, "are you alone?"

I said that I was. I'd assumed she couldn't come because of the class she had to teach. She seemed disappointed. But she said I was right, she really couldn't take time off right now, there were a bunch of new people at La Jouissance to train, plus we really needed the money from the class. I told her I knew it wouldn't make sense to ask her to come with me. Maybe next week if the situation didn't resolve.

"I'm suggesting a harm reduction option," she said, "which is that you ask one of our friends who needs a break from New York to go with you."

I hadn't thought of that, and it seemed impossible. "Like who?"

She named a few people. Trina, an old friend and lover of Nautica's. We had a great friendship but I didn't feel comfortable asking her for this. Dane, a feisty pro-sub who worked at La Jouissance. We'd worked together and she was a great femme bottom and we'd had some good social time together. Maybe, I said. I thought of Griffin. I did not suggest him.

By the end of the convo, I had agreed to put real effort toward getting someone to come with me, and we had bought me a one-way ticket leaving in two days. We booked me five nights in a cheap hotel near the intersection Rodney had told me about. I thought I should sleep on the desire to bring Griffin.

I called Rodney and left him a voicemail letting him know I was coming. "Let's hope no one moves his stuff in the next two days," I said. I didn't know what to say about Riley. I decided to wait to think about it.

It was almost intolerably warm inside the apartment when I got home from work the next day.

"I'm going to get naked," I said. "Are you making martinis?" Nautica was wearing flip flops, black shorts, and a white tank top. Her hair was pulled back by a series of large elastics at the nape of her neck. Her breasts strained the ribbed pattern of the shirt.

"I'm making dinner," she said. I put my bags down, slipped out of my shoes. Then my pants. Some relief.

"Are you considering asking Griffin to go with you?" she asked.

"Goddamnit, Nautica!" It just shot out of me. "How the fuck do you read my mind like that?"

She just smiled and shook her head and told me what she'd been thinking.

While she'd had masculine partners, Nautica's sexual desire did not extend to cisgender men. She didn't love their angular hard edges or rough hair the way I did. She could understand that my desire for her and my desire for Griffin would be different, and she didn't feel threatened sexually. But. If I took him, Griffin was going to see a part of my life she wanted access to, and he wouldn't be able to appreciate it the way she could, and what was most uncomfortable for her was imagining him and I spinning ourselves into an intimate little cocoon without her in a moment of crisis. She was envious of the closeness we'd build. She still didn't approve of not calling the cops. She worried about Carl. She was also pitifully imagining herself lonely, working too much, and jealous all the time while Griffin and I had mad constant highly-charged emotional sex.

So earlier that day, she had gone to a two-hour African dance class and meditated on how to feel deeper love. She made plans to spend the first night of my trip with an old lover of hers who liked occasional meet-for-drinks-and-sex dates. She had arranged a new configuration of stones on the witchy shelf in the apartment where she kept all her ritual objects. She had grocery shopped at the place that was farther away but had more stuff she liked. She was feeling better.

"But I still have some concerns," she said, "and they're not all about my personal comfort." She was worried that Griffin might be a liability around the people I'd be talking to on Skid Row, instead of a help to me.

"Why?"

"Oh, I don't know," she said sarcastically. "Maybe he stinks of rich white boy? People might get a cop vibe from him?"

"I was thinking he'd be able to help me fit in some places," I said.

"But what about the places where he'll make you stand out? You take him to Skid Row, he'll say the wrong thing so many times! He'll silence people just by being there, being white, being hip, looking like that kind of boy."

I groaned and pressed my palms into my eyes.

Maybe Griffin's presence would stifle people who didn't trust white people they didn't already know, and I was already a white person they didn't know. She was right that it was always worse when we brought numbers. On the other hand, I could leave him out of those situations, and when having a white man around was useful, it could be the difference between finding Carl or not. Especially if we had to deal with police at all. It still seemed like the whole trip could be better for me if he was there. It was a capitulation of sorts, like wearing a more conservative outfit to visit an old person. I said so.

"Or you can leave him in the hotel," she said.

"Or I can leave him in the hotel."

"Tied to the bed."

"Now we're talking," I said. I nudged her to turn her back to me, pushed an arm gently between her belly and the counter, leaned into her ass and rested my face at the base of her neck. I nuzzled to the side of her hair, until I could feel her skin.

I took a deep inhale of her scent and the food. "It smells like cinnamon and a night of storytelling in the desert," I said.

"That's the curry," she said. "It's evoking your memories of media representations of Indian stereotypes." She shimmied her hips to loosen my hold. She spooned me some stew. It was fantastic. She moved me away from the stove and pointed her wooden spoon at me, shaking her head. "A night of storytelling. Jesus."

Nautica. Queen of the Sea.

She went back to her cooking. "I'm pretty sure Griffin doesn't know how to handle the fact that you're a sex worker," she said. "I'm worried about that, too."

"He was so chill about it that first night," I said.

Side-eye. "It's hot to fuck one," she said. "It's emasculating and terrifying to them to date one."

I assented. It was impossible to know whether people

would be able to handle it, even when their initial response was positive or curious or even familiar. I set the table with Nautica's mismatched plates, her hand-made placemats, and her thick blue wine glasses. I poured us some Syrah. It looked black against the glass, a murky world behind the bright trapped bubbles.

"I'm going to call him," I said.

"Carl?"

"No. Griffin. I don't even have Carl's mysterious cell phone number."

"Alright," she said. She sighed a little. "Yep. Alright."

Griffin didn't answer. Call me, I said. I texted it too. Call me.

"I really, really don't get this 'other daughter' thing," I said. "Riley? I've never heard of this person."

Nautica shook her head. "I don't know, baby," she said. "I'm not really surprised to hear he might have another kid. People do it all the time."

We ate the stew on the floor in the living room. We lit candles. We talked about our clients. We talked about her tendonitis. We talked about someday building a website for the scent-fetishists. There would be special categories: stripper's costume bag, stripper shoes, Domme's corset, in addition to the regular dirty panties, scat, feet. We'd send them smell samples (our old shoes, girlfriends' outdated dance wear, and so on) in poly bags and they could sign up for monthly deliveries. We'd never have to haul our overused work outfits to the Goodwill again, and we'd make money giving men our body fluids. Fluids we produced while taking money from other clients, most likely. It was satisfying to think about. Wasting nothing.

"You haven't said anything about how you actually feel," Nautica said, while we cleared dishes. "You've got to be twisted up inside about all this."

The pang of worry was severe, this time.

"I'm avoiding it," I said. "I'm really avoiding thinking about it until I get there. I can't do anything."

"You can run but you can't hide," she said.

We cleaned up with music on, giving each other affectionate pats and swats in between putting the dishes away.

"Let's get yogurt," she said.

We walked three blocks to the new frozen yogurt shop. The fluorescents were obnoxiously bright in the all-white interior. I felt I was squinting unless I was looking down at my feet.

"I really don't understand how you can still be attracted to men," Nautica said.

"I'm not attracted to men in general," I said. I tried to focus on her face without wincing at the bright light.

She rolled her eyes and scraped the side of her Styrofoam cup with her plastic spoon.

"I think there's a big difference between having all your objects of desire be men, you know, to be looking at men, attempting to see their sexiness, which is what I used to do, and having one boy kind of break through."

"You want affirmation for liking a boy against your better judgment?"

"No," I said. I had gotten too much frozen yogurt, again. "Want any of mine?" I said, showing her the nicely carved mounds of cake batter and mango I still had left.

Of course she did, and she took my cup, and she gave me an extra rub with her hand as she did. I felt lucky in the midst of the other internal chaos.

"I guess I'm prejudiced," she said. "But the problem is how many of them actually do just consistently suck."

I understood that.

"So what do you like about Griffin again?" she asked.

I talked it through. I liked that he was so excited to submit to me without even knowing that was what he was doing. I enjoyed having him as a pet, but I especially liked talking to him about sex like we were fifteen-year-old boys together on a camp-out. He listened pretty well. He lied a lot less than most people. His response to me talking about my mom dying was more relaxed than most people. He was so *cute*. And so *weird*.

"All good things for you," Nautica said, nodding. She piled our cups together and took them out to the trash. That butt of hers! I wanted to touch her before she sat down, but I didn't. "Ok," she said.

"Ok, what?"

"Go with him to LA, but, find a way to take me with you, too."

"What?"

"Find a way. I'm going to stay in New York physically, so, you'll have to be creative."

I didn't really know what to say except, "Ok." With Nautica's blessing, I could more easily take the trip. And as if that relief removed a dam, the severity of Carl's absence flooded over me. She saw it.

"Baby," she said, and it was her gentle voice now, and her hands went on both my knees under the table—how did she do stuff like that without looking?—and her eyes were wide and deep, "I'm sorry for all this. I'm sorry I can't come with you. I'm sorry for all the stress. I'm worried about Carl. I know it seems like I'm worried about me, but I'll figure out how to live well and I'll be fine no matter what. Mostly I'm worried about *you*."

I said thank you, even though I wanted to remind her how good I was at surviving. I moved toward leaving. We walked without talking. We entwined our fingers and squeezed hands a little here and there, and I tried to believe it, believe that she loved me as much as she seemed to and said she did, and that she was going to be there for me when I got back. My old therapist's voice reminded me: I had evidence now. Nautica meant her commitment. We chose each other, over and over again.

The vendors were starting to pack up their plastic sandals and vinyl purses and stacks of incense. Behind the concrete skyline the colors were lovely: dark reds and purples and pinks. When we got to our door, Nautica squeezed my hand, then let go, rummaged in her purse, and pulled out a plastic tube with a joint in it.

"Smoke for the sunset?" she said.

"Yes please," I said. "I love that idea." We lay in bed together with our feet on the windowsill, smoked the joint, and watched the sky. At some point we rolled onto our sides and I spooned her. I started to fall asleep with my arm over her, feeling her precious breath on my hand.

"Thank you," I said, and kissed the back of her shoulder.

"You're welcome," she said quietly.

The phone rang. Griffin.

I wrenched myself from the comfort of Nautica's body and told him the scenario. I left out the part about Riley. I asked if he wanted to fly to LA with me tomorrow. "You don't have to do much," I said. "But obviously you have to be able to leave ASAP. I can pay for most of your way if you're willing to put some hours into helping me look for my Dad. I'll buy your ticket, I've already booked the motel."

He said yes on the spot. Then he asked to have two hours to think about it. Then he said yes again.

We arranged for him to come over the afternoon before our flight to get to know Nautica just a little better before we went off together. I texted Jason that I was leaving town for a few days but I wanted him to book a session with me when I was home next week. I put a vacation message on my Domme account so potential clients would think I was popular and happy and frolicking somewhere.

Nautica and I slept for a few hours coiled together.

In the morning, I stayed quiet. I thought about Carl, but my mind wouldn't stay with him. I tried to understand that he might have another daughter. A blood- related daughter, even. Nautica cleaned and made us food.

I did the horrible task of calling hospitals within ten miles of Skid Row that had Emergency Rooms and asked for Carl Baker. Nothing.

When Griffin got there, I stranded him with Nautica while I packed. They had a moment of genuine-sounding laughter. I drained our shampoo bottle into a travel tube.

I remembered being in a playpen. Mom and Carl were on the couch. They were wrestling, laughing, they said "yes!" a lot, and they both held me on the couch afterward, and I loved how warm they were, I could smell them, these bodies I called my home, and there was no fear, no trauma, no horrifying Freudian revelation that I must kill anyone. I learned about sex as happiness and family.

As a child, I masturbated with anything smooth-surfaced that I could wash off. I was told that it was a wonderful private activity to do with clean hands, and that it was important to clean up after myself, and to talk to my Mom if anything painful or unexpected ever happened. The early experimentation with toys was my own addition. I tried things inside, things outside, flat erasers, curvy candlestick, mascara tube. I did not imagine myself sticking a (phallic) *thing* into a (vestibular) *place*. I was getting nice feelings, I was figuring out how to maximize pleasure for myself using whatever appealed to me. I wanted to rub things on myself. I put things in my mouth. I put things in my eyes. I put things in my nose. I put things in my ears. I put things in my vagina. I put things in my anus. There was always a reason to put something in my body somewhere.

A penis is no more a thing than a place, and a vagina is no more a place than a thing. They are alive and in motion. But even if a penis were a thing and a vagina was a place, what is the anus? And are my eyes and ears places or things? Why did the kids believe that each girl carried around some demonic spiritual quotient of the boys she'd been with, such that she was "dirty" where the other boys had "been?" Why did they think girls couldn't make other girls feel as good as the boys did? I didn't ask anyone. I felt different from other kids.

The first time I wore a strap-on, I felt disgraced. I felt silly and nervous, but more than that, the deadweight, cold cock itself made me angry. I simply wished to have genitals that could respond with fleshly transmogrification to my desire. I wanted a flesh cock of my own, which could magically also return to being my vagina, and I wanted the power to use either or both, depending on the need I wanted to fill in myself or someone else. It seemed wrong and embarrassing to settle for a silicone dildo in a patent leather harness, especially as the harness needed to be navigated in a well-lit room with a mirror, just to get put on correctly. The strap on made me feel sexually incompetent, which I resented.

Eventually I learned to heat up the cock in the sink under hot water while I navigated the harness in low or no light, and, I got better with the buckles. I learned to feel comfortable. I learned to feel sexy and powerful. I tried different cocks in different colors. My favorite one was glittery and black with a rainbow around the flared base. Not too hard, not too soft, not too fat, not too long. If I stood up straight and put my fists on my hips I looked like a queer superhero of sex.

Griffin made me want to penetrate. He seemed like he

needed it. But I wasn't sure exactly which hole he needed it in most.

Fucking a penis hole changed my understanding of the world in a fundamental way. It had not ever occurred to me that the penetrating organ, that almighty dick, could be enjoyably penetrated. That some dicks crave it. That some dicks open up wide for a half-inch thick stick of chrome that slides in and out. Bodies do so much more than we think they can. Seeing is believing, Mom was fond of saying.

Take extra-special care with cleaning your urethral sounds, Nautica told me. Sanitize them. Use sanitary hospital-grade lubricant. Don't let a cock-owner get an infection up there because of you. I knew I was still on the right side of loving humanity because I followed through. I always took care with my boys' tender tiny external dick-vaginas.

Just in case, I packed my small leather case of urethral sounds. I packed my steel-reinforced paddle, a midsize butt plug, and I packed enough rope for cuffs and a harness or a hogtie. I was going to need to get some stress relief, I told myself, and if I was going to be in LA for more than a few days, I was going to need to pick up some clients. Having my own gear with me gave me options.

I went back in the living room. Nautica was clearing water glasses and showing off her waist-to-hip ratio.

Griffin looked at me with an electric panic, the tight smile of someone desperate to understand the social rules he was supposed to play by.

"Don't you want to fuck her?" I said.

"Who wouldn't?" he said, without looking at Nautica. She laughed.

"Don't be mean," she said to me. "He's already paralyzed."

"I'm not," he said. He adjusted himself on the couch, almost touched his crotch, but put his hand on his pocket for a second instead. Then he looked at me, rolled his eyes, and said, "Fine. This is terrifying. Ok? Everyone happy?"

"Everyone's happy!" I said.

"This is your bodyguard?" Nautica said to me.

"I'm not a good bodyguard," Griffin said, and tapped both his hip bones. "I'm slight."

"You're clearly a boy, and that's all that really matters," I said.

"I wish you had a man suit you could wear when you needed it," he said.

"I wish I didn't live in a sexist world where a man suit seems like a good idea," I said.

I waltzed Nautica into the kitchen. We held on. She bit my bottom lip. I squeezed the sides of her thighs. We kissed hard enough to feel our teeth behind our lips.

"Let me know what I can do to help," she said. "I wish I was going."

"I figured out how to take you with me," I said. I held up a ring I'd made out of a piece of leather I cut off her favorite flogger. It was just a sliver, tied into a tiny knot, but it fit on my pinkie.

"You're a shit!" she said, smiling. "That's perfect." She hugged me. "Don't take it off," she said.

I told her I would call. I told her I loved her. I felt that beautiful ache, the bittersweet crushing inside my ribs at the thought of not seeing her for a week, maybe longer. I tried to look forward to that precious delight at our returning to each other.

13

EN ROUTE

We left JFK at 11:38PM. I watched the lights zoom away, while a baby screamed and screamed and screamed. I imagined simultaneously: Carl's broken, bleeding body twisted and discarded in an alley; and the Christmas day in 1989 when the cat, who lived with us for only a few months before escaping into the world, pounced and then scuffled helplessly around with its head stuck in a Kleenex box while Carl laughed hard and had to wipe his eyes.

Why does it smell so horrible on airplanes? Gas, cleanser, synthetic fabrics, the accumulated dead skin and hair of a few hundred people, stuck inside the cracks of the windows, coating the bolts on the floor. Or maybe it's only the fuel and the food. The smell of the air coming through those twisty vents made me nauseous. Made me want to punch someone. The baby seemed to have endless energy for screaming. I finally understood people who spent their money on First Class.

I suddenly felt so tired I couldn't talk. I leaned on Griffin and gave in, grateful to exit.

I woke up kicking out. Griffin put his hand on my arm.

"You ok?" it sounded like real concern.

"Sort of," I said. "I think I was having this old chase dream I have when I'm stressed out."

He leaned over and kissed my cheek, blotting out the whining of the plane just for a second. Someone had gotten the baby to sleep. "I have a problem a lot like yours," he whispered.

"No, you don't," I whispered back. I was certain whatever was chasing him was significantly different.

Griffin reached up to turn off his overhead light, I smelled him, and felt a swell of wanting.

"In SA they say that whatever is chasing you is what you hope to change in yourself."

"I'm getting chased by death," I said.

He took a breath. Over his left shoulder, the oval window was fogging around the edges. The sky was black. I reached over him and pulled down the shade. He kissed my forearm. "I never know what you're going to say," he said.

"Thank you."

I bit him on the earlobe. I whispered a few things I'd like to do to his sorry ass in the bathroom at the back of the plane. He sighed. His eyes rolled back in pleasure. I wanted his face in my lap. I ordered him to fold over and massage my calves for five minutes each. He whispered his thanks and did it. The people across the aisle were asleep. The airplane crew ignored us.

When he was done, he lay his head still in my lap and fell asleep immediately.

I tried to imagine Los Angeles. I tried to remember Carl's face in its perfect moments of love and excitement. I twisted my leather ring around and around. I tried to imagine Nautica giving me a hug.

But I was not stronger than the visions of Carl in pain. Carl dead. Carl full of tubes in a hospital, with a bracelet that called him John Doe. I couldn't stop those pictures from coming. And who. The fuck. Was Riley. Let's say he had another daughter. Who was her mom? Why didn't he tell me about her? How old was she? Old enough to be telling Rodney she couldn't help with this situation.

Questions that couldn't be answered before the flight ended. I wrote a few of them down, pressing my notebook on the side of Griffins cheek a bit. His eyelashes. So cute. I drew a picture of what was right in front of me: the tray, the seat, the knees, the head, the stuff sticking out of the pocket. Eventually I accepted that I was probably going to feel bad for a while, got a few inches more horizontal, and stared into the stitching on the seat in front of me.

When I was little, I would turn Carl's hands over and back, over and back, looking at our palms together, looking at the backs of our hands together. I knew the word for the difference in color, melanin, but I didn't understand the point.

There's no point, honey, he told me once. No point at all. Except that we'd get bored if we looked at the same flower every day, don't you think?

Flowers don't kill each other, I told him. The pink ones don't gang up on the purple ones and put them in jail.

I stand by my original point, then, he said. There's no point at all.

Fifteen years later, he was urging me to read Huey P. Newton, to understand Black liberation struggles in Africa and the rest of the world, and writing me about how the racial categories of the prison were enforced. There was a point. Race had a point to someone. Coercion. Control. And also, pride.

We landed, deplaned, trudged through the quiet early-morning airport, and I became desperately bored at the baggage claim. Trapped. The fluorescent track lights. The thin smell of industrial disinfectant, and the small piles of grey detritus creeping in from the corners. Griffin was absorbed in his phone.

"Do you remember the first time you thought the world was really unfair?" I asked him.

"No," he said. "Do you?"

I didn't. "Do you remember a time from childhood when it sunk in, though?"

He smiled. He did. "Fabio's face got busted on a roller coaster at Busch Gardens."

"Fabio the model?"

"Yes. I saw it on the news. I went on the same ride endlessly right when it first opened. Before the ride operator pushed the green button that sent Fabio to get his face bashed, he undoubtedly said, 'Sit back, relax, and enjoy the maximum airtime on the wings of Apollo's Chariot, and enjoy your day at Busch Gardens!'"

"You memorized that."

"I couldn't help it. The cadence was intoxicating."

The baggage belt to our right started up, and I wondered if we were all going to have to shuffle over there instead. The buzzing of the lights seemed designed to make me unconsciously desire violence. I punched Griffin lightly in the chest.

"Thanks," he said. And, "You can do that harder." I punched him again, a little harder. We both felt a tiny bit better.

When Fabio got injured, Griffin was twelve years old and lived an hour from Busch Gardens. His parents took him there the week before the accident.

"For your birthday?"

"No, just because."

I didn't understand that, and he couldn't explain it.

"You don't always need a reason," he said.

"You do when you're poor," I said, irritated again.

"Ok, ok," he said, holding his palms up, and it seemed like I'd gotten through.

"Anyway, this isn't the kind of story I was asking for," I said.

"But it was so unfair! Fabio got hit in the face by a goose that was just flying by, minding its own business, and the ride was brand new, so of course everyone blamed the ride."

"Your sympathy goes to Apollo's Chariot? That's when you knew life was unfair?"

"It was a great ride."

"What about the goose?"

"They found a dead one not far away."

Our baggage belt started up. "If the TSA stole my vibrator again I'm going to complain," I said.

"That's happened?"

"Twice. They leave me little notes that say they went through my bag, and I discover my vibrator is missing. The first time they took the whole thing--the lube, the nice velvet bag, the charger. Ugh. Assholes."

"I can't believe that," he said.

"I didn't either, until the second time it happened," I said. "That time they left me the note, and left me the case and the other stuff. Just took the vibe." The innards of the airport vomited my bag. I reached, pulled, felt a hard twinge in my neck, stumbled a little backward.

He asked if I was okay.

"Yes," I said, "except this pervert I'm traveling with watches everything I do all day."

He looked at the bags on the carousel, a tiny smile at the edge of his mouth. "Sorry," he said. Had to press the smile down with his lips.

Outside, I was startled to think the air smelled like home. We got a little rental car--silver and four doors and smelling like old cigarette smoke and plastic. When we arrived at the motel, we got an old-school cherry red gummy-tag key ring with our room number painted in white and a menu for a Brazilian restaurant next door. The whole place was cracked and slouching, heavy with age.

Griffin seemed a little scared. I ignored it. We unpacked. We listened to a jazz station. I tried to stretch out a little bit. I must have looked stressed.

Griffin came over and sat on the edge of the bed and asked if he could put his hand on my leg. I nodded. He held me gently just above my knee.

"Can I do anything for you? Like a foot massage or something? Do you want to talk about your dad or anything? No pressure."

"Thanks," I said. "I don't think I want to talk right now."

"Cool, cool," he said. "Maybe checking in with Nautica would be good?"

"Yeah," I said. "Good idea."

"I'm gonna see if I can find a meeting nearby."

"A shoplifter's anonymous meeting?"

"Yes'm."

"Another good idea," I said. "You're just full of them."

He made himself busy on his phone while I called Nautica. She picked up, in a noisy place. I got the point across that we'd made it to our motel and were going to wind down. She got some love to me. I tried to give some back. I asked her to text me her schedule for the next day so I could call her up when she was free. She told me to rest and let her know my plan once I'd made one. I felt scared of meeting Rodney and then ashamed of being childish. I told her so. She said I was on a crisis-trip, I could expect to feel scared, and that she was rooting for me, and for Carl.

I motioned Griffin over so he could rub my feet. He stopped talking when I asked him to, and I fell asleep after only a few more terrifying visions of what might have happened to Carl.

In my dream there was thunder, lightning, heavy rain. Long bright sheets of water cutting fog under the street lights, as if rain falling on rain broke the rain into mist.

I carried precious cargo under an umbrella, in my old black Jansport backpack. A cell phone, a charger, some pills in a plastic bag, a notebook, a zipper pouch with makeup essentials, a small folded envelope with six hundred dollars in it, the latest letter from Carl, some black cotton clothes, some glittery dirt and small pieces of trash. A few pens and pencils, too.

I walked for two Brooklyn miles in the storm, wearing strappy short-heel sandals. I knew where I was going but I didn't know how to get there. I'd been dropped off at the wrong corner by a cabbie who seemed perfectly friendly, and because I was so tired, and so distracted, and the rain was so heavy, I didn't notice where I was, or really where I wasn't, until he was gone.

It had taken me a long time to catch a cab in the first place, standing in the downpour. It would only take me longer to get another, now that I was down so far on Nostrand Ave.

I walked. I walked and walked, nearly blind, wondering if I was going to absorb ambient New York City rat poison through the thin skin of my feet, as it got washed along the uneven sidewalk.

My Mom's smiling face in bad weather. The squish-squeak of her wet pantyhose foot coming out of her heavy work shoes. The aluminum pot she gave me to hold on my head and collect rain water in, so we could have a cup of rainwater tea. The plinky sound of rain in the pot. The deep thudding of the rain on this umbrella.

"Hey, pretty face there," someone said behind me.

I'd finally reached the brownstone I'd been aiming for all along.

"I said, 'hey, pretty face,'" the voice said again. This time I knew it was for me. I put my hand on the gate I needed to open. It was locked. I turned around.

The person was under their own umbrella. I knew it was Claudia. I could only see her bright red lips.

14

THE DAC

I woke up a few hours later. My neck was sore. Griffin navigated us to the address Rodney had given me over the phone.

We were in downtown Los Angeles, and although I'd been there once or twice as a younger person, I didn't recognize anything. The buildings were fantastic. They had art deco details caked in years of city dirt. Enormous wrought metal doors and inlaid stone address markers. Small piles of trash snaked down the street. I imagined the street Nautica and I lived on, awash in rusty brown and graying black, concrete, and lumpy paint on metal. The grass was brighter here, and the blue of the sky a truer blue, with puffy clouds, like a child had painted it. The shop signs in this neighborhood were hand-painted, in primary colors and pleasing block fonts. Tents and tarps appeared.

We parked in a thickly painted, forest green two-story lot.

"Ok honey," I said to Griffin. "I want you to make yourself scarce for a few hours. Keep your phone on you. There's a lot of fun stuff in this city, you should be able to entertain yourself on foot from here."

He looked panicked for a second. "I don't get to come with you?"

"Not for this part," I said. "I need to meet up with this Rodney guy on my own."

"Okay," he said. "But why?"

"We can talk about that later," I said. How do you tell a young white cisgendered man that his very presence in a room can be experienced as an act of aggression?

He sighed a little. "Call me the instant you need to, ok?"

I knew I wasn't going to need to. "I'll call you in about two hours," I said, "and see where we're at."

He took off, up Fifth Street. I walked into the diner Rodney had named, got a menu, and sat. The sign above my table said: *It's all been done before, but you must never stop trying to cook it up fresh* in cross stitch. The images were irresistible: bright yolks in a shiny blue pan, a spherical red apple shaded with pink. Each stitch had taken two pull-throughs. People did such inexplicable things with their time.

Sharon Jones and the Dap Kings sang the long-censored version of "This Land is Your Land," each glissando dripping, a threat of insurrection and an invitation to sex. The counter's beige Formica split into fractals or seashells. I was not ready for Carl to be gone. I could have at least told him I loved him, sometime in the past month. I could have asked him if he wanted to come live with me and Nautica in New York. I could have done that for years. I had a flash of my Mom, one of the cloudy ones, where I couldn't quite remember her face, reaching for Carl from the kitchen, telling him she wanted some sugar.

"Hello?" a person I expected to be Rodney said, his voice lilting like he was answering a phone. He was at the edge of the table. He wore a red, black and grey blanket-weave poncho with a fading pot leaf screen printed on the belly. The mirror behind him blasted outside's blue-white light, a fuzzy halo at the edges of the windows.

"Rodney?" I croaked a little. I cleared my throat.

"Yeah? Kindred?" He had short gray dreadlocks. Kind eyes. His cuticles were thick and splitting.

"That's me," I said, and held out my hand.

His black-brown eyes stayed locked. He shook my hand, said it was good to meet me. He'd been sitting at a back table waiting for me to arrive. He held a cup of water, a copy of *The Unbearable Lightness of Being*, and two menus.

He sat across from me, a server dressed like Rosie the Riveter took our order for two coffees, and I asked how long Rodney had been waiting for me.

He smiled. "Since they opened." He showed me his book. "You ever seen this movie? The book is so much better."

I said I hadn't, but of course the book was better.

He said, "Let's move to my table in the back so we can talk."

We moved to a table in the back corner of the place. He already had reserved it, by placing his overstuffed black backpack on the seat. He signaled to our server and she nodded.

"It took me two years, but I figured out this is the best spot," he said. I looked around. The only difference was that our corner was covered, booth-to-ceiling, with cork board. I pointed at it, and asked if that was the reason?

He nodded. "The acoustics are perfect for a private conversation."

"I like the way you think," I said.

We sat, drank a pot of coffee, ate somewhere between five and seven eggs, at least eight biscuits, and between us a stack of Smucker's strawberry and another stack of butter pads. No bacon. Rodney didn't eat pork. Our server had half-inch long purple glittering nails and smelled like sandalwood. Her black apron held enough pens for her to throw two bad ones behind the counter while she was taking our orders.

Rodney's eyes kept darting at the door, scanning out the windows, and then, he would look at me directly and my diaphragm would scoot up. It happened with people I wanted to fuck, and with generally confident people I admired. I didn't think he was either. Things are just weird, I told myself. You're going to react weirdly to weird things.

Rodney told me a long story about his traveling by bus from North Carolina to get away from his family; his problem with them loosely fell in the "all fucked up" category. He scooped his eggs with his elbow out and I remembered how Carl did that after prison, and when I ran out of steam for chatting, Rodney saw it.

"When's the last time you talked to Carl?" he asked.

"Weeks ago," I said. Guilt.

Rodney nodded. "I don't know much about you," he said.

"So you've got no reason to trust me," I said, but before I could continue, he interrupted.

"Yes, I do. Carl gave me your number and said to contact you if I ever thought something may have happened to him. That's trust."

"Whatever he's into, I'm not sure I want to know about it. I just want to know he's still breathing," I said.

Rodney shook his head and sipped coffee. "I know some of what your family's been through," he said. He checked the person coming in the door, decided they weren't a threat, and then returned his gaze to mine. "With your mom and all. I can tell you Carl's been working hard every day and every night to serve the people out here and it ain't like him to run out on us or his program."

I admitted to having no idea what he meant. I said I thought he was mostly volunteering. Did "his program" mean he was sober?

"He worked," Rodney said. "He worked six days a week at the DAC. He was still sleeping out, but he was working. He wasn't exactly sober, no. But he wasn't in trouble like that. His program was about showing up for the work he was doing, feel me?"

He worked at the what?

"The Downtown Action Center." It sounded familiar. "I work there too. You want to come see? It's next door."

So I had been brought to the safe place next to the real place. I felt tricked by that, for a second. But then I realized Rodney was showing me his and probably Carl's world one piece at a time. Rodney stayed on one of the blocks adjacent; this was his neighborhood. This was his diner, and next door, his office.

"Yes," I said. Then, "Where do you think he is?"

"I called you because I tried my ideas and he didn't turn up," Rodney said. "I don't know anymore. I was hoping you'd have some insight."

"He kept a lot from me," I said. "For instance, Riley."

"That's a bombshell," Rodney said, nodding. He picked up a spoon and spun it around, catching it before it toppled off his hand. "She's a good kid. Younger than you."

"Let's start next door, I guess," I said.

I insisted on paying the bill when he reached into his pockets. He nodded and thanked me.

He asked me what I did for a living while we slid out of our booth seats and over toward the bright outside.

"What did Carl tell you?"

Rodney shrugged. "Nothing," he said. "It wasn't my business without knowing you myself."

"I'm a professional dominatrix."

"Oh yeah?" he held the diner door open for me, and I walked through.

"Yeah."

"I've never gone to one of those, but it sounds interesting," he said.

I laughed.

"What?" he looked a little embarrassed. "Is that a bad thing to say?"

I told him no, it was a perfect thing to say. I thanked him for not being scared or evangelical or concerned. I imagined him submitting and he seemed like he could love it. I was glad I had told him. It was always a gamble, coming out like that.

He steered me toward the metal gate at the entrance of the Downtown Action Center. "You're grown," he said. "And I think people who do sex work on their own choice are offering a great service to society." I smiled at him, surprised. "You should meet the Hookers' Army," he said then. "They have a sex workers' meeting twice a month. It's not a rescue thing. They train self-defense. They're some of the most badass comrades in the city."

I didn't have time to think of a response, except, "I'd like to." I didn't know if I should do anything about him intimating that I was a sex worker, because of course I was, but people weren't supposed to assume that I considered myself a sex worker until I told them myself, I thought. I was confused by his utterly friendly aspect about the whole thing.

We entered the DAC office.

It was vibrant, frenetic, full of stuff. One wall was plastered with political posters and flyers for upcoming events, another wall rose into the second-floor stairs with a mural of faces. I couldn't tell if I was supposed to recognize them or if they were representations of "the people." They were all shades, a few pinky-peach and mostly brown and dark brown, in T-shirts and some in black or brown berets.

Rodney clapped his hands on the black leather-clad back of a person sitting at what seemed like a front desk repurposed from a high school principle. Years of dirt had embedded in the wood grain of the desk and the sheen of the sealant was worn down on the panel that hid the rest of the person's body.

I got ready to ask about their pronoun, since I wasn't confident of which one to use. Soft features, large breasts, whiskers. Just then Rodney called him "brother" and introduced me as "Carl's girl." The person made a noise of happy recognition, stood up, and was asking me how I was doing when Rodney interrupted him to call up the stairs, "Hey Sadie!"

I held out my hand and we shook. His name was Curly.

"Y'all enjoy yourselves," Curly said, and sat.

"Don't holler at me, Rodney," Sadie called from the top of the stairs. Her red Converse All Stars came padding down. I admired her painter's jeans, her unbuttoned flannel shirt and black T-shirt with "Rebel Against Empire" printed in silver Star Wars font. Her wild hair was flying, or floating, in a shimmering henna-red frizz around her heavily freckled face. She turned her serious eyes to me and introduced herself. I had a strong desire to know where she had come from and wondered if she had the same for me.

"I'm so glad to meet you," she said, and squeezed my triceps before she shook my hand. "Even with the circumstances we're under."

I told her I'd just met Rodney that morning, and was here looking for Carl.

She smelled like oatmeal soap and fresh coffee. She invited me and Rodney into her "cubby." I watched her ass walk up the stairs. In my mind, Nautica and I winked at each other, and a pang of missing Nautica shot through me. She was probably teaching her workshop right now.

Sadie's cubby was not much larger than a refrigerator box, stuffed perilously high with papers and books. She shifted a stack to make room on a folding chair, and pulled another chair just outside the doorway of the room. We were as close as New Yorkers on a rush-hour train in there.

"Welcome!" Sadie said. "Join the fray."

"This is a busy place," I said.

"Rodney said you were flying in from New York? Where do you stay out there?" Sadie asked. Rodney settled into the farthest chair so I sat in the folding chair across from her over-burdened desk. She leaned against its wooden edge with her arms crossed, but genially.

"Brooklyn," I said.

"Oh! Where!"

I told her I lived in Bed Stuy, near the Bushwick border. She and Rodney exchanged a glance and she made a noise like a chuckle.

"Oh Bushwick," she sighed dramatically, "where you live in squalor but you eat organic."

"Exactly. Cat shit and coconut water," I said.

Sadie dropped into a cross-legged shape on the floor without disturbing any of her piles. She beckoned to Rodney to come in. He had to ditch the chair, close the door, and get on the floor too.

"You can stay in your chair," Sadie told me as I cast around for more floor space. "The main thing is getting the door closed." I could see a little farther down her shirt. I wondered if Rodney thought she was sexy too. I wondered how old she was. I wondered where the hell those freckles came from; her skin was more olive than pink. I wondered if she liked her ears sucked. Focus, Kindred.

"I don't know where Carl is," she said.

Something in me shifted, although I'd already known it, somehow.

"But what do you think?" Rodney said. "He left all his stuff out on Towne and he ain't in any of the jails in the county? Kindred checked the hospitals nearby too. It's just not his way."

"You checked hospitals how far out?"

I said I had called from Venice up to Glendora.

She shook her head. "People disappear from Skid Row all the time," she said heavily. "It's more normal than knowing where they are, actually. They don't always give their real names at hospitals if they're in for an OD, you know? It's just so tough to find someone down here."

"I thought he was working here?" I said. I wondered why she'd mentioned an OD.

"Until he went missing," Rodney said. "He was."

"He could have just said 'fuck it' and taken one little baggie to a motel with a new girlfriend," Sadie said. "Or he could have taken a bus out of the city for a while. Taken a break. It's not like a regular job. He got a little stipend from the grant we're on right now, but he wasn't on a regular job schedule."

I said, "Sounds like you know him pretty well," and she flashed a sad smile at me. "You think he was getting high?"

Sadie shrugged. "Not necessarily. I just know it's a possibility. People need breaks. The pressure he was living under was constant. Constant."

Rodney was shaking his head now too. "He takes care of his stuff, though. His books and papers especially. It don't make sense."

Sadie patted my knee. It may have been motherly from her end, but it was sexy on mine.

"Of course, you could file a missing person's report, it's your prerogative," she said.

"I just can't," I said. "I don't think he'd want me to."

Sadie and Rodney shared a look. "Carl has been doing a lot of work down here to help the people organize for their rights," Sadie said. "We've been fighting a huge development project and he's been a leader on that campaign."

I had never heard someone call him a leader out loud.

"You busy tomorrow morning?" she said. "I'm teaching a workshop for a school group, it's the kind of thing Carl's been doing, you could see what his work is, come on the Skid Row tour? Then Rodney can take you around and maybe some more information will pop up."

"Can I bring my friend with me?"

"Of course," she said. "The more the merrier!"

She hugged me goodbye. Her breasts were small, her chest was strong. I wanted to linger, but I knew better. She hugged Rodney too.

"Good to see you, honey," she said to him, and then thumped his back like a boy.

We left.

"An S.R.O is subsidized housing?" I asked Rodney.

"That's right," he said. "Most of us try to get one. You get on a list while you sleep out. You check with them, maybe they gave your room away, maybe you get a room. You stay the month. You have to move at the end of twenty-eight days or you get tenant's rights. So they make you check out for three days and then maybe you get to move back in. We call it the Twenty-Eight-day shuffle. You sleep out again. Maybe you get your room back after a few days, or you start over, get on another list."

"I thought that was illegal," I said.

Rodney clenched his jaw. Of course it was illegal. "Lawsuit's been won," he said, but that hadn't stopped the practice. "Skid Row has its own rules."

"Take me to where he stays," I said. I felt lightheaded and wanted to go back to sleep. But it had to be done.

We walked over to Towne. Someone sitting on a milk crate yelled "Jesus said, 'I am the way and the truth and the Life!'"

"Who the fuck would trust a guy who says that about himself?" Rodney said to him.

It made me chuckle. "You don't trust that guy?" I asked.

"Him? That's just Pickles, he's okay," Rodney said. "I don't trust Jesus. And I don't understand how anyone does. He was a megalomaniac."

That made me actually laugh. "I trust a guy who hung out with prostitutes and didn't hide it," I said. "And I trust a guy who knew a party needs wine."

"Valid points," Rodney said. "He was right about the redistribution of wealth thing, too."

"But it's weird to claim you're the son of God and have people believe you."

"That's one word for it. It's madness to have thousands of people believe you, and then for them to kill thousands of other people who don't believe you? And then for it to continue until it's millions of people, believing and not believing and killing each other for it. Fucking insanity."

"I used to strip at this one place in New York," I said, "and the DJ looked like Jesus."

"I bet there were a lot of jokes."

"Sure," I said. "But never to his face. He had a lot of power over how our shifts played out."

Rodney nodded thoughtfully. "Yes, I can see how he would."

We turned a corner and Rodney stopped cold.

"What," I said.

"Motherfucking piece of shit pigs!" he ignored me and walked fast and hard up the block. "I fucking *knew* those assholes were coming, I fucking *knew* they were." He was pacing. He got out his phone.

"What's happening?" I couldn't see anything different from the last two blocks we'd walked down.

"This is the place," Rodney said to me. Then "Yeah, hello?" into his phone. "Dee, man, I told you to stay with Carl's motherfucking shit! It was just a few hours motherfucker, what the fuck! Where you at? The shit is gone, asshole. The shit is gone!"

He paused and I heard a loud protesting voice but couldn't make out the words. We were just a few feet away from someone's tent. I wondered if they were inside.

I pieced it together. Carl's camp had been confiscated and dumped by the cops. No one had been there to claim it, because Dee had taken a break to go piss and get a sweet tea around the corner. When he came back, it was happening. He didn't fight. He couldn't without risking arrest. He had two outstanding tickets of his own.

I didn't know how to feel. I didn't know what exactly had been lost, besides some dignity. And some camping equipment. And maybe some part of both mine and Rodney's hearts, the parts that expected Carl to walk around the corner any minute now, with a cast on his arm, and a story to tell us, and a new project he'd cooked up while lying in bed at a hospital I'd already called and failed to find him in.

"He's gonna be so mad," Rodney said, sitting on the curb. I smelled air freshener and rotting food and athletic shoes and cooking pavement. The sun was inexplicably cheerful and enveloping.

I checked my neck, stretching. Not as bad as the morning, but still painfully stiff.

"There's some good news, though," Rodney said, without

sounding happy. "Which is that I'm pretty sure Carl sent some of his stuff up to The Spot."

"The Spot."

"Our boy Michel has a camp up on the Avenue 26 overpass," he said, and brushed his pants leg straight, tucked his laces into his boots. "Carl has some boxes up there."

"That's good," I said.

"Shit," Rodney said. "I should call Riley and let her know."

"You get it that I've never met this person?" I said. I was so tired, so tired.

"I understand the words coming out your mouth," Rodney said, and smiled. He had a brown tooth back on one side I hadn't noticed before. "But I don't 'get it,' no."

"I don't either," I said. "Carl's never said anything about having another daughter. Like not even wondered to me if he might have one because of that one girl that one time, you know? Nada."

Rodney nodded thoughtfully. He pulled a purple velvet bag from his backpack and started packing a bowl. "Time to chill out," he said, to no one. Then, to me, "How old are you?"

"I'm about to be thirty."

"Riley is nineteen."

"Wow."

"She was born when you were ten."

"So Carl cheated on my mom."

We both shuffled around a little. Stared at our hands or something. It was too insane to feel anything but bad.

"They might have had an agreement," Rodney said.

"Even if they fucked other people and were okay with it," I said. "A pregnancy, a kid, changes things. My mom's dead, Rodney." He nodded. He knew. He was listening. "I don't even know if she knew, if she kept this a secret from me."

"He loved her and he loves you. Those are facts. But shit

happens, too. I don't know what to tell you. You could ask Riley what she knows." He pulled out his phone and dialed. "I'm just saying, it's possible he didn't betray your mom. And even if he did, I don't think any of that old history is what matters now."

"Easy for you to say," I spat. "My mom would have been furious."

I heard a feminine voice answer. I couldn't understand her words. Rodney reported that Carl's stuff was gone, most of it anyway, and that he was with "Kindred, your sister that got here from New York this morning," out on the Row.

There was a pause. Her voice said something short.

Rodney held the phone out. "She wants to talk to you."

My stomach went sour and heavy. I thought I might pass out. It would be so nice to sleep through this part of my life, I thought, and wake up with some clarity and purpose and vision, next to Nautica, and without dread.

"Hello?" The sun was really too much now. I hunched between my knees.

"This is Kindred?"

"Yes," I said. I heard the fizz-click of the lighter and Rodney's inhale. "I'm Kindred." I compulsively thought, we're kindred. Who the fuck am I if she's my sister. Smelled the weed.

"Nice to meet you," she said stiffly, "although these are terrible circumstances." She sounded grown.

"I'd like to meet in person," I said, before I'd had a chance to think about it. "As soon as we can. I think every day that passes without word from Carl is..." and I didn't have words for what I thought there.

"I know," she said. She sighed. "I know. And I know he didn't get a chance to talk with you about me before all this, so."

He didn't get a chance. I wondered what that chance

would have looked like. It seemed a strange thing to say. But could she have said anything that sounded sane to me?

"I gotta go back to work," she said. "But can you come meet me tomorrow afternoon? We can get a coffee."

"You're only nineteen?" I said.

"Huh?"

"Sorry, yeah, that sounds good," I said. "I'll get your number from Rodney and be in touch tomorrow after I do this Skid Row tour-thing at the DAC."

"Oh, you're doing that?" she said. "Cool, that's probably a good thing. Anyways, it's good to meet you sort of. I'll talk with you tomorrow."

She hung up.

I handed the phone back to Rodney. He offered me the pipe, a thick bulb of glass, a thin curl of smoke, a corner of green. I took it, I hit it, I put it out and emptied it. The lightness came quickly.

I got Riley's number and put it in my phone. I told Rodney I needed to go back to my motel and take a nap. Another memory of Mom came. Then another. I contacted Griffin, met him at the car, forced myself to stay awake enough to drive us back. I had forgotten how powerfully psychedelic California weed could be. Hospital memories. Conversations en route to the prison. A wave of unanswerable questions pounded through. Did she know about Riley? Did she want another baby, ever? Did Carl keep a double life from her?

The colors of the world were vibrant and clear, but inside I was a cloud. I didn't recognize Riley's voice. I didn't recognize my own memories. I had trouble seeing my mom's pre-cancer face up close in my mind. I couldn't talk to Griffin, but he stayed close to me walking into the motel room, asking me if I wanted anything, suggesting that I eat some food. I shook my head.

I got inside the door, lay across the bedspread in my clothes, and let the darkness take me. I slept through the rest of the afternoon. I woke up after the sun went down. I could hear Griffin puttering. I went back to sleep.

In the morning, I got up.

"You can come with me today," I said. "We're going on a tour of Skid Row."

Griffin was excited to have something to do.

"I've never been to a real Skid Row before," he said. He tied his sneakers. He was wearing a T-shirt I hadn't seen yet, that said "I Live Among You" in a font I could tell I was supposed to recognize from something in pop culture.

"This isn't just *a* Skid Row," I said, "it's *the* Skid Row." I stood in front of the mirror, twisted my hair into a bun at the nape of my neck. Decided against makeup today. I just couldn't. Crisis time, I told myself. No one is paying you, you don't have to work at the femme stuff right now. I took a picture of my naked face and sent it to Nautica. Then I remembered she'd had a date either last night or the night before and had a pang. Missing her, jealousy, something. Focus, I told myself. Focus on getting to the DAC right now. Nautica loves you and things are fine with her.

"What does that mean it's *the* Skid Row?" He was putting things in his little blue backpack. He always brought a jacket. Cute kid.

I repeated what Carl had told me. "It was partly haphazard and partly designed to be a contained environment for recently released prisoners, winos, drug addicted homeless," I said. "It's been there since the 1930s." I packed a jacket, too.

His eyebrows went up. "No shit?"

"Don't you ever read?" I said. "Like even Wikipedia could help you a lot today."

"I told you, I'm reading women's journals. But I really like learning from people better than from books," he said. He gave me some teeth in his smile.

I recognized the theme of excuses I'd given to Carl before. Especially when I was feeling insecure about not reading the books he'd asked me to before our visits. Inappropriately, "The Circle of Life" started playing in my head.

"I'll tell you two things that should curl your pubes," I said. "First, they actually shortened the time on the walk signals down there in order to be able to give homeless people more jaywalking tickets, and some lawyers proved it." I'd read that on a sign at the DAC office.

"What the fuck for?"

"Because when poor people don't pay their tickets, cops can get warrants, and then clean up the streets by putting people in jail."

He shook his head. "That's so fucked up," he said.

"Here's another one: just a few years ago they finally were able to prove that hospitals and jails were doing this thing they called 'dumping' people there, bringing them to Skid Row on a bus and being like, 'go for it, make a life for yourself' in front of a mission or an S.R.O. hotel." I scanned the room. We'd cleaned up ok.

"I can't believe that," he said. "I mean, I guess I can believe it, I just, how can they get away with it, you know?"

I made a cynical raspberry sound. "Because they can get away with anything they want. Because no one wants to deal with Skid Row."

"But Carl wanted to?" Griffin said.

"Don't use the past tense for him," I snapped. "He wants

to," I said. "Yeah. Sadie and Rodney do too, I guess. Ready to go?"

"I'm hungry," he said.

"We'll stop at Jack in the Box on the way there," I said. "You can eat a meaty breakfast burrito and pretend it's my cock."

He scrunched his face in grossed-out amusement. "Ew. You're amazing."

I thanked him. We listened to the news in the car. A shooting at a school, a new tax on plastic bags, a demonstration in Washington about healthcare. A new drone attack confirmed in Afghanistan.

We got the food and then parked at a lot across the street from the DAC. Because it was a rental car.

"This shit is too expensive," I said. "I think we should ditch it and take the bus."

"Whatever you want," he said.

Nice boy.

A different person was sitting at the old desk in the front. She was extremely thin and expertly femme.

"Can I help you?" she asked, and tapped her orange nails on the desk.

"Sadie told us to come today, for a workshop?" I said.

She smiled without showing her teeth and gestured to the stairs. "Go on upstairs, they're just getting started."

We walked past the mural of all the faces, up the stairs, and found a room with four big tables pushed together. There were people in most of the chairs. I saw two seats directly across from Sadie, who was looking at a binder, standing in the front with a whiteboard behind her. She was wearing a different flannel shirt, same wild hair.

She looked up and winked at me. "Folks I'd like to get started," she said, and nodded toward the chairs in front of her. "Everybody find a seat?"

We milled around and settled in. Griffin seemed a tiny bit uncomfortable. I liked it. All eyes turned to Sadie.

"Let's talk about what kinds of associations we have with homelessness," she said, pulling the cap off a white-board marker. She turned her back and poised to write. "What stereotypes, images, or memories do you have associated with Skid Row? What kinds of things do you remember from movies? Don't be shy. We're just naming the things, not endorsing them."

Eyes darted. People didn't want to do it.

"It stinks," I said. "Like piss." Someone had to break the seal.

"Ok, perfect," Sadie said, and wrote *smells like human defecation* on the board. "What else?"

"People live in tents?" Griffin said.

"Good," Sadie said, and wrote it up. She turned halfway, looked at us, and crossed her arms. "That's all?"

One of the students raised her hand. Her red T-shirt said "Superstar" in white script. "Drugs," she said.

"What about drugs?"

"Um, there's a lot of them?"

"Yes, people living here use the same pharmaceutical drugs, over-the-counter medicines, alcohol, and processed sugar that you'd find in most of our houses," Sadie said. I snorted a little.

"Illegal drugs," said the girl, like duh. She was certain of this one. It had been in the news recently. "There's a big drug problem with the homeless."

Sadie had been nodding slowly as the girl talked. I could see her breathe in, the way I did when a client had made me angry, or, when I was in an argument with Nautica and she was interrupting me every time I talked. Sadie wrote *drugs* on the board. "Here at the DAC, you'll hear us using words like 'houseless,' 'marginally housed,' or 'sleeping out,'" Sadie said. "The word 'homeless' tends to make people feel stigmatized, and like their whole identity is now about this one part of their life. So, I encourage you to try using other terms, while we brainstorm what associations we have with Skid Row itself," she said. "And, there are definitely a lot of people struggling with addiction here, but there are also a lot of people in active recovery. Most of the drugs consumed in this country are sold in the suburbs, it might surprise you to know. Next?"

A few more ideas went up: *mental illness, violence, panhandling, unemployment.*

"Ok! Now, how do you imagine people come to Skid Row?" Sadie asked. "What might precipitate a person coming here?"

A few suggestions came forward: *home foreclosure, drug addiction, getting released from prison with nowhere to go, abuse at home,* and Sadie stopped writing when one of the girls at the table said: "a series of bad choices."

"I'm not going to try to debunk or debate these ideas," Sadie said, capping her pen. "What I'm going to suggest to you today is that the stereotypical narrative of how people come to live in a community like Skid Row is not the only, or even the most accurate one, and, that there are multiple forces acting to create a community like this, especially one this large. I'd like to offer some of the explanations we use here for how the cycle of poverty gets maintained over time, who benefits from this situation, and how the Downtown Action Center is involved in Skid Row residents' fight for their human rights."

Sadie drew a rhombus-like shape on the board and labeled the edges: Main, 3rd, Alameda, 7th. She asked who of us knew about the Safer Cities Initiative.

No one raised a hand. Again, she took a slow breath. This seemed hard for her today. I felt for her. I raised my hand. She nodded at me.

"Can I take a guess and say it hasn't made life safer for people who live in Skid Row?"

"Good guess!" she said.

She walked to the table and leaned toward us. "There are around eighty thousand unhoused individuals living in Los Angeles proper. The impact of the Safer Cities Initiative on the nearly ten thousand people who stay down here on Skid Row has been profoundly negative. I'll write some information on the board for you and we can discuss. While I do that, I'd like for you to write something too."

She handed out blank baby-blue copy paper and blue ballpoint pens. I drew a few spirals in the corners until the ink was consistent.

"I want you to write down a stream-of-consciousness list of images, feelings, thoughts, as you tour your own neighborhood in your mind," Sadie said. "You're out on a walk from the front door of where you stay now. What do the houses or apartments look like? Are there dogs you say hello to? What colors catch your eye? Is there a lot of trash on the ground? Are the lawns all mowed the same? Are there any houseless people, camping at the overpass or sitting outside the grocery store? Describe the scene as you would for a news story, for someone who has never been there."

Griffin looked at me, with something like fear in his eyes.

I mouthed, what?

He gave me one dimple and shook his head. I glanced at him a few times while we all wrote. His concentration face was so endearing, chewing on the insides of his cheeks and pressing his pen too hard.

I thought about a string of apartments I'd lived in with

Mom and Carl. The last one, especially, and then the neighborhood I'd lived in with Angie, then the place I'd couch surfed for a few weeks, then that other place I'd stayed in with KC, and then there was the little room in Bushwick I'd called "mine," but the neighborhood I'd been in the longest, I realized, still "belonged" somehow to Nautica in my mind. It was her neighborhood, even though I lived there too, because she'd gotten there first. And maybe I'd never thought of myself as really living anywhere, I moved so often.

You've lived with Nautica in that apartment for five of your nine years together, said a reasonable voice in my head. Like an adult.

I wrote some lists of things and people. I got bored. I tried to draw Sadie's profile but she moved too much. She was setting something up on the white board. I read her facts and was quietly enraged at what the city was doing. I nudged Griffin and nodded at his paper. He handed it to me.

Spotted, cracked pavement. Buildings rise low. Red rust orange. Trimmed toward the back at an angle. Sense of lacking.

Meatpacking plant in two parts. Yellow cake frosting crust paint job. Always someone outside looking mad.

"You're a good writer," I whispered to him.

He looked like I'd handed him two thousand dollars. "Really?!"

Sadie and two of the other students glanced at us.

"Everyone finished?" Sadie said.

We all murmured and nodded.

"Great," she said. "Let's get ready for our tour." She gestured to the board. On the left, she'd written "SCI" in big letters at the top and a short list of what looked like promises from the cops about cleaning up the streets. On the other side, she'd written statistics about arrests, and people gone missing, and tickets issued for infractions like jaywalking. Griffin looked shocked. I felt a little sorry for him, and then I realized he was a grown man who needed to know things about the world he lived in. I wondered what he knew about policing in NYC. He'd probably never thought about it.

Nautica and I had been stopped and frisked twice together, and once they threatened to arrest us because we both were carrying boxes of condoms in our bags. That's probable cause, they said. You're fucking with me, right? Nautica had said. You've got to be fucking with me. I squeezed her hand. Oh please shut up, I thought. She didn't think it was legal for them to search her bag. They told her they didn't like her attitude.

One of them got in my face and said, you don't have anything to say, pretty lady? Who you having this much sex with, honey? Is he big? I made eye contact then and kept my mouth shut. Something happened on their walkie-talkies. They let us go. I was numb. Nautica cursed them for the whole walk back home. They saw us kissing, she said, fucking perverts. Fucking power-abusing assholes. 'Probable cause' my ass. We looked it up, and it was bad news: they could have used the condoms against us in court as evidence that we intended to commit prostitution. Nautica laughed. Then she sent an email to all the Dommes at the dungeon reminding them that their rental fees covered condoms and that they could keep their personal gear and costumes in their lockers. "Let's not let homophobic, misogynist, slut-shaming attacks from the police ruin a perfectly lovely day of beating up our little men and taking their money," she concluded. "Stay safe," she signed it, "from pathogens and persecution."

I thought about Carl, and how much he'd taught me over the years, even without my full presence or participation. Broken Windows Theory. The criminalization of homelessness. Sundown Towns. "Ugly" laws.

Sadie was trying to explain why it was so dangerous for

people to stay in such a heavily policed area, and yet, how they were trapped there because all the social services were there.

"Ok, but what are people supposed to do when something bad happens to them?" The same girl who'd wanted to talk about "bad choices" asked. "Don't they need cops down here because of, like, real crimes?"

"That depends on whether you are a person who is traditionally protected by the cops, or traditionally victimized by the cops," Sadie answered. "You, for instance, are a feminine-presenting person with white skin. You might feel safer when a cop arrives on the scene. But a lot of people don't, because the cops have a negative history with them. Does that make sense?"

"Ok," she said. I knew what she was thinking.

I raised my hand. "Isn't there a lot of rape down here, though?"

Sadie nodded. "Rape is definitely an issue for cisgender women, trans women, and also for men, especially those who identify as gay or queer," she said. "The problem is that the police don't go after rapists, even in rich neighborhoods. Frankly it's a low priority for them here, even when someone is brave enough to come forward and report."

She was quiet for a moment. "You understand we aren't meeting here today to solve all the social problems associated with homelessness?" she started erasing the board. "That's a years-long task that will require more thinking and a lot more action, especially from the people most affected by the system. I want to remind you all that solving the problems is not actually your job, even though of course it makes sense that you'd want to help. But sometimes the people who want to help come in here and try to solve problems they really don't understand. That is the mistake made by the Business Improvement District, which has paid for all the private security around here. They've caused more problems, not solved them. As I see it, your job is to listen to the people most affected by Skid Row policies, who are the residents, and do your part to support their choices, their plans for change. Do not make the mistake of thinking your ideas about what to do next are brand new, just because they are new to you." She let us stare at her in silence for a beat.

"The DAC helps people who live down here take care of themselves, and we refer to them as 'Skid Row residents,' not 'the homeless.' Our 'help' isn't the same as charity. It comes in the form of support for the residents' organizing for their own rights. We believe in the self-determination of the people, and we proceed from the fact that we are in an ongoing, racial class struggle over land and resources. This isn't just about individual stories, although all the people have important stories to tell. What you all are here to do is self-educate, and hopefully, motivate yourselves to make some changes in your own lives. When you want to try out that new expensive restaurant that popped up where the old fish market used to be, we'd like you to consider learning about where you're going, where you're putting your money. Gentrification is not good for everyone." She smiled with some real kindness. "If you want to help, start listening to the people who don't normally have a voice in the media. Listen when they speak up for their experience." I nodded. I wanted to hug her. No wonder Carl got along with her so well. "Now," she said, "Who's ready to walk?"

We left the DAC office in a lumpy talkative group.

We heard from Sadie that thousands of people had "gone missing" from Skid Row in the past few years. When students asked why, she said it depended who you talked to.

"Everyone has an individual story," she said. "It's important not to forget that. People experience negative impacts in different ways. But systemically, the war on the poor has intensified in most of the major cities. Los Angeles has the most punitive laws and the most reliably racist enforcement of any city in the country."

That seemed impossible to me, somehow. Worse than New York? Worse than Orlando, Atlanta, Dallas, Chicago? We passed a pile of what looked like trash and then several tents clustered together. There was also a shopping cart full of gray, flecked blankets. Sadie pointed at the cart. "We're seeing people's property get destroyed all the time, even though we won a lawsuit to prevent it. So why do people go missing?" She shot me a glance to make sure I was paying attention.

"Some people have one or two particularly difficult interactions with the police and they move to another area where they feel they may not be targeted. Some people get moved off their block because the city needs to come in and power wash the streets to meet a new health code, and then, when they try to move back, they get arrested because of city ordinances that weren't getting enforced the week before. Some people walk away and don't come back, change their name, or get temporary housing somewhere else in the city. Some people get arrested and then held for old warrants, or they catch another criminal case while they are inside, and stay imprisoned. Some get sick and can't get medical care. Some die."

We walked past a building that looked strangely familiar to me. "What's that place?" I asked Sadie.

"You recognize it, right?" she smiled.

"Yeah," Griffin piped in. "I recognize it too."

The building stood three stories, with sandy decorative bricks offsetting the brown. A beautiful archway framed the front door, which desperately needed some love and more red paint.

Sadie spoke to the whole group. "That's Fire Station 23! It was a working Fire Station for many years, and it was considered one of the nicest stations in the country because of the architect's choices for the finest materials. They used to call it the Taj Mahal of Fire Stations. You recognize it because it was the building facade they used for the original *Ghostbusters* movie," she said. "And about fifty films since then."

"This is so weird," said one of the students. She was pulling at a piece of her hair, over and over. "I mean, that's like a historical landmark or something, right? And it looks, like, kind of janky now."

"Sure," said Sadie. "It's a historical building, but the nonprofit that was administering the renovations took money from donations and film shooting fees, and pocketed them. Meanwhile, Skid Row keeps expanding around it." She led us up another block.

"Let's stop here," she said. We all bumbled to a halt.

Sadie pointed out a few more things. An enormous LAPD building. The toy district. A few old hotels that had been remodeled into SROs, single-room-occupancy subsidized housing. I wondered which ones kicked people out after twenty-eight days. "Once you know what you're looking for," she said, "Skid Row becomes a place full of history, art, culture, community."

Someone, not from our group, walked behind her. "Mornin' Miss Sadie," he said, solemnly, and nodded.

She smiled at him and made way for him to pass. "Brother Martin," she said to him, and he moved along.

We all waited for her to continue. She took a breath, and told us that man had been sleeping "rough" for nearly thirty years. He swept his entire block, no matter who was staying there, twice a day. He collected cans. He ate at the Mission, and volunteered at the DAC. "He's part of our fight against the City's football stadium project," she said. Something perked up in me. Carl had said something about a stadium the last time I talked with him.

"What football stadium," I whispered to Griffin.

He shrugged. "I don't do sports stuff," he said. "I wonder what that guy's story is," about Brother Martin. I wondered if he and Carl knew each other. If they talked about God and the world and revolution out on this block.

Sadie brought us back to the DAC and let the group go.

Griffin and I hung back.

"Who were those people?" I asked her.

She shrugged. "A school group from the Valley," she said. "Not a bad bunch." We stood by the reception desk, where Curly was sitting, and she patted him on the shoulder.

"You hooking up with Rodney today?" she said to me, while rubbing Curly's back.

"I don't know," I said. "I think I'm going to meet Riley."

Sadie nodded. "She's a good kid," she said. "I hope you two can support each other through this."

"We've never met," I said.

Sadie's eyes flickered but she didn't ask me to explain. "I didn't know that," she said. "You enjoy the tour?" she said to Griffin.

"It was great," he said. "I mean, I learned a lot."

"Good, good." She glanced around. I could tell she needed to go do things. She squeezed and massaged Curly's neck. He drooped his head little with his eyes closed.

"See you tomorrow maybe?" I said.

She reached out to shake my hand. "Sounds good." She asked Curly to take messages for her for an hour while she made calls upstairs. He nodded.

Griffin looked at me, waiting to leave until I moved to the door.

He was trying to take my cues. It was endearing.

We left, and I asked him to drive us back to the hotel.

15

PLAYING

On our second date, Nautica asked me to assign a symbolic animal to my brain.

"Goldfish," I had said.

She asked me why.

"My brain fidgets, and swims back stupidly to traumatic memories or self-harming thoughts," I said. "But, it's kind of cute in there too."

"I think you may be my perfect bottom," she said calmly. "Of course, you are probably a brat, too, but, I want to try some real power exchange and do some kinky stuff to you. What do you think?"

"I think you look so good I don't care whose side you're on here," I said.

She swatted at me and smiled.

"I'm on both our sides because we're a team right now," she said.

It was the best I'd felt in the presence of another person. It was like warm hands gently shaking out all my joints. It was like having a family you really, really like as people.

. . .

Griffin and I got into the motel room. It smelled like socks and old cigarettes. I was tired, achey, irritated all over, like wool scratching every inch of me.

"Can I help you feel better?" Griffin said. His face looked sweet, hopeful.

"You probably can," I said. "But you're going to have to come up with some ideas on your own at first."

"Are you hungry?"

"Not really."

He folded his jacket and put it on his suitcase.

"Do you want me to give you some head?"

"No thanks." I sat on the bed. What did I want.

"Do you want me to leave you alone?"

"No," I said. "Pretty sure I don't want to be alone." What did I want? I wanted Carl to be safe and in contact with me. I wanted to *do more* to ensure that he had every opportunity to let me know he was alright. I wanted him to be alright. I felt like I'd gotten to LA and done nothing useful to find Carl.

You're taking a break now, the Nautica in my head said. Take some deep breaths and enjoy it. Get some rest and some energy for the next steps you need to take. Stay focused and let the boy help you feel good for an hour or two.

Griffin got in the shower and started singing "California Love." He was shaving. I knew it was for me, just in case. A little squeeze on my heart released. A muscle jumped in my neck and then relaxed.

He emerged, toweling off. His floppy hair stuck in wet strands to his face.

"Ok I have an idea," I said.

The unmistakable disturbance of an ice cream truck broke the quiet. It changed my mind immediately.

"I want ice cream," I said, as if I'd conjured the jangly song of the truck myself. "Can you catch that truck?"

He threw down his razor with one hand and wiped his face with the other. He dashed past me, pulled on his pants and shoes, rummaged for his wallet, and ran out the door.

He hadn't asked me which ice cream I wanted. I arranged myself on the bed with all the pillows and waited, so I could critique his choices and then reward him for his effort.

What you wanted was some power play, said the Nautica in my head. Never forget that sometimes you just need to be in control of one tiny situation to relax about not being in control of the rest.

I called Riley. She was in college and worked on campus. "I've got some free time later this afternoon," she said. "Can you meet me at a coffee shop near my school at like four?"

Of course I could. She gave me an address and we said goodbye.

I called Nautica.

"Hi honey," she said. "How's today going?"

"Remember when you had that cat who ate the crotch out of my bloody underwear and then puked them onto your bed?" I said.

"Jesus, ugh, of course I do. Why the hell would you make me imagine that right now?"

"Sorry," I said. "It just came to me as the moment when I realized I loved you."

She laughed. "Really."

"Yes. I realized I was supposed to feel shame, but I didn't. About how gross it was."

"Love as the absence of shame," she said. "Interesting." It sounded like she was walking somewhere.

"No," I said. "The absence of shame helped me relax into an already-growing feeling of love."

"I see," she said.

"What about you?" I said.

"It didn't work like that for me," she said.

"Like what."

"In an instant like that. Kapow. I'm a slow-and-controlled style attacher."

"Ok, tell me one time you liked me before you loved me then."

I could hear her smile through the phone somehow. "When you locked yourself out of my place, the first time," she said.

I couldn't remember that time exactly.

"You locked yourself out and you called the manager and got him to let you in," she said. "Instead of calling me at work."

"Oh yeah, I remember. I thought you got mad about that."

"I did," she said. "But I was impressed by it, too. And that's a winning combination. You made a set of choices that I would not have been able to predict," she said.

"You're such a fucking Domme," I said.

"Thank you," she said. "For understanding that."

The door clicked and Griffin was back in the hotel room, out of breath.

"I think I need to do some power stuff with Griffin now," I said.

"Do it."

"I love you," I said. "I miss you."

"Call me later and tell me about what's happening with Carl."

"Okay."

"I love you too. The kitchen is very clean without you here."

"Sorry 'bout that. I'll make some messes in there soon."

She kissed into the phone and we said goodbye.

Griffin threw four packaged ice cream treats on the bed, one after another.

"You made it," I said.

"There's chocolate, vanilla, raspberry," he paused to gasp for breath, "and orange creamsicle. I didn't know what you'd want."

I picked up the orange creamsicle. "This is my favorite," I said.

"I'll remember that," he said.

"Atta boy," I said. Then I patted the bed next to me. "Deal with the rest of these and then come here."

He put them in the ice drawer of the mini fridge and lay with his head in my lap.

"Don't move," I said. I unwrapped the treat slowly. Then I rubbed the edge of the popsicle lightly on his cheek, ran it up to his temple, held it above him, and dripped it onto the side of his face a few times. Then I bent down to lick it off.

"You like that?" I whispered in his ear.

"I love it when you touch me," he said. "Any way you want to touch me."

"Then get naked," I said.

He did.

"Get a wide stance and lean your belly onto the bed," I said.

He did.

Thin legs covered in tiny wire hairs. That perfect little bubble butt.

"Hold your hands in prayer position above your head and don't move," I said. He moved his arms, fidgeted his head a little until he was comfortable, and closed his eyes. I warmed him up with some rubs and pinches, cooed a little at his cuteness. I reached under his butt a bit and tickled his balls, stroked his perineum, then slapped his right cheek. "More?" I said.

He nodded.

"Say 'yes, please,'" I instructed.

"Yes, please," he said, his eyes still closed.

I leaned over him, let him feel my weight, the curves of my body, and I spoke softly, directly into his ear. "You're a thief," I said. "And a liar. You don't deserve to read my private thoughts, you don't deserve to read anyone's without asking them to share with you. You know that right? Say 'yes, ma'am,' if you understand."

He didn't look quite as serene. "Yes ma'am," he said softly.

"So I'm going to punish you now," I told him. "Because you need it. Because you need to show me some respect."

"Yes ma'am. Thank you, ma'am."

I worked him over for twenty minutes. I started slow, slapping his calves, the backs of his thighs, varying intensity, hitting him hardest in the fleshiest mounds of his ass. I rubbed and hit, scratched and hit, cupped and hit, took breaks to stretch and breathe and then hit. He kept his honor bondage, he said many "Thank you ma'ams." When I got a good one in, my whole body would flush with Yes.

Eventually, I was done. I told him he was a good boy and he was free. He scooted his legs together and crawled on the bed. We met eyes.

"That was awesome," he said. He was pink and high.

"You did well," I said. "Clean up that popsicle."

He did. Then we lay still in the bed, side by side, with just our arms touching.

My mind felt quiet for a few more minutes. But the world never waits for long.

"What time is it?" I asked.

He rummaged around. "It's two. What's next?"

"What do you want to do?"

Griffin wanted to go to see the Scientology Center in

Hollywood. I told him he was free to enjoy himself; I was going to get ready to meet my sister. He asked if he could kiss my corset tattoo. His feathery mouth on the small of my back warmed me, from top to toe.

I took a shower. I tried to think about anything but Carl being dead.

Nautica had a suggestion box in the dressing room at La Jouissance labeled "Ways to say No." It was a shoebox she had covered with pictures of hands and eyes from magazines. Every new Domme or sub who worked there was encouraged to write down experiences of effective negotiations or deflections that required some form of saying "no" to a client, lover, or co-worker.

"Power exchange requires that all parties are free to say no, and excellent power exchange occurs among people who are skilled at it," she would say. I liked to think I was the first baby Domme she said that to, but she did say it every time she hired someone.

One day, before I had started taking clients as a Domme, I was helping her clean the space. I asked her if she ever checked inside the box.

"Almost never," she said.

"Then what's the point?"

"I like for the people who work here to think about saying 'no' as an art," she said. "That box is a reminder that we are always searching for more effective, elegant, precise, unhurtful ways to redirect if we need to."

"But if no one is putting suggestions in there," I said, "then how do you know people are thinking that way?" I shook the box. It sounded like there were a few pieces of paper in it. I opened it. There were two.

"I guess I haven't cared enough to wonder about that," she said.

The first small paper was completely filled with perfectly proportioned capital letters. They read: THAT IS A TOTALLY INAPPROPRIATE QUESTION TO ASK ME RIGHT NOW

"Good one," Nautica said, and pulled one of her favorite floggers from the top of the lockers, definitely not where it was supposed to be. "Bitches!" she said, half playful, half angry. She shook out the suede tails and smoothed them. She twirled, then folded it into her purse.

The second paper was less legible, written in a tighter script I associated with old people. It said: *I was able to exit a stupid argument by saying "I won't talk with you about that any more tonight" and then repeating it.*

Nautica made a whistling approval. "That's really good," she said.

"I think this thing could be really useful," I said. "Will you remind the Dommes to put ideas in here? I'll collect them, write them down somewhere. Maybe I'll make a zine."

She leaned half way in and said, "Kiss me."

I did.

"You're right," she said. "It's a good idea. Thank you."

I asked if she was making fun of me.

"I wasn't, but now I want to," she said. Such a babe.

16

RILEY

G riffin dropped me off to meet Riley near the address she'd given me.

The place was through some large hedges, a little house with a tiny sign that said "Coffee and Lemon Tea."

I wondered how I would recognize her, but I didn't need to. The bottom fell off my stomach. She looked more like Carl than I expected. She was reading, with earphones in. I recognized not just her face, but the face she was making. Concentration. Turning the corners of her mouth down just like he did. Suddenly I needed to gasp for air.

A cup of coffee, a cell phone, pens and highlighters out. I approached her table. She looked up when I got close, pulled the earbuds out, and stood.

"Kindred?" she said, and I nodded. She smiled and opened her arms and we hugged. She smelled like a stripper. Wait, I told myself, she just smells like plumeria body spray. She smells like nineteen years old.

We sat.

"You want a coffee or something?" she said.

"Yeah, ok," I said. I walked around a few mismatched tables to the front service counter, which was a taller table in front of the door to the kitchen. I was in a sorority house afternoon tea party from 1960. I ordered a Lemon Tea. A woman in a teddy-bear apron took my three dollars and told me to go ahead and sit down, they'll bring it to me.

Riley struck me as truly uncanny, again, on my second approach.

I sat. "I am really surprised at how much you look like Carl," I said. "I'm sorry if that's not the right thing to say, I just, I don't know. It's really noticeable. For me."

She listened. She didn't seem offended. "I get it," she said. "I had the same experience."

I didn't understand. I didn't look like him at all.

"I met Carl for the first time last year," she said. "I saw him and I was like, holy shit, that's me as an old man."

Oh, right. "He's only sixty!" I said, too defensively, aware that I didn't know his actual age and this could lose me points in the brand-new competition I'd just entered to see who was the best daughter, now that there were two of us.

"Yeah, well, that's an older man," she said.

I told myself I should not compete with this person. We were on the same team. The team of people who cared about what happened to Carl.

"You've only known him a year?"

"We were writing emails and stuff for a few months before we met," she said. "But yeah, I guess I've known him a little over a year."

"How often do you see each other? Do you talk?" I told her I was still dealing with the shock that he'd kept the relationship from me.

She didn't seem nearly as perplexed by his secrecy. They talked a little more often than he and I did. They saw each other about once a month, for coffee or dinner. Riley was studying business. She was determined to get a "good" job. I wondered what that meant for her. She said she was embarrassed to learn that her biological father was homeless, but she felt better after she met him. Her mother had told her her father was dead, then thought better of the lie when Riley was about thirteen. It was shocking to hear that actually he was quite alive and lived in the same city, of course.

I'd been asking her questions nonstop and I had so many more. My lemon tea arrived, and I took a few seconds to sip, breathe, look at Riley's face.

"Carl has told me a little bit about you," she said. "But he also seems really protective of your privacy."

"What has he told you about me?"

"That you live in New York with your partner, I'm sorry I forgot her name. That you work a lot, and that you like to draw."

So he'd told her I was in a relationship with a woman, but hadn't talked to her about sex work. I guessed it made sense, as far as managing someone else's closets could make sense.

"Did you go to college?" she asked me.

"I've taken some classes here and there," I said.

"I'm the first in my family to go," she said. "My mom likes to talk about that a lot."

"That's awesome," I said. "How's it going? Do you like it?"

She lit up a bit. "I love it," she said. "I wish I didn't have to work, too. I'd read all day every day."

I asked her if she had any ideas about where Carl might be. She sighed.

"When I met him, I knew he was going to be one of those people you can't really get attached to," she said. "I mean, that's what my mom said and I think she was right."

"Ok," I said, avoiding the temptation to talk about how

attached I was to him, "so you don't feel like you have any idea where he is, I'm guessing."

"Nope, and I don't expect to see him again, at this point." She was so calm as she said it.

"Why not?" I had acid in my throat.

"It's just been too many days," she said. "If he wanted us to know where he was, he would have found a way by now, that's what I think. He's either dead or he's completely left his life as it was, and he's capable of doing that, right?"

"He wouldn't just leave without telling me," I said. But I couldn't be sure. I realized she wasn't helping me find him. She had wanted to meet me out of her own curiosity.

"He said he was going to try to get you out here to meet me someday, he talked like he could just buy you a plane ticket. He said it might be hard for you to understand and adjust, I guess because he got my mom pregnant when he and your mom were broken up or something?"

I tried to remember being ten. A fuzzy story about Carl being out of town surfaced. I strained for it and couldn't remember more. I wasn't ever going to know what happened. "I thought he might have cheated on my mom," I said. "I guess at this point it doesn't really matter. Here we are."

"Honestly? I didn't expect you to be white," she said. "I don't mean it in a bad way? But he just never mentioned it."

That made me smile. "Carl's my dad," I said, "but my mom was white and so was the guy she fucked to get pregnant. She met Carl after I was born."

Riley looked genuinely surprised for the first time. "I didn't know that," she said. "So I'm his only real daughter? I mean, like biological daughter."

Ouch. "As far as I know," I said. "But now that you're in the picture, I'm wondering how many other kids he may have out there."

"I don't think he has any more," she said. But I didn't know why she'd think that, or how she could know.

We talked about her classes. We talked a little bit about New York and how much she wanted to go there someday, wanted to work there, wanted to live there. Her mom had married an insurance adjuster, lived in the Inland Empire, made crafts and sold them on the internet.

"That's a good hustle," I said.

She pulled back. "I don't like that word," she said.

"Oh, sorry?" I said. "I mean, it sounds like it's working out for her."

"She is doing what she loves," Riley said. "She's making an honest living doing something that makes her happy, and that's what's most important."

I wondered if Riley could get on board with sex work as a form of making an "honest" living. I didn't think so. So I chose to stay in my closet, at least for the moment. "You can't always love your work," I said. "I mean, it's tough to make a living, and we don't all have the same options. Like you and I have had different choices to make, been helped or hurt in different ways."

"If you get your mind right," she said, "You can do anything. I stay positive and apply myself, and see?" she gestured at her pile of study materials. "I'm going to get a good education and then a good job. The only thing standing in your way, if you want to be successful, is you."

I remembered so many conversations I'd had with Carl about this very thing. About what "work" and "labor" and "doing a job" and "success" meant under capitalism and patriarchy and racist regimes. About what a hustle is. Suddenly here was a person I was supposed to see as my sister, a young black woman getting ready to succeed, telling me that I'd sabotaged myself somehow by my negative thinking. I wanted her to graduate from college and do well. But there was something ugly rooted in her ideas too, and I had no way to address it with her. I had a flash of myself at nineteen, getting drunk and scaring people at a party by talking about my dead mom's morphine rambles. Riley was self-confident. I wanted to encourage that, without signing on to some pull-yourself-up-by-your-bootstraps pseudo-spiritual idea about the power of positive thinking, divorced from the realities of the unjust system we were both part of.

I imagined the kinds of things Riley's mom had probably said about Carl's life choices. It was difficult to admit that I'd been ashamed of him, too. Maybe if he'd found a job he could stay in for a few years, keep an apartment, keep a relationship going, we wouldn't be here now. On the other hand, his vulnerability to prejudice and especially the limitations he faced once he had a record were real. It wasn't just that he didn't think positive enough. I couldn't be that simple about it, anymore.

Riley asked me almost no questions. She was happy to talk about her life, her plans, her program, her ambitions. Carl did not raise this person, I kept thinking. She's trying to have something she thinks will be a good life, but she doesn't think like him, doesn't agree with him about what a "good life" is, at all.

And I do. And now I'm lonely and sad and... bored.

We said goodbye after an hour. I told her I'd be in touch, about Carl, before I went home to New York, and that she could look me up if she ever went out there.

I texted Nautica: I don't have anything in common with her. She's very put together and made me feel bad about myself for a minute.

Nautica wrote back: Sorry sweet pea. But that does sound like normal family, ironically. No info from her on Carl?

Nothing helpful, I wrote. Back to the drawing board. It's weird to have a sister.

. . .

I called Griffin and he didn't pick up. I decided to walk for a while, think, make a plan, clear my head.

I felt terrible. My heart could stop at any moment, I thought. I can't keep going like this.

But I kept going. I walked.

I got lost in a never-ending alley built for cars only. In the heat, surrounded by concrete, I did some deep breathing. A red 1980s Honda hatchback pulled up to my left. A large bearded man rolled down his window and leaned over the passenger seat to speak to me. He had a sweet face and a lot of friendship bracelets on.

"Hey, um, would you like some strawberries?" he said.

"Yeah, I guess so," I said.

He got out of the car and opened the back. He had a flat in there, and the berries were startlingly bright and shiny. "Take as much as you want," he said.

"You're trying to get rid of these?" I said.

"Yeah, otherwise they'll get thrown away," he said.

"Right on," I said. I took a carton. "This is enough for me right now," I said. "But good luck."

"You have a great day," he said. He drove to the end of the alley and turned right.

I walked for another ten minutes before the sweat was intolerable. I'd made it to Hope Street, and was in sighting distance of an arts and craft supply. I stopped in the shade of a warehouse to eat some strawberries.

Maybe I could get some beads. I could put them on some fishing line. I could touch each one and think of reasons to live, things I was grateful for. Maybe Riley was on to something with the part about getting your mind right. I kept thinking about her face. And her deep lack of panic.

A twenty-something sexy boy dressed in all white came around the corner of the warehouse. His skin was dark enough to hide all his tattoos--sleeves, neck, chest--until he was up close. He had small, even locks to the base of his neck.

"You look good," I said.

"It's too hot out here today, feel me?" he said. "I hate the sticky shit like this."

"Agreed." I held out my basket. "Want a strawberry?"

He took one. "It's good," he said. Then, "You stay out here?" He would have been surprised if I'd said yes, I thought.

So I said yes.

"Where at?" he said.

"Just a walk from here," I said.

"It's nice here," he said.

He turned a little so we were side-by-side, both looking at the street. "You working right now?" he said, slightly lower, slightly faster, tossed out the side of his mouth without eye contact. Aha.

"Not right now," I said, a little sly.

He started to cover the question with pleasantries, but I cut in, "I'm not offended you asked."

He relaxed back into himself. "I want to be in this whole city," he said, sweeping his hands at the skyline.

"I get that," I said, although I wasn't sure I did. "I'm going to go buy some plastic stuff at that craft store now."

"That's right," he said. "You have a beautiful day."

We said goodbye.

Just after I turned away, he said, "You're sexy as a mother-fucker, though."

I thanked him. "Stay cool," I said, now a little self-conscious.

"Yeah," he said, serious.

"Do you want these strawberries?" I said, turning back,

stretching out, "I can't eat them all and I need to get on with my day."

"Nah," he said. He gestured at his outfit.

"Oh right," I said. We both had higher priorities, for the moment, than not wasting food. And we left each other there, but gently.

I bought some big bright plastic beads and a yard of ribbon for $2.37.

But every thought I had about what I was grateful for got followed immediately by the thought:

It doesn't matter.

Griffin finally called me back, I gave him an address, and while I waited for him, I called Rodney.

"How'd it go with Riley?" he said.

"I don't know," I said. "Honestly, I don't think she's even that worried about Carl."

"I've got an idea," Rodney said. "There's some people gonna be out tonight we might want to talk to. But you'll have to be out on the Row with me, you cool with that?"

"Sure," I said.

"Are you ok with me bringing some stuff and staying *up?*" he said. There was something in his voice.

"Are you asking me if I party?" I said.

"Call it what you want. I'm asking if you're ok with me being up, and if you're gonna want to be with me."

He probably had some speed. It seemed like a smart way to go, considering what might be waiting for us on the Row.

"Yeah, I'm down," I said.

"Right on," he said. "Meet me outside the DAC at nine."

I confirmed, said goodbye, and wondered what Griffin would do with his night.

. . .

247

"Man, I wish I got to do some drugs," he whined, as we headed back to the motel.

"You could probably find some," I said.

"I'm not that brave," he said.

"Good to know yourself," I said. "How was your day?"

"It was awesome! I went to the Scientology Center and took the personality test. I had a wonderful conversation with a woman named Valerie."

"You took the Scientology personality test?"

"Yep."

"Of all the things to do in Los Angeles. Well, get ready for a flood of email."

"You doing ok?" he asked.

I thought about it. Nausea.

"Nope," I said, and breathed through it. "I'm really scared about Carl today. Nobody knows anything."

"When you get home later," Griffin said, "I'll put you in the bathtub and give you a massage and I'll get some food so you don't have to think about it."

"It's cute that you call our little shithole of a room 'home,'" I said. "And I like your plan. I'm going to need all that to recover right. Can you run some errands for me, actually?"

Of course he could. I gave him a list of supplements and groceries I wanted to soften my comedown. "The multivitamin, L-Tyrosine, and 5HTP are the most important," I said. "And the blueberries. I'm really going to need those."

He called me a grandma.

I reminded him that I'd spent a lot of my life in altered states. "Nowadays, if I'm gonna put my body through something, I like to take care of myself," I said. "But I can still put a cane on your ass."

He liked that. We held hands for a few seconds. I felt calmer, better.

"I'm going to text you a couple of video links I watched today," he said. "They're inspiring."

"Inspiring?"

He nodded.

Something in me pulled away from that, from him. The sparkle he had for Scientology. I didn't say anything.

17

FROM 4TH AND TOWNE TO THE SPOT

I got to the DAC office at nine PM. Rodney wasn't there yet. I watched Griffin's videos on my phone. They were insipid, offensive things from the Scientology website. A great way to remind me, at the very least, how much I preferred not being a straight woman. Before I had a chance to text anything to him, Rodney showed up.

He nodded, hugged me, and walked me a few blocks away. He had showered, smelled like Zest and patchouli. We leaned against the concrete wall of a fish shop. The street was lined with tents, carts, crates and people. One of them was singing. One of them was walking up the block, screaming at himself.

Rodney did a carefully concealed dealer handshake with someone much older than us both. Their wrinkles were age-spotted and their hands were curled with arthritis. They smelled so strongly, of urine, of something more sour too, my eyes threatened to water.

"Break time," Rodney said to them.

They nodded, and started shuffling off.

Rodney held up a tiny drug-bag to the light. A clouded

chunk, a thin pile of dust, probably enough to keep us both up for the night and a little more for Rodney.

"You got something we can cut lines on?" he asked me.

I set my pack down on the ground and started rummaging. I found something.

"Obviously, this glossy black junk mail from the credit card company was made for drugs," I said, and held it up.

"Well, you *are* entitled to incredible savings," he said, and took it.

He was careful but nimble, someone who knows how. I let him cut the lines. He didn't ask me anything about my habits or history. He trimmed a clean straw with his nail scissors, and I knew I could never thank him for that courtesy aloud. So I deferred the first line, which he offered like a host, and he nodded, and took it, the esteemed lord of our dirty little corner.

My turn. The fucking shitty burn and tears on one side. That acrid drip in the throat. The cobwebs cleared from my brain and peripheral vision and I bowed slightly to Rodney. We took turns once more, and then he checked in.

"You good?"

"I'm good," I said. I wanted more, but that is the least reliable measure of whether a person should continue ingesting methamphetamine. I could feel the energy without the nasty edge. I was good.

"I'm going one more," he said.

I nodded of course, whatever you want to do.

"Okay," I said. "I'll go one very small one more." So I did.

He folded the baggie into the black card stock and slid it into his inside jacket pocket. He rearranged his backpack, tightened a strap. "I'm carrying this for the pigs," he said. "If you want it at any time you can have it. Understand?"

"Sure," I said. "Thank you."

He smiled at me. "Relax your face." I did, by smiling back

like I meant it. He laughed once, a true and single "Ha!" and I felt ready to go.

"Let's go dancing," Rodney said.

"Let's," I said. "If we do nothing else with our lives, let us please begin this evening by dancing."

He rolled his eyes a little and gestured up the block, away from Skid Row. "It's that way," he said.

"Lead on," I said.

So we walked up Towne, took a few turns, and ended up at a small black-light bar with both a rainbow and a Mexican flag out front. The music had a thick fast bass and enough melody to make dancing possible, but the electronic sound effects must have grated on Rodney. I caught him wincing and called him old as we found space at the bar. It was musty, like the mopwater from last night's closing was still in the air. The music was absurdly loud and felt great to my thumping insides.

I bought us two Tecates and looked for a pair of seats somewhere. The lights flashed and I squinted to see past the dance floor. There was a back patio.

"Let's head out there?" I said, close to Rodney's ear. His hair tickled my face.

"Lead on," he said. I couldn't tell if he was repeating me unconsciously or to make fun of me. Luckily, I was high and I did not care at all.

On the back patio, people smoked cigarettes and laughed and talked in a rolling cadence of Spanish and English.

"The owners love us," he said. "They let us meet during the day back here. It's where we planned our last demo at the stadium negotiation meeting."

The stadium. I wanted to ask, and to find out who he meant by "us," but someone hollered "Rodney!" in a sing-song voice and he turned to look. She was tall, and wearing an enormous, perfectly coiffed blonde wig styled to look like Marilyn Monroe of the *Seven Year Itch*. Her blue eyeshadow rose up to her black brows. Ten bright red polished nails on bejeweled brown hands holding her waist. She was wearing a flowing white gown. "Honey! It's *so* good to see you," she said. She held out her hand and Rodney picked it up and kissed it. Then he turned to me.

"Kindred, this is my very good friend Frida Mall," he said.

I held out my hand for a shake and bowed a little. Her eyes were ringed with heavy liner. She smiled wide. "Great to meet you," I said to her.

"Ooh que linda," she said. "You got those thin shoulder bones, so nice."

"This is Carl Baker's girl," Rodney said, and Frida's eyes flickered. Surprise?

"Welcome baby," she said to me. "Your dad is a good man," she said. "And a fine one, too," she laughed.

"He's missing," I said.

Now she was openly surprised. "No baby," she said. "Really? Oh no no no." She gasped and shook her head. "That man better not be wasting hisself in the gutter, girl, or I will be furiosa, I will whip his motherfucking ass from here to Miami. I'm sorry," she put her hand on my arm, "to speak like that." She fanned herself. "I get mad when I worry, honey, it's just me."

"If he's not dead I'm ready to kill him," I said.

"He was sober last time I saw him," Rodney said, and although it seemed like a non sequitur, both Frida and I acknowledged it with nods. Then Rodney said, "You haven't heard anything from him, Frida?"

"No my love, I have *not* heard from Carl," she said. "You know, I haven't heard from any of your people for a long time. When's the next time I get to give a speech to all the gringos in those big leather chairs? You know they tried to sue us here saying we ain't had the right license? Then we paid and now we're fine. They so crooked, papa," she took a breath, "when do we tell them?"

"Next week," Rodney said. "We need you at the City Council meeting. I'll call you, ok?"

Frida tugged a little on her straps and nodded. "I'll be there honey, in my serious daytime dress." She shook her shoulder a little.

Rodney kissed her cheek and she made a demure smile. "You go on early tonight?" he said, looking at his watch. I drank some beer.

"As a matter of fact, I do, lucky for you bitches," she said, and winked at me. "If you see Carl tell him he better come see me?" Then she gave Rodney an extra beat of eye contact, with her hands enfolding his, and left us. I wished Frida was my friend too.

Rodney was smiling. His eyes got sweetly scrunched. He drank from his Tecate and looked around.

"Wait a second," I said. "You two?"

"She's a good friend," he said. "Let's dance."

"Rodney!" I was yelling but he was in front of me, the rainbow lights bouncing in his gray locks.

He refused any questions by entering a state of ecstatic dancing with his eyes closed. We each moved in rhythm on the dance floor for a few minutes to the overwhelmingly loud house beats and brass. Rodney put his hands up over his head, clapped occasionally, and did some step-touch move, or half a country line dance. Then the sound went off, the lights went up on the floor, and the first chords of Donna Summer's "Mac-Arthur Park" shocked my system in a wonderful new way.

Frida had impeccable control of her face, and she was able to breathe at all the right times, too. She danced lightly in her heels and shook her hips fast, surprisingly fast. I leaned over to Rodney and said into his ear, "I see why we came here."

"We got a few more places to try," he said back, "but we are going to watch her set first."

"She's awesome," I said.

He nodded.

Her face was artfully tortured, filled with exquisite anguish, while she lip-synched:

MacArthur Park is melting in the dark
All the sweet green icing flowing down
Someone left the cake out in the rain
I don't think that I can take it
'Cuz it took so long to make it
And I'll never have that recipe again!
Oh NOOOOO!

Frida broke into the higher-tempo disco section of the song, pointed in the air, and tipped a guy's cowboy hat off his head with a flick at his neck. She twirled and landed on Donna Summer's high note. I tipped her $5 even though I had planned to use it for alcohol that night.

"This song is insane," I said in his ear.

He grinned.

We watched her perform for another song, and then when the next queen came out Rodney caught my eye. He nodded at the door. I picked up my pack. We left.

"Strike one," he said on the street.

"What do we learn by this, though," I said. "We learn that Frida doesn't know where he is. Are they close? Is there a particular reason you expected her to know something and hadn't asked her yet?"

"She's tough to get in touch with," Rodney said. "So I knew I'd have to come down when she was working. But sometimes he's stayed at her place, when she had one up on the other side of the freeway, in Boyle Heights."

"Were they lovers?" I said. "Were you two lovers? Were you and Carl lovers?"

Rodney smiled. He pointed me toward a crosswalk. We were headed back into Skid Row.

"You know we didn't stay down here all the time, right?" Rodney said. "We both had places we stayed at here and there, sometimes together."

"That is not an answer to any of my questions." I said.

"Miss Kindred," he said, "Focus. I'm taking you to everyone I haven't hit up yet. After tonight, I'm done with my theories. I don't know what happened to him. And I'm not going to tell you all his business, at least not now. So stay with me, ok?"

"You haven't known him that long," I said. "But you act like you know him better than anyone."

"I know the Carl of last week better than anyone," he said. "Young people think you have to know someone a long time to know them well. The more you know yourself, the faster other people can know you. It's a gift of age."

It worked on me, softened something inside. I agreed I would ask no more intrusive tangential questions. "I keep feeling like I *don't* know him," I said. "It hurts my heart."

"Of course," Rodney said, "that's natural. But you do know him, you've loved him your whole life, and you know a piece of him none of the rest of us ever will."

He hugged me, and some tears came, and then I remembered where we were and pulled back.

"I like imagining you guys being happy together sometimes," I said.

Rodney patted me on the shoulder, just lightly. "Thank you," he said. "We were, sometimes. Happy as motherfuckers and free as men."

He lit up a cigarette. I had no idea he smoked. Maybe he was one of those people who only smoked cigarettes when he did other drugs.

"I will tell you that your dad and I aren't lovers," he said. He sucked in and blew the smoke along a breeze away from us.

"Ok," I said.

"I'm bisexual," he said, looking out into the street. "I would have. We had a talk. That man likes pussy."

"Hey that's great, ok," I said, hands up. "Got it. Thank you."

"I don't know about him and Frida," he said. "Maybe she was his special queer, you know? I don't know. I know they've been close in the past. That he stayed with her at her place sometimes. They talked politics a lot and laughed together. They'd read a lot of the same books. Made each other feel good in a family way. Doesn't always mean fucking. Feel me?"

I nodded. Gestured for his cigarette. Took the third and second-to last drags off it and handed it back for him to finish.

"Where to?" I said.

"We're gonna walk and see who's out," he said. "Couple more cats who might have seen him after me."

We walked back toward the DAC office. Outside it, Rodney said, "We call this block Beverly Hills."

"It's the nice part?" I said, looking at the barbed wire. The person a few feet away fumbling with something unrecognizable in their hand. An old shoe? Couldn't tell. "Carl always made fun of people who bought jeans with holes in them," I said.

Rodney smiled, "Yep, me too."

"Remind me how you met?" I said. "At the DAC?"

"Carl sat next to me out on the block, I was hungover as shit, and he told me he'd seen me out there without a book too often."

"Oh my god," I laughed. We were walking south.

"He gave me Alice in Wonderland," Rodney continued, waving at someone down the street, "and it was like an old friend had written me a letter reminding me of all the things I care about in this world."

"Shut up," I said. He couldn't be serious. But then he looked at me and I knew he was.

We got to a crosswalk. The light was red. I didn't look that far to the side because my neck hurt. I started into the street. Rodney grabbed at my back and yanked me back onto the sidewalk. I flipped around, grabbed his wrist, right fist ready, and then dropped them both, just as fast.

"I'm sorry," he said. He held kept his palms up, at his sides. Then his eyes slid to the side and he nodded over there. "That's a pig over there in his plainclothes who makes his whole life giving jaywalking tickets."

I turned, felt my adrenaline pushing still, and saw the black Crown Vic. "Shit," I said. "Thanks."

"People get tickets for jaywalking, sleeping on the sidewalk, then when they don't show up to their court dates, they get bench warrants." He was educating. He really was Carl's friend.

"And it's hard for people to get to court."

"Yep. Some are already on probation. It's hard to keep a calendar out here, to keep track of your nice shirt, to walk back into a building where you may have been traumatized before, and there's always something happening right in front of you on Skid Row that is the most urgent thing, needs attention, right now. Even if you aren't getting high."

"Then they get rounded up at night?"

"Or at five or six in the morning." The light changed. We crossed. "You do a martial art or something?" Rodney shook his wrist out in mock pain.

"Carl taught me some stuff when I was a kid," I said. "I've taken some self-defense classes. It's been useful more than once. That time I was just jumpy." On the other side of the street was a liquor store. I thought maybe we should get some juice. I suggested it. Rodney said he'd stand outside and wait for me. I got us two Vitamin Waters. Get some sugar in us since we probably weren't going to eat much tonight. There were big signs all over the store advertising their ability to accept EBT, Food Stamps, WIC. No grocery stores for miles, but Skid Row was well stocked with liquor and junk food. Outside, I said "I want to know about Alice in Wonderland. Why you loved it so much."

The sidewalk had flecks of silvery reflection and occasional black mounds of chewing gum-turned tar. It was slightly sticky under my boots. It wasn't the regular smell of a city that wrapped us up, it was the smell of people living outside, sour and heavy and musky-sweet and uncomfortably familiar.

"I followed a white rabbit down a hole and had wild visions too," he said. "And I spent a lot of my life getting lost and finding my way alone."

Me too, I thought. A memory ripped through me, quick and shocking: Mom in an orange button-up work shirt after she'd vomited, cleaned herself, and burned incense in the bathroom, emerging and glancing at me, looking away, saying, "I'm okay honey, I feel better now," with a face that said she felt worse. Sick mom, finding her way alone.

I realized I was staring at people, but I did not feel I could stop. I started nodding hello to those who made eye contact. A man in shorts, nice athletic socks pulled up to his knees, and an oversized polo shirt artfully hanging just over his belt, gestured at me to break ties with Rodney and come join him. But he seemed unsurprised when I got steely-eyed instead.

We had entered the fray. It was loud. Hundreds of people

were out on the street talking, greeting each other, catching up, playing games, playing drums, yelling at imagined opponents, and most were watching me as carefully as I was watching them. Someone near us was hollering, continuously. Rodney patted his pockets and found his cigarettes. A woman with a T-shirt wrapped around her head hailed him and he handed her one, without a conversation, and they moved on from the moment with respectful nods exchanged.

I wanted to ask. I decided to stop externalizing every question. I remembered that this drug made me have laser-like focus, but I had to direct it. Carl, I told myself. Focus on finding Carl. Listen and learn. I drank some Vitamin Water and felt the tightness in my jaw. My heart was pounding but I felt calm.

"Carl and I stayed over here on Towne together," Rodney pointed down the street to our left. It was lined with small, tidy camps. A few tents, a few forts built from large gray blankets, tarps, and plastic crates. An older woman in a graying sleeveless T-shirt and jeans called me baby and asked for money. She was sitting on an egg crate, wrapping her hair into curlers.

Rodney shook his head, just slightly, still smiling, and we stopped walking. He addressed her.

"Barbara, this is Carl's daughter. She's visiting us from New York City, believe that? Kindred, this is Barbara."

Barbara straightened her back, gave me serious eyes, and then narrowed them. Her dark brown skin was taught and shiny over her round cheeks. She didn't stop twisting her hair.

"You ain't his," she said.

"Not by blood," I said, "but he raised me."

"Where's your mama?"

"She died," I said.

Barbara's eyes opened wider. She nodded. "Where's Carl?"

I told her I didn't know. That I was here to try and find out. I asked if she'd heard from him. She hadn't.

"He owes me three dollars," she said. She clipped in a curler and wiped her hands on her pants.

I gave her three crumpled dollars from the side pocket of my bag. She smoothed them out, folded them, and tucked them into her bra strap, next to what looked like an old scar from a haphazard cigarette burn.

"Thank you baby," Barbara said. "What's your name again?"

"Kindred." I held my hand out, and she shook it.

"You have such nice hands!" she said, suddenly, smiling wide, and I felt Rodney's light touch on the small of my back.

I thanked her, said I needed to keep on for now, but I'd see her again soon. It felt like she may not let go of my hand. But she did.

Rodney gestured about fifty feet from where we stood to another section of the block. "Barbara's the last on this side of the street who crosses the line here," he pointed at the intersection.

"That's right," she said. She put a hand on her hip and we all watched a cop car cruise through. People out on the block mostly ignored them, but there was a nearly imperceptible rigidity that took over a few of our bodies until the car had turned another corner. "I stay with the junkies on that side, but I'm still welcome on the straight side," Barbara said.

"I'm gonna take Kindred to see one of Carl's old spots," Rodney told her.

"That's nice," she said. Then to me, "I hope he ain't dead too, honey. I like him. I think he's a good person."

"Me too," I said.

We moved away from Barbara, who sat where we left her, watching us.

We approached the quieter end of the block. The people thinned out some, but we were headed to a more cohesive camp, a series of well-organized temporary homes using plywood, tarps, ropes, and chairs in addition to the tents, in a cluster on Towne. As soon as we got there Rodney was giving high-fives and hugs and I was introduced to a small crowd of men, one of them as white as me and definitely the youngest.

"My man," Rodney said to him, and they gave an extended hug.

"How you been, Pops?" the guy said.

"Call me Pops again and I'll pop you one good, boy!" Rodney said, smiling. That was something Carl said. Ache. "Say hi to my friend Kindred, Jay."

We shook hands, and he called me "Miss Kindred." His greasy curls seemed more Hollywood than Skid Row. My mother's voice in my head called him cute-as-a-button.

Rodney relaxed a little, stretched his back, sat on an upturned egg crate, and twisted his hair. The crate was in front of a large orange tent, with a blue tarp thrown overtop and secured by zip ties.

"Get off my porch," someone growled from inside the tent.

"Fuck you, Compton," Rodney said good-naturedly. He gestured for me to sit on the crate next to him. "You've got company here."

The tent rustled and I caught a waft of the unmistakable smell of grown man mixed with some rancid shoes. The zipper came undone. The top half of Compton's face was shadowed, the bottom half a yellow-tooth grin in an unruly salt-and-pepper beard. "Rod-man!" he said. "You came to check on the poor folks today?" He came all the way out of the tent.

"Captain," Rodney said, "This is Kindred, Carl's girl. She's in from New York looking for him."

"Cap'n Compton," the man said to me, with a tip of an imagined hat. "Pleased."

I bowed slightly. "The pleasure is all mine, Captain," I said.

"Carl's girl, eh? Call me Compton," he said. "It's what my friends call me. Carl said you're a lesbian?"

"Sure," I said, "we'll go with that." Rodney shook his head and smiled a little at his shoes.

"Well goddamn! You're the first lesbian to visit me in my kingdom here," Compton said. "Not the first *lady*, not the last one neither," he jabbed Rodney in the ribs, "but I got some questions for you!"

"Alright old man," Rodney said. "Kindred gets to ask the questions. She's here to figure out what's going on with Carl." Compton and Rodney's eyes connected and some kind of message seemed to be granted between them.

"Well, then." Compton said, and straightened up just slightly. He gestured for me to sit on his other crate. I sat. "Miss Kindred looking for Carl. His place used to be right here," he pointed to his left, where a twin mattress, blankets tucked in the corners, on a carefully stacked pile of cardboard, was shaded by a rainbow-paneled umbrella.

"Now that's my spot," Jay said.

Compton coughed, a long hacking wet cough, and spit into a small cup he pulled from his pocket. The cup went behind his feet. "Me, Rod, and Carl used to run this block like a program, feel me? No church meeting to sit through, no contract to sign."

"Run it like what kind of a program?" I asked.

Rodney explained that they'd built a community on that block, the three of them, along with some other guys, who wanted to have some stability but didn't want to keep getting their hands slapped by the Mission.

"At the Mission you can't come in late, you can't get high, you can't see a woman, you can't make no money," Compton recited. "You got to do everything they say or they throw the book at you in there."

"The Bible?" I said. "Or the law books?"

"Yes ma'am," Compton said. Then he whistled softly.

I shifted my weight on the crate to avoid getting red lattice dents on my thighs. Even though no one was going to see them.

What Compton knew about Carl's disappearance was sketchy. He'd spent less time with him than Rodney recently. What Compton had were narratives about Carl's life on Towne that I'd never heard. How he organized among the people he stayed with, read books with them, shared his food, brought people in to Sadie's office when they had a formal complaint to file with the city or the police, and how he slept in his tent just past the time when the "skirts" usually started bothering people. Compton said Carl knew how to handle them.

"He had the mouth. He told them they'd watch his morning routine or take him to jail for brushing his teeth and combing his hair in public." He slapped a thigh. "Man, that was some *shit!*" Coughing, laughing, he spit in his cup, hid it again, and then patted himself for cigarettes.

"He always told them to hang on until he got dressed in his tent," Rodney said. "He never let the skirts get in his head. 'I'm a man,' he'd say, 'you wait for me to answer my door before you recite the law to me.'"

"So why did he move to the other block?" I said.

They didn't answer me.

"He's fucking missing," I said. "The cops took his stuff. I'm his daughter. If you know something. Please."

Compton met my gaze. "Miss Kindred, I respect that you're down here looking for your family. No one came after me when I fell out."

"Just Kindred, no Miss," I said. "What do you think happened to him?"

"Did you ask Miss Frida Mall?"

"We just saw her, she didn't know he was gone."

"And he ain't at Twin Towers? Ain't turned up in the hospital?"

I shook my head.

"Ma'am if it were any other cat? I'd say he dead."

"How."

"Don't know. You can die a hundred ways out here. Carl never ghosted without letting someone know what his plan was."

"God*damn* it," I said. The tears came back, all hot and pressing in my throat.

Rodney pulled a knotted bandana from a pocket. "You gotta cry about it, that's alright," he said. He handed it to me. It smelled clean. I wiped my eyes and nose. Compton nodded. He and Rodney shared a cigarette with me. We didn't talk for a minute.

"Carl had beef all over this place," Compton said. "Shit, he thought Skid Row should strap up and defend ourselves by any means necessary. He helped people get theirselves fed, but he didn't help them the way the charities like to do it. He made them political, saw every meal as a chance to talk about injustice. Some people down here thought he was just a troublemaker, made everything harder on us when it's already hard. He coulda been snatched by the police just as easy as stabbed by an old homie out on the Row, understand?"

"So some people are glad he's gone," I said.

"Some people, yes indeed. He upset the balance."

"You call this balanced?" I said, gesturing to the street.

Rodney put his hand on my arm. "Carl was working against the City, the Edelweiss people, and the NFL. He was a burr in their ass. You need to be patient to get info down here," he said. "Shit, I'm in danger being seen with you."

"Why?" I became aware of Jay, who could hear everything

we were saying, but was busily tidying up his spot just a few feet away.

"I don't walk around with a white woman down here unless she's doing good work in the community. You draw suspicion because no one knows you. It's not good attention."

"Down here on the Row, it's *different*," Compton said.

"You think I should stop looking?" I said to Compton.

"Your daddy always had courage," I heard him use the past tense and it cut my heart. "And according to Captain Compton, that's one of the best things you can say about a man."

I thanked him, stood, and signaled to Rodney that it was time to move on.

We got half a block before Jay caught up to us.

"Miss Kindred I hate to interrupt you but I got a question?" he said.

I told him, just Kindred, no Miss.

"Does the stadium plan have anything to do with the power washes they been doing down here?"

Rodney nodded to Jay while I said I didn't know what he was talking about. "It does," Rodney said.

"What's a power wash?" I asked. Jay gave me a confused look. He assumed I knew things I didn't, because I was Carl's daughter, maybe.

"There's no public restroom facilities here," Rodney said to me. "They don't pick up the trash, either. We try to take care of our own streets, but without facilities? People get kicked out of the McDonalds, the public library, the CVS. They have nowhere to go. People urinate and defecate on the sidewalks and in the park. The City and the BID uses the skirts to roust people from their camps. Then the City come in and power wash the streets, and we all gotta go or the LAPD confiscate our property and arrest us. Usually, once they've washed, we can set up our camps again. But recently they've been telling us we can't set up on the same blocks, making us move on or threatening to arrest. The space we've got to set up camps in is shrinking."

"And that's because of the stadium plan?" I said.

"They won't say so," said Rodney. "But it's pretty clear when you look at a map, which side of the Row is getting cleaned up the fastest."

Jay said he needed to head back. He thanked Rodney.

"Come over to the DAC on Wednesday at nine AM," Rodney said to him. "We're going to go all together to the City Council Meeting and speak against the stadium."

Jay said he might. We said goodbye.

It was nearly one AM. "We've got one more stop," Rodney said. "This one we gonna have to take a bus for."

We rode an empty bus up into the hills near the 110 Freeway. We got off on a residential street and walked toward an overpass. Rodney told me I needed to follow in single file. We climbed up the side of a hill and came out on top of a tunnel, crossed over the concrete and came upon a tall black tarp hanging all the way to the ground. I couldn't see where it was attached at the top, but it extended out a few feet to trees on either side. It was hung so that there was a flap in the middle, a door.

"Welcome to The Spot," Rodney said. "Home of the Lost Boys of Avenue 26." We went through the opening in the black tarp.

The Spot was a surprisingly large, layered tent made of tarps. The outer layer was black and dusty. The second layer was bright blue, and clean. We were inside, but still standing on the dirt.

"This is the vestibule," Rodney said. He held one end of the blue tarp open like a curtain and I went in ahead of him.

I was inside a large round, open air room made of tarps and

rugs. The whole thing seemed to be propped up by one large pole, like a circus tent. The pole had a round table mounted on it, covered in things like flashlights, batteries, and utility knives. The pole entered the dirt through a hole in an enormous rug with an animal print. Maybe buffalo. Legs stretched out, running. I stepped onto the rug. A large couch sat to my right, with the tarp tucked in behind it. To my left was a sea of city lights and the concrete edges of the tunnel. The view was unreal. Los Angeles opening her coat, miles of sparkling shapes in my eyes.

"Come in! Come in!" said a voice, urgent and cheerful, from farther inside the home. I walked carefully through.

Just on the other side of the rug and around a corner, a man was cooking on a small stove. His kitchen was lit with a propane camping lamp. He looked about sixty. His thick gray hair was combed back. He had enormous hands and a bulbous, pocked nose. His body was soft and his elbows were sharp. He wore a black T-shirt and long blue basketball shorts. Soccer sandals. His kitchen set up leaned on the concrete wall of the tunnel with the vast city view to his right.

"This place is gorgeous!" I said. "And no neighbors!"

"We've got them," he said. "Tweakers who hang out in the park on the other side of this hill. They know better than to come over this side, though."

I felt a spark of self-protection since I was high on the same shit he was insulting. He wiped his hands on his pants and held one out for me to shake.

"I'm Michel," he said. "It's not Michelle, but you can say it that way if you're too American to say anything else."

"Pleased to meet you, Michel," I said, and we shook. "I'm Kindred. What are you making?"

"Stir fry. Hungry?"

Of course not, but I didn't want to put him out. "I'll try it," I said, which sounded wrong as I said it.

"Have a look around," he said.

Rodney stepped in front of me. He and Michel thumped each other's back in a loving, masculine hug. They called each other Big Man and Baby Boy, and Rodney sniffed and approved of the food. Michel smiled out at the city and then to me. "Go!" he said. "Let Rodney give you a tour."

I saw the showers, the latrine, the dishwashing system, the platforms for sleeping. I learned that Michel had been living at the Spot for a year and a half.

"And no cops come out here?"

"They haven't yet," Rodney said. "You can't see the place from the freeway, and the boys don't bother anybody, but, we'll see how long it lasts. Someone's gonna want to build something here sometime."

About fifteen feet from the pole-room, Rodney and I sat on another couch facing the city. Someone had rigged a tarp behind and above the couch.

"This is a real nice cabana," I said. The last cabana I'd sat in was with Jason, in Hawai'i. It had cost him thousands of dollars to get that particular view of the ocean, with drinks and food that would please him.

Now, I had a view of Los Angeles for free. Michel joined us, and brought three bowls of steaming tofu stir fry. It smelled hearty, like garlic and butter.

"So you're looking for Carl," he said. He handed me a fork. I thanked him. He nodded and sat. He took a deep breath, a bite, and chewed slowly. He scanned the cityscape and then met my eyes. "You know I'm sorry, girl."

"For what."

"For your worry."

"Oh, thanks." I acknowledged that the past week had been

tough.

Then there was a rustle of the tarp and someone called out from inside the pole-room. "Yo! Where's a bitch with my money!"

Michel hollered back, "Watch your mouth, kid! We have company!"

A young person with a strut appeared. Black hoodie over black jeans. Hood came off. They had short dirty blonde hair, narrow brown eyes. A small jaw, pert mouth. "Aw my bad," they said. "'Sup," they said to me. They stood square with hands in pants pockets. "Angel," they said.

"Kindred," I said.

"Dope," they said. They nodded at Rodney. Rodney nodded back. "Cool, well, I'll see y'alls later then," Angel said, and went to get a bowl of Michel's stir fry.

Rodney said to Michel, "Tell her about how you got this place, man, she needs to hear that story!"

Michel leaned back and stretched a bit. "Where do I start? Would you believe in my country I had a maid?"

"Sure," I said. "Things change fast."

Michel told me he'd immigrated from Colombia with his wife. "My wife got really sick," he said. "I couldn't keep up with all the paperwork for her and then for citizenship and then to keep my architect's license. I lost my job. We got evicted. She went into the hospital, and she died there. I went crazy, man, I went off. I was drunk and high and, well, that was that."

"Shit," I said.

"Shit is right," he said. "But now, I've got this view, I've got my sobriety." He ate. I ate. Rodney was finished with his bowl. Michel said he'd been staying in an SRO hotel on the Row when someone told him there was a sweet camp spot, away from the madness, up in the hills. When he got here the people who had been staying here were packing up and getting ready to move on to Arizona. "They were old hippies, man," Michel laughed. "They wanted to smoke weed and talk to me about who all their bird friends were around here. I mean real birds, owls and ravens and shit they'd named. But they'd made a real nice camp. They did that kitchen set up so that all the gray water drains down the mountainside. It was a good change for me to have a place I could take care of. I like it here, and there's always some lost boys who need to live away from the Row."

I asked if Carl had ever lived here.

Michel said no, but he'd come to visit for a quiet night or two, cook some meals, read and write, before going back down to the city.

"Rod," Michel said, "did I tell you I got that job at the market downtown?"

"Naw," Rodney said. "Right on, brother."

"So you live in New York?" Michel said to me.

I affirmed it.

"Yeah? How is it out there? I always wanted to go there. See the snow."

"The snow is pretty if you catch it at the right time," I said. I ate another bite.

Michel and Rodney looked at each other, and Rodney made a gesture I didn't quite read. Michel nodded.

"I've got something to show you," Michel said. He took his bowl with him, kept eating. He went into the sleeping area.

"What did you just say to him?" I asked Rodney.

"Nothing," Rodney said.

I gave him an angry face.

He smiled. "All I said was, 'go ahead.'"

Michel came back with a mid-size cardboard box, his bowl balanced on top. It looked heavy. He set the cargo carefully at my feet and took his dinner back.

"That's some of Carl's shit," he said.

I wanted to ask why Michel had it, of course.

Rodney opened it. "Your dad is always writing," he said. "I think he keeps his notebooks up here with Michel so they'll stay a little safer than on the Row."

"And because he knows I don't snoop," said Michel, to Rodney.

The box was full of books.

Half of them were from Carl's library, artifacts from my own childhood. My heart clenched. His copies of *The Making of Black Revolutionaries*, *Revolutionary Suicide*, *The Dispossessed*, and *The Ugly American* sat on top. In the other half of the box were notebooks, probably filled with his writing. The clenching got more painful.

"You think I should read these," I said to Rodney.

"I do," he said. "I'm sick of waiting for this motherfucker to tell us where he's at."

"Michel?" I asked.

He held his hands out, palms up. "On the one side," he said, raising one hand, "you got a lot of intel here." Then he switched, raising the other hand, "On the other side, you may not want to see what ain't meant for you. There's no guarantee it'll help you find him, and that box *is* the man's private property."

"It is," I said. "I'm going to take it with me and think on it."

"Respect," Michel said, and bowed his head a bit to me.

We smoked a joint and talked for hours. The sunrise edged in, the drugs wore off. I finally got tired and Michel covered me with a sleeping bag.

Griffin texted. What time did I think I'd be back?

I told him a few more hours probably.

I want to do something, he said. I'm stir crazy.

I told him to do whatever he wanted.

. . .

I woke up hot, and it was very bright. My body ached and I wanted a shower. Rodney and Michel were standing inside the Spot's pole-room to my left, talking quietly, sounding serious. I strained but I couldn't hear them.

I got up and they stopped talking. I walked to them, carrying the sleeping bag in front of me.

"Just leave it on the couch," Michel said to me.

So I did. "Can we go?" I said to Rodney.

"Of course," he said. He and Michel hugged and thumped and eye-gazed again.

"Your box is in the vestibule," Michel said, and winked at me. Did he know both those words pertained to vaginas? Was that why he winked? I wasn't sure.

I thanked him for dinner and for being a good friend to Carl and he opened his arms for a hug. He reminded me of a pterodactyl, we squeezed each other, and I wondered where his former maid was today, and if she'd forgiven him, and if he and Angel were lovers.

I went through the black tarp and found the box. Michel had written "TAKE ME WITH YOU" in black Sharpie across the top flap and put new tape on it for us.

"I'll get that," Rodney said.

I let him. We were quiet on the bus. I called Griffin and asked him to pick me up at the DAC office. Rodney and I hugged goodbye outside the front door.

"I'm sorry," he said. "I wish we'd gotten more answers."

"I'm grateful you took me through that night," I said. The words were anemic, the feeling overwhelming.

"See you soon," he said.

Griffin shuffled awkwardly, a few feet away at the car.

"See you soon," I said. Pressure built up behind my throat,

so much I wanted to say or ask Rodney. But it wasn't the time. I swallowed it back and he turned from us and headed towards Towne. I wondered who he'd run into, what he'd do today, how and where he'd find some rest.

I drove the five minutes to the motel. Griffin was talking and I barely heard him. He sounded happy. The box was like a third person in the back of the car. When I opened the door to our room, I was surprised by how fast Griffin had taken over. His stuff was thrown everywhere. The room smelled like a boy.

"Yay!" he said, and fell onto the bed. The TV had been on while we were gone. Something starring Meryl Streep, with long hair looking fearful. Griffin came over and hugged me too hard and fast over the box I carried and then bounded backward. "I stayed home waiting for you! I didn't really want to go out."

"You didn't?" I said. I set the box on the floor next to my bed.

"No," he said. "Are you glad I waited for you?"

"Sure," I said, "that was nice."

"Are you depressed?" he said. "You seem kind of out of it."

"I'm tired," I said. "I'm really tired. It's time for me to rest and take all those supplements you got me."

He sat on the bed and put his hands in his lap. "Okay," he said. "Can I rub your feet?"

I told him he could after I took a shower. In the shower, I cried some more, thinking about the last time I talked to Carl and feeling it was the last time I would ever talk to him.

Griffin did a nice job on my feet, strong but tender, and I let him lick and kiss them a bit as a reward.

"Let me sleep," I said.

He cuddled in.

"Let me sleep without getting crushed," I said.

He scooted two inches away from me. I patted him. Then I

knocked out.

Carl's Notebook

Self Discipline is Key

Ask yourself questions about your habits. See if what you say
you do with your time is what you actually do with your time.
To do this honestly takes courage, because the answer you find
will be: you lie to yourself and everyone else about what you do
with your time. The real answer for you to find is: how much
lying? And about what to whom most often?

Day 1

6:00 AM Wake up, pack up, talk to crew

7:00 AM Food line, read paper

8:00 AM Food line, talk to brother William

9:00 AM Breakfast, talk to Rod about campaign

10:00 AM

Forms of revenge should be tailored to their target. For some,
destruction is called for. For others, a clear and consistent with-
drawal of attention is the worst-feeling thing you can do to
them.

Know when your friends and lovers are facing fears and help
them do it.

Last night I got sick of hearing the cats make fun of Marble
Man. I went over and told them fuck you assholes, I'm going to
play a game of his imaginary marbles with him. So I sat down,
and I told him, Marble Man, I'm here to play a game with you.
He grunted and told me to go ahead. I tried to remember the
rules to marbles. I shot an imaginary marble at his imaginary
circle. We hadn't played five minutes before he pulled out a

knife, held it six inches from my face, and accused me of cheating. How do you cheat at imaginary marbles, I said. But of course that's the wrong question. You can't win at it either. I told him thanks for the game, don't spread rumors about me. He put his knife away. I left him alone, and he kept playing his imaginary game. I still think it's wrong to make fun of the man the way the cats do down there when they're feeling mean and sick of the bullshit. But now I know for sure that Marble Man is no joke.

Length of a written work is not directly related to depth or potential impact. History teaches us that millions have died on behalf of slogans.

When trust is suffering or nonexistent, predict yourself, and then follow through. Make eight hundred tiny plans. Accomplish them. Proceed.

A Binge is an acknowledgment that health is mostly mythology and death is real. A Binge stops short of suicide because it hopes for life after craving.
Bingeing to feel good is not the same as creating a life where feeling good matters, but they can feel the same, while you're bingeing.

Big Jack says: Every four years the wolves and the foxes argue about who gonna guard the henhouse. I don't know who gonna win the fight this time, but I do know one thing. The hens are fucked.

Anastasia asked me to play the harmonica. Then she said, "If I don't like your music, we will not have a good time fucking." But she liked it. She took her hand off her hip and clapped.

18

IN THE SHADOW OF THE STADIUM

I slept until three PM. I woke up a little crunchy, but not too bad feeling. Griffin had gone to a corner store and brought back cheap donuts and burnt coffee that tasted like heaven.

"What's your plan today?" he asked with a note of urgency.

"You got something to do?"

"Well," his eyes darted. "I was hoping to go to this free workshop at the Scientology Center."

My mouth was full of cinnamon powder donut love joy and I refrained from spitting. I swallowed calmly instead.

We arranged for him to drop me off at the DAC and go to his thing. I told him I'd figure out my own way back on the bus or I'd do Carl-related stuff until he called me later in the evening.

I had no new ideas for what to do about Carl. I had relied on Rodney and he'd shown me that there weren't any forthcoming answers. I was hoping Sadie might be able to give me some more time, some more stones to check under.

Nautica called on our short drive to the DAC. She was furious.

"I know Carl's your number one problem right now but I'm not okay out here," she said. She had bad news. The rent was going to get nearly tripled at La Jouissance after a planned remodel of the building, and we had to be out within the month, and we weren't going to get back in until after a year, and there was no way we could afford that new lease anyway. The new owner of the building was getting ready to gut the adorable brownstone we'd been in and turn it into higher-end condos.

"It's not an option to find another space in that part of town, the rents are too damn high," Nautica said.

"Move the dungeon closer to home in Brooklyn?" I said.

"Who's going to pay to store all that equipment? To move it? To get a new space ready to be a commercial dungeon? You never saw what I had to do to get La Jouissance started in the first place. Our neighborhood is getting more expensive, too."

"What's going to happen to all the furniture and equipment?" I said.

"This is the part that makes me want to kill someone," she said. Another pro Domme in the New York scene, who ran kinky play parties and coordinated all kinds of BDSM social events had offered to take over. She wanted to buy the dungeon furniture, store it or use it until the building was done, she could afford to pay much higher rent for a space nearby, she would run a new business using our stuff. "She'd let me keep the name," Nautica said bitterly. "But all our people just got fucked out of their jobs as of next month no matter what, and I'm sorry to tell you baby but that's you too."

"Shit!" Of course, it meant me, too.

"That bitch is about ready to steal my life," she said. "I wouldn't be surprised if she showed up in your bed tomorrow, either."

"Hey now," I said.

"We need to make some decisions," Nautica said. "And my workshop is over and you're still in LA."

I looked out the window at the blue sky. I definitely was still in LA.

"Come out here," I said.

"What?"

"Just catch a plane. We can figure it out if we're together." Then from somewhere deep inside me came a string of words. "Carl is gone, just gone no one knows anything, or they won't tell me what they know I can't tell, he actually disappeared and I went with Rodney to talk to all these people but no one will tell me what the fuck and I can't, it's like a nightmare sometimes what I'm thinking and this girl Riley was just like who cares? You can't rely on him anyway I couldn't believe it, I just can't..." I suddenly imagined her looking at her watch, timing my tantrum, and telling me later exactly how much emotional labor she'd had to perform to support me.

"Sweetie," she said.

"What?" Of course I was asking too much.

"I've been feeling like I should come out there, too. Remember I trained Lady June last week to run the place while I'm gone on trips? I think she'll do fine. I'll get a flight. We've got a few days before I have to tell this boss lady yes or no. I just got some money from that workshop, I can get there. Let's do this one together. Ok?"

"Yes. Please, ok," I said. "Thank you." She was on my side. I felt instantly a tiny bit of relief.

"What's happening right now, though?" she said.

"I'm tired because I'm coming down, Griffin is off on some Scientology trip, a lead I was hoping for didn't work out last night, I feel stressed about needing to make some money, all the bullshit that can happen seems to happen around here, on a constant loop."

"Have you eaten food today?"

"Yeah," I said, but then I thought about it, and I hadn't eaten anything since donuts after I woke up. "Well, definitely not enough food."

"Ok, so I'm going to guess your water intake is low, based on that," she said. "So can we agree that your next step is to put some food and water in you?"

"Yes," I said.

"Thanks," she said.

"I love you," I said.

"I know," she said.

"Why are you always Han and I'm always Leia?"

"I don't need to answer that," she said, with a little smile I could hear in her voice.

"I'm sorry about the dungeon, honey. I'm going to miss it."

"Me too. I'm so pissed. We had a good run, I guess. We'll figure something out. I'll try to get an offer from the bitch for us to discuss. I'll let you know when I have a flight."

She told me she was sorry to hear that I hadn't found any helpful information about Carl, but she also sounded unsurprised.

"I want you," I said. "I miss you."

"Are you feeling horny or romantic or both?" she said.

"Romantic," I said.

"Mmmmmm," she sounded happy about it. "Thank you."

When we hung up, Griffin stayed quiet.

"Nautica is going to come out here," I said. "Some shit just got real at home and we need to make some decisions."

He nodded. He pulled up to the DAC office. "Talk to you soon," he said.

"You don't have anything to say?"

"No."

"Fine," I said. He probably didn't like it that I told Nautica he was "off on a Scientology trip." I couldn't deal with that right now. I got out of the car and he pulled away.

Rodney was inside the DAC office laughing with the person at the front desk. He held a Styrofoam coffee cup and wore the same clothes I'd seen him in last. The front desk person today was a young man in nice jeans and red sneakers. He had a close fade and hipster glasses on. He and Rodney noticed me at the same time. Rodney and I hugged and he introduced me to Kris.

"Kris is one of our gentrifiers," Rodney said. "He's trying to offset his footprint by volunteering."

"Jesus, Rod," Kris said and slapped him playfully on the chest. "That's not going to help me make friends." He turned to me and whispered, "it's true, though. I'm a little too bougie of a queen for this place."

"I'm going to let you two resolve your differences in peace," I said as good-naturedly as I could. "Is Sadie around?"

Rodney told me to go ahead upstairs. Then he patted me on the back lightly and asked how I was holding up.

"Not great," I said.

He nodded and told me to stay strong.

I went up the creaking stairs, knocked on her office door, and Sadie said, "Come."

I suppressed a Domme joke about ordering someone to orgasm as I pushed her door farther open.

She was at her desk, reading something that made her angry. She wore thin glasses perched low on her freckled nose and flannel shirt opened down to her cleavage. She rubbed her eyes and groaned.

"These motherfuckers," she said. "These goddamn mother-fucking assholes." She slammed a stack of paper down. She glanced up at me and pulled the glasses off her face. "I'm sorry Kindred, please come in."

"What's going on?" I moved a small pile of books off an open folding chair and sat.

"You know about the football stadium bid we're fighting?" she said. I shook my head. Finally. "Carl didn't tell you about it?" she seemed surprised. "This is one of his main projects," she said. "Well, okay. We're having an action for it tomorrow you might want to come to. It would mean a lot to people, since it looks like Carl won't be there and Riley doesn't do this stuff."

I told her if I went, I'd go as myself, not as Carl's daughter.

"But you are his daughter," she said. Then, "You still get to do exactly what you think is right, whatever, of course." She leaned back in her chair and rubbed her eyes again. She looked so tired, so stressed. I wanted to rub her neck or get her drunk or something. I wanted to get drunk. Normal for me, on the tail end of staying up all night. "You knocked on my door for something else," Sadie said. "What's up?"

"I'm just hitting a lot of dead ends and I was hoping you could help me."

She looked thoughtful. "I'll try," she said.

"Do you think he has any real enemies? I mean, could someone have wanted to hurt him? I've been reading his writing and I can't tell exactly how much danger he was in. Everything seems ominous. There's real threat, and then there's also paranoia, in every page."

"I don't tend to give out advice," she said, and I wondered if that could possibly be true, "But if you want to find a conspiracy on Skid Row, you'll find one. You can go crazy that way. There actually *is* a corrupt collaboration happening right now with the City and Edelweiss and the NFL. But I don't think it'll help you find him to imagine that he was targeted for something like getting beat up or disappeared by a bunch of secret strong-arms. If something that shady were happening, you probably wouldn't be able to figure it out on your own anyway."

I nodded.

"I'm sorry," she said. "There's just so many ways a man can go missing down here and political conspiracy is usually reserved for people in more visible positions of power? I mean, it happens. It's real. I don't know. If it helps your heart to look for him with suspicion of something like that, because it keeps you angry and fired up? Do it. But if it helps your heart to accept that we don't have answers right now, then do that. You've already done more than most people would. Most people would have filed a report with the cops and then given up."

"I don't know what to do next."

Sadie cracked her neck. "What do you think Carl would want you to do?"

I tried to imagine what Carl would want. I wasn't sure what would help my heart. "I wish I could get you and my girlfriend Nautica in the same room," I said.

A ripple of something, I wasn't sure what, went through the conversation. Had I embarrassed her somehow?

"I think Carl would want me to take care of myself and offer help where I was needed," I said. "I think he'd want me to keep my spirits up, stay healthy, and not give up on him. I think he'd want me to respect his life's work. That means no police."

"I'll support you in any way I can," Sadie said.

I felt numb. "I guess there's not much more I can do today," I said. It sounded wrong, and empty.

Sadie sat in silence with me for a stretch.

"What are you working on?" I asked her.

She blinked. "You sure you want to go there?"

"I'm probably there already."

"So you know how LA doesn't have an NFL team?" Sadie asked, and shifted in her chair.

I hadn't known LA didn't have a team, but it sounded strange. "Football isn't really my thing," I said.

"Me neither," she said, "and I'm glad. Because the people who are desperate to get a team here, the people who are in love with the NFL? Are the biggest pain in my ass right now."

I knew what she was doing—trying to keep me motivated by helping me find purpose in The Struggle. It was an act of kindness and an organizing tactic at the same time. Also, I'd asked for it. I really liked her.

"The context is that for years we've been trying to get more funding for services and housing, but the city keeps voting for measures that give more funding only to the police. Plus, the big businesses in the area—the banks, the hotel chains—already formed an association and hired their own security, who now harass Skid Row residents more often, more hours of the day."

I nodded. "The skirts," I said.

"The skirts," she said, and rolled her eyes. And I felt a breath of familiarity, a whisper of home in the conversation, because she reminded me of Carl.

"Okay so now, this enormous development company called Eidelweiss got in bed with the City and the NFL to build a new football stadium in Downtown so they can bring a team here. They're pretty far along in the approvals process. But their development deal sucks. There's no viable plan for the poor.

"Carl has been working to help organize the community here, to get some residents at the table because these deals will have serious impact on their daily lives."

The DAC landline rang. Sadie picked it up on the third ring. "Downtown Action Center," she said, "How can I be there for you today?" She gave someone some meeting times and names of people to contact. She told them they could come by the office anytime before 5PM. She hung up. "I wonder who is supposed to be on the phones downstairs," she said. I almost suggested Kris or Rodney but it felt like snitching so I didn't. "Anyway, we can go down the American caste-system rabbit hole another time. I'll try to stick to the current battle." She smiled and fished in her bag for a water bottle. She drank. She offered it to me.

I drank. "It's nice that you put lemon wedges in here."

She stretched her arms over her head, brought them down. I imagined her doing it naked in bed in the morning. "Ok where was I," she said.

"Some powerful people were all in bed together," I said.

She caught it, and gave me a flicker of a flirtatious smile. "Right. If the deal goes forward, we'd lose a ton of low income housing units, the traffic and environmental impacts would be horrible, and the City would continue on its project of dismantling the Skid Row services network so that they can come in and buy up this real estate. With no plan for the humans who live here."

"Jesus."

"The DAC has partnered up with a couple other small nonprofits," she said. "We've got a Legal Aid team that is all fired up about this because the current EIR doesn't measure up."

"You lost me."

She shook her head. "It's so complicated. Sorry. An Environmental Impact Report, we call it an EIR, is this document that any new proposed development has to file with the city, and if you do a shitty one, people can appeal. So that's what we're doing. Even more importantly though, we are suing the State of California for passing an unconstitutional law a little while back that basically destroyed any mechanisms the people had to slow or stop the development project."

"Wait, they passed laws to make building the stadium easier for them?"

"Yes."

"They can do that?"

"They can do that."

I sat with that discomfort for a moment. "What is Carl's role in all this?"

"He's been helping us translate the jargon into the real-life consequences and impacts for Skid Row residents, and organizing their response. This is a billion-dollar project that's going to have consequences for fifty years. He has recruited people to join the campaign against the stadium and put in work, come to community meetings, help make decisions about what to do. He's the one making sure that this isn't just policy people talking to developers, or, on our side, lawyers talking to policy people, but that residents of the area have a say in what happens to them."

I remembered him saying he was trying to get some real work done. I was proud of him, and I said so.

"Me too," Sadie said.

"I want to come tomorrow," I said. "To whatever the action is. I'll bring my boy, too."

They were going to make a final vote on the stadium project at a City Council Meeting, and the DAC was planning to protest the vote both outside and inside the meeting. The City Council didn't seem conflicted about the decision. They had sports celebrities scheduled to appear at the meeting to welcome the new stadium.

"They're not going to care about our public comments," Sadie said, "but we have to say them anyway." She sighed again. "Carl was looking forward to this meeting," she said, and gave me a sad smile. "He really gets a kick out of the political pageantry. He loves getting up on that mike when people are having petty disputes about crumbs of the budget, and saying things about the constitution."

"Maybe he'll turn up to it and we can kick his ass after the City Council leaves the room," I said.

"Sure," she said. So she thought Carl was gone for good, too. I thanked her for giving me some time. She said it was her pleasure. I thought it couldn't be true, considering how busy and stressed out she seemed, but it was titillating to hear her say the word "pleasure."

I waited for Griffin to pick me up and wondered if I'd ever feel like I belonged at a job, or in a city, or in a community.

On my first day working as a Domme, I spent six hours in professional grade fishnets, which was a mistake. I wore Danskin backseam beauties with the elastic waist cut down to a thin line, so none of my flesh was getting pinched or pouchy, but I did get some serious net burn on my thighs and calves. These are the kinds of mistakes you make when you haven't put in your time.

I wore a tight black body-shaping slip I got at Ross three years earlier, an old push-up bra with pink satin discolored by age and use on the inner cups. My rough edges were uncomfortably well-hidden. Eyebrows waxed. Lip, too. Manicure *and* pedicure. The stronger deodorant. An extra look at the shave job on inner thighs, crack, labia. Flossing. Makeup. The only thing I didn't do was false lashes. I didn't like them. Nautica wore them every day, all day, no matter what she was doing. She told me once that eyelashes make a person seem more *there*, somehow.

I did a two-hour session with a guy who called himself John

and had bad back acne. About an hour in, he told me I was more beautiful in person than on my website. He told me I hit harder than I looked like I could.

He took three increasingly larger sizes of butt plug. He told me he was "all cleaned out" which was not quite true, once we got to the largest, cock-shaped, jelly-black-rubber one. Stink.

There was a moment, leaning into him, when I thought: Hmm, I wonder if I'm getting any shit on my fishnets.

Then, a few hours later on with another guy, I crawled on top of his chest and he did a sniffing breath that could have been hoping for a whiff of my vagina, or, an unconscious attempt to scout out some ambient shit smell.

I moved my leg, I'll never know what he thought, and it doesn't matter because neither of us broke the scene at that moment. When I was leaving he asked if I ever wore shorts. Sure, I told him. I never heard from either one of those first clients again.

"What do I do when I break the scene?" I asked Nautica afterward. "Like when something goes wrong?"

"Like what?"

"Like someone farts or pukes or says the wrong thing or gets stuck?"

"Well there's only a few things to do anytime something goes wrong," she said, "and they all start with breathing."

She told me to get my training. Get my first aid, my CPR, my self-defense, and to get confident handling the most common problems that might happen. La Jouissance Dommes were meticulous and calculating and careful and she expected me to "step it up" like everyone else had.

I didn't know what that meant. I was thinking about all the things I'd done to be ready for those first two clients. Hours of preparation seemed like stepping it up just fine.

You're a beginner, she said. You're doing really really well for a beginner. But you can't help that you're new to it. Everyone learns their own lessons in their own time.

I hated that conversation, but I couldn't argue with her, of course. And years later, I said something very similar to someone else after their first day.

19

LIVING IN REALITY

W e were going to take it easy for the night in the motel room. Griffin looked at me with wild eyes and said, "I'm really learning about myself. I loved this workshop I went to today. Things are falling into place. I get why my life has been so hard, you know? I made it happen myself. I figured out that life is a game but I'm still playing it like it's American football."

I didn't know what to say. "Good for you," I said.

"I want to bring you to one," he said.

"No," I said. "And don't ask me again."

"Wow, can you be more rigid?" he said. "I feel like I finally don't need to read women's journals anymore, like I can just be authentically myself and trust that people who deserve to talk to me are going to be authentically themselves back."

"Please don't," I said. "I watched the videos you sent. I'm glad you feel better. I am. But I don't buy it. Don't try to make me go."

He slipped a hand around my waist and dragged his short

nails across my skin. "I just want you to be happy," he said, quietly, and leaned in to kiss my neck.

"Get off me," I said, and shoved him a little. "Manipulative little slut. Go fall in love with another religion."

He was completely ignoring the journal on the table. He didn't see that it was Carl's. He didn't care. Something in him definitely had changed. I didn't like it. But, he was happier. Something is so broken here, I thought. I wished it wasn't me, but of course, it probably was.

He sighed. "I'm sorry," his hands were up, then back at his sides.

"Thank you," I said.

"Can I help you here?" he said.

"No," I said. "And did you even watch their fucking video about 'Don't Do Anything Illegal?'" I said.

"I watched all of them. You take what works for you, you know? Like A.A."

"I don't think Scientology wants you to do that," I said.

"Well, that's how I'm doing it," he said.

"They don't even really want you," I said. "Unless you're willing to give them all of Mommy's money."

"My self-respect is what they want," he said, puffing up a little.

I gave up.

I pulled out way too much hair in the shower. I hadn't lost hair like that since I moved out of Angie's place. Griffin is going to age me, I thought. This is terrible. We broke the scene somehow. It had started to feel bad and we needed to re-negotiate. I was annoyed that I hadn't seen it coming.

When I got out of the shower, I sat on the bed in my towel and told Griffin I wanted him to go back to New York after the City

Council Meeting. Like, fly home in the next few days. I told him I'd pay for his flight.

He looked stricken.

"I've enjoyed sex and S&M with you," I said. "I've been comforted by your presence a few times," I said. "But you are now stressing me out and distracting me from the most important thing in front of me, which is Carl being gone. Second to that is the big changes Nautica and I need to make."

"I'm sorry that I stopped being useful to you," Griffin said, bitterly.

"I don't like your tone," I said. I got out of the bed and started rooting for my underwear.

"I'm sure you don't," he said, "I'm sure you'd prefer I just said 'yes, ma'am, whatever you want.'"

I put on some shorts, patted around, found my shirt. Griffin was rigid on his back, holding the sheet to his chest. I looked at his unhappy face.

"You've got the lowest standards for self-awareness of anyone I've ever fucked for free," I spat. "You came with me on this trip to help, I paid for you to come, you never actually helped that much, now I'm asking you to leave so I can focus on what matters to me, and you're blaming me for your bad feelings? No. Fuck that."

He couldn't speak. Or didn't.

"Let's stop this for tonight," I said. I sat on the bed. I tried to soften, and could, enough to want it to end. I said, "I'm exhausted, I'm angry, I'm sad, I'm scared, but I'm not trying to make this worse." I got back under the covers. "Let's just go to sleep."

"Okay, FINE," he said, and turned away.

Fury rose again. "Seriously!?"

He flopped onto his back and his fists snapped into his eye

sockets. "What?!" he said, in a fake whisper that was actually a yell.

I slowed my breathing down again.

"This is too dramatic," I said.

"I'm sorry!" he whined, and turned away.

"That is dramatic, too," I said. "This isn't how I want to do things."

"Oh of course not," he said, sarcastic, with his back to me, "you don't want to do things that involve difficult emotions, you've had enough in your life, it's all manipulation. I get it, okay? Put your armor away. I'll be fine. Goodnight." For three seconds I couldn't understand how ugly he had become. Then I did.

"Fuck. You." I said. But I couldn't move. It was his first real retaliation. Something had gone so wrong. How? I scanned and scrutinized and kept feeling baffled. How had it gone so wrong?

"Fuck me?!" he said. He flopped over again to face me. "You just announce I need to leave, so I get hurt and start having traumatic recall about abandonment and you're mad at me for it, because you can't control me now. That's what I see. And honestly? I'm not really open to your opinion on it yet." He turned back over.

I suppressed an urge to yell "Bullshit!"

He must not know about the long-term consequences of behavior like this yet, I thought. He's just a kid. And, he's probably right about me wanting control, somehow. So. I'll focus on that.

I could stop the tantrum from taking over my body too, if I wanted to. I decided to figure out if I needed to apologize to him, and discovered that I did. Goddamnit. I was going to hate it for a minute, but I was going to bigger-person my way through this.

"Hey Griffin," I said gently.

He didn't answer.

"I will say this again when we are looking each other in the eye," I said, "but I'm sorry for saying 'Fuck you' when I got frustrated, and, I'm really sorry for the times you've tried to talk to me about your experience and I have not listened that carefully to you."

"Thanks," he said.

A hot ghost of all the things I wanted to say was pushing its way out of me. Like, 'You steal my energy all the time and only sometimes give it back.'

I pulled up a guided visualization Nautica had recorded for me on my phone. She used it with clients, but it was one of my favorite things. I put my earphones in. The calmest, kindest version of her voice washed over me.

Sit comfortably, and relax your mind. Try to stay focused on the images that come to you. Take deep breaths and enjoy the journey.

You are walking in a dense, soft forest. The sun occasionally reaches through the foliage to warm your head and neck. The air smells clean and fresh, and soothes your nose, throat and lungs as you inhale. You are dressed in soft, comfortable, flattering clothes in deep sensual colors. Your shoes are light, and you can feel the contours of even the grass through their soles. As you walk through this lush forest, you feel the desire to sit down and rest in the shade. You sit cross-legged in front of an enormous tree. You can feel the strength of the tree against your lower, middle and upper back. You are settled into your position and a wave of relaxation, beginning at the crown of your head, flows all throughout your body.

As you become more and more relaxed, you notice there are a few places in your body holding on to their tension with more force than the others. These places are tight, feel out of sync, and need adjusting. Unexpectedly, you are also struck with a dangerous realization that each of these painful places in your body are at risk for infection, and you must take immediate action to care for them.

The tree you sit under is, luckily, known for its anti-microbial sap and sturdy needles. Your internal tension congeals into a few balls of sludgy black waste just under the skin of your shoulders, thighs, and belly. You gather a needle for each one, dip it in sap, and pierce a tiny hole in your skin. The black sludge shoots out of you and immediately dissolves in the air. You tenderly pat and probe your body for swelling and bruising, but the tiny punctures have already sealed, and your whole body feels lighter, cleaner, and fresher.

The sun finds you. It brightens the colors behind your closed eyelids, warms your face and inner thighs, fucks you slowly, and you have an incredibly deep, strong orgasm.

Griffin came with me the next morning, still radiating hurt and anger. We took the bus. It was full. I got a little nauseated, thought about how Nautica would have told me to eat. We got off the bus a few blocks from City Hall and found a coffee shop. Griffin sulked outside while I got us both coffees and thick pieces of carrot-zucchini bread. He didn't thank me.

At the bottom of the main steps of City Hall, there was a crowd of around a hundred people milling. There were many handmade signs--I imagined a group of three or four people from the DAC making them last night, mock-fighting over the last good permanent marker. I saw Frida Mall, who was in a black pantsuit, a brunette wig, and perfectly oversized sunglasses. Sadie was up front, standing in the middle of the steps, with her back to the building. Curly was there, in a DAC

T-shirt, holding a sign that read "Community Benefits Agreements require Input from the Community." Jay was there, and I had a flashing vision of tying him and Griffin together, side by side, and making them do household chores with only one right and one left hand. Rodney found us. He was wearing a DAC shirt, too. He hugged me first, then Griffin, who seemed surprised. There was one camera that looked professional, but no news vans.

Sadie turned her mic on and spoke into a small PA about what our purpose was for being there. She reminded everyone that we were going to make public comments inside the meeting at the appropriate time, that we were presenting information to the Council that should affect their vote on the stadium, and that we had a follow-up plan for the possibility that it didn't.

"We're already involved in legal action against this football stadium plan," Sadie said. "They don't think we can pull it off, so it's good to see so many faces here today saying that we can." She was dressed the same as always, in a soft flannel button down shirt, loose fitting jeans, and Converse. Her wild hair moved a little in the air, like an anime character having a lot of feelings. I wanted her, but it was a kind of special quiet wanting, not the urge to rub up on her immediately that I sometimes got when I was attracted to someone. I wanted something sturdier, in a long game, a slow and steady progression toward making her feel better than she ever had. With Nautica. What if we all three fell in love. Some organ I didn't know I had jumped towards that hope from deep in my guts. I tried to focus on Sadie's words.

"I stand with my friends and comrades and coworkers from Skid Row, from the Downtown Action Center," I watched her mouth as she listed a series of organizations. "This development plan has been pushed through many stages of the process in an incorrect way," she said. "We are here to correct some errors. We are here to voice real concerns about how this project impacts the lives of people who live here. The fat cats at Eidelweiss and the NFL may be able to impress the City Council, and even some of the unions, with stories of more sports and entertainment dollars and service and construction jobs coming into the city, but we won't be silenced by their empty promises. We demand that provision be made for replacing the affordable housing we will lose, that the environmental impact report adheres to the state regulations already in place, with no special shortcuts, and that the negative outcomes, including ones we predict and ones that are already happening to Skid Row residents be heard and fairly evaluated."

People clapped and pumped fists. Sadie probably hadn't had a real night's sleep for a week.

Rodney was next to speak. He told a story about meeting an Edelweiss executive who was looking at buildings and talking to the cops out on Towne. "The guy didn't know I was an activist for housing rights," Rodney said with a chagrined smile, "and he told me he was looking forward to cleaning up downtown. I asked him where he thought the people would go, the people who were surviving on the street. He said he didn't care, as long as they weren't in his way. He said they weren't his problem, that he was there for the hardworking people who were paying taxes. This is how capitalism warps our understanding of the value of human life." He gave some statistics about Skid Row residents' employment. He told us that there were more empty homes due to bank foreclosures than there were houseless people in Los Angeles county, but there were nearly four times the number of houseless people as there were shelter beds. "Housing is a human right," he said. "And it isn't impossible for us all to be housed."

Eventually we made our way to the meeting. We stood in

line. We went through a metal detector. We talked quietly, walking down the sterile hallways, under the fluorescent lights. The building was newer, freshly painted, no visible stains on the industrial gray carpet. I could feel my adrenaline.

Out of the corner of my eye, I saw Carl on the edge of the crowd. My body slammed backwards out of my skin for an instant, then I lurched forward.

I dodged around a few people.

But of course.

It wasn't him.

That's when it was real. That he wasn't just about to show up. That he'd been missing for a long time now and no one had anything helpful to tell me. That he'd been working on something complicated and important to a lot of people, a difficult project within a longer life's work, a life's work with a scope that had been larger than I'd understood. It was real, too, that he'd not tried to introduce Riley to me. That he was gone now, and for the foreseeable future, and I had to accept it or I would self-destruct. I wasn't going to know if he was suffering, or if he was dead, or if he was starting over. I wasn't going to know if he'd made choices I agreed with or not. I would have to enter a grieving process, in which I would not be able to predict the waves of fear or anger or despair. I wasn't going to smell Carl or hug Carl or hear Carl's voice today, and maybe never again.

I knew it so well, that state of loss, that moment of enormity so painful it can't be contained by the boundaries of my own body. The pain that turns the body into a contorted twisted broken thing. I felt I had lost a vital piece of my living flesh and I couldn't keep standing, and I'd been there before and I didn't know if I'd make it out the first time.

I told myself: You may be having a panic attack.

I told myself: dying right now would be ok though, I don't think I'd mind.

I told myself: That definitely sounds like a panic attack.

I told myself: I can't see very well. I can't see.

I told myself: I am sitting down.

I told myself: Breathe.

I told myself: Breathe.

I told myself: Head down. Breathe.

I told myself: you look weird but it's working right? Or are you going to have a heart attack? You act like a teenager but you're almost thirty now, and you did all those drugs all those years, and now look what you've done.

I told myself: Drink some water.

I told myself: Keep breathing.

I told myself: Get outside the building. You're going to throw up now.

And so I left the meeting, and ran into someone who was tossing a football to himself on my way out, and mumbled "sorry, excuse me," and threw up in the decorative river stones just to the left of the main entrance.

Loss that feels like a piece of my guts has been scooped out. The back of my throat, constricted, the burning in my face, the crying, my center had been hollowed out, scraped. Squeezed. Black, orange, red in my eyes.

I searched for a part of my body that didn't hurt. I found a toe. I concentrated on the toe. I wanted to go back in time, forward in time. I wondered if it would be okay to not get up again.

No, it would not. A reflex of the mind. All that therapy. You know how to handle a panic attack. You do.

But the desire to stop thinking, stop seeing and hearing things, stop having to respond, stop feeling the pain, was stronger than my desire to make it through. I imagined a car accident. Hurtling toward something too large to survive, and feeling the calm of release.

People die so easily. They step off a platform at just the wrong angle. They fall off a ladder. They get a clot in their heart that couldn't have been detected. They develop cancer quietly and in secret, while having perfectly healthy habits and enacting future plans. I could just slip away. The waters would close over me. Nautica would heal. My mom will not miss me. Carl will not miss me. None of my friends will lose their own will to live, and they may even be emboldened to greater acts of creation or joy or resistance to status quo, grief can be such a catalyst. Dying might be my greatest gift to the people I love.

Do not tell anyone you feel this way, a voice in my head said. They will not understand and they will want to put you in a hospital. I remembered Griffin's roommate, with his gasoline and his anger.

I'm not actually suicidal, I told myself. I don't have a plan. A fantasy about a car accident is not a plan. If I were about to buy three bottles of Tylenol, that could be considered a plan.

The muscles in my shoulders felt permanently contracted. The band of tension around my waist, like a belt holding my pain in. Empty of something, burning with something else.

Breathing in, hello suffering.

Breathing out, hello suffering, I am here.

Breathing in, I'd like to die.

Breathing out, I will not do it on purpose today.

What's wrong with you? Why can't you get your life together? So you've had some struggle, so has everyone else, and most people have worse. What's so horrible that you want to stare into your own shit so hard and stay there? You're a narcissist. You're useless. You don't care about the world, you only care about yourself, and you think your suffering is unique and precious when it isn't. You've failed yourself, you've failed everyone you've ever said you loved. You don't know how to love anyone but yourself, and you suck at that too.

Don't be that whore who proves them right about whores. Don't be that queer who justifies parents telling their kids "You're choosing a hard life." Straight people who don't know you think you brought this on yourself. Don't let them be right. It's true that Carl is missing, and may not be coming back. Might be dead. It's true. You've lived through death before. You know people die. You know that you got to love them when you have them and that you're going to die too. Pick your goddamn self up, get stronger, and finish this fight. Fight to live. Fight to live well. Make a decision.

I knew I was in the fetal position. I knew I was looking at the ground. I knew I was worrisome, that it wasn't good. But I couldn't move. I didn't want to move. I couldn't feel any reason to move. I had to try to take breaths. If I didn't think about it, my breaths were too shallow and short. My eyes stayed slightly out of focus. Breathing in. Breathing out.

It isn't fair.

Security was on me. Ma'am are you alright, Ma'am do you need an ambulance, Ma'am you can't sit here do I need to call someone for you.

It isn't fair.

Then another voice. A new one. She said, Fairness is for children. This voice wasn't angry with me. This voice wasn't desperate. This voice was calm. Fairness isn't the goal, baby. Justice is the goal.

Justice is for adults. You are grown. Go for justice. You don't have to do that alone. You can love and be loved and fight for justice and you won't be alone.

I struggled, but I stood. Spirals of black nothing threatened the edges of my vision. They receded as I breathed in and out, in and out. I got my water out of my bag. Swished. Spit. You don't have to do this alone.

Griffin appeared. He completely ignored the security

guard and threaded his arm through mine and said, "Ready to walk to the bus?" The guard retreated a few feet and watched.

"I want to go back in there," I said. I found some gum in my bag, unwrapped it, and put it in my mouth.

I could see how badly he wanted to tell me no. "You sure about that? You look bad. I mean, I'm sorry, but--you just, you know," he pointed at the place where I'd vomited.

"I'm ok," I said. "I thought I saw Carl. I panicked. I feel bad, I'm sure I look bad. It'll pass. I want to be in there for this. Then we eat a real meal."

"I don't get it," Griffin said. "But I'll support whatever you want to do."

"Good boy."

We nodded at the security guard, who was talking into his walkie-talkie, and we reentered the building. We went back into the meeting room. I looked at my shoes and let Griffin lead, let him make the eye contact, let him get me through. My shoes were clean, at least.

The suit with the football was leaning against the wall behind the low wooden partition that separated the Council from the people. He tossed the ball in the air and caught it idly, scanning the room. Some Council members were seated, looking down at their notes, but most of them were milling around behind their little wall.

A person from the Downtown Action Center was on the mike in the people's section, giving a comment about the provisions for housing that were missing from the stadium plan. I realized that the City Council was actively discouraging anyone from making or listening to public comment. There was the suit tossing a ball, three Council members out of their seats, all of them not looking us in the eye.

Sadie stood in line to make a comment, motioned for me to

come next to her and I did, pulling Griffin along. She whispered, "You ok?"

"I'm ok," I said, trying to angle my breath away from her face. I was wobbly and the room was spinning gently.

"You're not ok," she said.

"Don't worry about me," I said.

She narrowed her eyes. She accepted my deflection, but she didn't like it.

"You see this shit?" she said, gesturing at the guy with the football.

I nodded, yes, I saw what was happening. And it made me angry. "Rude," I said.

She gave me a tiny "humpf."

Griffin begged with his eyes to sit down, stop being looked at. I let him go with a nod and pointed at the open seats in the back. "Thank you," I whispered at him. He squeezed my hand and went.

I stood with Sadie. I twisted my leather ring, finding the knot and sending it around, around, around. I wished Nautica was there.

Sadie spoke her piece to the dissolved, distracted audience. She was clear and strong and direct. The guy with the football just kept tossing it and ignoring her on the side of the room and I thought, I would like to get him alone, take all his money, and humiliate the shit out of him. He stood there in his collared button-down and his blue suit jacket with an arrogant smirk, leaning over to his friend and whispering and laughing, while Sadie discussed the potential harms to Skid Row residents inherent to his plan.

Who is this demonstration for? I wondered. Why are we even here? I couldn't see what the point was, how we were going to win against the NFL with our dirty clothes and handwritten signs and unstable minds.

But Sadie seemed sure of what she was doing, and I believed her, and I'd been in enough BDSM situations to know that when you really want to follow someone, it's best to do it wholeheartedly.

Later that night, Sadie sent me an email with a link. She had added me to the DAC newsletter list.

The link took me to YouTube. Title: "Los Angeles City Council Approves Economic Development Project of our Generation Despite Community Concern about Unconstitutional Policy, Environmental Impacts, Housing." I watched a minute-thirty of a cell phone video from the City Council meeting with captions from the DAC. Sadie's well-written points were scrolling while a red arrow pointed at the football every time the guy tossed it in the air. A few slides at the end of the video gave viewers contact info for the DAC, and a list of services they provided in addition to this campaign they were on. They needed volunteers and were happy to train, and they gave "Skid Row Tours" to activists and school groups interested in supporting Skid Row Residents' human rights campaigns. I loved the way Football Asshole had been shamed. I loved the way the DAC kept fighting.

I love it here, I thought. I love Los Angeles. I have missed her.

She was just as messy and full of madness as New York, but brighter and greener and smelled better too, somehow.

I sent Sadie a text affirming the video with my hopes for its viral capacity. I told her I admired her and that she did great work.

Griffin packed. He was watching Scientology videos on his phone.

Nautica called. She was arriving in the morning. I already

felt embarrassed for all the problems I was going to have to hand her when she did. But my embarrassment was nearly submerged in relief, at knowing we'd at least be together for solving the problems and walking through the grief. Nautica was such a great reason to live.

And she was bringing my Mom's ashes. I wasn't certain of why I'd asked her to, but it felt right.

20

LIFE AFTER REALITY

Nautica arrived at LAX wearing a new coat. She and Griffin were about to overlap by one night.

I watched her stride past a struggling family with toppling luggage, not ignoring them, not offering to help them, but holding her free hand out, as if spotting the youngest's vulnerable head and wanting to offer an alternative to his crashing into her. She stopped to scan the monitors, and I watched people notice her, get momentarily hypnotized, and then look away. She moved like water.

I tried to wet my mouth and swallow and breathe.

"Hi!" she said. She smelled like the airplane. I wanted to strip her and bury my face in her tummy skin, where her scent had been protected from industrial progress.

"You got a new coat," I said.

She put her bag down and twirled. The plum fabric rustled behind her. She caught a corner and brought up the edge to my face. "Feel it," she whispered, "Look at how well this is made!"

"I really don't know anything about coats," I said.

"It's waterproof," she said, "but breathable. Which is genius. It was a gift."

"From who?"

"New client," she said. Then she stopped to stare into my eyes. "I'm so excited to see you! How are you feeling about everything today?"

"Pretty heartbroken," I said, and the tears started rising.

She squeezed me, said, "Yeah, makes sense," and picked up her bag.

"Did you bring my mom?" I asked.

"Yes," she said. "She's in my carryon, which was really stressful."

"Thank you," I said. "Really. Thank you."

She met my eyes again and I felt her there. "You're my love," she said. "Of course."

Nautica didn't plan to stay long, and she wanted a car. I'd made Griffin return ours, so we got a new one, a little blue Kia that seemed more like a joke than a car. I looked at the LA Weekly in the rental office, and saw an ad for an amateur night tonight at a downtown strip club. I showed it to Nautica. I'd thought about trying to get a kink client but this would be much easier.

"Maybe I should do this tonight," I said. The prize was $500.

"Looks good," she said. "Maybe the boy and I will come watch you. Stripping's like riding a bike, right?"

Griffin and Nautica drank beer together and helped me win third place, which was $200, by screaming and clapping as loud as they could. I got invited to work the rest of the night. I decided to do it so I could pay for Griffin's ticket and put the whole thing behind me financially.

They kissed my cheeks simultaneously and I felt strong, but almost immediately after they left I had some trouble with my ankle and by the end of the night it was swollen and hurt to walk on. I'd been in heels for four hours, taking breaks to perch at the bar or even to put my feet up for a minute on a barstool until the bouncer, or the bartender, or manager, snapped or glared at me. Not allowed to be on our phones. Not allowed to recline. I didn't remember stripping feeling so restrictive. Maybe I was spoiled now that I was a Domme.

"Are you at work, or are you watching TV at home?" the manager said. He had thick dark hair parted in the middle like a 1930s gangster. He wore a black suit. He liked to call us all "girls," even the ones who were ten years older than him.

"I just feel so comfortable here," I said.

He snapped his fingers anyway. I moved my feet. The relief ended and the throbbing resumed. I got a cup of ice from the bar.

In the dressing room, I asked around for a painkiller. I got one, a Percocet, for an inflated ten dollars from a dancer I didn't want to fight with. With the ice on, and the pill in, I fixed my makeup. I bolded my eyeliner. I painted a new layer of dark wine lip stain.

My face looked stressed. I tried to relax it, to smile. I messed with my hair a little, wished I'd brought my flatiron, considered using one that was left on the counter, decided against it.

But what am I really doing with my life, my eyes said,

I was getting money. So I could eat. So I could pay for Griffin to go home and a place to sleep. I was just getting money with these hours. True answers, but so unsatisfying.

"There's got to be more to life than this," said a dancer at the mirror, to my right.

"I was just thinking something like that," I said.

"You're new, right?" she said. She was doing some low-impact primping of her perfect brown curls. I wondered if she was wearing a wig and tried to see her part.

"I'm visiting from New York," I said. Then wanted to fix it if it made me sound stuck up. "What's your name?" I asked her.

"Kelly," she said.

"I'm Melissa," I said. We shook hands.

"So cool that you're from New York!" she said. "I've only been there once, but it was awesome."

"I'm actually from here," I said. "I've lived in Brooklyn for like ten years though."

She nodded. She didn't seem to care much about the "from" or "lived in" part. Very LA of her.

We chatted. She was funny. She said surprising things. Like, "I told the girls once I thought we should pool our tips. One of them was super into it. The rest were like, not happy imagining giving their money to a collective."

"There's a place in San Francisco where they do that," I said. "But I think it's a peep show, not a strip club."

She looked thoughtful. "I wonder if we could get in touch with someone there and find out how it works for them."

Suddenly I remembered something Rodney had said to me about a sex worker organization in LA. "Hey," I said, feeling strangely vulnerable, "have you ever heard of the Hookers Army?"

She smiled at me. "Is that a band?"

"It's a sex worker group someone told me about," I said.

She asked me if I was part of it.

I told her I'd just heard of them but I was interested.

"Sounds cool," she said. "Can I go if I'm just a dancer?"

"No idea," I said.

"Take me with you if you go to a meeting?"

I said I would. We exchanged numbers.

I was attracted to her. It was a nice feeling. Life-affirming. She had pillow lips.

I hobbled back out onto the floor and got lucky. I found a guy who wanted me to lay down on him and barely move. I made three hundred dollars. Since five hundred had been my goal I decided to call it a win and leave early so I could take care of my ankle. I hadn't realized how high the tip-out would be. I left with less than four hundred, but it was enough for Griffin's ticket.

When I got back to the motel, Griffin and Nautica were watching an action movie. They seemed contented. They'd smoked some weed and talked about me, Nautica said.

I wondered where they got the weed but it didn't seem polite to ask them as they'd bonded somehow.

"You never told me that much about growing up here," Griffin said, as if we'd known each other for years and I'd been withholding. "Nautica says you lived in your car."

"Yeah, I slept in my car a lot for a few months," I said. "Griffin, can you rip yourself away from this movie and get me some ice?"

"Of course," he said, and took a long time to find the ice bucket. I counted out my money. Three hundred ninety after the high tip-out. Well. It was three hundred ninety I didn't have yesterday.

"You okay?" Nautica asked me as I peeled off the post-work sweatpants and stepped into the shower.

"My ankle hurts and I'm tired," I said. "But I'm okay." I told her I'd met a cute dancer.

"Is she queer?"

"I don't know."

"Did you get her number?"

"Of course I did!" I yelled from the shower.

I heard her laughing.

The water was a sweet relief from the grime. I soaped my feet gently and watched small eddies of gray water flow to the drain.

The following day, we put Griffin on a plane back to NYC. He'd spent the morning at the Scientology Center. I don't know what happened there, but he was serene and very kind when he left. Hugging him goodbye, I felt sad. Like I would miss him. But still, I knew it was best for him to go. "I'm sorry about your dad," he said, after hugging and kissing me. "Call me when you're back in town?"

I said I would. But I wasn't sure it was a good idea.

I scattered my Mom's ashes at Dockweiler Beach twelve years after I put them in the coffee can. I wrote a letter to Carl and then burned it in a barbecue. I invited Riley but she said she wasn't into "ritual stuff." Nautica stood with me, held me, and took me to eat Thai food in the middle of the night. She fucked me carefully and slowly and with love, and I slept deeply for the first time in a week. We spent a few more days talking with people, collecting pieces of Carl's stuff. I was right about the potential for a mutual respect between Nautica and Sadie. I was also right that they'd have some chemistry. I enjoyed watching them look at each other.

Nautica and I spent three more months in New York, handling the sale of La Jouissance, spending time with friends and lovers, closing up shop. We decided to move to LA.

After we had a coffee date to catch up and Griffin told me he was dating on a fetish site now, we said a gentle goodbye.

Griffin wrote one very long, very thoughtful email to me in which he critiqued us both for some sloppy boundaries and poor communication. It was true and very boring and I hoped he felt better for it.

The original stadium plan was defeated, by the DAC and their coalition's lawsuit about the Environmental Impact Report. It took months of tedious, constant work after that City Council meeting to get it done. The *LA Times* called it a "David and Goliath" story. Someone high up at Eidelweiss got fired. The DAC and their partners had been fighting nonstop for a year, while still providing housing aid, legal clinics, organizing space, and other policy advocacy.

Nautica and I made it back to LA in time for the DAC's announcement that they'd settled the lawsuit. We celebrated victory over the stadium development scam by getting drunk en masse at the bar where Rodney and I had seen Frida's show. I drunk-dialed Angie and we talked for ten minutes and I cried and I told her I'd moved back to LA and Carl was gone and she said she hoped I could find peace in my life soon and I realized she thought something was worse than it was, because I was drunk, so I told her she should call me when she came out to visit her parents and said goodbye.

Nautica and Sadie made out on the dance floor and we took her home and stayed up laughing and dancing and occasionally letting out enormous, guttural groans. The kind that come when something difficult is finished. We wanted to have sex that night but I told them both I'd be too sad if it was just a fun drunk one-off because of what a strong fantasy I had about the three of us actually dating. So we waited until the morning, and then we had the threesome that changed everything. We love telling the story that way, dripping with poly queer nearly-unbelievable romance.

. . .

In the last few weeks of my mother's life a doctor who had generally avoided eye contact with me brought two students into her room. He had a forced friendly bedside manner and called her by her name, as if he'd always known it. He told his students I was her guard dog. I barked at them.

When he left with his minions, Mom told me that she liked it, how fiercely protective of her I was. I thought, what if she'd been ugly? Rude? Unable to speak English? Or alone? She'd be dead. I walked a mile or so to the nearest liquor store, and waited until a guy in an ironed white T-shirt bought me a six-pack of Pabst and told me to be careful. I was not careful, not for years.

Carl taught me things that played in my head like old songs. You must not back down from a righteous fight, even though it means you will probably fight someone, something, somewhere, every day. Your wildness will keep you soft in the right places, and allow the collective power of your loving and being loved to heal you when you lose. When you are betrayed, your wildness will cry out for trust. When you are locked up, your wildness will search for a way out. When you are lonely, you can rely on your wildness to attract love.

My mom never said "you can be anything you want" because she knew it wasn't true, and so she tried to teach me to want less. Her response to what was true and necessary about life was to suffer it, tolerate it, compromise with it. She thought "healthy" meant: not being addicted, graduating from high school, seeming cheerful, getting a nice boyfriend, and making legal money at a job I could tell people about.

In a fight one night, Carl told her that she was and would remain passively racist, that being in love with one black man was not the cure, and that she had lied about her passion for making social change. I don't remember what she said, but I'm pretty sure she didn't understand what the hell he meant.

Somehow, they made up from that fight. Or at least, they moved on.

I wish I could talk to Mom and Carl about these things. I'd set up a table with some macaroni and cheese, a bottle of four-dollar Chardonnay, and one of those apple-cinnamon candles Carl always bought at the 99-cent store. I miss even Mom's heavy sighs and dismissive eye-rolls. I miss the horrible sound of her panty-hose feet rubbing against the floor under the table. I miss Carl's dry, warm hands. I even miss his frustrating way of preaching in between saying things that meant something to me.

When I can feel the pain returning to me, when I miss them both so much it feels like I'm poisoned, I turn my mind to a memory of Carl and Mom, holding each other with their eyes closed. Carl's left hand sits gently on Mom's lower back, his right holds her hand over his heart, and their foreheads lean together. Sometimes they open their eyes and smile. Otherwise their faces are relaxed, almost serious. Swaying, turning in a small circle, they both lift their feet just a centimeter, and that is enough to keep them moving along the same track, in time.

ACKNOWLEDGMENTS

From beginning to end, this book was inspired, co-created, and supported by a large cast of incredible people. I won't be able to name them all, but I feel my indebtedness to each one. Thank you to Lisa Kastner and Peter Wright at Running Wild Press for seeing the value in this manuscript and helping it take clearer shape and material form.

I am grateful to all my writing mentors, but especially Aimee Bender, who gave me time, attention, and support when I needed it most at USC. A special thank you to Dana Johnson, for gently reshaping my vision and staying interested in what I was doing when she could have just canceled me for my ignorance. Thanks to Nomi Stolzenberg, for offering me confidence in my abilities and sympathy for my struggles as I moved through the work. Percival Everett, every day I hear you in my head, admonishing me to stay courageous and keep putting pen to paper.

I am indebted and grateful to the people who shared their lives and life's work with me so I could write a few of Skid Row's complexities. At the time, many of them were a part of the Los Angeles Community Action Network (LA CAN) family: Jojo, Adam, Sean, I miss hearing you yell lovingly at each other; Eric, for spending precious time explaining the football stadium deal; and Becky, you're just a badass and a half. Very special gratitude for Bilal, without whom this book would truly not exist.

To the people in my family and family of choice who read drafts, wrote thoughts, let me steal conversations, and patiently allowed this project to take so many years: thank you. I'm so lucky to have so many of you who believe in what I do. To the people who are no longer in contact, I thank you too, for the truths that emerged in both our closeness and our separating.

Thank you to my goddessmother Susan, aka SARK, for creating the micromovement method which helped me finish this manuscript and submit it to publishers as many times as I needed to; thank you also for loving me so ferociously, all these years, whether I'm writing or in-between writings.

I thank every comrade in LA, the Bay Area, New York, and on the internet who has been a part of my political education, challenged me, and helped me grow. Thank you to every sex worker I've ever known who shared their life with me, each person who has written to me from inside prison, all the activists who smoked and talked with me late into the night or on a long drive, anyone who has put their own self on the line, seeking justice and the creation of the next and better world. May we all outdo ourselves, again and again.

AUTHOR'S BIO

Vanessa Carlisle, PhD is an LA-based queer, polyamorous, sex working writer, educator, death doula, and consultant. A graduate of the University of Southern California's PhD program in Creative Writing, English Literature and Gender Studies, Vanessa also holds a BA in Psychology from Reed College, and an MFA in Creative Writing from Emerson College. Vanessa appeared on Season One of Showtime's docuseries *Polyamory: Married and Dating* and co-hosted *Sex, Please!* the only show about sexuality ever to air on KPFK Los Angeles 90.7FM, which later became the groundbreaking podcast *On the Dresser*. With twenty-one years of experience as a sex worker and ten as an activist for sex workers' rights, Vanessa leads trauma-informed anti-stigma workshops for college students, therapists, social workers, and others seeking to support the health and wellbeing of people with lived experience in the criminalized sex trades. Her writing has appeared in literary, academic, and trade publications, including the essay "How to Build a Hookers Army" in *#WeToo: Essays on*

Sex Work and Survival (Feminist Press). When not writing, teaching, organizing in her community, or working with clients, Vanessa trains jujitsu and Conscious Breathwork. Also, she loves being a crazy aunt.

OTHER TITLES BY RUNNING WILD

Past Titles

Running Wild Stories Anthology, Volume 1
Running Wild Anthology of Novellas, Volume 1
Jersey Diner by Lisa Diane Kastner
Magic Forgotten by Jack Hillman
The Kidnapped by Dwight L. Wilson
Running Wild Stories Anthology, Volume 2
Running Wild Novella Anthology, Volume 2, Part 1
Running Wild Novella Anthology, Volume 2, Part 2
Running Wild Stories Anthology, Volume 3
Running Wild's Best of 2017, AWP Special Edition
Running Wild's Best of 2018
Build Your Music Career From Scratch, Second Edition by Andrae Alexander
Writers Resist: Anthology 2018 with featured editors Sara Marchant and Kit-Bacon Gressitt
Magic Forbidden by Jack Hillman
Frontal Matter: Glue Gone Wild by Suzanne Samples
Mickey: The Giveaway Boy by Robert M. Shafer

Dark Corners by Reuben "Tihi" Hayslett
The Resistors by Dwight L. Wilson
Open My Eyes by Tommy Hahn
Legendary by Amelia Kibbie
Christine, Released by E. Burke
Running Wild Stories Anthology, Volume 4
Running Wild Novella Anthology, Volume 4
Magpie's Return by Curtis Smith
Suicide Forrest by Sarah Sleeper
Tough Love at Mystic Bay by Elizabeth Sowden
The Faith Machine by Tone Milazzo
Recon: The Anthology by Ben White
The Self Made Girl's Guide by Aliza Dube
Sodom & Gomorrah on a Saturday Night by Christa Miller

Running Wild Press publishes stories that cross genres with great stories and writing. Our team consists of:

Lisa Diane Kastner, Founder and Executive Editor
Barbara Lockwood, Editor
Peter A. Wright, Editor
Rebecca Dimyan, Editor
Benjamin White, Editor
Andrew DiPrinzio, Editor
Lisa Montagne, Director of Education

Learn more about us and our stories at www.runningwild-press.com

Loved this story and want more? Follow us at www.running-wildpress.com, www.facebook/runningwildpress, on Twitter @lisadkastner @RunWildBooks

CPSIA information can be obtained
at www.ICGtesting.com
Printed in the USA
FSHW021813280521
81903FS